Patricia Cornwell sold her first novel, *Postmortem*, while working as a computer analyst at the Office of the Chief Medical Examiner in Richmond, Virginia. It would go on to win the Edgar, Creasey, Anthony, and Macavity awards as well as the French Prix du Roman d'Aventure prize – the first book ever to claim all these distinctions in a single year. To date, Cornwell's books have sold some 100 million copies in thirty-six languages in over 120 countries, winning Cornwell the Sherlock Award for best detective created by an American author, the Gold Dagger Award, the RBA Thriller Award, and the Medal of Chevalier of the Order of Arts and Letters for her contributions to literary and artistic development.

Though Cornwell now lives in Boston, she was born in Miami and grew up in Montreat, North Carolina. After earning her degree in English from Davidson College in 1979, she began working at the *Charlotte Observer*, then moving to a job with the Office of the Chief Medical Examiner of Virginia – a post she would later bestow upon the fictional Kay Scarpetta.

When not writing from her Boston home, Patricia tirelessly researches cutting-edge forensic technologies to include in her work. Her interests span outside the literary: Patricia co-founded of the Conservation Scientist Chair at the Harvard University Art Museums. She appears as a forensic consultant on CNN and serves as a member of Harvard-affiliated McLean Hospital's National Council, where she advocates for psychiatric research. She's helped fund the ICU at Cornell's Animal Hospital, the scientific study of a Confederate submarine, the archaeological excavation of Jamestown, and a variety of law enforcement charities.

Also by Patricia Cornwell

Patricia Cornwell
Unnatural Exposure

SPHERE

SPHERE

First published in the United States in 1997 by G. P. Putnam's Sons
First published in Great Britain in 1997 by Little, Brown and Company
This reissue published in 2010 by Sphere
This edition published in 2020 by Sphere

3 5 7 9 10 8 6 4 2

A CIP catalogue record for this book is available from the British Library.

ISBN 978-0-7515-8264-2

Printed and bound in Great Britain by Clays Ltd, Elcograf S.p.A.

Papers used by Sphere are from well-managed forests
and other responsible sources.

Sphere
An imprint of
Little, Brown Book Group
Carmelite House
50 Victoria Embankment
London EC4Y 0DZ

An Hachette UK Company
www.hachette.co.uk

www.littlebrown.co.uk

And there came unto me one of the seven angels which had the seven vials full of the seven last plagues . . .

Revelation 21:9

NIGHT FELL CLEAN and cold in Dublin, and wind moaned beyond my room as if a million pipes played the air. Gusts shook old windowpanes and sounded like spirits rushing past as I rearranged pillows one more time, finally resting on my back in a snarl of Irish linen. But sleep would not touch me, and images from the day returned. I saw bodies without limbs or heads, and sat up, sweating.

I switched on lamps, and the Shelbourne Hotel was suddenly around me in a warm glow of rich old woods and deep red plaids. I put on a robe, my eyes lingering on the phone by my fitfully-slept-in bed. It was almost two A.M. In Richmond, Virginia, it would be five hours earlier, and

1

Pete Marino, commander of the city police department's homicide squad, should be up. He was probably watching TV, smoking, eating something bad for him unless he was on the street.

I dialed his number, and he grabbed the phone as if he were right next to it.

'Trick or treat.' He was loudly on his way to being drunk.

'You're a little early,' I said, already regretting the call. 'By a couple of weeks.'

'Doc?' He paused in confusion. 'That you? You back in Richmond?'

'Still in Dublin. What's all the commotion?'

'Just some of us guys with faces so ugly we don't need masks. So every day is Halloween. Hey! Bubba's bluffing,' he yelled out.

'You always think everybody's bluffing,' a voice fired back. 'It's from being a detective too long.'

'What you talking about? Marino can't even detect his own B.O.'

Laughter in the background was loud as the drunk, derisive comments continued.

'We're playing poker,' Marino said to me. 'What the hell time is it there?'

'You don't want to know,' I answered. 'I've got some unsettling news, but it doesn't sound like we should get into it now.'

'No. No, hold on. Let me just move the phone. Shit. I hate the way the cord gets twisted, you know what I mean? Goddamn it.' I could hear his heavy footsteps and a chair scraping. 'Okay, Doc. So what the hell's going on?'

'I spent most of today discussing the landfill cases with the state pathologist. Marino, I'm increasingly suspicious

2

that Ireland's serial dismemberments are the work of the same individual we're dealing with in Virginia.'

He raised his voice. 'You guys hold it down in there!'

I could hear him moving farther away from his pals as I rearranged the duvet around me. I reached for the last few sips of Black Bush I had carried to bed.

'Dr Foley worked the five Dublin cases,' I went on. 'I've reviewed all of them. Torsos. Spines cut horizontally through the caudal aspect of the fifth cervical vertebral body. Arms and legs severed through the joints, which is usual, as I've pointed out before. Victims are a racial mix, estimated ages between eighteen and thirty-five. All are unidentified and signed out as homicides by unspecified means. In each case, heads and limbs were never found, the remains discovered in privately owned landfills.'

'Damn, if that don't sound familiar.' he said.

'There are other details. But yes, the parallels are profound.'

'So maybe the squirrel's in the U.S. now,' he said. 'Guess it's a damn good thing you went over there, after all.'

He certainly hadn't thought so at first. No one really had. I was the chief medical examiner of Virginia, and when the Royal College of Surgeons had invited me to give a series of lectures at Trinity's medical school, I could not pass up an opportunity to investigate the Dublin crimes. Marino had thought it a waste of time, while the FBI had assumed the value of the research would prove to be little more than statistical.

Doubts were understandable. The homicides in Ireland were more than ten years old, and as was true in the Virginia cases, there was so little to go on. We did not have fingerprints, dentition, sinus configurations or witnesses for identification. We did not have biological samples from people missing to compare to the victims' DNA. We did not know the means of death. Therefore, it was very difficult to say much about the killer, except that I believed he was experienced with a meat saw and quite possibly used one in his profession, or had at one time.

'The last case in Ireland, that we know of, was a decade ago,' I was saying to Marino over the line. 'In the past two years we've had four in Virginia.'

'So you're thinking he stopped for eight years?' he said. 'Why? He was in prison, maybe, for some other crime?'

'I don't know. He may have been killing somewhere else and the cases haven't been connected,' I replied as wind made unearthly sounds.

'There's those serial cases in South Africa,' he thickly thought out loud. 'In Florence, Germany, Russia, Australia. Shit, now that you think of it, they're friggin' everywhere. Hey!' He put his hand over the phone. 'Smoke your own damn cigarettes! What do you think this is? Friggin' welfare!'

Male voices were rowdy in the background, and someone had put on Randy Travis.

'Sounds like you're having fun,' I dryly said. 'Please don't invite me next year, either.'

'Bunch of animals,' he mumbled. 'Don't ask me why I do this. Every time they drink me outa house, home. Cheat at cards.'

'The M.O. in these cases is very distinctive.' My tone was meant to sober.

'Okay,' he said. 'So if this guy started in Dublin, maybe we're looking for someone Irish. I think you should hurry back home.' He belched. 'Sounds like we need to go to Quantico and get on this. You told Benton yet?'

Benton Wesley headed the FBI's Child Abduction Serial Killer Unit, or CASKU, for which both Marino and I were consultants.

'I haven't had a chance to tell him yet.' I replied, hesitantly. 'Maybe you can give him a heads-up. I'll get home as soon as I can.'

'Tomorrow would be good.'

'I'm not finished with the lecture series here,' I said.

'Ain't a place in the world that don't want you to lecture. You could probably do that and nothing else,' he said, and I knew he was about to dig into me.

'We export our violence to other countries,' I said. 'The least we can do is teach them what we know, what we've learned from years of working these crimes . . .'

'Lectures ain't why you're staying in the land of leprechauns, Doc,' he interrupted as a flip-top popped. 'It ain't why, and you know it.'

'Marino,' I warned. 'Don't do this.'

But he kept on. 'Ever since Wesley's divorce, you've found one reason or another to skip along the Yellow Brick Road, right on out of town. And you don't want to come home now, I can tell from the way you sound, because you don't want to deal, take a look at your hand and take your chances. Let me tell you. Comes a time when you got to call or fold . . .'

'Point taken.' I was gentle as I cut off his besotted good intentions. 'Marino, don't stay up all night.'

The Coroner's Office was at No. 3 Store Street, across from the Custom House and central bus station, near docks and the river Liffey. The brick building was small and old, the alleyway leading to the back barred by a heavy black gate with MORGUE painted across it in bold white letters.

Climbing steps to the Georgian entrance, I rang the bell and waited in mist.

It was cool this Tuesday morning, trees beginning to look like fall. I could feel my lack of sleep. My eyes burned, my head was dull, and I was unsettled by what Marino had said before I had almost hung up on him.

'Hello.' The administrator cheerfully let me in. 'How are we this morning, Dr Scarpetta?'

His name was Jimmy Shaw, and he was very young and Irish, with hair as fiery as copper ivy, and eyes as blue as sky.

'I've been better,' I confessed.

'Well, I was just boiling tea,' he said, shutting us inside a narrow, dimly lit hallway, which we followed to his office. 'Sounds like you could use a cup.'

'That would be lovely, Jimmy,' I said.

'As for the good doctor, she should be finishing up an inquest.' He glanced at his watch as we entered his cluttered small space. 'She should be out in no time.'

His desk was dominated by a large Coroner's Inquiries book, black and bound in heavy leather, and he had been reading a biography of Steve McQueen and eating toast before I arrived. Momentarily, he was setting a mug of tea within my reach, not asking how I took it, for by now he knew.

'A little toast with jam?' he asked as he did every morning.

'I ate at the hotel, thanks.' I gave the same reply as he sat behind his desk.

'Never stops me from eating again.' He smiled, slipping on glasses. 'I'll just go over your schedule, then. You lecture at eleven this morning, then again at one P.M. Both at the college, in the old pathology building. I should expect about seventy-five students for each, but there could be more. I don't know. You're awfully popular over here, Dr Kay Scarpetta,' he cheerfully said. 'Or maybe it's just that American violence is so exotic to us.'

'That's rather much like calling a plague *exotic*,' I said.

'Well, we can't help but be fascinated by what you see.'

'And I guess that bothers me,' I said in a friendly but ominous way. 'Don't be too fascinated.'

We were interrupted by the phone, which he snapped up with the impatience of one who answers it too often.

Listening for a moment, he brusquely said. 'Right, right.

Well, we can't place an order like that just yet. I'll have to ring you back another time.

'I've been wanting computers for years,' he complained to me as he hung up. 'No bloody money when you're the dog wagged by the Socialist tail.'

'There will never be enough money. Dead men don't vote.'

'The bloody truth. So what's the topic of the day?' he wanted to know.

'Sexual homicide,' I replied. 'Specifically the role DNA can play.'

'These dismemberments you're so interested in.' He sipped tea. 'Do you think they're sexual? I mean, would that be the motivation on the part of whoever would do this?' His eyes were keen with interest.

'It's certainly an element,' I replied.

'But how can you know that when none of the victims has ever been identified? Couldn't it just be someone who kills for sport? Like, say, your Son of Sam, for example?'

'What the Son of Sam did had a sexual element,' I said,

looking around for my pathologist friend. 'Do you know how much longer she might be? I'm afraid I'm in a bit of a hurry.'

Shaw glanced at his watch again. 'You can check. Or I suppose she may have gone on to the morgue. We have a case coming in. A young male, suspected suicide.'

'I'll see if I can find her.' I got up.

Off the hallway near the entrance was the coroner's court, where inquests for unnatural deaths were held before a jury. This included industrial and traffic accidents, homicides and suicides, the proceedings *in camera*, for the press in Ireland was not allowed to print many details. I ducked inside a stark, chilly room of varnished benches and naked walls, and found several men inside, tucking paperwork into briefcases.

'I'm looking for the coroner,' I said.

'She slipped out about twenty minutes ago. Believe she had a viewing,' one of them said.

I left the building through the back door. Crossing a small parking lot, I headed to the morgue as an old man came out of it. He seemed disoriented, almost stumbling as he looked about, dazed. For an instant, he stared at me as if I held some answer, and my heart hurt for him. No business that had brought him here could possibly be kind. I watched him hurry toward the gate as Dr Margaret Foley suddenly emerged after him, harried, her graying hair disarrayed.

'My God!' She almost ran into me. 'I turn my back for a minute and he's gone.'

The man let himself out, the gate flung open wide as he fled. Foley trotted across the parking lot to shut and latch it again. When she got back to me, she was out of breath and almost tripped over a bump in the pavement.

'Kay, you're out and about early,' she said.

'A relative?' I asked.

'The father. Left without identifying him, before I could even pull back the sheet. That will foul me up the rest of the day.'

She led me inside the small brick morgue with its white porcelain autopsy tables that probably belonged in a medical museum and old iron stove that heated nothing anymore. The air was refrigerated-chilly, modern equipment nonexistent except for electric autopsy saws. Thin gray light seeped through opaque skylights, barely illuminating the white paper sheet covering a body that a father could not bear to see.

'It's always the hardest part,' she was saying. 'No one should ever have to look at anyone in here.'

I followed her into a small storeroom and helped carry out boxes of new syringes, masks and gloves.

'Strung himself up from the rafters in the barn,' she went on as we worked. 'Was being treated for a drink problem and depression. More of the same. Unemployment, women, drugs. They hang themselves or jump off bridges.' She glanced at me as we restocked a surgical cart. 'Thank God we don't have guns. Especially since I don't have an X-ray machine.'

Foley was a slight woman with old-fashioned thick glasses and a penchant for tweed. We had met years ago at an international forensic science conference in Vienna, when female forensic pathologists were a rare breed, especially overseas. We quickly had become friends.

'Margaret, I'm going to have to head back to the States sooner than I thought,' I said, taking a deep breath, looking about, distracted. 'I didn't sleep worth a damn last night.'

She lit a cigarette, scrutinizing me. 'I can get you copies of whatever you want. How fast do you need them? Photographs may take a few days, but they can be sent.'

'I think there is always a sense of urgency when someone like this is on the loose,' I said.

'I'm not happy if he's now your problem. And I'd hoped after all these years he had bloody quit.' She irritably tapped an ash, exhaling the strong smoke of British tobacco. 'Let's take a load off for a minute. My shoes are already getting tight from the swelling. It's hell getting old on these bloody hard floors.'

The lounge was two squat wooden chairs in a corner, where Foley kept an ashtray on a gurney. She put her feet up on a box and indulged her vice.

'I can never forget those poor people.' She started talking about her serial cases again. 'When the first one came to me, I thought it was the IRA. Never seen people torn asunder like that except in bombings.'

I was reminded of Mark in a way I did not want to be, and my thoughts drifted to him when he was alive and we were in love. Suddenly he was in my mind, smiling with eyes full of a mischievous light that became electric when he laughed and teased. There had been a lot of that in law school at Georgetown, fun and fights and staying up all night, our hunger for each other impossible to appease. Over time we married other people, divorced and tried again. He was my leitmotif, here, gone, then back on the phone or at my door to break my heart and wreck my bed.

I could not banish him. It still did not seem possible that a bombing in a London train station would finally bring the tempest of our relationship to an end. I did not imagine him dead. I could not envision it, for there was no last image that might grant peace. I had never seen his body, had fled from any chance, just like the old Dubliner who could not view his son. I realized Foley was saying something to me.

'I'm sorry,' she repeated, her eyes sad, for she knew my history well. 'I didn't mean to bring up something painful. You seem blue enough this morning.'

'You made an interesting point.' I tried to be brave. 'I suspect the killer we're looking for is rather much like a bomber. He doesn't care who he kills. His victims are people with no faces or names. They are nothing but symbols of his private, evil credo.'

'Would it bother you terribly if I asked a question about Mark?' she said.

'Ask anything you want.' I smiled. 'You will anyway.'

'Have you ever gone to where it happened, visited that place where he died?'

'I don't know where it happened,' I quickly replied.

She looked at me as she smoked.

'What I mean is, I don't know where, exactly, in the train station.' I was evasive, almost stuttering.

Still she said nothing, crushing the cigarette beneath her foot.

'Actually,' I went on, 'I don't know that I've been in Victoria at all, not that particular station, since he died. I don't think I've had reason to take a train from there. Or arrive there. Waterloo was the last one I was in, I think.'

'The one crime scene the great Dr Kay Scarpetta will not visit.' She tapped another Consulate out of the pack. 'Would you like one?'

'God knows I would. But I can't.'

She sighed. 'I remember Vienna. All those men and the two of us smoking more than they did.'

'Probably the reason we smoked so much was all those men,' I said.

'That may be the cause, but for me, there seems to be no cure. It just goes to show that what we do is unrelated to what we know, and our feelings don't have a brain.' She shook out a match. 'I've seen smokers' lungs. And I've seen my share of fatty livers.'

'My lungs are better since I quit. I can't vouch for my liver,' I said. 'I haven't given up whiskey yet.'

'Don't, for God's sake. You'd be no fun.' She paused, adding pointedly, 'Course, feelings can be directed, educated, so they don't conspire against us.'

'I will probably leave tomorrow.' I got back to that.

'You have to go to London first to change planes.' She met my eyes. 'Linger there. A day.'

'Pardon?'

'It's unfinished business, Kay. I have felt this for a long time. You need to bury Mark James.'

'Margaret, what has suddenly prompted this?' I was tripping over words again.

'I know when someone is on the run. And you are, just as much as this killer is.'

'Now, that's a comforting thing to say,' I replied, and I did not want to have this conversation.

But she was not going to let me escape this time. 'For very different reasons and very similar reasons. He's evil, you're not. But neither of you wants to be caught.'

She had gotten to me and could tell.

'And just who or what is trying to catch me, in your opinion?' My tone was light but I felt the threat of tears.

'At this stage, I expect it's Benton Wesley.'

I stared off, past the gurney and its protruding pale foot tied with a tag. Light from above shifted by degrees as clouds moved over the sun, and the smell of death in tile and stone went back a hundred years.

'Kay, what do you want to do?' she asked kindly as I wiped my eyes.

'He wants to marry me,' I said.

I flew home to Richmond and days became weeks with the weather getting cold. Mornings were glazed with frost and evenings I spent in front of the fire, thinking and fretting. So much was unresolved and silent, and I coped the way I always did, working my way deeper into the labyrinth of my profession until I could not find a way out. It was making my secretary crazy.

'Dr Scarpetta?' She called out my name, her footsteps loud and brisk along the tile floor in the autopsy suite.

'In here,' I answered over running water.

It was October 30. I was in the morgue locker room, washing up with antibacterial soap.

'Where have you been?' Rose asked as she walked in.

'Working on a brain. The sudden death from the other day.'

She was holding my calendar and flipping pages. Her gray hair was neatly pinned back, and she was dressed in a dark red suit that seemed appropriate for her mood. Rose was deeply angry with me and had been since I'd left for Dublin without saying good-bye. Then I forgot her birthday when I got back. I turned off the water and dried my hands.

'Swelling, with widening of the gyri, narrowing of the

sulci, all good for ischemic encephalopathy brought on by his profound systemic hypotension,' I cited.

'I've been trying to find you,' she said with strained patience.

'What did I do this time?' I threw up my hands.

'You were supposed to have lunch at the Skull and Bones with Jon.'

'Oh, God,' I groaned as I thought of him and other medical school advisees I had so little time to see.

'I reminded you this morning. You forgot him last week, too. He really needs to talk to you about his residency, about the Cleveland Clinic.'

'I know, I know.' I felt awful about it as I looked at my watch. 'It's one-thirty. Maybe he can come by my office for coffee?'

'You have a deposition at two, a conference call at three about the Norfolk-Southern case. A gunshot wound lecture to the Forensic Science Academy at four, and a meeting at five with Investigator Ring from the state police.' Rose went down the list.

I did not like Ring or his aggressive way of taking over cases. When the second torso had been found, he had inserted himself into the investigation and seemed to think he knew more than the FBI.

'Ring I can do without,' I said, shortly.

My secretary looked at me for a long moment, water and sponges slapping in the autopsy suite next door.

'I'll cancel him and you can see Jon instead.' She eyed me over her glasses like a stern headmistress. 'Then rest, and that's an order. Tomorrow, Dr Scarpetta. Don't come in. Don't you dare let me see you darken the door.'

I started to protest and she cut me off.

'Don't even think of arguing,' she firmly went on. 'You need a mental health day, a long weekend. I wouldn't say that if I didn't mean it.'

She was right, and as I thought about having a day to myself, my spirits lifted.

'There's not a thing I can't reschedule,' she added. 'Besides.' She smiled. 'We're having a touch of Indian summer and it's supposed to be glorious, in the eighties with a big blue sky. Leaves are at their peak, poplars an almost perfect yellow. Maples look like they're on fire. Not to mention, it's Halloween. You can carve a pumpkin.'

I got suit jacket and shoes out of my locker. 'You should have been a lawyer,' I said.

T HE NEXT DAY, the weather was just what
Rose predicted, and I woke up thrilled. As stores
were opening, I set out to stock up for trick-
or-treaters and dinner, and I drove far out on
Hull Street to my favorite gardening center. Summer plant-
ings had long since faded around my house, and I could not
bear to see their dead stalks in pots. After lunch, I carried
bags of black soil, boxes of plants and a watering can to my
front porch.

I opened the door so I could hear Mozart playing inside
as I gently tucked pansies into their rich, new bed. Bread
was rising, homemade stew simmering on the stove, and I
smelled garlic and wine and loamy soil as I worked. Marino

was coming for dinner, and we were going to hand out chocolate bars to my small, scary neighbors. The world was a good place to live until three-thirty-five when my pager vibrated against my waist.

'Damn,' I exclaimed as it displayed the number for my answering service.

I hurried inside, washed my hands and reached for the phone. The service gave me a number for a Detective Grigg with the Sussex County Sheriff's Department, and I immediately called.

'Grigg,' a man answered in a deep voice.

'This is Dr Scarpetta,' I said as I stared dismally out windows at large terra cotta pots on the deck and the dead hibiscus in them.

'Oh good. Thank you for getting back to me so quick. I'm out here on a cellular phone, don't want to say much.' He spoke with the rhythm of the old South, and took his time.

'Where, exactly, is *here?*' I asked.

'Atlantic Waste Landfill on Reeves Road, off 460 East. They've turned something up I think you're going to want to take a look at.'

'Is this the same sort of thing that has turned up in similar places?' I cryptically asked as the day seemed to get darker.

'Afraid that's what it's looking like,' he said.

'Give me directions, and I'm on my way.'

I was in dirty khakis, and an FBI tee shirt that my niece, Lucy, had given to me, and did not have time to change. If I didn't recover the body before dark, it would have to stay where it was until morning, and that was unacceptable. Grabbing my medical bag, I hurried out the door, leaving soil, cabbage plants and geraniums scattered over the porch. Of course my black Mercedes was low on gas. I stopped at Amoco first and pumped my own, then was on my way.

The drive should have taken an hour, but I sped. Waning light flashed white on the underside of leaves, and rows of corn were brown in farms and gardens. Fields were ruffled green seas of soybeans, and goats grazed unrestrained in the yards of tired homes. Gaudy lightning rods with colored balls tilted from every peak and corner, and I always wondered what lying salesman had hit like a storm and played on fear by preaching more.

Soon grain elevators Grigg had told me to look for came into view. I turned on Reeves Road, passing tiny brick homes and trailer courts with pickup trucks and dogs with no collars. Billboards advertised Mountain Dew and the Virginia Diner, and I bumped over railroad tracks, red dust billowing up like smoke from my tires. Ahead, buzzards in the road picked at creatures that had been too slow, and it seemed a morbid harbinger.

At the entrance of the Atlantic Waste Landfill, I slowed my car to a stop and looked out at a moonscape of barren acres where the sun was setting like a planet on fire. Flatbed refuse trucks were sleek and white with polished chrome, crawling along the summit of a growing mountain of trash. Yellow Caterpillars were striking scorpions. I sat watching a moiling storm of dust heading away from the landfill, rocking over ruts at a high rate of speed. When it got to me it was a dirty red Ford Explorer driven by a young man who felt at home in this place.

'May I help you, ma'am?' he said in a Southern drawl, and he seemed anxious and excited.

'I'm Dr Kay Scarpetta,' I replied, displaying the brass

shield in its small black wallet that I always pulled at scenes where I did not know anyone.

He studied my credentials, then his eyes were dark on mine. He was sweating through his denim shirt, hair wet at his neck and temples.

'They said the medical examiner would get here, and for me to watch for him,' he said to me.

'Well, that would be me,' I blandly replied.

'Oh yes, ma'am. I didn't mean anything . . .' His voice trailed off as his eyes wandered over my Mercedes, which was coated in dust so fine and persistent that nothing could keep it out. 'I suggest you leave your car here and ride with me,' he added.

I stared up at the landfill, at Caterpillars with rampant blades and buckets immobile on the summit. Two unmarked police cars and an ambulance awaited me up where the trouble was, and officers were small figures gathered near the tailgate of a truck smaller than the rest. Near it someone was poking the ground with a stick, and I got increasingly impatient to get to the body.

'Okay,' I said. 'Let's do it.'

Parking my car, I got my medical bag and scene clothes out of the trunk. The young man watched in curious silence as I sat in my driver's seat with the door open wide, and pulled on rubber boots, scarred and dull from years of wading in woods and rivers for people murdered and drowned. I covered myself with a big faded denim shirt that I had appropriated from my ex-husband, Tony, during a marriage that now did not seem real. Then I climbed inside the Explorer and sheathed my hands in two layers of gloves. I pulled a surgical mask over my head and left it loose around my neck.

'I can't say that I blame you,' my driver said. 'The smell's pretty rough. I can tell you that.'

'It's not the smell,' I said. 'Microorganisms are what make me worry.'

'Gee,' he said, anxiously. 'Maybe I should wear one of those things.'

'You shouldn't be getting close enough to have a problem.'

He made no reply, and I had no doubt that he already had gotten that close. Looking was too much of a temptation for most people to resist. The more gruesome the case, the more this was true.

'I sure am sorry about the dust,' he said as we drove through tangled goldenrod on the rim of a small fire pond populated with ducks.'You can see we put a layer of tire chips everywhere to keep things settled, and a street cleaner sprays it down. But nothing seems to help all that much.' He nervously paused before going on. 'We do three thousand tons of trash a day out here.'

'From where?' I asked.

'Littleton, North Carolina, to Chicago.'

'What about Boston?' I asked, for the first four cases were believed to be from as far away as that.

'No, ma'am.' He shook his head. 'Maybe one of these days. We're so much less per ton down here. Twenty-five dollars compared to sixty-nine in New Jersey or eighty in New York. Plus, we recycle, test for hazardous waste, collect methane gas from decomposing trash.'

'What about your hours?'

'Open twenty-four hours a day, seven days a week,' he said with pride.

'And you have a way to track where the trucks come from?'

21

'A satellite system that uses a grid. We can at least tell you which trucks would have dumped trash during a certain time period in the area where the body was found.'

We splashed through a deep puddle near Porta-Johns, and rocked by a powerwash where tracks were being hosed off on their way back out to life's roads and highways.

'I can't say we've ever had anything like this,' he said. 'Now, they've had body parts at the Shoosmith dump. Or at least, that's the rumor.'

He glanced at me, assuming I would know if such a rumor were true. But I did not verify what he had just said as the Explorer sloshed through mud strewn with rubber chips, the sour stench of decomposing garbage drifting in. My attention was riveted to the small truck I had been watching since I had gotten here, thoughts racing along a thousand different tracks.

'By the way, my name's Keith Pleasants.' He wiped a hand on his pants and held it out to me. 'Pleased to meet you.'

My gloved hand shook his at an awkward angle as men holding handkerchiefs and rags over their noses watched us pull up. There were four of them, gathered around the back of what I now could see was a hydraulic packer, used for emptying Dumpsters and compressing the trash. *Cole's Trucking Co.* was painted on the doors.

'That guy poking garbage with a stick is the detective for Sussex,' Pleasants said to me.

He was older, in shirtsleeves, wearing a revolver on his hip. I felt I'd seen him somewhere before.

'Grigg?' I guessed, referring to the detective I had spoken to on the phone.

'That's right.' Sweat was rolling down Pleasants' face, and he was getting more keyed up. 'You know, I've never had any dealings with the sheriff's department, never even got a speeding ticket around here.'

We slowed down to a halt, and I could barely see through the boiling dust. Pleasants grabbed his door handle.

'Sit tight just a minute,' I told him.

I waited for dust to settle, looking out the windshield and surveying as I always did when approaching a crime scene. The loader's bucket was frozen midair, the packer beneath it almost full. All around, the landfill was busy and full of diesel sounds, work stopped only here. For a moment, I watched powerful white trucks roar uphill as Cats clawed and grabbed, and compactors crushed the ground with their chopper wheels.

The body would be transported by ambulance, and para-medics watched me through dusty windows as they sat in air conditioning, waiting to see what I was going to do. When they saw me fix the surgical mask over my nose and mouth and open my door, they climbed out, too. Doors slammed shut. The detective immediately walked to meet me.

'Detective Grigg, Sussex Sheriff's Department,' he said. 'I'm the one who called.'

'Have you been out here the entire time?' I asked him.

'Since we were notified at approximately thirteen hundred hours. Yes, ma'am. I've been right here to make sure nothing was disturbed.'

'Excuse me,' one of the paramedics said to me. 'You going to want us right now?'

'Maybe in fifteen. Someone will come get you,' I said as they wasted no time returning to their ambulance. 'I'm going to need some room here,' I said to everybody else.

Feet crunched as people stepped out of the way, revealing what they had been guarding and gawking at. Flesh was unnaturally pale in the dying light of the autumn afternoon, the torso a hideous stub that had tumbled from a scoop of trash and landed on its back. I thought it was Caucasian, but was not sure, and maggots teeming in the genital area made it difficult for me to determine gender at a glance. I could not even say with certainty whether the victim was pre- or postpubescent. Body fat was abnormally low, ribs protruding beneath flat breasts that may or may not have been female.

I squatted close and opened my medical bag. With forceps, I collected maggots into a jar for the entomologist to examine later, and decided upon closer inspection that the victim was, in fact, a woman. She had been decapitated low on the cervical spine, arms and legs severed. Stumps were dry and dark with age, and I knew right away that there was a difference between this case and the others.

This woman had been dismembered by cutting straight through the strong bones of the humerus and femur, versus the joints. Getting out a scalpel, I could feel the men staring as I made a half-inch incision on the torso's right side, and inserted a long chemical thermometer. I rested a second thermometer on top of my bag.

'What are you doing?' asked a man in a plaid shirt and baseball cap, who looked like he might get sick.

'I need the body's temperature to help determine time of death. A core liver temperature is the most accurate,' I patiently explained. 'And I also need to know the temperature out here.'

'Hot, that's what it is,' said another man. 'So, it's a woman, I guess.'

'It's too soon to say,' I replied. 'Is this your packer?'

'Yeah.'

He was young, with dark eyes and very white teeth, and tattoos on his fingers that I usually associated with people who have been in prison. A sweaty bandanna was tied around his head and knotted in back, and he could not look at the torso long without averting his gaze.

'In the wrong place at the wrong time,' he added, shaking his head with hostility.

'What do you mean?' Grigg had his eye on him.

'Wasn't from me. I know that,' the driver said as if it were the most important point he would ever make in his life. 'The Cat dug it up while it was spreading my load.'

'Then we don't know when it was dumped here?' I scanned faces around me.

It was Pleasants who replied, 'Twenty-three trucks unloaded in this spot since ten A.M., not counting this one.' He looked at the packer.

'Why ten A.M.?' I asked, for it seemed like a rather arbitrary time to start counting trucks.

'Because that's when we put down the last cover of tire chips. So there's no way it could have been dumped before then,' Pleasants explained, staring at the body. 'And in my opinion, it couldn't have been out long, anyway. It doesn't exactly look the way you'd expect if it's been run over by a fifty-ton compactor with chopper wheels, trucks or even this loader.'

He stared off at other sites where compacted trash was being gouged off trucks as huge tractors crushed and spread. The driver of the packer was getting increasingly agitated and angry.

'We got big machines all over the place up here,' Pleasants added. 'And they pretty much never stop.'

I looked at the packer, and the bright yellow loader with

its empty cab. A tatter of black trash bag fluttered from the raised bucket.

'Where's the driver of the loader?' I asked.

Pleasants hesitated before answering, 'Well, I guess that would be me. We had somebody out sick. I was asked to work on the hill.'

Grigg moved closer to the loader, looking up at what was left of the trash bag as it moved in the hot, barren air.

'Tell me what you saw,' I said to Pleasants.

'Not much. I was unloading him.' He nodded at the driver. 'And my bucket caught the garbage bag, the one you see there. It tore and the body fell out to where it is now.' He paused, wiping his face on his sleeve and swatting at flies.

'But you don't know for sure where this came from,' I tried again, while Grigg listened, even though he probably had already taken their statements.

'I could've dug it up,' Pleasants conceded. 'I'm not saying it's impossible. I just don't think I did.'

'That's 'cause you don't want to think it.' The driver glared at him.

'I know what I think.' Pleasants didn't flinch. 'The bucket grabbed it off your packer when I was unloading it.'

'Man, you don't *know* it came from me,' the driver snapped at him.

'No, I don't know it for a fact. Makes sense, that's all.'

'Maybe to you.' The driver's face was menacing.

'Believe that will be about enough, boys,' Grigg warned, moving close again, his presence reminding them he was big and wore a gun.

'You got that right,' said the driver. 'I've had enough of this shit. When can I get out of here? I'm already late.'

'Something like this inconveniences everyone,' Grigg said to him with a steady look.

Rolling his eyes and muttering profanity, the driver stalked off and lit a cigarette.

I removed the thermometer from the body, and held it up. The core temperature was eighty-four degrees, the same as the ambient air. I turned the torso over to see what else was there and noted a curious crop of fluid-filled vesicles over the lower buttocks. As I checked more carefully, I found evidence of others in the area of the shoulders and thighs, at the edges of deep cuts.

'Double-pouch her,' I directed. 'I need the trash bag it came in, including what's caught on the bucket up there. And I want the trash immediately around and under her, send all of it in.'

Grigg unfolded a twenty-gallon trash bag and shook it open. He pulled gloves out of a pocket, squatted and started grabbing up garbage by the handful while paramedics opened the back of the ambulance. The driver of the packer was leaning against his cab, and I could feel his fury like heat.

'Where was your packer coming from?' I asked him.

'Look at the tags,' he replied in a surly tone.

'Where in Virginia?' I refused to be put off by him.

It was Pleasants who said, 'Tidewater area, ma'am. The packer belongs to us. We got a lot of them we lease.'

The landfill's administrative headquarters overlooked the fire pond and was quaintly out of sync with the loud, dusty surroundings. The building was pale peach stucco, with flowers in window boxes and sculpted shrubs bordering the walk. Shutters were painted cream, a brass pineapple knocker on the front door. Inside, I was greeted by clean, chilled air that was a wonderful relief and I knew why Investigator Percy Ring had chosen to conduct his interviews here. I bet he had not even been to the scene.

He was in the break room, sitting with an older man in shirtsleeves, drinking Diet Coke and looking at computer-printed diagrams.

'This is Dr Scarpetta. Sorry,' Pleasants said, adding to Ring, 'I don't know your first name.'

Ring gave me a big smile and a wink. 'The doc and I go way back.'

He was in a crisp blue suit, blond and exuding pure youthful innocence that was easy to believe. But he had never fooled me. He was a big-talking charmer who basically was lazy, and it had not escaped me that the moment he had become involved in these cases, we had been besieged by leaks to the press.

'And this is Mr Kitchen,' Pleasants was saying to me. 'The owner of the landfill.'

Kitchen was simple in jeans and Timberland boots, his eyes gray and sad as he offered a big rough hand.

'Please sit down,' he said, pulling out a chair. 'This is a bad, bad day. Especially for whoever that is out there.'

'That person's bad day happened earlier,' Ring said. 'Right now, she's feeling no pain.'

'Have you been up there?' I asked him.

'I just got here about an hour ago. And this isn't the crime scene, just where the body ended up,' he said. 'Number five.' He peeled open a stick of Juicy Fruit. 'He's not waiting as long, only two months in between 'em this time.'

I felt the usual rush of irritation. Ring loved to jump to conclusions and voice them with the certainty of one who doesn't know enough to realize he could be wrong. In part this was because he wanted results without work.

'I haven't examined the body yet or verified gender,' I said, hoping he would remember there were other people in the room. 'This is not a good time to be making assumptions.'

'Well, I'll leave ya,' Pleasants said nervously, on his way out the door.

'I need you back in an hour so I can get your statement,' Ring loudly reminded him.

Kitchen was quiet, looking at diagrams, and then Grigg walked in. He nodded at us and took a chair.

'I don't think it's an assumption to say that what we got here is a homicide,' Ring said to me.

'That you can safely say.' I held his gaze.

'And that it's just like the other ones.'

'That you can't safely say. I haven't examined the body yet,' I replied.

Kitchen shifted uncomfortably in his chair. 'Anybody want a soda. Maybe coffee?' he asked. 'We got rest rooms in the hall.'

'Same thing,' Ring said to me as if he knew. 'Another torso in a landfill.'

Grigg was watching with no expression, restlessly tapping his notebook. Clicking his pen twice, he said to Ring, 'I agree with Dr Scarpetta. Seems we shouldn't be connecting this case to anything yet. Especially not publicly.'

'Lord help me. I could do without that kind of publicity,' Kitchen said, blowing out a deep breath. 'You know, when you're in my business, you accept this can happen, especially when you're getting waste from places like New York, New Jersey, Chicago. But you never think it's going to land in your yard.' He looked at Grigg. 'I'd like to offer a reward to help

29

catch whoever did this terrible thing. Ten thousand dollars for information leading to the arrest.'

'That's mighty generous,' Grigg said, impressed.

'That include investigators?' Ring grinned.

'I don't care who solves it.' Kitchen wasn't smiling as he turned to me. 'Now you tell me what I can do to help you, ma'am.'

'I understand you use a satellite tracking system,' I said. 'Is that what these diagrams are?'

'I was just explaining them,' Kitchen said.

He slid several of them to me. Their patterns of wavy lines looked like cross sections of geode, and they were marked with coordinates.

'This is a picture of the landfill face,' Kitchen explained. 'We can take it hourly, daily, weekly, whenever we want, to figure out where waste originated and where it was deposited. Locations on the map can be pinpointed by using these coordinates.' He tapped the paper. 'Sort of similar to how you plot a graph in geometry or algebra.' Looking up at me, he added, 'I reckon you suffered through some of that in school.'

'*Suffer* is the operative word.' I smiled at him. 'Then the point is you can compare these pictures to see how the landfill's face changes from load to load.'

He nodded. 'Yes, ma'am. That's it in a nutshell.'

'And what have you determined?'

He placed eight maps side by side. The wavy lines in each were different, like different wrinkles on the faces of the same person.

'Each line, basically, is a depth,' he said. 'So we can pretty much know which truck is responsible for which depth.'

Ring emptied his Coke can and tossed it in the trash.

He flipped through his notepad as if looking for something.

'This body could not have been buried deep,' I said. 'It's very clean, considering the circumstances. There are no postmortem injuries, and based on what I observed out there, the Cats grab bales off the trucks, smash them open. They spread the trash on the ground so the compactor can doze it with the straight blade, chopping and compressing.'

'That's pretty much it.' Kitchen eyed me with interest. 'You want a job?'

I was preoccupied with images of earth-moving machines that looked like robotic dinosaurs, claws biting into plastic-shrouded bales on trucks. I was intimately acquainted with the injuries in the earlier cases, with human remains crushed and mauled. Except for what the killer had done, this victim was intact.

'Hard to find good women,' Kitchen was saying.

'You ain't kidding, brother,' Ring said as Grigg watched him with growing disgust.

'Seems like a good point,' Grigg said. 'If that body had been on the ground for any time at all, it would be pretty chewed up.'

'The first four were,' Ring said. 'Mangled like cube steak.' He eyed me. 'This one look compacted?'

'The body doesn't appear crushed,' I replied.

'Now that's interesting, too,' he mused. 'Why wouldn't it be?'

'It didn't start out at a transfer station where it was compacted and baled,' Kitchen said. 'It started in a Dumpster that was emptied by the packer.'

'And the packer doesn't pack?' Ring dramatically asked.

'Thought that's why they were called *packers*.' He shrugged and grinned at me.

'It depends on where the body was in relation to the other garbage when the compacting was done,' I said. 'It depends on a lot of things.'

'Or if it was compacted at all, depending on how full the truck was,' Kitchen said. 'I'm thinking it was the packer. Or at most, one of the two trucks before it, if we're talking about the exact coordinates where the body was found.'

'I guess I'm going to need the names of those trucks and where they're from,' Ring said. 'We gotta interview the drivers.'

'So you're looking at the drivers as suspects,' Grigg said, coolly, to him. 'Got to give you credit, that's original. The way I look at it, the trash didn't originate with them. It originated with the folks who pitched it. And I expect one of those folks is who we need to find.'

Ring stared at him, not the least bit perturbed. 'I'd just like to hear what the drivers have to say. You never know. It'd be a good way to stage something. You dump a body in a place that's on your route and make sure you deliver it yourself. Or, hell, you load it into your own truck. No one suspects you, right?'

Grigg pushed back his chair. He loosened his collar and worked his jaw as if it hurt. His neck popped, then his knuckles. Finally, he slapped his notebook down on the table and everybody looked at him as he glared at Ring.

'You mind if I work this thing?' he said to the young investigator. 'I'd sure hate not to do what the county hired me for. And I believe this is my case, not yours.'

'Just here to help,' Ring said easily as he shrugged again.

'I didn't know I needed help,' Grigg replied.

'The state police formed the multijurisdictional task force on homicides when the second torso showed up in a different county than the first one,' Ring said. 'You're a little late in the game, good buddy. Seems like you might want some background from somebody who's not.'

But Grigg had tuned him out, and he said to Kitchen, 'I'd like that vehicle information, too.'

'How about I get it for the last five trucks that were up there, to be safe,' Kitchen said to all of us.

'That will help a lot,' I said as I got up from the table. 'The sooner you could do that, the better.'

'What time you going to work on it tomorrow?' Ring asked me, remaining in his chair, as if there were little to do in life and so much time.

'Are you referring to the autopsy?' I asked.

'You bet.'

'I may not even open this one up for several days.'

'Why's that?'

'The most important part is the external examination. I will spend a very long time on that.' I could see his interest fade. 'I'll need to go through trash, search for trace, degrease and deflesh bones, get with an entomologist on the age of the maggots to see if I can get an idea of when the body was dumped, et cetera.'

'Maybe it's better if you just let me know what you find,' he decided.

Grigg followed me out the door and was shaking his head as he said in his slow, quiet way, 'When I got out of the army a long time ago, state police was what I wanted to be. I can't believe they got a bozo like that.'

'Fortunately, they're not all like him,' I said.

We walked out into the sun as the ambulance slowly made

its way down the landfill in clouds of dust. Trucks were chugging in line and getting washed, as another layer of shredded modern America was added to the mountain. It was dark out when we reached our cars. Grigg paused by mine, looking it over.

'I wondered whose this was,' he said with admiration. 'One of these days I'm going to drive something like that. Just once.'

I smiled at him as I unlocked my door. 'Doesn't have the important things like a siren and lights.'

He laughed. 'Marino and me are in the same bowling league. His team's the Balls of Fire, mine's the Lucky Strikes. That ole boy's about the worst sport I ever seen. Drinks beer and eats. Then thinks everybody's cheating. He brought a girl the last time.' He shook his head. 'She bowled like the damn Flintstones, dressed like them, too. In this leopard-skin thing. All that was missing was a bone in her hair. Well, tell him we'll talk.'

He walked off, his keys jingling.

'Detective Grigg, thanks for your help,' I said.

He gave me a nod and climbed into his Caprice.

When I designed my house, I made sure the laundry room was directly off the garage because after working scenes like this one, I did not want to track death through the rooms of my private life. Within minutes of my getting out of my car, my clothes were in the washing machine, shoes and boots in an industrial sink, where I scrubbed them with detergent and a stiff brush.

Wrapping up in a robe I kept hanging on the back of the door, I headed to the master bedroom and took a long, hot shower. I was worn out and discouraged. Right now, I did not have the energy to imagine her, or her name, or who she had been, and I pushed images and odors from my mind. I fixed myself a drink and a salad, staring dismally at the big bowl of Halloween candy on the counter as I thought of plants waiting to be potted on the porch. Then I called Marino.

'Listen,' I said to him when he answered the phone. 'I think Benton should be here for this in the morning.'

There was a long pause. 'Okay,' he said. 'Meaning you want me to tell him to get his ass to Richmond. Versus your telling him.'

'If you wouldn't mind. I'm beat.'

'No problem. What time?'

'Whenever he wants. I'll be down there all day.'

I went back to the office in my house to check e-mail before I went to bed. Lucy rarely called when she could use the computer to tell me how and where she was. My niece was an FBI agent, the technical specialist for their Hostage Rescue Team, or HRT. She could be sent anywhere in the world at a moment's notice.

Like a fretful mother, I found myself frequently checking for messages from her, dreading the day her pager went off, sending her to Andrews Air Force Base with the boys, to board yet another C-141 cargo plane. Stepping around stacks of journals waiting to be read and thick medical tomes that I recently had bought but had not yet shelved, I sat at my desk. My office was the most lived-in room in my house, and I had designed it with a fireplace and large windows overlooking a rocky bend in the James River.

Logging on to America Online, or AOL, I was greeted by a mechanical male voice announcing that I had mail. I had e-mail about various cases, trials, professional meetings and journal articles, and one message from someone I did not recognize. His user name was *deadoc*. Immediately, I was uneasy. There was no description of what this person had sent, and when I opened what he had written to me, it simply said, *ten*.

A graphic file had been attached, and I downloaded and decompressed it. An image began to materialize on my screen, rolling down in color, one band of pixels at a time. I realized I was looking at a photograph of a wall the color of putty, and the edge of a table with some sort of pale blue cover on it that was smeared and pooled with something dark red. Then a ragged, gaping red wound was painted on the screen, followed by flesh tones that became bloody stumps and nipples.

I stared in disbelief as the horror was complete, and I grabbed the phone.

'Marino, I think you'd better get over here,' I said in a scared tone.

'What's wrong?' he said, alarmed.

'There's something here you need to see.'

'Are you okay?'

'I don't know.'

'Sit tight, Doc.' He took charge. 'I'm coming.'

I printed the file and saved it on my A drive, fearful it would somehow vanish before my eyes. While I waited for Marino, I dimmed the lights in my office to make details and colors brighter. My mind ran in a terrible loop as I stared at the butchery, the blood forming a vile portrait that for me, ordinarily, wasn't rare. Other physicians, scientists, lawyers and law enforcement officers frequently sent me photographs like this over the Internet. Routinely, I was asked, via e-mail, to examine crime scenes, organs, wounds, diagrams, even animated reconstructions of cases about to go to court.

This photograph could easily have been one sent by a detective, a colleague. It could have come from a Commonwealth's Attorney or CASKU. But there was one thing obviously wrong. So far we had no crime scene in this case, only a landfill where the victim had been dumped, and the trash and tattered bag that had been around her. Only the killer or someone else involved in the crime could have sent this file to me.

Fifteen minutes later, at almost midnight, my doorbell rang, and I jumped out of my chair. I ran down the hall to let Marino in.

'What the hell is it now?' he said right off.

He was sweating in a gray Richmond police tee shirt that was tight over his big body and gut, and baggy shorts and athletic shoes with tube socks pulled up to his calves. I smelled stale sweat and cigarettes.

'Come on,' I said.

He followed me down the hall into my office, and when he saw what was on the computer screen, he sat in my chair, scowling as he stared.

'Is this what the shit I think it is?' he said.

'Appears the photograph was taken where the body was dismembered.' I was not used to having anyone in the private place where I worked, and I could feel my anxiety level rise.

'This is what you found today.'

'What you're looking at was taken shortly after death,' I said. 'But yes, this is the torso from the landfill.'

'How do you know?' Marino said.

His eyes were fastened to the screen, and he adjusted my

chair. Then his big feet shoved books on the floor as he made himself more comfortable. When he picked up files and moved them to another corner of my desk, I couldn't stand it any longer.

'I have things where I want them,' I pointedly said as I returned the files to their original messy space.

'Hey, chill out, Doc,' he said as if it didn't matter. 'How do we know that this thing ain't a hoax?'

Again, he moved the files out of his way, and now I was really irritated.

'Marino, you're going to have to get up,' I said. 'I don't let anybody sit at my desk. You're making me crazy.'

He shot me an angry look and got up out of my chair. 'Hey, do me a favor. Next time call somebody else when you got a problem.'

'Try to be sensitive . . .'

He cut me off, losing his temper. 'No. *You* be sensitive and quit being such a friggin' fussbudges. No wonder you and Wesley got problems.'

'Marino,' I warned, 'you just crossed a line and better stop right there.'

He was silent, looking around, sweating.

'Let's get back to this.' I sat in my chair, readjusting it. 'I don't think this is a hoax, and I believe it's the torso from the landfill.'

'Why?' He would not look at me, hands in his pockets.

'Arms and legs are severed through the long bones, not the joints.' I touched the screen. 'There are other similarities. It's her, unless another victim with a similar body type has been killed and dismembered in the same manner, and we've not found her yet. And I don't know how someone could have perpetrated a hoax like this without knowing how the victim was dismembered. Not to mention, this case hasn't hit the news yet.'

'Shit.' His face was deep red. 'So, is there something like a return address?'

'Yes. Someone on AOL with the name D-E-A-D-O-C.'

'As in *Dead-Doc*?' He was intrigued enough to forget his mood.

'I can only assume. The message was one word: *ten*.'

'That's it?'

'In lowercase letters.'

He looked at me, thinking. 'You count the ones in Ireland, this is number ten. You got a copy of this thing?'

'Yes. And the Dublin cases and their possible connection to the first four here have been in the news.' I handed him a printout. 'Anybody could know about it.'

'Don't matter. Assuming this is the same killer and he's just struck again, he knows damn well how many he's killed,' he said. 'But what I'm not getting is how he knew where to send this file to you?'

'My address in AOL wouldn't be hard to guess. It's my name.'

'Jesus, I can't believe you would do that,' he erupted again. 'That's like using your date of birth for your burglar alarm code.'

'I use e-mail almost exclusively to communicate with medical examiners, people in the Health Department, the police. They need something easy to remember. Besides,' I added as his stare continued to pass judgment on me, 'it's never been a problem.'

'Well, now it sure as hell is,' he said, looking at the printout. 'Good news is, maybe we'll find something in here that will help. Maybe he left a trail in the computer.'

'On the Web,' I said.

'Yeah, whatever,' he said. 'Maybe you should call Lucy.'

'Benton should do that,' I reminded him. 'I can't ask her help on a case just because I'm her aunt.'

'So I guess I got to call him about that, too.' He picked his way around my clutter, walking to the doorway. 'I hope you've got some beer in this joint.' He stopped and turned toward me. 'You know, Doc, it ain't none of my business, but you got to talk to him eventually.'

'You're right,' I said. 'It's none of your business.'

THE NEXT MORNING, I woke up to the muffled drumming of heavy rain on the roof and the persistent beeping of my alarm. The hour was early for a day that I was supposed to be taking off from work, and it struck me that during the night the month had turned into November. Winter was not far away, another year gone. Opening shades, I looked out at the day. Petals from my roses were beaten to the ground, the river swollen and flowing around rocks that looked black.

I felt bad about Marino. I had been impatient with him when I had sent him home without a beer last night. But I did not want to talk with him about matters he would not understand. For him, it was simple. I was divorced. Benton Wesley's wife had left him for another man. We'd been having an affair, so we might as well get married. For a while I had gone along with the plan. Last fall and winter, Wesley and I went skiing, diving, we shopped, cooked in and out and even worked in my yard. We did not get along worth a damn.

In fact, I didn't want him in my house any more than I wanted Marino sitting in my chair. When Wesley moved a piece of furniture or even returned dishes and silverware to the wrong cabinets and drawers, I felt a secret anger that surprised and dismayed me. I had never believed that our relationship was right when he was still married, but back then we had enjoyed each other more, especially in bed. I feared that my failure to feel what I thought I should revealed a trait that I could not bear to see.

I drove to my office with the windshield wipers working hard as the relentless downpour thrummed the roof. Traffic was thin because it was barely seven, and Richmond's downtown skyline came into view slowly and by degrees in the watery fog. I thought of the photograph again. I envisioned it slowly painting down my screen, and the hairs on my arms stood up as a chill crept over me. I was disturbed in a way I could not define as it occurred to me for the first time that the person who had sent it might be someone I knew.

Turning on the Seventh Street exit, I wound around Shockoe Slip, with its wet cobblestones and trendy restaurants that were dark at this hour. I passed parking lots barely beginning to fill, and turned into the one behind my four-story stucco building. I couldn't believe it when I found a television news van waiting in my parking place, which was clearly designated by a sign that read CHIEF MEDICAL EXAMINER. The crew knew that if they waited there long enough, they would be rewarded with me.

I pulled up close and motioned for them to move as the van's doors slid open. A cameraman in a rain suit jumped out, coming my way, a reporter in tow with a microphone. I rolled my window down several inches.

'Move,' I said, and I wasn't nice about it. 'You're in my parking place.'

They did not care as someone else got out with lights. For a moment I sat staring, anger turning me hard like amber. The reporter was blocking my door, her microphone shoved through the opening in the window.

'Dr Scarpetta, can you verify that the Butcher has struck again?' she asked, loudly, as the camera rolled and lights burned.

'Move your van,' I said with iron calm as I stared right at her and the camera.

'Is it in fact a torso that was found?' Rain was running off her hood as she pushed the microphone in farther.

'I'm going to ask you one last time to move your van out of my parking place,' I said like a judge about to cite contempt of court. 'You are trespassing.'

The cameraman found a new angle, zooming in, harsh lights in my eyes.

'Was it dismembered like the others . . .?'

She jerked the microphone away just in time as my window went up. I shoved the car in gear and began backing, the crew scrambling out of the way as I made a three-hundred-and-sixty-degree turn. Tires spun and skidded as I parked right behind the van, pinning it between my Mercedes and the building.

'Wait a minute!'

'Hey! You can't do that!'

Their faces were disbelieving as I got out. Not bothering with an umbrella, I ran for the door and unlocked it.

'Hey!' the protests continued. 'We can't get out!'

Inside the bay, water was beaded on the oversized maroon station wagon and dripping to the concrete floor. I opened another door and walked into the corridor, looking around to see who else was here. White tile was spotless, the air heavy with industrial strength deodorizer, and as I walked to the morgue office, the massive stainless steel refrigerator door sucked open.

'Good morning!' Wingo said with a surprised grin. 'You're early.'

'Thanks for bringing the wagon in out of the rain,' I said.

'No more cases coming in that I know of, so I didn't think it would hurt to stick it in the bay.'

'Did you see anybody out there when you drove it?' I asked.

He looked puzzled. 'No. But that was about an hour ago.'

Wingo was the only member of my staff who routinely got to the office earlier than I did. He was lithe and attractive, with pretty features and shaggy dark hair. An obsessive-compulsive, he ironed his scrubs, washed the wagon and anatomical vans several times a week, and was forever polishing stainless steel until it shone like mirrors. His job was to run the morgue, and he did so with the precision and pride of a military leader. Carelessness and callousness were not allowed down here by either one of us, and no one dared dispose of hazardous waste or make sophomoric jokes about the dead.

'The landfill case is still in the fridge,' Wingo said to me. 'Do you want me to bring it out?'

'Let's wait until after staff meeting.' I said. 'The longer she's refrigerated, the better, and I don't want anybody wandering in here to look.'

'That won't happen,' he said as if I had just implied he might be delinquent in his duties.

'I don't even want anybody on the staff wandering in out of curiosity.'

'Oh.' Anger flashed in his eyes. 'I just don't understand people.'

He never would, because he was not like them.

'I'll let you alert security,' I said. 'The media's already in the parking lot.'

'You got to be kidding. This early?'

'Channel Eight was waiting for me when I pulled in.' I handed him the key to my car. 'Give them a few minutes, and then let them go.'

'What do you mean, let them go?' He frowned, staring at the remote control key in his hand.

'They're in my parking place.' I headed toward the elevator.

'They're what?'

'You'll see.' I boarded. 'If they so much as touch my car, I'll charge them with trespassing and malicious property damage. Then I'm going to have the A.G.'s office call their station's general manager. I might sue.' I smiled at him through shutting doors.

My office was on the second floor of the Consolidated Lab Building, which had been constructed in the seventies and was soon to be abandoned by us and the scientists upstairs. At last, we were to get spacious quarters in the city's new

Biotech Park just off Broad Street, not far from the Marriott and the Coliseum.

Construction was already under way, and I spent far too much time arguing over details, blueprints and budgets. What had been home to me for years was now in disarray, stacks of boxes lining hallways, and clerks not wanting to file, since everything would have to be packed anyway. Averting my gaze from more boxes, I followed the hallway to my office, where my desk was in its usual state of avalanche.

I checked my e-mail again, almost expecting another anonymous file like the last, but only the same messages were there, and I scanned through them, sending brief replies. The address *deadoc* quietly waited in my mailbox, and I could not resist opening it and the file with the photograph. I was concentrating so hard, I did not hear Rose walk in.

'I think Noah had better build another ark,' she said.

Startled, I looked up to see her in the doorway adjoining my office and hers. She was taking off her raincoat, and looked worried.

'I didn't mean to scare you,' she said.

Hesitating, she stepped inside, scrutinizing me.

'I knew you'd be here, despite all advice,' she said. 'You look like you've seen a ghost.'

'What are you doing here so early?' I asked.

'I had a feeling you'd have your hands full.' She took off her coat. 'You saw the paper this morning?'

'Not yet.'

She opened her pocketbook and got out her glasses. 'All this *Butcher* business. You can imagine the uproar. While I was driving, I heard on the news that since these cases started, more handguns are being sold than you can shake a stick at. I sometimes wonder if the gun shops aren't behind things like this. Frighten us out of our wits so we all make a mad dash for the nearest .38 or semiautomatic pistol.'

Rose had hair the color of steel that she always wore up, her face patrician and keen. There was nothing she had not seen, and she was not afraid of anyone. I lived in the uneasy shadow of her retirement, for I knew her age. She did not have to work for me. She stayed only because she cared and had no one left at home.

'Take a look,' I said, pushing back my chair.

She came around to my side of the desk and stood so close I could smell White Musk, the fragrance of everything she had concocted at the Body Shop, where they were against testing with animals. Rose had recently adopted her fifth retired greyhound. She bred Siamese cats, kept several aquariums and was one step short of being dangerous to anyone who wore fur. She stared into my computer screen, and did not seem to know what she was looking at. Then her demeanor stiffened.

'My God,' she muttered, looking at me over the top of her bifocals. 'Is this what's downstairs?'

'I think an earlier version of it,' I said. 'Sent to me on AOL.'

She did not speak.

'Needless to say,' I went on, 'I will trust you to keep an eagle eye on this place while I'm downstairs. If anybody comes into the lobby we don't know or aren't expecting, I want security to intercept them. Don't you even think about going out to see what they want.' I looked pointedly at her, knowing what she was like.

'You think he would come here?' she matter-of-factly stated.

'I'm not sure what to think except that he clearly had

some need to contact me.' I closed the file and got up. 'And he has.'

At not quite half past eight, Wingo rolled the body onto the floor scale, and we began what I knew would be a very long and painstaking examination. The torso weighed forty-six pounds and was twenty-one inches in length. Livormortis was faint posteriorly, meaning when her circulation had quit, blood had settled according to gravity, placing her on her back for hours or days after death. I could not look at her without seeing the savaged image on my computer screen, and believed it and the torso before me were the same.

'How big do you think she was?' Wingo glanced at me as he parallel parked the gurney next to the first autopsy table.

'We'll use heights of lumbar vertebrae to estimate height, since we obviously don't have tibias, femurs,' I said, tying a plastic apron over my gown. 'But she looks small. Frail, actually.'

Moments later, X-rays had finished processing and he was attaching them to light boxes. What I saw told a story that did not seem to make sense. The faces of the pubic symphysis, or the surfaces where one pubis joins the other, were no longer rugged and ridged, as in youth. Instead, bone was badly eroded with irregular, lipped margins. More X-rays revealed sternal rib ends with irregular bony growths, the bone very thin-walled with sharp edges, and there were degenerative changes to the lumbosacral vertebrae, as well.

Wingo was no anthropologist, but he saw the obvious, too.

'If I didn't know better, I'd think we got her films mixed up with somebody else's,' he said.

'This lady's old,' I said.

'How old, would you guess?'

'I don't like to guess.' I was studying her X-rays. 'But I'd say seventy, at least. Or to play it really safe, between sixty-five and eighty. Come on. Let's go through trash for a while.'

The next two hours were spent sifting through a large garbage bag of trash from the landfill that had been directly under and around the body. The garbage bag I believed she had been in was black, thirty-gallon size, and had been sealed with a yellow plastic-toothed tie. Wearing masks and gloves, Wingo and I picked through shredded tire and the fluff from upholstery stuffing that was used as a cover in the landfill. We examined countless tatters of slimy plastic and paper, picking out maggots and dead flies and dropping them into a carton.

Our treasures were few, a blue button that was probably unrelated, and, oddly, a child's tooth, which I imagined was tossed, a coin left under a pillow. We found a mangled comb, a flattened battery, several shards of broken china, a tangled wire coat hanger, and the cap of a Bic pen. Mostly, it was rubber, fluff, torn black plastic and soggy paper that we threw into a garbage can. Then we circled bright lights around the table and centered her on a clean white sheet.

Using a lens, I began going over her an inch at a time, her flesh a microscopic landfill of debris. With forceps, I collected pale fibers from the dark bloody stump that once had been her neck, and I found hairs, three of them, grayish-white, about fourteen inches long, adhering to dried blood, posteriorly.

'I need another envelope.' I said to Wingo as I came across something else I did not expect.

Embedded in the ends of each humerus, or the bone of the

49

upper arm, and also in margins of muscle around it were more fibers and tiny fragments of fabric that looked pale blue, meaning the saw had to have gone through it.

'She was dismembered through her clothes or something else she was wrapped in,' I said, startled.

Wingo stopped what he was doing and looked at me. 'The others weren't.'

Those victims appeared to have been nude when they were sawn apart. He made more notes as I moved on, peering through the lens.

'Fibers and bits of fabric are also embedded in either femur.' I looked more closely.

'So she was covered from the waist down, too?' he said.

'That's the way it's looking.'

'So someone waited until after she was dismembered, and then took all her clothes off?' He looked at me, emotion in his eyes as he started to envision it.

'He wouldn't want us to get the clothes. There might be too much information there,' I said.

'Then why didn't he undress her, unwrap her or whatever to begin with?'

'Maybe he didn't want to look at her while he was dismembering her,' I said.

'Oh, so now he's getting sensitive on us,' Wingo said, as if he hated whoever it was.

'Make a note of the measurements,' I told him. 'Cervical spine is transected at the level of C-5. Residual femur on the right measures two inches below the lesser trochanter, and two and a half inches on the left, with saw marks visible. Right and left segments of humerus are one inch, saw marks visible. On the upper right hip is a three-quarters-of-an-inch old, healed vaccination scar.'

'What about that?' He referred to the numerous raised, fluid-filled vesicles scattered over buttocks, shoulders and upper thighs.

'I don't know,' I said, reaching for a syringe. 'I'm guessing herpes zoster virus.'

'Whoa!' Wingo jumped back from the table. 'I wish you'd told me that earlier.' He was scared.

'Shingles.' I began labeling a test tube. 'Maybe. I must confess, it's a little weird.'

'What do you mean?' He was getting more unnerved.

'With shingles,' I replied, 'the virus attacks sensory nerves. When the vesicles erupt, they do so in a swath along nerve distributions. Under a rib, for example. And the vesicles will be of varying ages. But this is a crop, and they all look the same age.'

'What else could it be?' he asked. 'Chicken pox?'

'Same virus. Children get chicken pox. Adults get shingles.'

'What if I get it?' Wingo said.

'Did you have chicken pox as a kid?'

'Got no idea.'

'What about the VZV vaccine?' I asked. 'Have you had that?'

'No.'

'Well, if you have no antibody to VZV, you should be vaccinated.' I glanced up at him. 'Are you immunosuppressed?'

He did not say anything as he went to a cart, snatching off his latex gloves and slamming them into the red can for biologically hazardous trash. Upset, he snatched a new pair made of heavier blue Nitrile. I stopped what I was doing, watching him until he returned to the table.

'I just think you could have warned me before now,' he

said, and he sounded on the verge of tears. 'I mean, it's not like you can take any precautions in this place, like vaccinations, except for hepatitis B. So I depend on you to let me know what's coming in.'

'Calm down.'

I was gentle with him. Wingo was too sensitive for his own good, and that was really the only problem I ever had with him.

'You can't possibly get chicken pox or shingles from this lady unless you have an exchange of body fluids,' I said. 'So as long as you're wearing gloves and going about business in the usual way, and don't cut yourself or get a needle stick, you will not be exposed to the virus.'

For an instant, his eyes were bright, and he quickly looked away.

'I'll start taking pictures,' he said.

MARINO AND BENTON WESLEY appeared
midafternoon, when the autopsy was well under
way. There was nothing further I could do with
the external examination, and Wingo had taken a
late lunch, so I was alone. Wesley's eyes were on me as he
walked through the door, and I could tell by his coat that it
was still raining.

'Just so you know,' Marino said right off, 'there's a flood
warning.'

Since there were no windows in the morgue, I never knew
the weather.

'How serious a warning?' I asked, and Wesley had come
close to the torso, and was looking at it.

'Serious enough that if this keeps up, somebody'd better start piling up sandbags,' Marino replied as he parked his umbrella in a corner.

My building was blocks from the James. Years ago, the lower level had flooded, bodies donated to science rising in overflowing vats, water poisoned pink with formalin seeping into the morgue and the parking lot in back.

'How worried should I be?' I asked with concern.

'It's going to stop,' Wesley said, as if he could profile the weather, too.

He took off his raincoat, and the suit beneath it was a dark blue that was almost black. He wore a starched white shirt and conservative silk tie, his silver hair a little longer than usual, but neat. His sharp features made him seem even keener and more intimidating than he was, but today his face was grim, and not just because of me. He and Marino went to a cart to put on gloves and masks.

'I'm sorry we're late,' Wesley said to me as I continued working. 'Every time I tried to get away from the house, the phone rang. This thing's a real problem.'

'Certainly for her it is,' I said.

'Shit.' Marino stared at what was left of a human being. 'How the hell does anybody do something like that?'

'I'll tell you how,' I said, cutting sections of spleen. 'First you pick an old woman and make sure she isn't properly watered or fed, and when she gets sick, forget medical care. Then you shoot or beat her in the head.' I glanced up at them. 'My bet is that she has a basilar skull fracture. Maybe some other type of trauma.'

Marino looked baffled. 'She doesn't have a head. How can you say that?'

'I can say it because there's blood in her airway.'

They got closer to see what I was talking about.

'One way that could have happened,' I went on, 'is if she had a basilar skull fracture and blood dripped down the back of her throat, and she aspirated it into her airway.'

Wesley looked carefully at the body with the demeanor of one who has seen mutilation and death a million times. He stared at the space where the head should be, as if he could imagine it.

'She has hemorrhage in muscle tissue.' I paused to let this sink in. 'She was still alive when the dismemberment began.'

'Jesus Christ,' Marino exclaimed in disgust as he lit a cigarette. 'Don't tell me that.'

'I'm not saying she was conscious,' I added. 'Most likely this was at or about the time of death. But she still had a blood pressure, feeble as it might have been. This was true around the neck, anyway. But not the arms and legs.'

'Then he severed her head first,' Wesley said to me.

'Yes.'

He was scanning X-rays on the walls.

'This doesn't fit with his victimology,' he said. 'Not at all.'

'Everything about this case doesn't fit,' I replied. 'Except that once again, a saw was used. I've also found some cuts on bone that are consistent with a knife.'

'What else can you tell us about her?' Wesley said, and I could feel his eyes on me as I dropped another section of organ into the stock jar of formalin.

'She has some sort of eruptions that might be shingles, and two scars of the right kidney that would indicate pyelonephritis, or kidney infection. Cervix is elongated and stellate, which could suggest she's had children. Her myocardium, or heart muscle, is soft.'

'Meaning?'

'Toxins do that. Toxins produced by microorganisms.' I looked up at him. 'As I've mentioned, she was sick.'

Marino was walking around, looking at the torso from different angles. 'Do you have any idea with what?'

'Based on secretions in her lungs, I know she had bronchitis. At the moment, I don't know what else, except her liver's in pretty grim shape.'

'From drinking,' Wesley said.

'Yellowish, nodular. Yes,' I said. 'And I would say that at one time she smoked.'

'She's skin and bones,' Marino said.

'She wasn't eating,' I said. 'Her stomach is tubular, empty and clean.' I showed them.

Wesley moved to a nearby desk and pulled out a chair. He stared off in thought as I yanked a cord down from an overhead reel and plugged in the Stryker saw. Marino, who liked this part of the procedure the least stepped back from the table. No one spoke as I sawed off the ends of arms and legs, a bony dust drifting on the air, the electric whir louder than a dentist's drill. I placed each section into a labeled carton, and said what I thought.

'I don't think we're dealing with the same killer this time.'

'I don't know what to think,' Marino said. 'But we got two big things in common. A torso, and it was dumped in central Virginia.'

'He's had a varied victimology all along,' said Wesley, wearing his surgical mask loose around his neck. 'One black, two whites, all female, and one black male. The five in Dublin were mixed, as well. But again, all were young.'

'So would you now expect him to choose an old woman?' I asked him.

'Frankly, I wouldn't. But these people aren't an exact science, Kay. This is somebody who does whatever the hell he feels like whenever he feels like it.'

'The dismemberment isn't the same, it's not through the joints,' I reminded them. 'And I think she was clothed or wrapped in something.'

'This one may have bothered him more,' Wesley said, taking the mask off altogether and dropping it on top of the desk. 'His urge to kill again may have been overwhelming, and she may have been easy.' He looked at the torso. 'So he strikes, but his M.O. shifts because the victimology has suddenly shifted, and he doesn't really like it. He leaves her at least partially dressed or covered because raping and killing an old woman aren't what turn him on. And he cuts off her head first so he doesn't have to look at her.'

'You see any sign of rape?' Marino asked me.

'You rarely do,' I said. 'I'm about to finish up here. She'll go in the freezer like the other ones in the hope we eventually get an identification. I've got muscle tissue and marrow for DNA, hoping that we'll eventually have a missing person to compare it with.'

I was discouraged, and it showed. Wesley collected his coat from the back of a door, leaving a small puddle on the floor.

'I'd like to see the photograph sent to you over AOL,' he said to me.

'That doesn't fit the M.O., either, by the way,' I said as I began suturing the Y-incision. 'I wasn't sent anything in the earlier cases.'

Marino was in a hurry, as if he had somewhere else to go.

'I'm heading out to Sussex,' he said, walking to the door. 'Gotta meet Lone Ranger Ring so he can give me lessons in how to investigate homicides.'

He abruptly left, and I knew the real reason why. Despite his preaching to me about marriage, my relationship with Wesley secretly bothered Marino. A part of him would always be jealous.

'Rose can show you the photograph,' I said to Wesley as I washed the body with hose and sponge. 'She knows how to get into my e-mail.'

Disappointment glinted in his eyes before he could mask it. I carried the cartons of bone ends to a distant counter where they would be boiled in a weak solution of bleach, to completely deflesh and degrease them. He stayed where he was, waiting and watching until I got back. I did not want him to go, but I did not know what to do with him anymore.

'Can't we talk, Kay?' he finally said. 'I've hardly seen you. Not in months. I know we're both busy, and this isn't a good time. But . . .'

'Benton,' I interrupted with feeling. 'Not here.'

'Of course not. I'm not suggesting we talk here.'

'It will just be more of the same.'

'I promise it won't.' He checked the clock on the wall. 'Look, it's already late. Why don't I just stay in town. We'll have dinner.'

I hesitated, ambivalence bouncing from one end of my brain to the other. I was afraid to see him and afraid not to see him.

'All right,' I said. 'My house at seven. I'll throw together something. Don't expect much.'

'I can take you out. I don't want you to go to any trouble.'

'The last place I want to be right now is out in public,' I said.

His eyes lingered on me a little longer as I labeled tags and tubes and various types of containers. The strike of his heels was sharp on tile as he left, and I heard him speak to someone as elevator doors opened in the hall. Seconds later, Wingo walked in.

'I would have got here sooner.' He went to a cart and began putting on new shoe covers, mask and gloves. 'But it's a zoo upstairs.'

'What's that supposed to mean?' I asked, untying my gown in back as he slipped into a fresh one.

'Reporters.' He put on a face shield and looked at me through clear plastic. 'In the lobby. Casing the building in their television vans.' He looked tensely at me. 'Hate to tell you, but now Channel Eight's got you blocked in. Their van's right behind your car so you can't get out, and nobody's in it.'

Anger rose like heat. 'Call the police and get them towed,' I said from the locker room. 'You finish up here. I'm going upstairs to take care of this.'

Slamming my balled-up gown into the laundry bin, I grabbed off gloves, shoe covers and cap. I vigorously scrubbed with antibacterial soap and yanked open my locker, my hands suddenly clumsy. I was very upset, this case, the press, Wesley, everything was getting to me.

'Dr Scarpetta?'

Wingo was suddenly in the doorway as I fumbled with buttons on my blouse, and his walking in on me while I was dressing was nothing new. It never bothered either of us, for I was as comfortable with him as I would be with a woman.

'I was wondering if you had time . . .' He hesitated. 'Well, I know you're busy today.'

I tossed bloody Reeboks into my locker and slipped on the shoes I had worn to work. Then I put on my lab coat.

'Actually, Wingo' – I checked my anger so I did not take it out on him – 'I'd like to talk to you, too. When you finish down here, come see me in my office.'

He did not have to tell me. I had a feeling I knew. I rode the elevator upstairs, my mood darkened like a storm about to strike. Wesley was still in my office, studying what was on my computer screen, and I walked past in the hallway without slowing my stride. It was Rose I wanted to find. When I got to the front office, clerks were frantically answering phones that would not stop, while my secretary and administrator were before a window overlooking the front parking lot.

The rain had not relented, and this had not seemed to deter a single journalist, cameraman or photographer in this town. They seemed crazed, as if the story must be huge for everyone else to be braving a downpour.

'Where are Fielding and Grant?' I asked about my deputy chief and this year's fellow.

My administrator was a retired sheriff who loved cologne and snappy suits. He stepped away from the window, while Rose continued to look out.

'Dr Fielding's in court,' he said. 'Dr Grant had to leave because his basement's flooding.'

Rose turned around with the demeanor of one ready to fight, as if her nest had been invaded. 'I put Jess in the filing room,' she said of the receptionist.

'So there's no one out front.' I looked toward the lobby.

'Oh, there are plenty of people, all right,' my secretary

angrily said as phones rang and rang. 'I didn't want anybody sitting out there with all those vultures. I don't care if there is bulletproof glass.'

'How many reporters are in the lobby?'

'Fifteen, maybe twenty, last I checked,' my administrator answered. 'I went out there once and asked them to leave. They said they weren't going until they had a statement from you. So I thought we could write something up and . . .'

'I'll give them a statement, all right,' I snapped.

Rose put her hand on my arm. 'Dr Scarpetta, I'm not sure it's a good idea . . .'

I interrupted her, too. 'Leave this to me.'

The lobby was small, and the thick glass partition made it impossible for any unauthorized person to get in. When I rounded the corner, I could not believe how many people were crammed into the room, the floor filthy with footprints and dirty puddles. As soon as they saw me, camera lights blazed. Reporters began shouting, shoving microphones and tape recorders close as flash guns went off in my face.

I raised my voice above all of them. 'Please! Quiet!'

'Dr Scarpetta . . .'

'Quiet!' I said more loudly, as I blindly stared out at aggressive people I could not make out. 'Now, I am going to ask you politely to leave,' I said.

'Is it the Butcher again?' a woman raised her voice above the rest.

'Everything is pending further investigation,' I said.

'Dr Scarpetta.'

I could just barely make out the television reporter as Patty Denver, whose pretty face was on billboards all over the city.

'Sources say you're working this as another victim in these serial killings,' she said. 'Can you verify that?'

I did not respond.

'Is it true the victim is Asian, probably prepubescent, and came off a truck that is local?' she went on, to my dismay. 'And are we to assume that the killer may now be in Virginia?'

'Is the Butcher killing in Virginia now?'

'Possible he deliberately wanted the other bodies dumped here?'

I held up a hand to quiet them. 'This is not the time for assumptions,' I said. 'I can tell you only that we are treating this as a homicide. The victim is an unidentified white female. She is not prepubescent but an older adult, and we encourage people who might have information to call this office or the Sussex County Sheriff's Department.'

'What about the FBI?'

'The FBI is involved,' I said.

'Then you are treating this as the Butcher . . .'

Turning around, I entered a code on a keypad and the lock clicked free. I ignored the demanding voices, shutting the door behind me, my nerves humming with tension as I walked quickly down the hall. When I entered my office, Wesley was gone, and I sat behind my desk. I dialed Marino's pager number, and he called me right back.

'For God's sake, these leaks have got to stop!' I exclaimed over the line.

'We know damn well who it is,' Marino irritably said.

'Ring.' I had no doubt, but could not prove it.

'The drone was supposed to meet me at the landfill. That was almost an hour ago,' Marino went on.

'It doesn't appear the press had any trouble finding him.'

I told him what *sources* allegedly had divulged to a television crew.

'Goddamn idiot!' he said.

'Find him and tell him to keep his mouth shut,' I said. 'Reporters have practically put us out of business today, and now the city's going to believe there's a serial killer in their midst.'

'Yeah, well, unfortunately, that part could be true,' he said.

'I can't believe this.' I was only getting angrier. 'I have to release information to correct misinformation. I can't be put in this position, Marino.'

'Don't worry, I'm going to take care of this and a whole lot more,' he promised. 'I don't guess you know.'

'Know what?'

'Rumor has it that Ring's been seeing Patty Denver.'

'I thought she was married,' I said as I envisioned her from a few moments earlier.

'She is,' he said.

I began dictating case 1930–97, trying to focus my attention on what I was saying and reading from my notes.

'The body was received pouched and sealed,' I said into the tape recorder, rearranging paperwork smeared with blood from Wingo's gloves. 'The skin is doughy. The breasts are small, atrophic and wrinkled. There are skin folds over the abdomen suggestive of prior weight loss . . .'

'Dr Scarpetta?' Wingo was poking his head in the doorway. 'Oops. Sorry,' he said when he realized what I was doing. 'I guess now's not a good time.'

'Come in,' I said with a weary smile. 'Why don't you shut the door.'

He did and closed the one between my office and Rose's, too. Nervously, he pulled a chair close to my desk, and he was having a hard time meeting my eyes.

'Before you start, let me.' I was firm but kind. 'I've known you for many years, and your life is no secret to me. I don't make judgments. I don't label. In my mind, there are only two categories of people in this world. Those who are good. And those who aren't. But I worry about you because your orientation places you at risk.'

He nodded. 'I know,' he said, eyes bright with tears.

'If you're immunosuppressed,' I went on, 'you need to tell me. You probably shouldn't be in the morgue, at least not for some cases.'

'I'm HIV positive.' His voice trembled and he began to cry.

I let him go for a while, his arms over his face, as if he could not bear for anyone to see him. His shoulders shook, tears spotting his greens as his nose ran. Getting up with a box of tissues, I came over to him.

'Here.' I set the tissues nearby. 'It's all right.' I put my arm around him and let him weep. 'Wingo, I want you to try to get hold of yourself so we can talk about this, okay?'

He nodded, blowing his nose and wiping his eyes. For a moment he nuzzled his head against me, and I held him like a child. I gave him time before I faced him straight on, gripping his shoulders.

'Now is the time for courage, Wingo,' I said. 'Let's see what we can do to fight this thing.'

'I can't tell my family,' he choked. 'My father hates me anyway. And when my mother tries, he gets worse. To her. You know?'

I moved a chair close. 'What about your friend?'

'We broke up.'

'But he knows.'

'I just found out a couple weeks ago.'

'You've got to tell him and anybody else you've been intimate with,' I said. 'It's only fair. If someone had done that for you, maybe you wouldn't be sitting here now, crying.'

He was silent, staring down at his hands. Taking a deep breath, he said, 'I'm going to die, aren't I.'

'We're all going to die,' I gently told him.

'Not like this.'

'It could be like this,' I said. 'Every physical I get, I'm tested for HIV. You know what I'm exposed to. What you're going through could be me.'

He looked up at me, his eyes and cheeks burning. 'If I get AIDS, I'm going to kill myself.'

'No, you're not,' I said.

He began to cry again. 'Dr Scarpetta, I can't go through it! I don't want to end up in one of those places, a hospice, the Fan Free Clinic, in a bed next to other dying people I don't know!' Tears flowed, his face tragic and defiant. 'I'll be all alone just like I've always been.'

'Listen.' I waited until he calmed down. 'You will not go through this alone. You have me.'

He dissolved in tears again, covering his face and making sounds so loud I was certain they could be heard in the hall.

'I will take care of you,' I promised as I got up. 'Now I want you to go home. I want you to do what's right and tell your friends. Tomorrow, we'll talk more and figure out the best way to handle this. I need the name of your doctor and permission to talk to him or her.'

'Dr Alan Riley. At MCV.'

I nodded. 'I know him, and I want you to call him first thing in the morning. Let him know I'll be contacting him and that it's all right for him to talk to me.'

'Okay.' He looked furtively at me. 'But you'll be . . . You won't tell anyone.'

'Of course not,' I said with feeling.

'I don't want anyone here to know. Or Marino. I don't want him to.'

'No one will know,' I said. 'At least not from me.'

He slowly got up and stepped toward the door with the unsteadiness of someone drunk or dazed. 'You won't fire me, will you?' His hand was on the knob as he cast blood-shot eyes my way.

'Wingo, for God's sake,' I said with quiet emotion. 'I would hope you would think more of me than that.'

He opened the door. 'I think more of you than anyone.' Tears spilled again, and he wiped them on his scrubs, exposing his thin bare belly. 'I always have.'

His footsteps were rapid in the hall as he almost ran, and the elevator bell rang. I listened as he left my building for a world that did not give a damn. I rested my forehead on my fist and shut my eyes.

'Dear God,' I muttered. 'Please help.'

T HE RAIN WAS still heavy as I drove home, and traffic was terrible because an accident had closed lanes in both directions on I-64. There were fire trucks and ambulances, rescuers prying open doors and hurrying with stretchers and boards. Broken glass glistened on wet pavement, drivers slowing to stare at injured people. One car had flipped multiple times before catching fire. I saw blood on the shattered windshield of another and that the steering wheel was bent. I knew what that meant, and said a prayer for whoever the people were. I hoped I would not see them in my morgue.

In Carytown, I pulled off at P. T. Hasting's. Festooned

with fish nets and floats, it sold the best seafood in the city. When I walked in, the air was spicy and pungent with fish and Old Bay, and filets looked thick and fresh on ice inside displays. Lobsters with bound claws crawled in their tank of water, and were in no danger from me. I was incapable of boiling anything alive and wouldn't touch meat if the cattle and pigs were first brought to my table. I couldn't even catch fish without throwing them back.

I was trying to decide what I wanted when Bev emerged from the back.

'What's good today?' I asked her.

'Well, look who's here,' she exclaimed warmly, wiping her hands on her apron. 'You're about the only person to brave the rain. So you sure got plenty to choose from.'

'I don't have much time, and need something easy and light,' I said.

A shadow passed over her face as she opened a jar of horseradish. 'I'm afraid I can imagine what you've been doing,' she said. 'Been hearing it on the news.' She shook her head. 'You must be plumb worn out. I don't know how you sleep. Let me tell you what to do for yourself tonight.'

She walked over to a case of chilled blue crabs. Without asking, she selected a pound of meat in a carton.

'Fresh from Tangier Island. Hand-picked it myself, and you tell me if you find even a trace of cartilage or shell. You're not eating alone, are you?' she said.

'No.'

'That's good to hear.'

She winked at me. I had brought Wesley in here before.

She picked out six jumbo shrimp, peeled and deveined, and wrapped them. Then she set a jar of her homemade cocktail sauce on the counter by the cash register.

'I got a little carried away with the horseradish,' she said, 'so it will make your eyes water, but it's good.' She began ringing up my purchases. 'You sauté the shrimp so quick their butts barely hit the pan, got it? Chill 'em, and have that as an appetizer. By the way, those and the sauce are on the house.'

'You don't need to . . .'

She waved me off. 'As for the crab, honey, listen up. One egg slightly beaten, one-half teaspoon dry mustard, a dash or two of Worcestershire sauce, four unsalted soda crackers, crushed. Chop up an onion, a Vidalia if you're still hoarding any from summer. One green pepper, chop that. A teaspoon or two of parsley, salt and pepper to taste.'

'Sounds fabulous,' I gratefully said. 'Bev, what would I do without you?'

'Now you gently mix all that together and shape it into patties.' She made the motion with her hands. 'Sauté in oil over medium heat until lightly browned. Maybe fix him a salad or get some of my slaw,' she said. 'And that's as much as I would fuss over any man.'

It was as much as I did. I got started as soon as I got home, and shrimp were chilling by the time I turned on music and climbed into a bath. I poured in aromatherapy salts that were supposed to reduce stress, and shut my eyes as steam carried soothing scents into my sinuses and pores. I thought about Wingo, and my heart ached and seemed to lose its rhythm like a bird in distress. For a while, I cried. He had started out with me in this city, then left to go back to school. Now he was back and dying. I could not bear it.

At seven P.M., I was in the kitchen again, and Wesley, always punctual, eased his silver BMW into my drive. He was still in the suit he had been wearing earlier, and he had a bottle of Cakebread chardonnay in one hand, and a fifth of Black Bush Irish whiskey in the other. The rain, at last, had stopped, clouds marching on to other fronts.

'Hi,' he said when I opened the door.

'You profiled the weather right.' I kissed him.

'They don't pay me this much money for nothing.'

'The money comes from your family.' I smiled as he followed me in. 'I know what the Bureau pays you.'

'If I was as smart with money as you are, I wouldn't need it from my family.'

In my great room was a bar, and I went behind it because I knew what he wanted.

'Black Bush?' I made sure.

'If you're serving it. Fine pusher that you are, you've managed to get me hooked.'

'As long as you bootleg it from D.C., I'll serve it any time you like,' I said.

I fixed our drinks on the rocks with a splash of seltzer water. Then we went into the kitchen and sat at a cozy table by an expansive window overlooking my wooded yard and the river. I wished I could tell him about Wingo and how it felt for me. But I could not break a confidence.

'Can I bring up a little business first?' Wesley took off his suit jacket and hung it on the back of a chair.

'I have some, too.'

'You first.' He sipped his drink, his eyes on mine.

I told him what had been leaked to the press, adding, 'Ring's a problem that's only getting worse.'

'If he's the one, and I'm not saying he is or isn't. The difficulty's getting proof.'

'There's no doubt in my mind.'

'Kay, that's not good enough. We can't just throw someone out of an investigation based on our intuition.'

'Marino's heard rumors that Ring's having an affair with a well-known local broadcaster,' I then said. 'She's with the same station that had the misinformation about the case, about the victim being Asian.'

He was silent. I knew he was thinking about proof again, and he was right. This all sounded circumstantial even as I said it.

Then he said, 'This guy's very smart. Are you aware of his background?'

'I know nothing about him,' I replied.

'Graduated with honors from William and Mary, double major in psychology and public administration. His uncle is the secretary of public safety.' He piled worse news upon bad. 'Harlow Dershin, who's an honorable guy, by the way. But it goes without saying this is not a good situation for making accusations unless you're one hundred percent damn sure of yourself.'

The secretary of public safety for Virginia was the immediate boss of the superintendent of the state police. Ring's uncle couldn't have been more powerful unless he had been the governor.

'So what you're saying is that Ring's untouchable,' I said.

'What I'm saying is, his educational background makes it clear he has high aspirations. Guys like him are looking to be a chief, a commissioner, a politician. They're not interested in being a cop.'

'Guys like him are interested only in themselves,' I impatiently said. 'Ring doesn't give a damn about the victims or the people left behind who have no idea what has happened to their loved one. He doesn't care if someone else gets killed.'

'Proof,' he reminded me. 'To be fair, there are a lot of people – including those working at the landfill – who could have leaked information to the press.'

I had no good argument, but nothing would shake me loose from my suspicions.

'What's important is breaking these cases,' he went on to say, 'and the best way to do that is for all of us to go about our business and ignore him, just like Marino and Grigg are doing. Follow every lead we can, steering around the impediments.' His eyes were almost amber in the overhead light, and soft when they met mine.

I pushed back my chair. 'We need to set the table.'

He got out dishes and opened wine as I arranged chilled shrimp on plates and spooned *Bev's Kicked By A Horse Cocktail Sauce* into a bowl. I halved lemons and wrapped them in gauze diapers, and fashioned crab cakes. Wesley and I ate shrimp cocktail as night drew closer and cast its shadow over the east.

'I've missed this,' he said. 'Maybe you don't want to hear it, but it's true.'

I did not say anything because I did not want to get into another big discussion that went on for hours, leaving both of us drained.

'Anyway.' He set his fork on his plate the way polite people do when they are finished. 'Thank you. I have missed you, Dr Scarpetta.' He smiled.

'I'm glad you're here, Special Agent Wesley.'

I smiled back at him as I got up. Turning on the stove, I heated oil in a pan while he cleared dishes.

'I want to tell you what I thought of the photograph that

was sent to you,' he said. 'First, we need to establish that it is, in fact, of the victim you worked on today.'

'I'm going to establish that on Monday.'

'Assuming it is,' he went on, 'this is a very dramatic shift in the killer's M.O.'

'That and everything else.' Crab cakes went into the pan and began to sizzle.

'Right,' he said, serving coleslaw. 'It's very blatant this time, as if he's really trying to rub our noses in it. And, of course, the victimology's all wrong, too. That looks great,' he added, watching what I was cooking.

When we were seated again, I said with confidence, 'Benton, this is not the same guy.'

He hesitated before replying, 'I don't think it is, either, if you want to know the truth. But I'm not prepared to rule him out. We don't know what games he might be into now.'

I was feeling the frustration again. Nothing could be proven, but my intuition, my instincts, were screaming at me.

'Well, I don't think this murdered old woman has anything to do with the earlier cases from here or Ireland. Someone just wants us to assume she does. I think what we're dealing with is a copycat.'

'We'll get into it with everybody. Thursday. I think that's the date we set.' He tasted a crab cake. 'This is really incredibly good. Wow.' His eyes watered. 'Now that's cocktail sauce.'

'Staging. Disguising a crime that was committed for some other reason,' I said. 'And don't give me too much credit. This was Bev's recipe.'

'The photograph bothers me,' he said.

'You and me both.'

'I've talked to Lucy about it,' he said.

Now he really had my interest.

'You tell me when you want her here.' He reached for his wine.

'The sooner the better.' I paused, adding, 'How is she doing? I know what she tells me, but I'd like to hear it from you.'

I remembered we needed water, and got up for it. When I returned, he was quietly staring at me. Sometimes it was hard for me to look at his face, and my emotions began clashing like instruments out of tune. I loved his chiseled nose with its clean straight bridge, his eyes, which could draw me into depths I had never known and his mouth with its sensuous lower lip. I looked out the window, and could not see the river anymore.

'Lucy,' I reminded him. 'How about a performance evaluation for her aunt?'

'No one's sorry we hired her,' he dryly said of someone we all knew was a genius. 'Or maybe that's the understatement of the century. She's simply terrific. Most of the agents have come to respect her. They want her around. I'm not saying there aren't problems. Not everybody appreciates having a woman on HRT.'

'I continue to worry that she'll try to push it too far,' I said.

'Well, she's fit as hell. That's for sure. No way I'd take her on.'

'That's what I mean. She wants to keep up with them, when it really isn't possible. You know how she is.' I gave him my eyes again. 'She's always got to prove herself. If the guys are fast-roping and running through the mountains wearing sixty-pound packs, she thinks she's got to keep up, when she should just be content with her technical abilities, her robots and all the rest of it.'

'You're missing her biggest motivation, her biggest demon,' he said.

'What?'

'You. She feels she has to prove herself to you, Kay.'

'She has no reason to feel that way.' What he said was piercing. 'I don't want to feel I'm the reason she takes her life into her hands with all of these dangerous things she feels she must do.'

'This is not about blame,' he said, getting up from the table. 'This is about human nature. Lucy worships you. You're the only decent mother figure she's ever had. She wants to be like you, and she feels people compare her to you, and that's a pretty big act to follow. She wants you to admire her, too, Kay.'

'I do admire her, for God's sake.' I got up, too, and we began clearing dishes. 'Now you really have me worried.'

He began rinsing, and I loaded the dishwasher.

'You probably should worry.' He glanced at me. 'I will tell you this, she's one of these perfectionists who won't listen to anyone. Other than you, she's the most stubborn human being I've ever come across.'

'Thanks a lot.'

He smiled and put his arms around me, not caring that his hands were wet. 'Can we sit and talk for a while?' he said, his face, his body close to mine. 'Then I've got to hit the road.'

'And after that?'

'I'm going to talk to Marino in the morning, and in the afternoon I've got another case coming in. From Arizona. I know it's Sunday, but it can't wait.'

He continued talking as we carried our wine into the great room.

'A twelve-year-old girl abducted on her way home from school, body dumped in the Sonora desert,' he said. 'We think this guy's already killed three other kids.'

'It's hard to feel very optimistic, isn't it,' I said bitterly as we sat on the couch. 'It never stops.'

'No,' he replied. 'And I'm afraid it never will. As long as there are people on the planet. What are you going to do with what's left of the weekend?'

'Paperwork.'

One side of my great room was sliding glass doors, and beyond, my neighborhood was black with a full moon that looked like gold, clouds gauzy and drifting.

'Why are you so angry with me?' His voice was gentle, but he let me know his hurt.

'I don't know.' I would not look at him.

'You do know.' He took my hand and began to rub it with his thumb. 'I love your hands. They look like a pianist's, only stronger. As if what you do is an art.'

'It is,' I simply said, and he often talked about my hands. 'I think you have a fetish. As a profiler, that should concern you.'

He laughed, kissing knuckles, fingers, the way he often did. 'Believe me, I have a fetish for more than your hands.'

'Benton.' I looked at him. 'I am angry with you because you are ruining my life.'

He got very still, shocked.

I got up from the couch and began to pace. 'I had my life set up just the way I wanted it,' I said as emotions rose to a crescendo. 'I am building a new office. Yes, I've been smart with my money, made enough smart investments to afford

76

this.' I swept my hand over my room. 'My own house that I designed. For me, everything was in its proper place until you . . .'

'Was it?' He was watching me intensely, wounded anger in his voice. 'You liked it better when I was married and we were always feeling rotten about it? When we were having an affair and lying to everyone?'

'Of course I didn't like that better!' I exclaimed. 'I just liked my life being mine.'

'Your problem is you're afraid of commitment. That's what this is about. How many times do I have to point that out? I think you should see someone. Really. Maybe Dr Zenner. You're friends. I know you trust her.'

'I'm not the one who needs a psychiatrist.' I regretted the words the instant I said them.

He angrily got up, as if ready to leave. It was not even nine o'clock.

'God. I'm too old and tired for this,' I muttered. 'Benton, I'm sorry. That wasn't fair. Please sit back down.'

He didn't at first, but stood in front of sliding glass doors, his back to me.

'I'm not trying to hurt you, Kay,' he said. 'I don't come around to see how badly I can fuck up your life, you know. I admire the hell out of everything you do. I just wish you'd let me in a little bit more.'

'I know. I'm sorry. Please don't leave.'

Blinking back tears, I sat down and stared up at the ceiling with its exposed beams and trowel marks visible on plaster. Wherever I looked there were details that had come from me. For a moment, I shut my eyes as tears rolled down my face. I did not wipe them away and Wesley knew when not to touch me. He knew when not to speak. He quietly sat beside me.

'I'm a middle-aged woman set in her ways,' I said as my voice shook. 'I can't help it. All I have is what I've built. No children. I can't stand my only sister and she can't stand me. My father was in bed dying my entire childhood, then gone when I was twelve. Mother's impossible, and now she's dying of emphysema. I can't be what you want, the good wife. I don't even know what the hell that is. I only know how to be Kay. And going to a psychiatrist isn't going to change a goddamn thing.'

He said to me, 'And I'm in love with you and want to marry you. And I can't seem to help that, either.'

I did not reply.

He added, 'And I thought you were in love with me.'

Still, I could not speak.

'At least you used to be,' he went on as pain overwhelmed his voice. 'I'm leaving.'

He started to get up again, and I put my hand on his arm.

'Not like this.' I looked at him. 'Don't do this to me.'

'To you?' He was incredulous.

I dimmed the lights until they were almost out, and the moon was a polished coin against a clear black sky scattered with stars. I got more wine and started the fire, while he watched everything I did.

'Sit closer to me,' I said.

He did, and I took his hands this time.

'Benton, patience. Don't rush me,' I said. 'Please. I'm not like Connie. Like other people.'

'I'm not asking you to be,' he said. 'I don't want you to be. I'm not like other people, either. We know what we see. Other people couldn't possibly understand. I could never

78

talk to Connie about how I spend my days. But I can talk to you.'

He kissed me sweetly, and we went deeper, touching faces, tongues and nimbly undressing, doing what we once did best. He gathered me in his mouth and hands, and we stayed on the couch until early morning, as light from the moon turned chilled and thin. After he drove home, I carried wine throughout my house, pacing, wandering with music on and flowing out speakers in every room. I landed in my office, where I was a master at distraction.

I began going through journals, tearing out articles that needed to be filed. I began working on an article I was due to write. But I was not in the mood for any of it, and decided to check my e-mail to see if Lucy had left word about when she might make it to Richmond. AOL announced I had mail waiting, and when I checked my box I felt as if someone had struck me. The address *deadoc* awaited me like an evil stranger.

His message was in lowercase, with no punctuation except spaces. It said, *you think you re so smart*. I opened the attached file and once again watched color images paint down my screen, severed feet and hands lined up on a table covered with what appeared to be the same bluish cloth. For a while I stared, wondering why this person was doing this to me. I hoped he had just made a very big mistake as I grabbed the phone.

'Marino!' I exclaimed when I got him on the line.

'Huh? What happened?' he blurted as he came to.

I told him.

'Shit. It's three friggin' o'clock in the morning. Don't you ever sleep?'

He seemed pleased, and I suspected he figured I wouldn't have called him if Wesley had still been here.

'Are you okay?' he then asked.

'Listen. The hands are palm up,' I said. 'The photograph was taken at close range. I can see a lot of detail.'

'Like what kind of detail? Is there a tattoo or something?'

'Ridge detail,' I said.

Neils Vander was the section chief of fingerprint examination, an older man with wispy hair and voluminous lab coats perpetually stained purple and black with ninhydrin and dusting powder. Forever in a hurry and prepossessed, he was from genteel Virginia stock. Vander had never called me by my first name or referred to anything personal about me in all the years I had known him. But he had his way of showing he cared. Sometimes it was a doughnut on my desk in the morning or, in the summer, Hanover tomatoes from his garden.

Known for an eagle eye that could match loops and whorls at a glance, he was also the resident expert in image enhancement and, in fact, had been trained by NASA. Over the years, he and I had materialized a multitude of faces from photographic blurs. We had conjured up writing that wasn't there, read impressions and restored eradications, the concept really very simple even if the execution of it was not.

A high-resolution image processing system could see two hundred and fifty-six shades of gray, while the human eye could differentiate, at the most, thirty-two. Therefore, it was possible to scan something into the computer and let it see what we could not. Deadoc may have sent me more than he bargained for. The first task this morning was to compare a morgue photograph of the torso with the one sent to me through AOL.

'Let me get a little more gray over here.' Vander said as he worked computer keys. 'And I'm going to tilt this some.'

'That's better,' I agreed.

We were sitting side by side, both of us leaning into the nineteen-inch monitor. Nearby, both photographs were on the scanner, a video camera feeding their images to us live.

'A little more of that.' Another shade of gray washed over the screen. 'Let me bump this a tad more.'

He reached over to the scanner and repositioned one of the photographs. He put another filter over the camera lens.

'I don't know,' I said as I stared. 'I think it was easier to see before. Maybe you need to move it a little more to the right,' I added, as if we were hanging pictures.

'Better. But there's still a lot of background interference I'd like to get rid of.'

'I wish we had the original. What's the radiometric resolution of this thing?' I asked, referring to the system's capability of differentiating shades of gray.

'A whole lot better than it used to be. Since the early days, I guess we've doubled the number of pixels that can be digitalized.'

Pixels, like the dots in dot matrix, were the smallest elements of an image being viewed, the molecules, the impressionistic points of color forming a painting.

'We got some grants, you know. One of these days, I want to move us into ultraviolet imaging. I can't even tell you what I could do with cyanoacrylate,' he went on about Super Glue, which reacted to components in human perspiration and was excellent for developing fingerprints difficult to see with the unaided eye.

'Well, good luck,' I said, because money was always tight no matter who was in office.

Repositioning the photograph again, he placed a blue filter over the camera lens, and dilated the lighter pixel elements, brightening the image. He enhanced horizontal details, removing vertical ones. Two torsos were now side by side. Shadows appeared, gruesome details sharper and in contrast.

'You can see the bony ends.' I pointed. 'Left leg severed just proximal to the lesser trochanter. Right leg' – I moved my finger on the screen – 'about an inch lower, right through the shaft.'

'I wish I could correct the camera angle, the perspective distortion,' he muttered, talking to himself, which he often did. 'But I don't know the measurements of anything. Too bad whoever took this didn't include a nice little ruler as a scale.'

'Then I would really worry about who we were dealing with,' I commented.

'That's all we need. A killer who's like us.' He defined the edges, and readjusted the positions of the photographs one more time. 'Let's see what happens if I superimpose them.'

He did, and the overlay was amazing, bone ends and even the ragged flesh around the severed neck, identical.

'That does it for me,' I announced.

'No question about it in my mind,' he agreed. 'Let's print this out.'

He clicked the mouse and the laser printer hummed on. Removing the photographs from the scanner, he replaced them with the one of the feet and hands, moving it around until it was perfectly centered. As he began to enlarge images, the sight became even more grotesque, blood staining the sheet bright red, as if it had just been spilled. The killer had neatly lined up feet like a pair of shoes, hands side by side like gloves.

'He should have turned them palm down,' Vander said. 'I wonder why he didn't?'

Using spatial filtering to retain important details, he began eliminating interference, such as the blood and the texture of the blue table cover.

'Can you get any ridge detail?' I asked leaning so close, I could smell his spicy aftershave.

'I think I can,' he said.

His voice was suddenly cheerful, for there was nothing he liked better than reading the hieroglyphics of fingers and feet. Beneath his gentle, distracted demeanor was a man who had sent thousands of people to the penitentiary, and dozens to the electric chair. He enlarged the photograph and assigned arbitrary colors to various intensities of gray, so we could see them better. Thumbs were small and pale like old parchment. There were ridges.

'The other fingers aren't going to work,' he said, staring, as if in a trance. 'They're too curled for me to see. But thumbs look pretty darn good. Let's capture this.' Clicking into a menu, he saved the image on the computer's hard disk. 'I'm going to want to work on this for a while.'

That was his cue for me to leave, and I pushed back my chair.

'If I get something, I'll run it through AFIS right away,' he said of the Automated Fingerprint Identification System, capable of comparing unknown latent prints against a databank of millions.

'That would be great,' I said. 'And I'll start with HALT.'

He gave me a curious look, because the Homicide Assessment and Lead Tracking System was a Virginia database maintained by the state police in conjunction with the FBI. It was the place to start if we suspected the case was local.

'Even though we have reason to suspect the other cases are not from here,' I explained to him, 'I think we should search everything we can. Including Virginia databases.'

Vander was still making adjustments, staring at the screen.

'As long as I don't have to fill out the forms,' he replied.

In the hallway were more boxes and white cartons marked *EVIDENCE* lining either side and stacked to the ceiling. Scientists walked past, preoccupied and in a hurry, paperwork and samples in hand that might send someone to court for murder. We greeted each other without slowing down as I headed to the fibers and trace evidence lab, which was big and quiet. More scientists in white coats were bent over microscopes and working at their desks, black counters haphazardly arranged with mysterious bundles wrapped in brown paper.

Aaron Koss was standing in front of an ultraviolet lamp that was glowing purple-red as he examined a slide through a magnifying lens to see what the reflective long wavelengths might tell him.

'Good morning,' I said.

'Same to you.' Koss grinned.

Dark and attractive, he seemed too young to be an expert in microscopic fibers, residues, paints and explosives. This morning, he was in faded jeans and running shoes.

'No court for you,' I said, for one could usually tell by the way people were dressed.

'Nope. Lucky me,' he said. 'Bet you're curious about your fibers.'

'I was in the neighborhood,' I said. 'Thought I'd drop by.'

I was notorious for making evidence rounds, and in the main, the scientists endured my intensity patiently, and in the end were grateful. I knew I pressured them when caseloads were already overwhelming. But when people were being murdered and dismembered, evidence needed to be examined now.

'Well, you've granted me a reprieve from working on our pipe-bomber,' he said with another smile.

'No luck with that,' I assumed.

'They had another one last night. I-195 North near Laburnum, right under the nose of Special Operations. You know, where Third Precinct used to be, if you can believe that?'

'Let's hope the person sticks with just blowing up traffic signs,' I said.

'Let's hope.' He stepped back from the UV lamp and got very serious. 'Here's what I've got so far from what you've turned in to me. Fibers from fabric remnants embedded in bone. Hair. And trace that was adhering to blood.'

'Her hair?' I asked, perplexed, for I had not receipted the long, grayish hairs to Koss. That was not his specialty.

'What I saw under the scope don't look human to me,' he replied. 'Maybe two different types of animal. I've sent them on to Roanoke.'

The state had only one hair expert, and he worked out of the western district forensic labs.

'What about the trace?' I asked.

'My guess is it's going to be debris from the landfill. But I want to look under the electron microscope. What I've got under UV now is fibers,' he went on. 'I should say they're fragments, really, that I gave an ultrasonic bath in distilled water to remove blood. You want to take a look?'

He gave me room to peer through the lens, and I smelled Obsession cologne. I could not help but smile, for I remembered being his age and still having the energy to preen. There were three mounted fragments fluorescing like neon lights. The fabric was white or off-white, one of them spangled with what looked like iridescent flecks of gold.

'What in the world is it?' I glanced up at him.

'Under the stereoscope, it looks synthetic,' he replied. 'The diameters regular, consistent like they would be if they were extruded through spinnerettes, versus being natural and irregular. Like cotton, let's say.'

'And the fluorescing flecks?' I was still looking.

'That's the interesting part,' he said. 'Though I've got to do further tests, at a glance it looks like paint.'

I paused for a moment to imagine this. 'What kind?' I asked.

'It's not flat and fine like automotive. This is gritty, more granular. Seems to be a pale, eggshell color. I'm thinking it's structural.'

'Are these the only fragments and fibers you've looked at?'

'I'm just getting started.' He moved to another countertop and pulled out a stool. 'I've looked at all of them under UV, and I'd say that about fifty percent of them have this paint-type substance soaked into the material. And although I can't definitively say what the fabric is, I do know that all of the samples you submitted are the same type, and probably from the same source.'

He placed a slide in the stage of a polarizing microscope, which, like Ray-Ban sunglasses, reduced glare, splitting light in different waves with different refractive index values to give us yet another clue as to the identity of the material.

'Now,' he said, adjusting the focus as he stared into the lens without blinking. 'This is the biggest fragment recovered, about the size of a dime. There are two sides to it.'

He moved out of the way and I looked at fibers reminiscent of blond hairs with speckles of pink and green along the shaft.

'Very consistent with polyester,' Koss explained. 'Speckles are delusterants used in manufacturing so the material isn't shiny. I also think there's some rayon mixed in, and based on all this would have decided what you've got here is a very common fabric that could be used in almost anything. Anything from blouses to bedspreads. But there's one big problem.'

He opened a bottle of liquid solvent used for temporary mountings, and with tweezers, removed the cover slide and carefully turned the fragment over. Dripping xylene, he covered the slide again and motioned for me to bend close.

'What do you see?' he asked, and he was proud of himself.

'Something grayish and solid. Not the same material as the other side.' I looked at him in surprise. 'This fabric has a backing on it?'

'Some kind of thermoplastic. Probably polyethylene terephthalate.'

'Which is used in what?' I wanted to know.

'Primarily soft drink bottles, film. Blister packs used in packing.'

I stared at him, baffled, for I did not see how those products could have anything to do with this case.

'What else?' I asked.

He thought. 'Strapping materials. And some of it, like bottles, can be recycled and used for carpet fibers, fiberfill, plastic lumber. Just about anything.'

'But not fabric for clothing.'

He shook his head, and said with certainty, 'No way. The fabric in question is a rather common, crude polyester blend lined with a plastic-type material. Definitely not like any clothing I've ever heard of. Plus, it appears to be saturated with paint.'

'Thank you, Aaron,' I said. 'This changes everything.'

When I got back to my office, I was surprised and annoyed to find Percy Ring sitting in a chair across from my desk, flipping through a notebook.

'I had to be in Richmond for an interview at Channel Twelve,' he innocently said, 'so I thought I might as well come by to see you. They want to talk to you, too.' He smiled.

I did not answer him, but my silence was loud as I sat in my chair.

'I didn't think you would do the interview. And that's what I told them,' he went on in his easy, affable way.

'And so tell me, what exactly did you say this time?' My tone was not nice.

'Excuse me?' His smile faded and his eyes got hard. 'What's that supposed to mean?'

'You're the investigator. Figure it out.' My eyes were just as hard as his.

He shrugged. 'I gave the usual. Just the basic information about the case and its similarities to the other ones.'

'Investigator Ring, let me make this very clear yet one more time,' I said with no attempt to hide my disdain for him. 'This case is not necessarily like the other ones, and we should not be discussing it with the media.'

'Well, now, it appears you and I have a different perspective, Dr Scarpetta.'

Handsome in a dark suit and paisley suspenders and tie, he looked remarkably credible. I could not help but recall what Wesley had said about Ring's ambitions and connections, and the idea that this egotistical idiot would one day run the state police or be elected to Congress was one I could not stand.

'I think the public has a right to know if there's a psycho in their midst,' he was saying.

'And that's what you said on TV.' My irritation flared hotter. 'That there's a psycho in our midst.'

'I don't remember my exact words. The real reason I stopped by is I'm wondering when I'm going to get a copy of the autopsy report.'

'Still pending.'

'I need it as soon as I can get it.' He looked me in the eye. 'The Commonwealth's Attorney wants to know what's going on.'

I couldn't believe what I'd just heard. He would not be talking to a C.A. unless there was a suspect.

'What are you saying?' I asked.

'I'm looking hard at Keith Pleasants.'

I was incredulous.

'There are a lot of circumstantial things,' he went on, 'not the least of which is how he just so happened to be the one operating the Cat when the torso was found. You know, he usually doesn't operate earth-moving equipment, and then just happens to be in the driver's seat at that exact moment?'

'I should think that makes him more a victim than a suspect. If he's the killer,' I continued, 'one might expect that he wouldn't have wanted to be within a hundred miles of the landfill when the body was found.'

'Psychopaths like to be right there,' he said as if he knew. 'They fantasize about what it would be like to be there when the victim is discovered. They get off on it, like that ambulance driver who murdered women, then dumped them in the area he covered. When it was time to go on duty, he'd call 911 so he was the one who ended up responding.'

In addition to his degree in psychology, he no doubt had attended a lecture on profiling, too. He knew it all.

'Keith lives with his mother, who I think he really resents,' he went on, smoothing his tie. 'She had him late in life, is in her sixties. He takes care of her.'

'Then his mother is still alive and accounted for,' I said.

'Right. But that doesn't mean he didn't take out his aggressions on some other poor old woman. Plus – and you won't believe this – in high school, he worked at the meat counter of a grocery store. He was a butcher's assistant.'

I did not tell him that I did not think a meat saw had been used in this case, but let him talk.

'He's never been very social, which again fits the profile.' He continued spinning his fantastic web. 'And it's rumored among the other guys who work at the landfill that he's homosexual.'

'Based on what?'

'On the fact he doesn't date women or even seem interested in them when the other guys make remarks, jokes. You know how it is with a bunch of rough guys.'

'Describe the house he lives in.' I thought of the photographs sent to me through e-mail.

'Two-story frame, three bedrooms, kitchen, living room. Middle class on its way to being poor. Like maybe in an earlier day when his old man was around, they had it pretty nice.'

'What happened to the father?'

'Ran off before Keith was born.'

'Brothers, sisters?' I asked.

'Grown, have been for a long time. I guess he was a surprise. I suspect Mr Pleasants isn't the father, explaining why he was already gone before Keith was even around.'

'And what is this suspicion based on?' I asked with an edge.

'My gut.'

'I see.'

'Where they live is remote, about ten miles from the landfill, in farmland,' he said. 'Got a pretty good-size yard, a garage that's detached from the house.' He crossed his legs, pausing, as if what he had to add next was important. 'There are a lot of tools, and a big workbench. Keith says he's a handyman and uses the garage when things need fixing around the house. I did see a hacksaw hanging up on a pegboard, and a machete he says he uses for cutting back kudzu and weeds.'

Slipping out of his jacket, he carefully draped it over his lap as he continued the tour of Keith Pleasants' life.

'You certainly had access to a lot of places without a warrant,' I cut him off.

'He was cooperative,' he replied, nonplussed. 'Let's talk about what's in this guy's head.' He tapped his own. 'First, he's smart, real smart, books, magazines, newspapers all over the place. Get this. He's been videotaping news accounts of this case, clipping articles.'

'Probably most of the people working at the landfill are,' I reminded him.

But Ring was not interested in one word I said.

'He reads all kinds of crime stuff. Thrillers. *Silence of the Lambs, Red Dragon*. Tom Clancy, Ann Rule . . .'

I interrupted again because I could not listen to him a moment longer. 'You've just described a typical American reading list. I can't tell you how to conduct your investigation, but let me try to persuade you to follow the evidence . . .'

'I am,' he interrupted right back. 'That's exactly what I'm doing.'

'That's exactly what you're not doing. You don't even know what the evidence is. You haven't received a single report from my office or the labs. You haven't received a profile from the FBI. Have you even talked to Marino or Grigg?'

'We keep missing each other.' He got up and put his jacket back on. 'I need those reports.' It sounded like an order. 'The C.A. will be calling you. By the way, how's Lucy?'

I did not want him to even know my niece's name, and it was evident by the surprised, angry look in my eyes.

'I wasn't aware the two of you were acquainted,' I coolly replied.

'I sat in on one of her classes, I don't know, a couple months back. She was talking about CAIN.'

I grabbed a stack of death certificates from the in-basket, and began initialing them.

'Afterwards she took us over to HRT for a robotics demo,' he said from the doorway. 'She seeing anyone?'

I had nothing to say.

'I mean, I know she lives with another agent. A woman. But they're just roommates, right?'

His meaning was plain, and I froze, looking up as he walked off, whistling. Furious, I collected an armload of paperwork and was getting up from my desk when Rose walked in.

'He can park his shoes under my bed anytime he wants,' she said in Ring's wake.

'Please!' I couldn't stand it. 'I thought you were an intelligent woman, Rose.'

'I think you need some hot tea,' she said.

'Maybe so.' I sighed.

'But we have another matter first,' she said in her business-like way. 'Do you know someone named Keith Pleasants?'

'What about him?' For an instant, my mind locked.

'He's in the lobby,' she said. 'Very upset, refuses to leave until he sees you. I started to call security, but thought I should check . . .' The look on my face stopped her cold.

'Oh my God,' I exclaimed in dismay. 'Did he and Ring see each other?'

'I have no idea,' she said, and now she was very perplexed. 'Is something wrong?'

'Everything.' I sighed, dropping the paperwork back on my desk.

'Then you do or don't want me to call security?'

'Don't.' I walked briskly past her.

My heels were sharp and directed as I followed the hallway to the front, and around a corner into a lobby that had never been homey no matter how hard I had tried. No amount of tasteful furniture or prints on walls could disguise the terrible truths that brought people to these doors. Like Keith Pleasants, they sat woodenly on a blue upholstered couch that was supposed to be unprovocative and soothing. In shock, they stared at nothing or wept.

I pushed open the door as he sprung to his feet, eyes bloodshot. I could not quite tell if he were in a rage or a panic as he almost lunged at me. For an instant, I thought he was going to grab me or start swinging. But he awkwardly dropped his hands by his sides and glared at me, his face darkening as his outrage boiled over.

'You got no right to be saying things like that about me!' he exclaimed with clenched fists. 'You don't know me! Don't know anything about me!'

'Easy, Keith,' I said, calmly, but with authority.

Motioning for him to sit back down, I pulled up a chair so I could face him. He was breathing hard, trembling, eyes wounded and filled with furious tears.

'You met me one time.' He shot a finger at me. 'One lousy time and then say things.' His voice was quavering. 'I'm about to lose my job.' He covered his mouth with a fist, averting his eyes as he fought for control.

'In the first place,' I said, 'I have not said a word about you. Not to anyone.'

He glanced at me.

'I have no idea what you're talking about.' My eyes were steady on him, and I spoke with quiet confidence that made him waver. 'I wish you'd explain it to me.'

He was studying me with uncertainty, lies he had been led to believe about me wavering in his eyes.

'You didn't talk to Investigator Ring about me?' he said.

I checked my fury. 'No.'

'He came to my house this morning while my mama was still in bed.' His voice shook. 'Started interrogating me like I was a murderer or something. Said you had findings pointing right to me, so I better confess.'

'Findings? What findings?' I said as my disgust grew.

'Fibers that according to you looked like they came from what I had on the day we met. You said my size fit what you think the size is of the person who cut up that body. He said you could tell by the pressure applied with the saw that whoever did it was about my strength. He said you were demanding all kinds of things from me so you could do all these tests. DNA. That you thought I was weird when I drove you up to the site . . .'

I interrupted him, 'My God, Keith. I have never heard so much bullshit in my life. If I said even one of those things, I would be fired for incompetence.'

'That's the other thing,' Pleasants jumped in again, fire in his eyes. 'He's been talking with everyone I work with! They're all wondering if I'm some kind of axe murderer. I can tell by the way they look at me.'

He dissolved in tears as doors opened and several state troopers walked in. They paid us no mind as they were buzzed inside, on their way down to the morgue, where Fielding was working on a pedestrian death. Pleasants was too upset for me to discuss this with him any further, and I was so incensed with Ring that I did not know what else to say.

'Do you have a lawyer?' I asked him.

He shook his head.

'I think you'd better get one.'

'I don't know any.'

'I can give you some names,' I said as Wingo opened the door and was startled by the sight of Pleasants crying on the couch.

'Uh, Dr Scarpetta?' Wingo said. 'Dr Fielding wants to know if he can go ahead and receipt the personal effects to the funeral home.'

I stepped closer to Wingo, because I did not want Pleasants further upset by the business of this place.

'The troopers are on their way down,' I said in a low voice. 'If they don't want the personal effects, then yes. Receipt them to the funeral home.'

He was staring hard at Pleasants, as if he knew him from somewhere.

'Listen,' I said to Wingo. 'Get him the names and numbers of Jameson and Higgins.'

They were two very fine lawyers in town whom I considered friends.

'Then please see Mr Pleasants out.'

Wingo was still staring, as if transfixed by him.

'Wingo?' I gave him a questioning look, because he did not seem to have heard me.

'Yes, ma'am.' He glanced at me.

I went past him, heading downstairs. I needed to talk to Wesley, but maybe I should get hold of Marino first. As I rode the elevator down, I debated if I should call the C.A. in Sussex and warn her about Ring. At the same time all of this was going through my mind, I felt dreadfully sorry for Pleasants. I was scared for him. As far-fetched as it might seem, I knew he could end up charged with murder.

In the morgue, Fielding and the troopers were looking at the pedestrian on table one, and there wasn't the usual banter because the victim was the nine-year-old daughter of a city councilman. She had been walking to the bus stop early this morning when someone had swerved off the road at a high rate of speed. Based on the absence of skid marks, the driver had hit the girl from the rear and not even slowed.

'How are we doing?' I asked when I got to them.

'We got us a real tough one here,' said one of the troopers, his expression grave.

'The father's going ape shit,' Fielding told me as he went over the clothed body with a lens, collecting trace evidence.

'Any paint?' I asked, for a chip of it could identify the make and model of the car.

'Not so far.' My deputy chief was in a foul mood. He hated working on children.

I scanned torn, bloody jeans and a partial grille mark imprinted in fabric at the level of the buttocks. The front bumper had struck the back of the knees, and the head had hit the windshield. She had been wearing a small red knapsack. The bagged lunch, and books, papers and pens that had been taken out of it pricked my heart. I felt heavy inside.

'The grille mark seems pretty high,' I remarked.

'That's what I'm thinking, too,' another trooper spoke. 'Like you associate with pickup trucks and recreational vehicles. About the time it happened, a black Jeep Cherokee was observed in the area traveling at a high rate of speed.'

'Her father's been calling every half hour.' Fielding glanced up at me. 'Thinks this was more than an accident.'

'Implying what, exactly?' I asked.

'That it's political.' He resumed work, collecting fibers and bits of debris. 'A homicide.'

'Lord, let's hope not,' I said, walking away. 'What it is now is bad enough.'

On a steel counter in a remote corner of the morgue was a portable electric heater where we defleshed and degreased bones. The process was decidedly unpleasant requiring the boiling of body parts in a ten-percent solution of bleach. The big, rattling steel pot, the smell, were dreadful, and I usually restricted this activity to nights and weekends when we were unlikely to have visitors.

Yesterday, I had left the bone ends from the torso to boil overnight. They had not required much time, and I turned off the heater. Pouring steaming, stinking water into a sink, I waited until the bones were cool enough to pick up. They were clean and white, about two inches long, cuts and saw marks clearly visible. As I examined each segment carefully, a sense of scary disbelief swept over me. I could not tell which saw marks had been made by the killer and which had been made by me.

'Jack,' I called out to Fielding. 'Could you come over here for a minute?'

He stopped what he was doing and walked to my corner of the room.

'What's up?' he asked.

I handed him one of the bones. 'Can you tell which end was cut with the Stryker saw?'

He turned it over and over, looking back and forth, at one end and then the other, frowning. 'Did you mark it?'

'For right and left I did,' I said. 'Beyond that, no. I should have. But usually it's so obvious which end is which, it's not necessary.'

'I'm not expert, but if I didn't know better, I'd say all these cuts were made with the same saw.' He handed the bone back to me and I began sealing it in an evidence bag. 'You got to take them to Canter anyway, right.'

'He's not going to be happy with me.' I said.

M Y HOUSE WAS built of stone on the edge of Windsor Farms, an old Richmond neighborhood with English street names, and stately Georgian and Tudor homes that some would call mansions. Lights were on in windows I passed, and beyond glass I could see fine furniture and chandeliers, and people moving or watching TV. No one seemed to close their curtains in this city, except me. Leaves had begun to fall. It was cool and overcast, and when I pulled into my driveway, smoke was drifting from the chimney, my niece's ancient green Suburban parked in front.

'Lucy?' I called out as I shut the door and turned off the alarm.

'I'm in here,' she replied from the end of the house where she always stayed.

As I headed for my office to deposit my briefcase and the pile I had brought home to work on tonight, she emerged from her bedroom, pulling a bright orange UVA sweatshirt over her head.

'Hi.' Smiling, she gave me a hug, and there was very little that was soft about her.

Holding her at arm's length, I took a good look at her, just like I always did.

'Uh oh,' she playfully said. 'Inspection time.' She held out her arms and turned around, as if about to be searched.

'Smarty,' I said.

In truth, I would have preferred it had she weighed a little more, but she was keenly pretty and healthy, with auburn hair that was short but softly styled. After all this time, I still could not look at her without envisioning a precocious, obnoxious ten-year-old who had no one, really, but me.

'You pass,' I said.

'Sorry I'm so late.'

'Tell me again what it was you were doing?' I asked, for she had called earlier in the day to say she could not get here until dinner.

'An assistant attorney general decided to drop in with an entourage. As usual, they wanted HRT to put on a show.'

We headed to the kitchen.

'I trotted out Toto and Tin Man,' she added.

They were robots.

'Used fiber optics, virtual reality. The usual things, except it's pretty cool. We parachuted them out of a Huey, and I maneuvered them to burn through a metal door with lasers.'

'No stunts with the helicopters, I hope,' I said.

'The guys did that. I did my shit from the ground.' She wasn't happy about it.

The problem was, Lucy wanted to do stunts with helicopters. There were fifty agents on the HRT. She was the only woman and had a tendency to overreact when they wouldn't let her do dangerous things that, in my opinion, she had no business doing anyway. Of course, I wasn't the most objective judge.

'It suits me fine if you stick with robots,' I said, and we were in the kitchen now. 'Something smells good. What did you fix your tired, old aunt to eat?'

'Fresh spinach sautéed in a little garlic and olive oil, and filets that I'm going to throw on the grill. This is my one day a week to eat beef, so tough luck if it's not yours. I even sprung for a bottle of really nice wine, something Janet and I discovered.'

'Since when can FBI agents afford nice wine?'

'Hey,' she said, 'I don't do too bad. Besides, I'm too damn busy to spend money.'

Certainly, she didn't spend it on clothes. Whenever I saw her, she was either in khaki fatigues or sweats. Now and then she wore jeans and a funky jacket or blazer, and made fun of my offers of hand-me-downs. She would not wear my lawyerly suits and blouses with high collars, and frankly, my figure was fuller than her firm, athletic one. Probably nothing in my closet would fit.

The moon was huge and low in a cloudy, dark sky. We put on jackets and sat out on the deck drinking wine while Lucy cooked. She had started baked potatoes first, and they were taking a while, so we talked. Over recent years, our relationship had become less mother-daughter as we evolved into colleagues and friends. The transition was not an easy one, for often she taught me and even worked on some of my cases. I felt oddly lost, no longer certain of my role and power in her life.

'Wesley wants me to track this AOL thing,' she was saying. 'Sussex definitely wants CASKU's help.'

'Do you know Percy Ring?' I asked as I thought of what he had said in my office, infuriated again.

'He was in one of my classes and was obnoxious, wouldn't shut up.' She reached for the bottle of wine. 'What a peacock.'

She began filling our glasses. Raising the hood of the grill, she poked potatoes with a fork.

'I believe we're ready,' she said, pleased.

Moments later, she was emerging from the house, carrying the filets. They sizzled as she placed them on the grill. 'Somehow he figured out you're my aunt.' She was talking about Ring again. 'Not that it's a secret, and he asked me about it after class once. You know, if you tutored me, helped me out with my cases, like I couldn't possibly do what I'm doing on my own, that sort of thing. I just think he picks on me because I'm a new agent and a woman.'

'That may be the biggest miscalculation he's ever made in his life,' I said.

'And he wanted to know if I was married.' Her eyes were shadowed as porch lights shone on one side of her face.

'I worry about what his interest really is,' I commented.

She glanced at me as she cooked. 'The usual.' She shrugged it off, for she was surrounded by men and paid no attention to their comments or their stares.

'Lucy, he made a reference to you in my office today,' I said. 'A veiled reference.'

'To what?'

'Your status. Your roommate.'

No matter how often or delicately we talked about this, she always got frustrated and impatient.

'Whether it's true or not,' she said, and the sizzling of the grill seemed to match her tone, 'there would still be rumors because I'm an agent. It's ridiculous. I know women married with kids, and the guys think all of them are gay, too, just because they're cops, agents, troopers, secret service. Some people even think it about you. For the same reason. Because of your position, your power.'

'This is not about accusations,' I reminded her, gently. 'This is about whether someone could hurt you. Ring is very smooth. He comes across as credible. I expect he resents that you're FBI, HRT and he's not.'

'I think he's already demonstrated that.' Her voice was hard.

'I just hope the jerk doesn't keep asking you out.'

'Oh, he already is. At least half a dozen times.' She sat down. 'He's even asked Janet out, if you can believe that.' She laughed. 'Talk about not getting it.'

'The problem is I think he does get it,' I said, ominously. 'It's like he's building a case against you, gathering evidence.'

'Well, gather away.' She abruptly ended our discussion. 'So tell me what else went on today.'

I told her what I had learned at the labs, and we talked about fibers embedded in bone and Koss's analysis of them as we carried steaks and wine inside. We sat at the kitchen table with a candle lit, digesting information few people would serve with food.

'A cheap motel curtain could have a backing like that,' Lucy said.

'That or something like a drop cloth, because of the paint-like substance,' I replied. 'The spinach is wonderful. Where did you get it?'

'Ukrops. I'd give anything to have a store like that in my neighborhood. So this person wrapped the victim in a drop cloth and then dismembered her through it?' she asked as she cut her meat.

'That's certainly the way it's looking.'

'What does Wesley say?' She met my eyes.

'I haven't had a chance to talk to him yet.' This wasn't quite true. I had not even called.

For a moment, Lucy was silent. She got up and brought a bottle of Evian to the table. 'So how long do you plan to run from him?'

I pretended not to hear her, in hopes she would not start in.

'You know that's what you're doing. You're scared.'

'This is not something we should discuss,' I said. 'Especially when we're having such a pleasant evening.'

She reached for her wine.

'It's very good, by the way,' I said. 'I like pinot noir because it's light. Not heavy like a merlot. I'm not in the mood for anything heavy right now. So you made a good choice.'

She stabbed another bite of steak, getting my point.

'Tell me how things are going with Janet,' I went on. 'Mostly doing white-collar crime in D.C.? Or is she getting to spend more time at ERF these days?'

Lucy stared out the window at the moon as she slowly swirled wine in her glass. 'I should get started on your computer.'

While I cleaned up, she disappeared into my office. I did not disturb her for a very long time, if for no other reason than I knew she was put out with me. She wanted complete openness, and I had never been good at that, not with anyone. I felt bad, as if I had let down everyone I loved. For a while, I sat at the kitchen desk, talking to Marino on the phone, and I called to catch up with my mother. I put on a pot of decaffeinated coffee and carried two mugs down the hall.

Lucy was busy at my keyboard, glasses on, a slight frown furrowing her young, smooth brow as she concentrated. I set her coffee down and looked over her head at what she was typing. It made no sense to me. It never did.

'How's it going?' I asked.

I could see my face reflected in the monitor as she struck the enter key again, executing another UNIX command.

'Good and not good,' she replied with an impatient sigh. 'The problem with applications like AOL is you can't track files unless you get into the original programming language. That's where I am now. And it's like following bread crumbs through a universe with more layers than an onion.'

I pulled up a chair and sat next to her. 'Lucy,' I said, 'how did someone send these photographs to me? Can you tell me, step by step?'

She stopped what she was doing, slipping off her glasses and setting them on the desk. She rubbed her face in her hands and massaged her temples as if she had a headache.

'You got any Tylenol?' she asked.

'No acetaminophen with alcohol.' I opened a drawer and got out a bottle of Motrin instead.

'For starters,' she said, taking two, 'this wouldn't have been easy if your screen name wasn't the same as your real one: KSCARPETTA.'

'I made it easy *deliberately*, for my colleagues to send me mail,' I explained one more time.

'You made it easy for anyone to send you mail.' She looked accusingly at me. 'Have you gotten crank mail before?'

'I think this goes beyond crank mail.'

'Please answer my question.'

'A few things. Nothing to worry about.' I paused, then went on, 'Generally after a lot of publicity because of some big case, a sensational trial, whatever.'

'You should change your user name.'

'No,' I said. 'Deadoc might want to send me something else. I can't change it now.'

'Oh great.' She put her glasses back on. 'So now you want him to be a pen pal.'

'Lucy, please,' I quietly said, and I was getting a headache, too. 'We both have a job to do.'

She was quiet for a moment. Then she apologized. 'I guess I'm just as overly protective of you as you've always been of me.'

'I still am.' I patted her knee. 'Okay, so he got my screen name from the AOL directory of subscribers, right?'

She nodded. 'Let's talk about your AOL profile.'

'There's nothing in it but my professional title, my office phone number and address,' I said. 'I never entered personal details, such as marital status, date of birth, hobbies, et cetera. I have more sense than that.'

'Have you checked out his profile?' she asked. 'The one for deadoc?'

'Frankly, it never occurred to me that he would have one,' I said.

Depressed, I thought of saw marks I could not tell apart, and felt I had made yet one more mistake this day.

'Oh, he's got one, all right.' Lucy was typing again. 'He wants you to know who he is. That's why he wrote it.'

She clicked to the Member Directory, and when she opened deadoc's profile, I could not believe what was before my eyes. I scanned key words that could be searched by anyone interested in finding other users to whom they applied.

Attorney, autopsy, chief, Chief Medical Examiner, Cornell, corpse, death, dismemberment, FBI, forensic, Georgetown, Italian, Johns Hopkins, judicial, killer, lawyer, medical, pathologist, physician, Scuba, Virginia, woman.

The list went on, the professional and personal information, the hobbies, all describing me.

'It's like deadoc's saying he's you,' Lucy said.

I was dumbfounded and suddenly felt very cold. 'This is crazy.'

Lucy pushed back her chair and looked at me. 'He's got your profile. In cyberspace, on the World Wide Web, you're both the same person with two different screen names.'

'We are not the same person. I can't believe you said that.' I looked at her, shocked.

'The photographs are yours and you sent them to yourself. It was easy. You simply scanned them into your computer. No big deal. You can get portable color scanners for four, five hundred bucks. Attach the file to the message *ten*, which you send to KSCARPETTA, send to yourself, in other words . . .'

'Lucy,' I cut her off, 'for God's sake, that's enough.'

She was silent, her face without expression.

'This is outrageous. I can't believe what you're saying.' I got up from the chair in disgust.

'If your fingerprints were on the murder weapon,' she replied, 'wouldn't you want me to tell you?'

'My fingerprints aren't on anything.'

'Aunt Kay, I'm just making the point that someone out there is stalking you, impersonating you, on the Internet. Of course you didn't do anything. But what I'm trying to impress upon you is every time someone does a search by subject because they need help from an expert like you, they're going to get deadoc's name, too.'

'How could he have known all this information about me?' I went on. 'It's not in my profile. I don't have anything in there about where I went to law school, medical school, that my heritage is Italian.'

'Maybe from things written about you over the years.'

'I suppose.' I felt as if I were coming down with something. 'Would you like a nightcap? I'm very tired.'

But she was lost again in the dark space of the UNIX environment with its strange symbols and commands like *cat*, *:q!* and *vi*.

'Aunt Kay, what's your password in AOL?' she asked.

'The same one I use for everything else,' I confessed, knowing she would be annoyed again.

'Shit. Don't tell me you're still using *Sinbad*.' She looked up at me.

'My mother's rotten cat has never been mentioned in anything ever written about me,' I defended myself.

I watched as she typed the command *password* and entered *Sinbad*.

'Do you do password aging?' she asked as if everyone should know what that meant.

'I have no idea what you're talking about.'

'Where you change your password at least once a month.'

'No,' I said.

'Who else knows your password?'

'Rose knows it. And of course, now you do,' I said. 'There's no way deadoc could.'

'There's always a way. He could use a UNIX password-encryption program to encrypt every word in a dictionary. Then compare every encrypted word to your password . . .'

'It wasn't that complicated,' I said with conviction. 'I bet whoever did this doesn't know a thing about UNIX.'

Lucy closed what she was doing, and looked curiously at me, swiveling the chair around. 'Why do you say that?'

'Because he could have washed the body first so trace evidence didn't adhere to blood. He shouldn't have given us a photo of her hands. Now we may have her prints.' I was leaning against the door frame, holding my aching head. 'He's not that smart.'

'Maybe he doesn't think her prints will ever matter,' she said, getting up. 'And by the way,' she said as she walked by. 'Almost any computer book's going to tell you it's stupid to choose a password that's the name of your significant other or your cat.'

'Sinbad's not my cat. I wouldn't have a miserable Siamese that always gives me the fisheye and stalks me whenever I walk into my mother's house.'

'Well, you must like him a little bit or you wouldn't have wanted to think of him every time you log on to your computer,' she said from down the hall.

'I don't like him in the least,' I said.

The next morning, the air was crisp and clean like a fall apple, stars were out, traffic mostly truckers in the midst of long hauls. I turned off on 64 East, just beyond the state fairgrounds, and minutes later was prowling rows in short-term parking at the Richmond International Airport. I chose a space in *S* because I knew it would be easy for me to remember, and was reminded of my password again, of other obvious acts of carelessness caused by overload.

As I was getting my bag out of the trunk, I heard footsteps behind me and instantly wheeled around.

'Don't shoot.' Marino held up his hands. It was cool enough out that I could see his breath.

'I wish you'd whistle or something when you walk up on me in the dark,' I said, slamming shut the trunk.

'Oh. And bad people don't whistle. Only good guys like me do.' He grabbed my suitcase. 'You want me to get that, too?'

He reached for the hard, black Pelican case I was taking with me to Memphis today, where it already had been numerous times before. Inside were human vertebrae and bone, evidence that could not leave me.

'This stays handcuffed to me,' I said, grabbing it and my briefcase. 'I'm really sorry to put you out like this, Marino. Are you sure it's necessary for you to come along?'

We had discussed this several times now, and I did not think he should accompany me. I did not see the point.

'Like I told you, some squirrel's playing games with you,' he said. 'Me, Wesley, Lucy, the entire friggin' Bureau think I should come along. For one thing, you've made this exact same trip in every case, so it's gotten predictable. And it's been in the papers that you use this guy at UT.'

Parking lots were well lit and full of cars, and I could not help but notice people slowly driving past, looking for a place that wasn't miles from the terminal. I wondered what else deadoc knew about me, and wished I had worn more than a trench coat. I was cold and had forgotten my gloves.

'Besides,' Marino added, 'I've never been to Graceland.'

At first, I thought he was joking.

'It's on my list,' he went on.

'What list?'

'The one I've had since I was a kid. Alaska, Las Vegas and the Grand Ole Opry,' he said as if the thought filled him with joy. 'Don't you have some place you would go if you could do anything you want?'

We were at the terminal now, and he held the door.

'Yes,' I said. 'My own bed in my own home.'

I headed for the Delta desk, picked up our tickets and went upstairs. Typical for this hour, nothing was open except security. When I placed my hard case on the X-ray belt, I knew what was going to happen.

'Ma'am, you're going to have to open that,' said the female guard.

I unlocked it and unsnapped the clasps. Inside, nestled in foam rubber, were labeled plastic bags containing the bones. The guard's eyes widened.

'I've been through here before with this,' I patiently explained.

She started to reach for one of the plastic bags.

'Please don't touch anything,' I warned. 'This is evidence in a homicide.'

There were several other travelers behind me, now, and they were listening to every word I said.

'Well, I have to look at it.'

'You can't.' I got out my brass medical examiner's shield and showed it to her. 'You touch anything here, and I'll have to include you in the chain of evidence when this eventually goes to court. You'll be subpoenaed.'

That was as much of an explanation as she needed, and she let me go.

'Dumb as a bag of hammers,' Marino mumbled as we walked.

'She's just doing her job,' I replied.

'Look,' he said. 'We don't fly back until tomorrow morning, meaning unless you spend the whole damn day looking at bones, we should have some time.'

'You can go to Graceland by yourself. I've got plenty of work to do in my room. I'm also sitting in nonsmoking.' I chose a seat at our gate. 'So if you want to smoke, you'll have to go over there.' I pointed.

He scanned other passengers waiting, like us, to board. Then he looked at me.

'You know what, Doc?' he said. 'The problem is you hate to have fun.'

I got the morning paper out of my briefcase, shook it open.

He sat next to me. 'I'll bet you've never even listened to Elvis.'

'How could I not listen to Elvis? He's on the radio, on TV, in elevators.'

'He's the king.'

I eyed Marino over the top of the paper.

'His voice, everything about him. There's never been anyone like him,' Marino went on as if he had a crush. 'I mean, it's like classical music and those painters you like so much. I think people like that only come along every couple hundred years.'

'So now you're comparing him with Mozart and Monet.' I turned a page, bored with local politics and business.

'Sometimes you're a friggin' snob.' He got up, grumpy. 'And maybe just once in your life you might think of going some place I want to go. You ever seen me bowl?' He glared down at me, getting out his cigarettes. 'You ever said anything nice about my truck? You ever gone fishing with me? You ever eat at my house? No, I gotta go to yours because you live in the right part of town.'

'You cook for me, I'll come over,' I said as I read.

He angrily stalked off, and I could feel the eyes of strangers on us. I supposed they assumed that Marino and I were an item, and had not gotten along in years. Smiling to myself, I turned a page. Not only would I go to Graceland with him, I planned to buy him barbecue tonight.

Since it seemed that one could not fly direct from Richmond to anywhere except Charlotte, we were routed to Cincinnati first, where we changed planes. We arrived in Memphis by noon and checked into the Peabody Hotel. I had gotten us a government rate of seventy-three dollars per night, and Marino looked around, gawking at a grand lobby of stained glass and a fountain of mallard ducks.

'Holy shit,' he said. 'I've never seen a joint that has live ducks. They're everywhere.'

We were walking into the restaurant, which was appropriately named Mallards, and displayed behind glass were duck objets d'art. There were paintings of ducks on walls, and ducks were on the staff's green vests and ties.

'They have a duck palace on the roof,' I said. 'And roll out a red carpet for them twice a day when they come and go to John Philip Sousa.'

'No way.'

I told the hostess that we would like a table for two. 'In nonsmoking,' I added.

The restaurant was crowded with men and women wearing big name tags for some real estate convention they were attending at the hotel. We sat so close to other people that I could read reports they were perusing and hear their affairs. I ordered a fresh fruit plate and coffee, while Marino got his usual grilled hamburger platter.

'Medium rare,' he told the waiter.

'Medium.' I gave Marino a look.

'Yeah, yeah, okay.' He shrugged.

'Enterohemorrhagic E. coli,' I said to him as the waiter walked off. 'Trust me. Not worth it.'

'Don't you ever want to do things bad for you?' he said.

He looked depressed and suddenly old as he sat across from me in this beautiful place where people were well dressed and better paid than a police captain from Richmond. Marino's hair had thinned to an unruly fringe circling the top of his ears like a tarnished silver halo shoved low. He had not lost an ounce since I had known him, his belly rising from his belt and touching the edge of the table. Not a day went by that I did not fear for him. I could not imagine his not working with me forever.

At half past one, we left the hotel in the rental car. He drove because he would never have it any other way, and we got on Madison Avenue and followed it east, away from the Mississippi River. The brick university was so close we could have walked it, the Regional Forensic Center across the street from a tire store and the Life Blood Donor Center. Marino parked in back, near the public entrance of the medical examiner's office.

The facility was funded by the county and about the size of my central district office in Richmond. There were three forensic pathologists, and also two forensic anthropologists, which was very unusual and enviable, for I would have loved to have someone like Dr David Canter on my staff. Memphis had yet another distinction which was decidedly not a happy one. The chief had been involved in perhaps two of the most infamous cases in the country. He had performed the autopsy of Martin Luther King and had witnessed the one of Elvis.

'If it's all the same to you,' Marino said as we got out of the car, 'I think I'll make phone calls while you do your thing.'

'Fine. I'm sure they can find an office for you to use.'

He squinted up at an autumn blue sky, then looked around as we walked. 'I can't believe I'm here,' he said. 'This is where he was posted.'

'No,' I said, because I knew exactly who he was talking about. 'Elvis Presley was posted at Baptist Memorial Hospital. He never came here, even though he should have.'

'How come?'

'He was treated like a natural death,' I replied.

'Well, he was. He died of a heart attack.'

'It's true his heart was terrible,' I said. 'But that's not what killed him. His death was due to his polydrug abuse.'

'His death was due to Colonel Parker,' Marino muttered as if he wanted to kill the man.

I glanced at him as we entered the office. 'Elvis had ten drugs on board. He should have been signed out an accident. It's sad.'

'And we know it was really him,' he then said.

'Oh for God's sake, Marino!'

'What? You've seen the photos? You know it for a fact?' he went on.

'I've seen them. And yes, I know,' I said as I stopped at the receptionist's desk.

'Then what's in them.' He would not stop.

A young woman named Shirley, who had taken care of me before, waited for Marino and me to quit disagreeing.

'That is none of your business,' I sweetly said to him. 'Shirley, how are you?'

'Back again?' She smiled.

'With no good news, I'm sorry to say,' I replied.

Marino began trimming his fingernails with a pocket-knife, glancing around like Elvis might walk in any minute.

'Dr Canter's expecting you,' she said. 'Come on. I'll take you back.'

While Marino ambled off to make phone calls somewhere down the hall, I was shown into the modest office of a man I had known since his residency days at the University of Tennessee. Canter had been as young as Lucy when I had met him for the first time.

A devotee of forensic anthropologist Dr Bass, who had begun the decay research facility in Knoxville known as The Body Farm, Canter had been mentored by most of the greats. He was considered the world's foremost expert in saw marks, and I wasn't quite sure what it was about this state famous for the Vols and Daniel Boone. Tennessee seemed to corner the market on experts in time of death and human bones.

'Kay.' Canter rose, extending his hand.

'Dave, you're always so good to see me on such short notice.' I took a chair across from his desk.

'Well, I hate what you're going through.'

He had dark hair combed straight back from his brow, so that whenever he looked down it fell in his way. He was constantly shoving it out of his way but did not seem aware of it. His face was youthful and interestingly angular, with closely set eyes and a strong jaw and nose.

'How are Jill and the kids?' I inquired.

'Great. We're expecting again.'

'Congratulations. That makes three?'

'Four.' His smile got bigger.

'I don't know how you do it,' I said sincerely.

'Doing it's the easy part. What goodies have you brought me?'

Setting the hard case on the edge of his desk, I opened it and got out the plastic-enclosed sections of bone. I handed them to him and he took out the left femur first. He studied it under a lamp with his lens, slowly turning it end over end.

'Hmmm,' he said. 'So you didn't notch the end you cut.' He glanced at me.

He wasn't chastising, just reminding, and I felt angry with myself again. Usually, I was so careful. If anything, I was known for being cautious to the point of obsession.

'I made an assumption, and I was wrong,' I said. 'I did not expect to discover that the killer used a saw with characteristics very similar to mine.'

'They usually don't use autopsy saws.' He pushed back his chair and got up. 'I've never had a case, really, just studied that type of saw mark in theory, here in the lab.'

'Then that's what this is.' I had suspected as much.

'I can't say with certainty until I get it under the scope. But both ends look like they've been cut with a Stryker saw.'

He gathered the bags of bones, and I followed him out into the hall as my misgivings got worse. I did not know what we would do if he could not tell the saw marks apart. A mistake like this was enough to ruin a case in court.

'Now, I know you're probably not going to tell much about the vertebral bone,' I said, for it was trabecular, less dense than other bone and therefore not a good surface for tool marks.

'Never hurts to bring it anyway. We might get lucky,' he said as we entered his lab.

There was not an inch of empty space. Thirty-five-gallon drums of degreaser and polyurethane varnish were parked wherever they would fit. Shelves from floor to ceiling were crammed with packaged bones, and in boxes and on carts were every type of saw known to man. Dismemberments were rare, and I knew of only three obvious motivations for taking a victim apart. Transporting the body was easier. Identification was slowed, if not made impossible. Or simply, the killer was malicious.

Canter pulled a stool close to an operating microscope equipped with a camera. He moved aside a tray of fractured ribs and thyroid cartilage that he must have been working on before I arrived.

'This guy was kicked in the throat, among other things,' he absently said as he pulled on surgical gloves.

'Such a nice world we live in,' I commented.

Canter opened the Ziploc bag containing the segment of right femur. Because he could not fit it on the microscope's stage without cutting a section that was thin enough to mount, he had me hold the two-inch length of bone against the table's edge. Then he bent a twenty-five-power fiber optics light close to one of the sawn surfaces.

'Definitely a Stryker saw,' he said as he peered into the lenses. 'You got to have a fast-moving, reciprocating motion to create a polish like this. It almost looks like polished stone. See?'

He moved aside and I looked. The bone was slightly beveled, like water frozen in gentle ripples, and it shone. Unlike other power saws, the Stryker had an oscillating blade that did not move very far. It did not cut skin, only the hard surface it was pressed against, like bone or a cast an orthopedist cut from a mending limb.

'Obviously,' I said, 'the transverse cuts across the mid-shaft are mine. From removing marrow for DNA.'

'But the knife marks aren't.'

'No. Absolutely not.'

'Well, we're probably not going to have much luck with them.'

Knives basically covered their own tracks, unless the victim's bone or cartilage was stabbed or hacked.

'But the good news is, we got a few false starts, a wider kerf and TPI,' he said, adjusting the microscope's focus as I continued holding the bone.

I had known nothing about saws until I began spending so much time with Canter. Bone is an excellent surface for tool marks, and when saw teeth cut into it, a groove or kerf is formed. By microscopically examining the walls and floor of a kerf, one can determine exit chipping on the side where the saw exited bone. Determining the characteristics of the individual teeth, the number of teeth per inch (TPI), the spacing of them and the striae, can reveal the shape of the blade.

Canter angled the optic light to sharpen the striations and defects.

'You can see the curve of the blade.' He pointed to several false starts on the shaft, where someone had pushed the saw blade into the bone, and then tried again in another spot.

'Not mine,' I said. 'Or at least I hope I'm more adept than that.'

'Since this also is the end where most of the knife cuts are, I'm going to agree that it wasn't you. Whoever did this had to cut first with something else, since an oscillating blade won't cut flesh.'

'What about the saw blade?' I asked, for I knew what I used in the morgue.

'Teeth are large, seventeen per inch. So this is going to be a round autopsy blade. Let's turn it over.'

I did, and he directed the light at the other end, where there were no false starts. The surface was polished and beveled like the other one, but not identical to Canter's discerning eye.

'Power autopsy saw with a large, sectioning blade,' he said. 'Multidirectional cut since the radius of the blade's too small to cut through the whole bone in one stroke. So, whoever did this just changed directions, going as it from different angles, with a great deal of skill. We have slight bending of the kerfs. Minimal exit chipping. Again denoting great skill with a saw. I'm going to bump up the power some and see if we can accentuate the harmonics.'

He referred to the distance between saw teeth.

'Tooth distance is point-oh-six. Sixteen teeth per inch,' he counted. 'Direction is push-pull, tooth-type chisel. I'm voting this is yours.'

'You caught me,' I said with relief. 'Guilty as charged.'

'I would think so.' He was still looking. 'I wouldn't think you use a round blade for anything.'

The large, round autopsy blades were heavy and continuous rolling, and destroyed more bone. Generally, this was a utility blade used in labs or in doctors' offices to saw off casts.

'The rare occasion I might use a round blade is on animals,' I said.

'Of the two-or four-legged variety?'

'I've taken bullets out of dogs, birds, cats and, on one fine occasion, a python shot in a drug raid,' I replied.

Canter was looking at another bone. 'And I thought I was the one who had all the fun.'

'Do you find it unusual that someone would use a meat saw in four dismemberments, and then suddenly switch to an electric autopsy saw?' I asked.

'If your theory's correct about the cases in Ireland, then you're talking nine cases with a meat saw,' he said. 'How about holding this right here so I can get a picture.'

I held the section of left femur in the tips of my fingers, and he pressed a button on the camera.

'To answer your question,' he said. 'I would find it extremely unusual. You're talking two different profiles. The meat saw is manual, physical, usually ten teeth per inch. It will go through tissue and takes a lot of bone with each stroke, the saw marks rougher-looking, more indicative of someone skilled and powerful. And it's also important to remember that in each of those earlier cases the perpetrator cut through joints, versus the shafts, which is also very rare.'

'It's not the same person.' I again voiced my growing belief.

Canter took the bone from my hand and looked at me. 'That's my vote.'

When I returned to the lobby of the M.E.'s office, Marino was still on the phone down the hall. I waited a little while, then stepped outside because I needed air. I needed sunshine and sights that weren't savage. Some twenty minutes passed before he finally walked out and joined me by the car.

'I didn't know you was here,' he said. 'If someone had told me, I would've got off the phone.'

'It's all right. What a gorgeous day.'

He unlocked the car.

'How'd it go?' he asked, sliding into the driver's seat.

I briefly summarized as we sat in the parking lot, not going anywhere.

'You want to go back to the Peabody?' he asked, tapping the steering wheel with his thumb.

I knew exactly what he wanted to do.

'No,' I said. 'Graceland might be just what the doctor ordered.'

He shoved the car in gear and could not suppress a big grin.

'We want the Fowler Expressway,' I said, for I had studied a map.

'I wish you could get me his autopsy report,' he started on that again. 'I want to see for myself what happened to him. Then I'll know and it won't eat at me anymore.'

'What do you want to know?' I looked at him.

'If it was like they said. Did he die on the toilet? That's always bothered the hell out of me. You know how many cases like that I've seen?' He glanced at me. 'Don't matter if you're some drone or the president of the United States. You end up dead with a ring around your butt. Hope to hell that don't happen to me.'

'Elvis was found on the floor of his bathroom. He was nude, and yes, it is believed that he slid off his black porcelain toilet.'

'Who found him?' Marino was entranced in an uneasy way.

'A girlfriend who was staying in the adjoining room. Or that's the story,' I said.

'You mean he walks in there, feels fine, sits down and boom? No warning signs or nothing?'

'All I know is he'd been playing racquetball in the early morning, and seemed fine,' I said.

'You're kidding.' Marino's curiosity was insatiable. 'Now, I never heard that part. I didn't know he played racquetball.'

We drove through an industrialized area, with trains and trucks, then past campers for sale. Graceland stood in the midst of cheap motels and stores, and it did not seem so grand given its surroundings. The white mansion with its columns was completely out of place, like a joke or a set for a bad movie.

'Holy shit,' Marino said, as he pulled into the parking lot. 'Will you look at that. Holy smoke.'

He went on as if it were Buckingham Palace as he parked beside a bus.

'You know, I wish I could've known him,' he wistfully said.

'Maybe you would have, had he taken better care of himself.' I opened my door as he lit a cigarette.

For the next two hours, we wandered through gilt and mirrors, shag carpeting and stained-glass peacocks as the voice of Elvis followed us through his world. Hundreds of fans had arrived on buses, and their passion for this man was on their faces as they walked around listening to the tour on cassette. Many of them placed flowers, cards and letters on his grave. Some wept as if they had known him well.

We wandered around his purple and pink Cadillacs, Stutz Blackhawk and museum of other cars. There were his planes and shooting range, and the Hall of Gold, with Grammy showcases of gold and platinum records, and trophies and other awards that amazed even me. The hall was at least eighty feet long. I could not take my eyes off splendid costumes of gold and sequins, and photographs of what was truly an extraordinarily and sensuously beautiful human being. Marino was blatantly gawking, an almost pained expression on his face that reminded me of puppy love as we inched our way through rooms.

'You know, they didn't want him to move here when he bought this place,' he announced, and we were outside now, the fall afternoon cool and bright. 'Some of the snobs in this city never did accept him. I think that hurt him, in a way, might be what got him in the end. You know, why he took painkillers.'

'He took more than that,' I made the point again as we walked.

'If you had been the medical examiner, could you have done his autopsy?' He got out cigarettes.

'Absolutely.'

'And you wouldn't have covered his face?' He looked indignant as he fired up his lighter.

'Of course not.'

'Not me.' He shook his head, sucking in smoke. 'No friggin' way I'd even want to be in the room.'

'I wish he had been my case,' I said. 'I wouldn't have signed him out as a natural death. The world should know the truth, so maybe somebody else would think twice about popping Percodan.'

We were in front of one of the gift shops now, and people were gathered around televisions inside, watching Elvis videos. Through outdoor speakers, he was singing 'Kentucky Rain,' his voice powerful and playful, unlike any other I had ever heard in my life. I started walking again and told the truth.

'I am a fan and have a rather extensive collection of his CDs, if you really must know,' I said to Marino.

He couldn't believe it. He was thrilled.

'And I'd appreciate it if you didn't spread that around.'

'All these years I've known you, and you never told me?' he exclaimed. 'You're not kidding me, right? I never would've thought that. Not in a million years. Hey, so maybe now you know I got taste.'

This went on as we waited for a shuttle to return us to the parking lot, and then it continued in the car.

'I remember watching him on TV once when I was a kid in New Jersey,' Marino was saying. 'My old man came in drunk, as usual, started yelling at me to switch the channel. I'll never forget it.'

He slowed and turned into the Peabody Hotel.

'Elvis was singing "Hound Dog," July 1956. I remember it was my birthday. My father comes in, cussing, turns the TV off, and I get up and turn it back on. He smacks the side of my head, turns the TV off again. I turn it back on and walk toward him. First time in my life I ever laid a hand on him. I slam him against the wall, get in his face, tell the son of a bitch he ever touches me or my mother again, I'm going to kill him.'

'And did he?' I asked as the valet opened my door.

'Shit no.'

'Then Elvis should be thanked,' I said.

7

TWO DAYS LATER, on Thursday, November 6, I started out early on the ninety-minute drive from Richmond to the FBI Academy at Quantico, Virginia. Marino and I took separate cars, since we never knew when something might happen to send us off somewhere. For me, it could be a plane crash or derailed train, while he had to deal with city government and layers of brass. I wasn't surprised when my car phone rang as we neared Fredericksburg. The sun was in and out of clouds, and it felt cold enough to snow.

'Scarpetta,' I said, on speakerphone.

Marino's voice erupted inside my car. 'City council's freaking,' he said. 'You got McKuen whose little kid's been hit by a car, now more crap about our case, on TV, in the papers, hear it on the radio.'

More leaks had occurred over the past two days. Police had a suspect in serial murders that included five cases in Dublin. An arrest was imminent.

'You believe this shit?' Marino exclaimed. 'We're talking about, what? Someone in his mid-twenties, and somehow he was in Dublin over the past few years? Bottom line is council's suddenly decided to have some public forum about this situation, probably because they think it's about to be resolved. Got to get that credit, right, make the citizens think maybe they did something for once.' He was careful what he said, but seething. 'So I gotta turn my ass right back around and be at city hall by ten. Plus, the chief wants to see me.'

I watched his taillights up ahead as he approached an exit. I-95 was busy this morning with trucks, and people who commuted every day to D.C. No matter how early I started, whenever I headed north, it seemed traffic was terrible.

'Actually, it's a good thing you're going to be there. Cover my back, too,' I said to him. 'I'll get up with you later, let you know what went on.'

'Yo. When you see Ring, do that to his neck,' he said.

I arrived at the Academy, and the guard in his booth waved me through because by now he knew my car and its license plate. The parking lot was so full, I ended up almost in the woods. Firearms training was already in progress on ranges across the road, and Drug Enforcement Agents were out in camouflage, gripping assault rifles, their faces mean. The grass was heavy with dew and soaked my shoes as I took a shortcut to the main entrance of the tan brick building called Jefferson.

Inside the lobby, luggage was parked near couches and the walls, for there were always National Academy, or N.A., police going somewhere, it seemed. The video display over the front desk reminded everyone to have a nice day and properly display his badge. Mine was still in my purse, and I got it out, looping the long chain around my neck. Inserting a magnetized card into a slot, I unlocked a glass door etched with the Department of Justice seal and followed a long glass-enclosed corridor.

I was deep in thought and scarcely cognizant of new agents in dark blue and khaki, and N.A. students in green. They nodded and smiled as they passed, and I was friendly, too, but I did not focus. I was thinking of the torso, of her infirmities and age, of her pitiful pouch in the freezer, where she would stay for several years or until we knew her name. I thought of Keith Pleasants, of deadoc, of saws and sharp blades.

I smelled Hoppes solvent as I turned into the gun-cleaning room with its rows of black counters and compressors blasting air through the innards of guns. I could never smell these smells or hear these sounds without thinking of Wesley, and of Mark. My heart was squeezed by feelings too strong for me when a familiar voice called out my name.

'Looks like we're heading the same way,' said Investigator Ring.

Impeccably dressed in navy blue, he was waiting for the elevator that would take us sixty feet below ground, where Hoover had built his bomb shelter. I switched my heavy briefcase to my other hand, and tucked the box of slides more snugly under an arm.

'Good morning,' I blandly said.

'Here, let me help with some of that.'

131

He held out a hand as elevator doors parted, and I noticed his nails were buffed.

'I'm fine,' I said, because I didn't need his help.

We boarded, both of us staring straight ahead as we began the ride down to a windowless level of the building directly beneath the indoor firing range. Ring had sat in on consultations before, and he took copious notes, none of which had ended up in the news thus far. He was too clever for that. Certainly, if information divulged during an FBI consultation was leaked, it would be easy enough to trace. There were only a few of us who could be the source.

'I was rather dismayed by the information the press somehow got access to,' I said as we got out.

'I know what you mean,' Ring said with a sincere face.

He held open the door leading into a labyrinth of hallways that comprised what once had begun as Behavioral Science, then changed to Investigative Support, and now was CASKU. Names changed, but the cases did not. Men and women often came to work in the dark and left after it was dark again, spending days and years studying the minutiae of monsters, their every tooth mark and track in mud, the way they think and smell and hate.

'The more information that gets out the worse it is,' Ring went on as we approched another door, leading into a conference room where I spent at least several days a month. 'It's one thing to give details that might help the public help us . . .'

He talked on, but I wasn't listening. Inside, Wesley was already sitting at the head of a polished table, his reading glasses on. He was going through large photographs stamped on the back with the name of the Sussex County

Sheriff's Department. Detective Grigg was several chairs away, a lot of paperwork in front of him as he studied a sketch of some sort. Across from him was Frankel from the Violent Criminal Apprehension Program, or VICAP, and at the other end of the table, my niece. She was tapping on a laptop computer, and glanced up at me but did not say hello.

I took my usual chair to the right of Wesley, opened my briefcase and began arranging files. Ring sat on the other side of me and continued our conversation.

'We got to accept as a fact that this guy is following everything in the news,' he said. 'That's part of the fun for him.'

He had everyone's attention, all eyes on him, the room silent except for his own sound. He was reasonable and quiet, as if his only mission was to convey the truth without drawing undue attention to himself. Ring was a superb con man, and what he said next in front of my colleagues incensed me beyond belief.

'For example, and I have to be honest about this,' he said to me, 'I just don't think it was a good idea to give out the race, age and all about the victim. Now maybe I'm wrong.' He looked around the room. 'But it seems like the less said, the better right now.'

'I had no choice,' I said, and I could not keep the edge out of my voice. 'Since someone had already leaked misinformation.'

'But that's always going to happen, and I don't think it should force us to give out details before we're ready,' he said in his same earnest tone.

'It is not going to help us if the public is focused on a missing prepubescent Asian female.' I stared at him, eye to eye, while everyone else looked on.

133

'I agree.' Frankel, from VICAP, spoke. 'We'd be getting missing person files from all over the country. An error like that has to be straightened out.'

'An error like that never should have happened to begin with,' Wesley said, peering around the room over the top of his glasses, the way he did when he was in a humorless mood. 'With us this morning is Detective Grigg of Sussex, and Special Agent Farinelli.' He looked at Lucy. 'She's the technical analyst for HRT, manages the Criminal Artificial Intelligence Network all of us know as CAIN, and is here to help us with a computer situation.'

My niece did not look up as she hit more keys, her face intense. Ring had her in his sights, staring as if he wanted to eat her flesh.

'What computer situation?' he asked, as his eyes continued to devour her.

'We'll get to that,' Wesley said, and briskly moved on. 'Let me summarize, then we'll move on to specifics. The victimology in this most recent landfill case is so different from the previous four – or nine, if we include Ireland – as for me to conclude that we are dealing with a different killer. Dr Scarpetta is going to review her medical findings which I think will make it abundantly clear that this M.O. is profoundly atypical.'

He went on, and we spent until midday going over my reports, diagrams and photographs. I was asked many questions, mostly by Grigg, who wanted very much to understand every facet and nuance of the serial dismemberments so he could better discern that the one in his jurisdiction was unlike the rest.

'What's the difference between someone cutting through joints and cutting through the bones?' he asked me.

'Cutting through joints is more difficult,' I said. 'It requires knowledge of anatomy, perhaps some previous experience.'

'Like if someone was a butcher or maybe worked in a meat-packing plant.'

'Yes,' I replied.

'Well, I guess that sure would fit with a meat saw,' he added.

'Yes. Which is very different from an autopsy saw.'

'Exactly how?' It was Ring who spoke.

'A meat saw is a hand saw designed to cut meat, gristle, bone,' I went on, looking around at everyone. 'Usually about fourteen inches long with a very thin blade, ten chisel-type teeth per inch. It's push action, requiring some degree of strength on the part of the user. The autopsy saw, in contrast, won't cut through tissue, which must first be reflected back with something like a knife.'

'Which was what was used in this case,' Wesley said to me.

'There are cuts to bone that fit the class characteristics of a knife. An autopsy saw,' I went on to explain, 'was designed to work only on hard surfaces by using a reciprocating action that is basically push-pull, going in only a little bit at a time. I know everyone here is familiar with it, but I've got photos.'

Opening an envelope, I pulled out eight-by-tens of the saw marks the killer had left on the bone ends I had carried to Memphis. I slid one to each person.

'As you can see,' I went on, 'the saw pattern here is multidirectional with a high polish.'

'Now let me get this straight,' said Grigg. 'This is the exact same saw you use in the morgue.'

'No. Not exactly the same,' I said. 'I generally use a larger sectioning blade than was used here.'

'But this is from a medical sort of saw.' He held up the photograph.

'Correct.'

'Where would your average person get something like that?'

'Doctor's office, hospital, morgue, medical supply company,' I replied. 'Any number of places. The sale of them is not restricted.'

'So he could have ordered it without being in the medical profession.'

'Easily,' I said.

Ring said, 'Or he could have stolen it. He could have decided to do something different this time to throw us off.'

Lucy was looking at him, and I had seen the expression in her eyes before. She thought Ring was a fool.

'If we're dealing with the same killer,' she said, 'then why is he suddenly sending files through the Internet when he's never done that before, either?'

'Good point.' Frankel nodded.

'What files?' Ring said to her.

'We're getting to that.' Wesley restored order. 'We've got an M.O. that's different. We've got a tool that's different.'

'We suspect she has a head injury,' I said, sliding autopsy diagrams and the e-mail photos around the table, 'because of blood in her airway. This may or may not be different from the other cases, since we don't know their causes of death. However, radiologic and anthropologic findings indicate that this victim is profoundly older than the others. We also recovered fibers indicating she was covered in something consistent with a drop cloth when she was dismembered, again, inconsistent with the other cases.'

I explained in more detail about the fibers and paint, all the while vividly aware of Ring watching my niece and taking notes.

'So she was probably cut up in someone's workshop or garage,' Grigg said.

'I don't know,' I answered. 'And as you've seen from the photos sent to me through e-mail, we can only know that she's in a room with putty-colored walls, and a table.'

'Let me again point out that Keith Pleasants has an area behind his house that he uses for a workshop,' Ring reminded us. 'It has a big workbench in it and the walls are unpainted wood.' He looked at me. 'Which could pass for putty-colored.'

'Seems like it would be awfully hard to get rid of all the blood,' Grigg dubiously mused.

'A drop cloth with a rubber backing might explain the absence of blood,' Ring said. 'That's the whole point. So nothing leaks through.'

Everyone looked at me to see what I would say.

'It would have been very unusual not to get things bloody in a case like this,' I replied. 'Especially since she still had a blood pressure when she was decapitated. If nothing else, I would expect blood in wood grain, in cracks of the table.'

'We could try some chemical testing for that.' Ring was a forensic scientist now. 'Like luminol. Any blood at all, it's going to react to it and glow in the dark.'

'The problem with luminol is it's destructive,' I replied. 'And we're going to want to do DNA, to see if we can get a match. So we certainly don't want to ruin what little blood we might find.'

'It's not like we got probable cause to go in Pleasants'

workshop and start any kind of testing anyway.' Grigg's stare across the table at Ring was confrontational.

'I think we do.' He stared back at him.

'Not unless they changed the rules on me.' Grigg spoke slowly.

Wesley was watching all this, evaluating everyone and every word the way he always did. He had his opinion, and more than likely it was right. But he remained silent as the arguing went on.

'I thought . . .' Lucy tried to speak.

'A very viable possibility is that this is a copycat,' Ring said.

'Oh, I think it is,' said Grigg. 'I just don't buy your theory about Pleasants.'

'Let me finish.' Lucy's penetrating gaze scanned the faces of the men. 'I thought I would give you a briefing on how the two files were sent via America Online to Dr Scarpetta's e-mail address.'

It always sounded odd when she called me by my professional name.

'I know I'm curious.' Ring had his chin propped on a hand now, studying her.

'First, you would need a scanner,' she went on. 'That's not hard. Something with color capabilities and decent resolution, as low as seventy-two dots per inch. But this looks like higher resolution to me, maybe three hundred dpi. We could be talking about something as simple as a hand-held scanner for three hundred and ninety-nine dollars, to a thirty-five-millimeter slide scanner that can run into the thousands . . .'

'And what kind of computer would you hook this up to,' Ring said.

'I was getting to that.' Lucy was tired of being interrupted by him. 'System requirements: Minimum of eight
megs RAM, a color monitor, software like Foto Touch or
ScanMan, a modem. Could be a Macintosh, a Performa
6116CD or even something older. The point is, scanning
files into your computer and sending them through the
Internet is very accessible to your average person, which
is why telecommunications crimes are keeping us so busy
these days.'

'Like that big child pornography, pedophile case you all
just cracked,' Grigg said.

'Yes, photos sent as files through the World Wide Web,
where children can talk to strangers again,' she said. 'What's
interesting in the situation at hand, is scanning black and
white is no big deal. But when you move into color, that's
getting sophisticated. Also the edges and borders in the
photos sent to Dr Scarpetta are relatively sharp, not much
background noise.'

'Sounds to me this is someone who knew what he was
doing,' Grigg said.

'Yes,' she agreed. 'But not necessarily a computer analyst
or graphic artist. Not at all.'

'These days, if you've got access to the equipment and a
few instruction books, anyone can do it,' said Frankel, who
also worked in computers.

'All right, the photos were scanned into the system,' I
said to Lucy. 'Then what? What is the path that led them
to me?'

'First you upload the file, which in this case is a graphic or
GIF file,' she replied. 'Generally, to send this successfully,
you have to determine the number of data bits, stop bits,
the parity setting, whatever the appropriate configuration

is. That's where it's not user-friendly. But AOL does all that for you. So in this case, sending the files was simple. You upload and off they go.' She looked at me.

'And this was done over the telephone, basically,' Wesley said.

'Right.'

'What about tracing that?'

'Squad Nineteen's already on it.' Lucy referred to the FBI unit that investigated illegal uses of the Internet.

'I'm not sure what the crime would be in this case,' Wesley pointed out. 'Obscenity, if the photos are fakes, and unfortunately, that isn't illegal.'

'The photographs aren't fake,' I said.

'Hard to prove.' He held my gaze.

'What if they're not fake?' Ring asked.

'Then they're evidence,' Wesley said, adding after a pause, 'A violation of Title Eighteen, Section Eight-seventy-six. Mailing threatening communications.'

'Threats towards who?' Ring asked.

Wesley's eyes were still on me. 'Clearly, towards the recipient.'

'There's been no blatant threat,' I reminded him.

'All we want is enough for a warrant.'

'We got to find the person first,' Ring said, stretching and yawning in his chair like a cat.

'We're watching for him to log on again,' Lucy replied. 'It's being monitored around the clock.' She continued hitting keys on her laptop, checking the constant flow of messages. 'But if you imagine a global telephone system with some forty million users, and no directory, no operators, no directory assistance, that's what you've got with the Internet. There's no list of membership, nor does AOL have one, unless you voluntarily choose to fill out a profile. In this case, all we have is the bogus name deadoc.'

'How did he know where to send Dr Scarpetta's mail?' Grigg looked at me.

I explained, and then asked Lucy, 'This is all done by charge card?'

She nodded. 'That much we've traced. An American Express Card in the name of Ken L. Perley. A retired high-school teacher. Norfolk. Seventy, lives alone.'

'Do we have any idea how someone might have gotten access to his card?' Wesley asked.

'It doesn't appear Perley uses his credit cards much. Last time was in a Norfolk restaurant, a Red Lobster. This was on October second, when he and his son went out to dinner. The bill was twenty-seven dollars and thirty cents, including the tip, which he put on AmEx. Neither he nor the son remembers anything unusual that night. But when it was time to pay the bill, the credit card was left on the table in plain view for quite a long interval because the restaurant was very busy. At some point while the card was out, Perley went to the men's room, and the son stepped outside to smoke.'

'Christ. That was intelligent. Did someone from the wait staff notice anyone coming over to the table?' Wesley said to Lucy.

'Like I said, it was busy. We're running down every charge made that night to get a list of customers. Problem's going to be the people who paid cash.'

'And I suppose it's too soon for the AOL charges to have come up on Perley's American Express,' he said.

'Right. According to AOL, the account was just opened recently. A week after the dinner at the Red Lobster, to be

141

exact. Perley's being very cooperative with us,' Lucy added. 'And AOL is leaving the account open without charge in the event the perpetrator wants to send something else.'

Wesley nodded. 'Though we can't assume it, we should consider that the killer, at least in the Atlantic landfill case, may have been in Norfolk as recently as a month ago.'

'This case is definitely sounding local.' I made that point again.

'Possible any of the bodies could have been refrigerated?' Ring asked.

'Not this one,' Wesley was quick to answer. 'Absolutely not. This guy couldn't stand looking at his victim. He had to cover her up, cut through the cloth, and my guess is, didn't go very far away to dispose of her.'

'Shades of "The Tell-Tale Heart,"' Ring said.

Lucy was reading something on her laptop screen, quietly hitting keys, her face tense. 'We just got something from Squad Nineteen,' she said, continuing to scroll down. 'Deadoc logged on fifty-six minutes ago.' She looked up at us. 'He sent e-mail to the president.'

The electronic mail was sent directly to the White House, which was no great feat since the address was public and readily available to any user of the Internet. Once again, the message was oddly in lowercase and used spaces for punctuation, and it read: *apologize if not I will start on france.*

'There are a number of implications,' Wesley was saying to me as gunshots from the range upstairs thudded like a distant, muffled war going on. 'And all of them make me nervous about you.'

He stopped at the water fountain.

'I don't think this has anything to do with me,' I said. 'This has to do with the president of the United States.'

'That's symbolic, if you want to know my guess. Not literal.' We started walking. 'I think this killer is disgruntled, angry, feels a certain person in power or perhaps people in power are responsible for his problems in life.'

'Like the Unabomber,' I said as we took the elevator up.

'Very similar. Perhaps even inspired by him,' he said, glancing at his watch. 'Can I buy you a beer before you leave?'

'Not unless someone else is driving.' I smiled. 'But you can talk me into coffee.'

We walked through the gun-cleaning room, where dozens of FBI and DEA agents were breaking down their weapons, wiping them and blasting parts with air. They glanced at us with curious eyes, and I wondered if they had heard the rumors. My relationship with Wesley had been an item of gossip for quite a long time at the Academy, and it bothered me more than I let on. Most people, it seemed, maintained their belief that his wife had left because of me when, in fact, she had left because of another man.

Upstairs, the line was long in the PX, a mannikin modeling the latest sweatshirt and range pants, and Thanksgiving pumpkins and turkeys in the windows. Beyond, in the Boardroom, the TV was loud, and some people were already into popcorn and beer. We sat as far away from everyone as we could, both of us sipping coffee.

'What's your slant on the France connection?' I asked.

'Obviously, this individual is intelligent and follows the news. Our relations with France were very strained during their nuclear weapons testing. You may recall the violence, vandalism, boycotting of French wine and other products.

143

There was a lot of protesting outside French embassies, the U.S. very much involved.'

'But that was a couple years ago.'

'Doesn't matter. Wounds heal slowly.' He stared out the window at darkness gathering. 'And more to the point, France would not appreciate our exporting a serial killer to them. I can only suppose that is what deadoc is implying. Cops from France and other nations have been worrying for years that our problem would eventually become theirs. As if violence is a disease that can spread.'

'Which it is.'

He nodded, reaching for his coffee again.

'Maybe that would make more sense if we believed the same person killed ten people here and in Ireland,' I said.

'Kay, we can't rule out anything.' He sounded tired as he said that again.

I shook my head. 'He's taking credit for someone else's murders and now threatening us. He probably has no idea how different his M.O. is from what we've seen in the past. Of course, we can't rule out anything, Benton. But I know what my findings tell me, and I believe identifying this recent victim is going to be the key.'

'You always believe that.' He smiled, playing with his coffee stirrer.

'I know who I work for. Right this minute, I work for that poor woman whose torso is in my freezer.'

It was now completely dark out, the Boardroom filling fast with healthy, clean-living men and women in color-coded fatigues. The noise was making it difficult to talk, and I needed to see Lucy before I left.

'You don't like Ring.' Wesley reached around to the back

of his chair and collected his suit jacket. 'He's bright and seems sincerely motivated.'

'You definitely profiled the last part wrong,' I said as I got up. 'But you are right about what you said first. I don't like him.'

'I thought that was rather obvious by your demeanor.'

We moved around people who were looking for chairs and setting down pitchers of beer.

'I think he's dangerous.'

'He's vain and wants to make a name for himself,' Wesley said.

'And you don't think that's dangerous?' I looked over at him.

'It describes almost everyone I've ever worked with.'

'Except for me, I hope.'

'You, Dr Scarpetta, are an exception to just about everything I can think of.'

We were walking through a long corridor, heading to the lobby, and I did not want to leave him right now. I felt lonely and wasn't sure why.

'I would love for us to have dinner,' I said, 'but Lucy's got something to show me.'

'What makes you think I don't already have plans?' He held the door for me.

The thought bothered me, even though I knew he was teasing.

'Let's wait until I can get away from here,' he said, and we were walking toward the parking lot now. 'Maybe over the weekend, when we can relax a little more. I'll cook this time. Where are you parked?'

'Over here.' I pointed the key's remote control.

Doors unlocked and the interior light went on. Typically,

we did not touch. We never had when someone might see.

'Sometimes I hate this,' I said as I got into my car. 'It's fine to talk about body parts, rape and murder all day long, but not to hug each other, hold hands. God forbid anybody should see that.' I started the engine. 'Tell me how normal that is? It's not like we're still having an affair or committing a crime.' I yanked my seatbelt across my chest. 'Is there some don't-ask-don't-tell FBI rule no one's let me in on?'

'Yes.'

He kissed me on the lips as a group of agents walked by.

'So don't tell anyone,' he said.

Moments later, I parked in front of the Engineering Research Facility, or ERF, a huge, space age-looking building where the FBI conducted its classified technical research and development. If Lucy knew all of what went on in the labs here, she did not tell, and there were few areas of the building where I was allowed, even when escorted by her. She was waiting by the front door as I pointed the remote control at my car, which was not responding.

'It won't work here,' she said.

I looked up at the eerie rooftop of antennae and satellite dishes, sighing as I manually locked doors with the key.

'You'd think I'd remember after all these times,' I muttered.

'Your investigator friend, Ring, tried to walk me over here after the consultation,' she said, scanning her thumb in a biometric lock by the door.

'He's not my friend,' I told her.

146

The lobby was high-ceilinged and arranged with glass cases displaying clunky, inefficient radio and electronic equipment used by law enforcement before ERF was built.

'He asked me out again,' she said.

Corridors were monochromatic and seemed endless, and I was forever impressed with the silence and sense that no one was here. Scientists and engineers worked behind shut doors in spaces big enough to accommodate automobiles, helicopters and small planes. Hundreds of Bureau personnel were employed at ERF, yet they had virtually no contact with any of us across the street. We did not know their names.

'I'm sure there are a million people who would like to ask you out,' I said as we boarded an elevator, and Lucy scanned her thumb again.

'Usually, not after they've been around me very long,' she said.

'I don't know, I haven't gotten rid of you yet.'

But she was very serious. 'Once I start talking shop, the guys turn off. But he likes a challenge, if you know the type.'

'I know it all too well.'

'He wants something from me, Aunt Kay.'

'Would you like to hazard a guess? And where are you taking me, by the way?'

'I don't know. But I just have this feeling.' She opened a door to the virtual environment lab, adding, 'I have a rather interesting idea.'

Lucy's ideas were always more than interesting. Usually they were frightening. I followed her into a room of virtual system processors and graphic computers stacked on top of each other, and countertops scattered with tools, computer boards, chips and peripherals like DataGloves and helmet-mounted displays. Electrical cords were bundled in thick hanks and tied back from the blank expanse of linoleum flooring where Lucy routinely lost herself in cyberspace.

She picked up a remote control and two video displays blinked on, and I recognized the photographs deadoc had sent to me. They were big and in color on the screens, and I began to get nervous.

'What are you doing?' I asked my niece.

'The basic question has always been, does an immersion into an environment actually improve the operator's performance,' she said, typing computer commands. 'You never got a chance to be immersed in this environment. The crime scene.'

Both of us stared at the bloody stumps and lined-up body parts on the monitors, and a chill crept through me.

'But suppose you could have that chance now?' Lucy went on. 'What if you could be inside deadoc's room?'

I started to interrupt, but she would not let me.

'What else might you see? What else might you do?' she said, and when she got like this, she was almost manic. 'What else might you learn about the victim and him?'

'I don't know if I can use something like this,' I protested.

'Sure you can. Now what I haven't had time to do is add the synthetic sound. Well, except for the typical canned auditory cues. So a squelch is something opening, a click's a switch being turned on or off, a ding usually means you've just bumped into something.'

'Lucy,' I said as she took my left arm, 'what the hell are you talking about?'

She carefully pulled a DataGlove over my left hand, making sure it was snug.

'We use gestures for human communication. And we can use gestures, or positions as we call them, to communicate with the computer, too,' she explained.

The glove was black lycra with fiber-optic sensors mounted on the back of it. These were attached to a cable that led to the high-performance host computer that Lucy had been typing on. Next she picked up a helmet-mounted display that was connected to another cable, and fear fluttered through my breast as she headed my way.

'One VPL Eyephone HRX,' she cheerfully said. 'Same thing they're using at NASA's Ames Research Center, which is where I discovered it.' She was adjusting cables and straps. 'Three hundred and fifty thousand color elements. Superior resolution and wide field of vision.'

She placed the helmet on top of my head, and it felt heavy and covered my eyes.

'What you're looking into are liquid crystal displays, or LCDs, your basic video displays. Glass plates, electrodes and molecules doing all kinds of cool things. How does it feel?'

'Like I'm going to fall down and suffocate.'

I was beginning to panic the way I had when I'd first learned how to scuba dive.

'You're not going to do either.' She was very patient, her hand steadying me. 'Relax. It's normal to be phobic at first. I'll tell you what to do. Now you stand still and take deep breaths. I'm going to put you in.'

She made adjustments, tightening the display around my head, then returned to the host computer. I was blind and off balance, a tiny TV in front of each eye.

'Okay, here we go,' she said. 'Don't know if it will do any good, but can't hurt to try.'

Keys clicked, and I was thrown inside that room. She began instructing me about what to do with my hand to fly forward or faster, or in reverse, and how to release and grab. I moved my index finger, made clicking motions, brought my thumb near my palm and moved my arm across my chest as I broke out in a sweat. I spent a good five minutes on the ceiling and walking into walls. At one point, I was on top of the table where the torso lay on its bloody blue cover, stepping on evidence and the dead.

'I think I might throw up,' I said.

'Just hold still for a minute,' Lucy said. 'Catch your breath.'

I gestured as I started to say something more, and was instantly on the virtual floor, as if I had fallen from the air.

'That's why I told you to hold still,' she said as she watched what I was doing on the monitors. 'Now move your hand in and point with your first two fingers toward where you hear my voice coming from. Better?'

'Better,' I said.

I was standing on the floor in the room, as if the photograph had come to life, three-dimensional and large. I looked around and did not actually see anything I hadn't before when Vander had done the image enhancement. It was what this made me feel, and what I felt changed what I saw.

Walls were the color of putty, with faint discolorations that until now I had attributed to water damage, which might be expected in a basement or garage. But they seemed different now, more uniformly distributed, some so faint I could barely see them. Paper had once covered the putty paint on these walls. It had been removed but not replaced, as had the cornice box or drapery rod. Above a window covered with shut Venetian blinds were small holes where brackets once had been.

'This isn't where it happened,' I said as my heart beat harder.

Lucy was silent.

'She was brought in here after the fact to be photographed. This is not where the killing and dismemberment took place.'

'What are you seeing?' she asked.

I moved my hand and walked closer to the virtual table. I pointed at the virtual walls, to show Lucy what I saw. 'Where did he plug in the autopsy saw?' I said.

I could find but one electrical outlet, and it was at the base of a wall.

'And the drop cloth is from here, too?' I went on. 'It doesn't fit with everything else. No paint, no tools.' I kept looking around. 'And look at the floor. The wood's lighter at the border as if there once was a rug. Who puts rugs in workshops? Who has wallpaper and drapes? Where are the outlets for power tools?'

'What do you feel?' she asked.

'I feel this is a room in someone's house where the furniture has been removed. Except there is some sort of table, which has been covered with something. Maybe a shower curtain. I don't know. The room feels domestic.'

I reached out my hand and tried to touch the edge of the table cover, as if I could lift it and reveal what was underneath, and as I looked around, details became so clear to me, I wondered how I could have missed them before. Wiring was exposed in the ceiling directly above the table, as if a chandelier or other type of light fixture had once hung there.

'What about my color perception right now?' I asked.

'Should be the same.'

'Then there's something else. These walls.' I touched them. 'The color lightens in this direction. There's an opening. Maybe a doorway, with light coming through it.'

'There's no doorway in the photo.' Lucy reminded me. 'You can only see what's there.'

It was odd, but for a moment I thought I could smell her blood, the pungency of old flesh that has been dead for days. I remembered the doughy texture of her skin, and the peculiar eruptions that made me wonder if she had shingles.

'She wasn't random,' I said.

'And the others were.'

'The other cases are nothing like this one. I'm getting double imagery. Can you adjust that?'

'Vertical retinal image disparity.'

Then I felt her hand on my arm.

'Usually goes away after fifteen or twenty minutes,' she said. 'It's time to take a break.'

'I don't feel too good.'

'Image rotation misalignment. Visual fatigue, simulation sickness, cybersick, whatever you want to call it,' she said. 'Causing image blurring, tears, even queasiness.'

I couldn't wait to remove the helmet and I was on the table again, facedown in blood before I could get the LCDs away from my eyes.

My hands were shaking as Lucy helped me take off the glove. I sat down on the floor.

'Are you all right?' she asked, kindly.

'That was awful,' I said.

'Then it was good.' She returned the helmet and glove to

a counter. 'You were immersed in the environment. That's what should happen.'

She handed me several tissues, and I wiped my face.

'What about the other photograph? Do you want to do that one, too?' she asked. 'The one with the hands and feet?'

'I've been in that room quite enough,' I said.

I DROVE HOME haunted. I had been going to
crime scenes most of my professional life, but
had never had one come to me. The sensation
of being inside that photograph, of imagining I
could smell and feel what was left of that body, had shaken
me badly. It was almost midnight by the time I pulled into
my garage, and I couldn't unlock my door fast enough.
Inside my house, I turned the alarm off, then back on the
instant I shut and locked the door. I looked around to make
sure nothing was out of place.

Lighting a fire, I fixed a drink and missed cigarettes again.
I turned on music to keep me company, then went inside my
office to see what might await me there. I had various faxes

and phone messages, and another communication in e-mail. This time, all deadoc had for me was to repeat, *you think you're so smart*. I was printing this and wondering if Squad 19 had seen it, too, when the telephone rang, startling me.

'Hi,' Wesley said. 'Just making sure you got in okay.'

'There's more mail,' I said, and I told him what it was.

'Save it and go to bed.'

'It's hard not to think about.'

'He wants you to stay up all night thinking. That's his power. That's his game.'

'Why me?' I was out of sorts and still felt queasy.

'Because you're the challenge, Kay. Even for nice people like me. Go to sleep. We'll talk tomorrow. I love you.'

But I did not get to sleep long. At several minutes past four A.M., my phone rang again. It was Dr Hoyt this time, a family practitioner in Norfolk, where he had served as a state-appointed medical examiner for the last twenty years. He was pushing seventy, but spry and as lucid as new glass. I'd never known him to be alarmed by anything, and I was instantly unnerved by his tone.

'Dr Scarpetta, I'm sorry,' he said, and he was talking very fast. 'I'm on Tangier Island.'

All I could think of, oddly, were crab cakes. 'What in the world are you doing there?'

I arranged pillows behind me, reaching for call sheets and pen.

'I got called late yesterday, been out here half the night. The Coast Guard had to bring me in one of their cutters, and I don't like boats worth a damn, beaten and whipped around worse than eggs. Plus it was cold as hell.'

I had no idea what he was talking about.

'The last time I saw anything like this was Texas, 1949,'

he went on, talking fast, 'when I was doing my residency and about to get married . . .'

I had to cut him off. 'Slow down, Fred,' I said. 'Tell me what's happened.'

'A fifty-two-year-old Tangier lady. Probably been dead at least twenty-four hours in her bedroom. She's got severe skin eruptions in crops, just covered with them, including the palms of her hands and the bottoms of her feet. Crazy as it sounds, it looks like smallpox.'

'You're right. That's crazy,' I said as my mouth got dry. 'What about chicken pox? Any way this woman was immunosuppressed?'

'I don't know anything about her, but I've never seen chicken pox look like this. These eruptions follow the small-pox pattern. They're in crops, like I said, all about the same age, and the farther away from the center of the body, the denser they get. So they're confluent, on the face, the extremities.'

I was thinking of the torso, of the small area of eruptions that I had assumed were shingles, my heart filled with dread. I did not know where that victim had died, but I believed it was somewhere in Virginia. Tangier Island was also in Virginia, a tiny barrier island in the Chesapeake Bay where the economy was based on crabbing.

'There are a lot of strange viruses out there these days,' he was saying.

'Yes, there are,' I agreed. 'But Hanta, Ebola, HIV, dengue, et al., do not cause the symptoms you have described. That doesn't mean there isn't something else we don't know about.'

'I know smallpox. I'm old enough to have seen it with my own two eyes. But I'm not an expert in infectious diseases,

Kay. And I sure as hell don't know the things that you do. But whatever it might be in this case, the fact is, the woman's dead and some type of poxvirus killed her.'

'Obviously, she lived alone.'

'Yes.'

'And she was last seen alive when?'

'The chief's working on that.'

'What chief?' I said.

'The Tangier police department has one officer. He's the chief. I'm in his trailer now, using the phone.'

'He's not overhearing this.'

'No, no. He's out talking to neighbors. I did my best to get information, without a whole lot of luck. You ever been out here?'

'No, I haven't.'

'Let's just say they don't exactly rotate their crops. There are maybe three family names on the whole island. Most folks grow up here, never leave. It's mighty hard to understand a word they're saying. Now that's a dialect you won't hear in any other corner of the world.'

'Nobody touches her until I have a better idea what we're dealing with,' I said, unbuttoning my pajamas.

'What do you want me to do?' he asked.

'Get the police chief to guard the house. No one goes in or near it until I say. Go home. I'll call you later in the day.'

The labs had not completed microbiology on the torso, and now I could not wait. I dressed in a hurry, fumbling with everything I touched, as if my motor skills had completely left me. I sped downtown on streets that were deserted, and at close to five was parking in my space behind the morgue. As I let myself into the bay, I startled the night security guard and he startled me.

'Lord have mercy, Dr Scarpetta,' said Evans, who had watched over the building for as long as I had been here.

'Sorry,' I said, my heart thudding. 'I didn't mean to frighten you.'

'Just making my rounds. Is everything all right?'

'I sure hope so.' I went past him.

'Is something coming in?'

He followed me up the ramp. I opened the door leading inside, and looked at him.

'Nothing I know of,' I replied.

Now he was completely confused, for he did not understand why I was here at this hour if no case was coming in. He started shaking his head as he headed back toward the door leading out into the parking lot. From there, he would go next door to the lobby of the Consolidated Labs, where he would sit watching a small, flickering TV until it was time to make his rounds again. Evans would not step foot into the morgue. He did not understand how anyone could, and I knew he was scared of me.

'I won't be down here long,' I told him. 'Then I'll be upstairs.'

'Yes, ma'am,' he said, still shaking his head. 'You know where I'll be.'

Midway along the corridor in the autopsy suite was a room not often entered, and I stopped there first, unlocking the door. Inside were three freezers unlike any normally seen. They were stainless steel and oversized, with temperatures digitally displayed on doors. On each was a list of case numbers, indicating the unidentified people inside.

I opened a door and thick fog rolled out as frigid air bit my face. She was in a pouch, and on a tray, and I put on gown, gloves, face shield, every layer of protection we had.

I knew I might already be in trouble, and the thought of Wingo and his vulnerable condition thrilled me with fear as I slid out the pouch and lifted it onto a stainless steel table in the middle of the room. Unzipping black vinyl, I exposed the torso to ambient air, and I went out and unlocked the autopsy suite.

Collecting a scalpel and clean glass slides, I pulled the surgical mask back down over my nose and mouth, and returned to the freezer room, shutting the door. The torso's outer layer of skin was moist as thawing began, and I used warm, wet towels to speed that along before unroofing vesicles, or the eruptions clustered over her hip and at the ragged margins of the amputations.

With the scalpel, I scraped vesicular beds, and made smears on the slides. I zipped up the pouch, marking it with blaze orange biological hazard tags, almost could not lift the body back up to its frigid shelf, my arms trembling under the strain. There was no one to call for help but Evans, so I managed on my own, and placed more warnings on the door.

I headed upstairs to the third floor, and unlocked a small lab that would have looked like most were it not for various instruments used only in the microscopic study of tissue, or histology. On a counter was a tissue processor, which fixed and dehydrated samples such as liver, kidney, spleen, and then infiltrated them with paraffin. From there the blocks went to the embedding center, and on to the microtome where they were shaved into thin ribbons. The end product was what kept me bent over my microscope downstairs.

While slides air-dried, I rooted around shelves, moving aside stains of bright orange, blue and pink in coplin jars, pulling out Gram's iodine for bacteria. Oil Red for fat in liver, silver nitrate, Biebrach Scarlet and Acridine Orange, as I thought about Tangier Island, where I'd never had a case before. Nor was there much crime, so I had been told, only drunkenness, which was common with men alone at sea. I thought of blue crab again, and irrationally wished Bev had sold me rock fish or tuna.

Finding the bottle of Nicolaou stain, I dipped in an eye dropper and carefully dripped a tiny amount of the red fluid on each slide, then finished with cover slips. These I secured in a sturdy cardboard folder, and I headed downstairs to my floor. By now, people were beginning to arrive for work, and they gave me odd looks as I came down the hall and boarded the elevator in scrubs, mask and gloves. In my office, Rose was collecting dirty coffee mugs off my desk. She froze at the sight of me.

'Dr Scarpetta?' she said. 'What in the world is going on?'

'I'm not sure, but I hope nothing,' I replied as I sat at my desk and took the cover off my microscope.

She stood in the doorway, watching as I placed a slide on the stage. She knew by my mood, if by nothing else, that something was very wrong.

'What can I do to help,' she said in a grim, quiet way.

The smear on the slide came into focus, magnified four hundred and fifty times, and then I applied a drop of oil. I stared at waves of bright red eosinophilic inclusions within infected epithelial cells, or the cytoplasmic Guarnieri bodies indicative of a pox-type virus. I fitted a Polaroid MicroCam to the microscope, and took instant high-resolution color photographs of what I suspected would have cruelly killed the old woman anyway. Death had given her no humane choice, but had it been me, I would have chosen a gun or a blade.

'Check MCV, see if Phyllis has gotten in,' I said to Rose. 'Tell her the sample I sent on Saturday can't wait.'

Within the hour, Rose had dropped me off at Eleventh and Marshall Streets, at the Medical College of Virginia, or MCV, where I had done my forensic pathology residency when I wasn't much older than the students I now advised and presented gross conferences to throughout the year. Sanger Hall was sixties architecture, with a facade of garish bright blue tiles that could be spotted for miles. I got on an elevator packed with other doctors I knew, and students who feared them.

'Good morning.'

'You, too. Teaching a class?'

I shook my head, surrounded by lab coats. 'Need to borrow your TEM.'

'You hear about the autopsy we had downstairs the other day?' a pulmonary specialist said to me as doors parted. 'Mineral dust pneumoconiosis. Berylliosis, specifically. How often you ever see that around here?'

On the fifth floor, I walked quickly to the Pathology Electron Microscopy Lab, which housed the only transmission electron microscope, or TEM, in the city. Typically, carts and countertops had not an inch of room to spare, crowded with photo and light microscopes, and other esoteric instruments for analyzing cell sizes, and coating specimens with carbon for X-ray microanalysis.

As a rule, TEM was reserved for the living, most often used in renal biopsies and specific tumors, and viruses rarely, and autopsy specimens almost never. In terms of my ongoing needs and patients already dead, it was difficult to get scientists and physicians very excited when hospital beds were filled with people awaiting word that might grant them a reprieve from a tragic end. So I never prodded microbiologist Dr Phyllis Crowder into instant action on the occasions I had needed her in the past. She knew this was different.

From the hall, I recognized her British accent as she talked on the phone.

'I know. I understand that,' she was saying as I knocked on the open door. 'But you're either going to have to reschedule or go on without me. Something else has come up.' She smiled, motioning me in.

I had known her during my residency days, and had always believed that kind words from faculty like her had everything to do with why I had come to mind when the chief's position had opened in Virginia. She was close to my age and had never married, her short hair the same dark gray as her eyes, and she always wore the same gold cross necklace that looked antique. Her parents were American, but she had been born in England, which was where she had trained and worked in her first lab.

'Bloody meetings,' she complained as she got off the phone. 'There's nothing I hate more. People sitting around talking instead of doing.'

She pulled gloves from a box and handed a pair to me. This was followed by a mask.

'There's an extra lab coat on the back of the door,' she added.

I followed her into the small, dark room, where she had been at work before the phone had rung. Slipping on the lab coat, I found a chair as she peered into a green phosphorescent screen inside the huge viewing chamber. The

TEM looked more like an instrument for oceanography or astronomy than a normal microscope. The chamber always reminded me of the dive helmet of a dry suit through which one could see eerie, ghostly images in an iridescent sea.

Through a thick metal cylinder called the scope, running from the chamber to the ceiling, a hundred-thousand-volt beam was striking my specimen, which in this case was liver that had been shaved to a thickness of six or seven one-hundredths of a micron. Smears like the ones I had viewed with my light microscope were simply too thick for the electron beam to pass through.

Knowing this at autopsy, I had fixed liver and spleen sections in glutaraldehyde, which penetrated tissue very rapidly. These I had sent to Crowder, who I knew would eventually have them embedded in plastic and cut on the ultramicrotome, then the diamond knife, before being mounted on a tiny copper grid and stained with uranium and lead ions.

What neither of us had expected was what we were looking at now, as we peered into the chamber at the green shadow of a specimen magnified almost one hundred thousand times. Knobs clicked as she adjusted intensity, contrast and magnification. I looked at DNA double-stranded, brick-shaped virus particles, two hundred to two hundred and fifty nanometers in size. I stared without blinking at smallpox.

'What do you think?' I said, hoping she would prove me wrong.

'Without a doubt, it's some type of poxvirus,' she hedged her bets. 'The question is which one. The fact that the eruptions didn't follow any nerve pattern. The fact that chicken pox is uncommon in someone this old. The fact that you may now have another case with these same manifestations causes me great concern. Other tests need to be done, but I'd treat this as a medical crisis.' She looked at me. 'An international emergency. I'd call CDC.'

'That's just what I'm going to do,' I replied, swallowing hard.

'What sense do you make of this being associated with a dismembered body?' she asked, making more adjustments as she peered into the chamber.

'I can make no sense of it,' I said, getting up and feeling weak.

'Serial killers here, in Ireland, raping, chopping people up.'

I looked at her.

She sighed. 'You ever wish you'd stayed with hospital pathology?'

'The killers you deal with are just harder to see,' I replied.

The only way to get to Tangier Island was by water or air. Since there wasn't a huge tourist business there, ferries were few and did not run after mid-October. Then one had to drive to Crisfield, Maryland, or in my case, go eighty-five miles to Reedville, where the Coast Guard was to pick me up. I left the office as most people were thinking about lunch. The afternoon was raw, the sky cloudy with a strong cold wind.

I had left instructions for Rose to call the Centers for Disease Control and Prevention (CDC) in Atlanta, because every time I had tried, I was put on hold. She was also to reach Marino and Wesley and let them know where I was going and that I would call as soon as I could.

I took 64 East to 360, and soon found myself in farm-land.

Fields were brown with fallow corn, hawks dipping and soaring in a part of the world where Baptist churches had names like *Faith, Victory* and *Zion*. Trees wore kudzu like chain mail, and across the Rappahannock River, in the Northern Neck, homes were sprawling old manors that the present-generation owner couldn't afford anymore. I passed more fields and crepe myrtles, and then the Northumberland Courthouse that had been built before the Civil War.

In Heathsville were cemeteries with plastic flowers and cared-for plots, and an occasional painted anchor in a yard. I turned off through woods dense with pines, passing cornfields so close to the narrow road, I could have reached out my window to touch brown stalks. At Buzzard's Point Marina, sailboats were moored and the red, white and blue tour boat, *Chesapeake Breeze*, was going nowhere until spring. I had no trouble parking, and there was no one in the ticket booth to ask me for a dime.

Waiting for me at the dock was a white Coast Guard boat. Guardsmen wore bright orange and blue antiexposure coveralls, known as mustang suits, and one of the men was climbing up on the pier. He was more senior than the others, with dark eyes and hair, and a nine-millimeter Beretta on his hip.

'Dr Scarpetta?' He carried his authority easily, but it was there.

'Yes,' I said, and I had several bags, including a heavy hard case containing my microscope and MicroCam.

'Let me help with those.' He held out his hand. 'I'm Ron Martinez, the station chief at Crisfield.'

'Thanks. I really appreciate this,' I said.

'Hey, so do we.'

The gap between the pier and the forty-foot patrol boat yawned and narrowed as the surge pushed the boat against the pier. Grabbing the rail, I boarded. Martinez went down a steep ladder, and I followed him into a hold packed with rescue equipment, fire hoses and huge coils of rope, the air heavy with diesel fumes. He tucked my belongings in a secure spot and tied them down. Then he handed me a mustang suit, life vest and gloves.

'You're going to need to put these on, in case you go in. Not a pretty thought but it can happen. The water's maybe in the fifties.' His eyes lingered on me. 'You might want to stay down here,' he added as the boat knocked against the pier.

'I don't get seasick but I am claustrophobic,' I told him as I sat on a narrow ledge and took off my boots.

'Wherever you want, but it's gonna be rough.'

He climbed back up as I began struggling into the suit, which was an exercise in zippers and Velcro, and filled with polyvinyl chloride to keep me alive a little longer should the boat capsize. I put my boots back on, then the life vest, with its knife and whistle, signal mirror and flares. I climbed back up to the cabin because there was no way I was going to stay down there. The crew shut the engine cover on deck, and Martinez strapped himself into the pilot's chair.

'Wind's blowing out of the northwest at twenty-two knots,' a guardsman said. 'Waves cresting at four feet.'

Martinez began pulling away from the pier. 'That's the problem with the bay,' he said to me. 'The waves are too close together so you never get a good rhythm like you do at sea. I'm sure you're aware that we could get diverted.

There's no other patrol boat out, so something goes down out here, there's no one but us.'

We began slowly passing old homes with widow's walks and bowling greens.

'Someone needs rescuing, we got to go,' he went on as a member of the crew checked instruments.

I watched a fishing boat go past, an old man in hip-high boots standing as he steered the outboard motor. He stared at us as if we were poison.

'So you could end up on anything.' Martinez enjoyed making this point.

'It wouldn't be the first time,' I said as I began to detect a very revolting smell.

'But one way or another, we'll get you there, like we did the other doctor. Never did get his name. How long have you worked for him?'

'Dr Hoyt and I go way back,' I said blandly.

Ahead were rusting fisheries with rising smoke, and as we got close I could see moving conveyor belts tilted steeply toward the sky, carrying millions of menhaden in to be processed for fertilizer and oil. Gulls circled and waited greedily from pilings, watching the tiny, stinking fish go by as we passed other factories that were ruins of brick crumbling into the creek. The stench now was unbearable, and I was certainly more stoical than most.

'Cat food,' a guardsman said, making a face.

'Talk about cat breath.'

'No way I'd live around here.'

'Fish oil's real valuable. The Algonquin Indians used cogies to fertilize their corn.'

'What the hell's a cogy?' Martinez asked.

'Another name for those nasty little suckers. Where'd you go to school?'

'Doesn't matter. Least I don't got to smell that for a living. Unless I'm out here with a schleps like you.'

'What the hell's a schlep?'

The banter continued as Martinez pushed the throttle up more, engines rumbling, bow dipping. We sailed by duck blinds and floats marking crab pots as rainbows followed in the spray of our wake. He pushed the speed up to twenty-three knots and we cut into the deep blue water of the bay, where no pleasure boats were out this day, only an ocean liner a dark mountain on the horizon.

'How far is it?' I asked Martinez, hanging on to the back of his chair, and grateful for my suit.

'Eighteen miles total.' He raised his voice, riding waves like a surfer, sliding in sideways and over, his eyes always ahead. 'Ordinarily, it wouldn't take long. But this is worse than usual. A lot worse, really.'

His crew continued checking depth and direction detectors as the GPS pointed the way by satellite. I could see nothing but water now, moguls rising in front, and behind, waves clapping hard like hands as the bay attacked us from all sides.

'What can you tell me about where we're going?' I almost had to shout.

'Population of about seven hundred. Until about twenty years ago they generated their own electricity, got one small airstrip made of dredge material. Damn.' The boat slammed down hard in a trough. 'Almost broached that one. That'll turn you over in a flash.'

His face was intense as he rode the bay like a bronco,

his crewmen unfazed but alert as they held on to whatever they could.

'Economy's based on blue crabs, soft-shell crabs, ship 'em all over the country,' Martinez went on. 'In fact, rich folks fly private planes in all the time just to buy crabs.'

'Or that's what they say they're buying,' someone remarked.

'We do have a problem with drunkenness, bootlegging, drugs,' Martinez went on. 'We board their boats when we're checking for life jackets, doing drug interdictions, and they call it being *overhauled*.' He smiled at me.

'Yeah, and we're *the guards*,' a guardsman quipped. 'Look out, here come *the guards*.'

'They use language any way they want,' Martinez said, rolling over another wave. 'You may have a problem understanding them.'

'When does crab season end?' I asked, and I was more concerned about what was being exported than I was about the way Tangiermen talked.

'This time of year they're dredging, dragging the bottom for crabs. They'll do that all winter, working fourteen, fifteen hours a day, sometimes gone a week at a time.'

Starboard, in the distance, a dark hulk protruded from the water like a whale. A crewman caught me looking.

'World War Two Liberty ship that ran aground,' he said. 'Navy uses it for target practice.'

At last, we were slowing as we approached the western shore, where a bulkhead had been built of rocks, shattered boats, rusting refrigerators, cars and other junk, to stop the island from eroding more. Land was almost level with the bay, only feet above sea level at its highest ground. Homes, a church steeple and a blue water tower were proud on the horizon on this tiny, barren island where people endured the worst weather with the least beneath their feet.

We chugged slowly past marshes and tidal flats. Old gap-toothed piers were piled high with crab pots made of chicken wire and strung with colored floats, and battle-scarred wooden boats with round and boxy sterns were moored but not idle. Martinez whelped his horn, and the sound ripped the air as we came through. Tangiermen with bibs turned expressionless, raw faces on us, the way people do when they have private opinions that aren't always friendly. They moved about in their crab shanties and worked on their nets as we docked near fuel pumps.

'Like most everybody else here, the chief's name is Crockett,' Martinez said as his crew tied us down. 'Davy Crockett. Don't laugh.' His eyes searched the pier and a snack bar that didn't look open this time of year. 'Come on.'

I followed him out of the boat, and wind blowing off the water felt as cold as January. We hadn't gone far when a small pickup truck quickly rounded a corner, tires loud on gravel. It stopped, and a tense young man got out. His uniform was blue jeans, a dark winter jacket and a cap that said *Tangier Police*, and his eyes darted back and forth between Martinez and me. He stared at what I was carrying.

'Okay,' Martinez said to me. 'I'll leave you with Davy.' To Crockett, he added, 'This is Dr Scarpetta.'

Crockett nodded. 'Y'all come on.'

'It's just the lady who's going.'

'I'll ride you to there.'

I had heard his dialect before in unspoiled mountain coves where people really are not of this century.

'We'll be waiting for you here,' Martinez promised me, walking off to his boat.

I followed Crockett to his truck. I could tell he cleaned it inside and out maybe once a day, and liked Armor All even more than Marino did.

'I assume you've been inside the house,' I said to him as he cranked the engine.

'I haven't. Was a neighbor that did. And when I was noticed about it, I called for Norfolk.'

He began to back up, a pewter cross swinging from the key chain. I looked out the window at small white frame restaurants with hand-painted signs and plastic sea-gulls hanging in windows. A truck hauling crab pots was coming the other way and had to pull over to let us pass. People were out on bicycles that had neither hand brakes nor gears, and the favorite mode of travel seemed to be scooters.

'What is the decedent's name?' I began taking notes.

'Lila Pruitt,' he said, unmindful that my door was almost touching someone's chain link fence. 'Widder lady, don't know how aged. Sold receipts for the tourists. Crab cakes and things.'

I wrote this down, not sure what he was saying as he drove me past the Tangier Combined School, and a cemetery. Headstones leaned every way, as if they had been caught in a gale.

'What about when she was last seen alive?' I asked.

'In Daby's, she was.' He nodded. 'Oh, maybe June.'

Now I was hopelessly lost. 'I'm sorry,' I said. 'She was last seen in some place called Daby's way back in June?'

'Yes'em.' He nodded as if this made all the sense in the world.

'What is Daby's and who saw her there?'

'The store. Daby's and Son. I can get you to it.' He shot

me a look, and I shook my head. 'I was in it for shopping and saw her. June, I think.'

His strange syllables and cadences sprung, tongued and rolled over each other like the water of his world. There was *thur*, can't was *cain't*, things was *thoings*, do was *doie*.

'What about her neighbors? Have any of them seen her?' I asked.

'Not since days.'

'Then who found her?' I asked.

'No one did.'

I looked at him in despair.

'Just Mrs Bradshaw come in for a receipt, went on in and had the smell.'

'Did this Mrs Bradshaw go upstairs?'

'Said she not.' He shook his head. 'She went on straight for me.'

'The decedent's address?'

'Where we are.' He was slowing down. 'School Street.'

Catty-corner to Swain Memorial Methodist Church, the white clapboard house was two stories, with clothes still on the line and a purple martin house on a rusting pole in back. An old wooden rowboat and crab pots were in a yard scattered with oyster shells, and brown hydrangea lined a fence where there was a curious row of white-painted cubbyholes facing the unpaved street.

'What are those?' I asked Crockett.

'For where she sold receipts. Quarter each. Drop it in a slot.' He pointed. 'Mrs Pruitt didn't do direct much with no one.'

I finally realized that he was talking about recipes, and pulled up my door handle.

'I'll here be waiting,' he said.

173

The expression on his face begged me not to ask him to go inside that house.

'Just keep people away.' I got out of his truck.

'Don't have to worrisome about that none.'

I glanced around at other small homes and trailers in their sandy-soil yards. Some had family plots, the dead buried wherever there was high ground, headstones worn smooth like chalk and tilted or knocked down. I climbed Lila Pruitt's front steps, noticing more headstones in the shadows of junipers in a corner of her yard.

The screen door was rusting in spots, and the spring protested loudly as I entered an enclosed porch sloping toward the street. There was a glider upholstered in floral plastic, and beside it a small plastic table, where I imagined her rocking and drinking iced tea while she watched tourists buying her recipes for a quarter. I wondered if she had spied to make sure they paid.

The storm door was unlocked, and Hoyt had thought to tape on it a homemade sign that warned, SICKNESS: DO NOT ENTER!! I supposed he had figured that Tangiermen might not know what a biological hazard was, but he had made his point. I stepped inside a dim foyer, where a portrait of Jesus praying to His Father hung on the wall, and I smelled the foul odor of decomposing human flesh.

In the living room was evidence that someone had not been well for a while. Pillows and blankets were disarrayed and soiled on the couch, and on the coffee table were tissues, a thermometer, bottles of aspirin, liniment, dirty cups and plates. She had been feverish. She had ached, and had come in here to make herself comfortable and watch TV.

Eventually, she had not been able to make it out of bed, and that was where I found her, in a room upstairs with rosebud wallpaper and a rocker by the window overlooking her street. The full-length mirror was shrouded with a sheet, as if she could not bear to see her reflection anymore. Hoyt, old-world physician that he was, had respectfully pulled bed covers over the body without disturbing anything else. He knew better than to rearrange a scene, especially if his visit was to be followed by mine. I stood in the middle of the room, and took my time. The stench seemed to make the walls close in and turn the air black.

My eyes wandered over the cheap brush and comb on the dresser, the fuzzy pink slippers beneath a chair that was covered with clothes she hadn't had the energy to put away or wash. On the bedside table was a Bible with a black leather cover that was dried out and flaking, and a sample size of Vita aromatherapy facial spray that I imagined she had used in vain to cool her raging fever. Stacked on the floor were dozens of mail-order catalogues, page corners folded back to mark her wishes.

In the bathroom, the mirror over the sink had been covered with a towel, and other towels on the linoleum floor were soiled and bloody. She had run out of toilet paper, and the box of baking soda on the side of the tub told me she had tried her own remedy in her bath to relieve her misery. Inside the medicine cabinet, I found no prescription drugs, only old dental floss, Jergens, hemorrhoid preparations, first-aid cream. Her dentures were in a plastic box on the sink.

Pruitt had been old and alone, with very little money, and probably had been off this island few times in her life. I expected that she had not attempted to seek help from any of her neighbors because she had no phone, and had feared that if anyone had seen her, they would have fled in horror.

Even I wasn't quite prepared for what I saw when I peeled back the covers.

She was covered in pustules, gray and hard like pearls, her toothless mouth caved in, and dyed red hair wild. I pulled the covers down more, unbuttoning her gown, noting the density of eruptions was greater on her extremities and face than on her trunk, just as Hoyt had said. Itching had driven her to claw her arms and legs, where she had bled and gotten secondary infections that were crusty and swollen.

'God help you,' I muttered in pain.

I imagined her itching, aching, burning up with fever, and afraid of her own nightmarish image in the mirror.

'How awful,' I said, and my mother flashed in my mind.

Lancing a pustule, I smeared a slide, then went down to the kitchen and set my microscope on the table. I was already convinced of what I'd find. This was not chicken pox. It wasn't shingles. All indicators pointed to the devastating, disfiguring disease *variola major*, more commonly known as smallpox. Turning on my microscope, I put the slide on the stage, bumped magnification up to four hundred, adjusted the focus as the dense center, the cytoplasmic Guarnieri bodies, came into view. I took more Polaroids of something that could not be true.

Shoving back the chair, I began pacing as a clock ticked loudly from the wall.

'How did you get this? How?' I talked to her out loud.

I went back outside to where Crockett was parked on the street. I didn't get close to his truck.

'We've got a real problem,' I said to him. 'And I'm not a hundred percent sure what I'm going to do about it.'

*   *   *

My immediate difficulty was finding a secure phone, which I finally decided simply was not possible. I couldn't call from any of the local businesses, certainly not from the neighbors' houses or from the chief's trailer. That left my portable cellular phone, which ordinarily I would never have used to make a call like this. But I did not see that I had a choice. At three-fifteen, a woman answered the phone at the U.S. Army Medical Research Institute of Infectious Diseases, or USAMRIID, at Fort Detrick, in Frederick, Maryland.

'I need to speak with Colonel Fujitsubo,' I said.

'I'm sorry, he's in a meeting.'

'It's very important.'

'Ma'am, you'll have to call back tomorrow.'

'At least give me his assistant, his secretary . . .'

'In case you haven't heard, all nonessential federal employees are on furlough . . .'

'Jesus Christ!' I exclaimed in frustration. 'I'm stranded on an island with an infectious dead body. There may be some sort of outbreak here. Don't tell me I have to wait until your goddamn furlough ends!'

'Excuse me?'

I could hear telephones ringing nonstop in the background.

'I'm on a cellular phone. The battery could die any minute. For God's sake, interrupt his meeting! Patch me through to him! Now!'

Fujitsubo was in the Russell Building on Capitol Hill, where my call was connected. I knew he was in some senator's office but did not care as I quickly explained the situation, trying to control my panic.

'That's impossible,' he said. 'You're sure it's not chicken pox, measles . . .'

'No. And regardless of what it is, it should be contained, John. I can't send this into my morgue. You've got to handle it.'

USAMRIID was the major medical research laboratory for the U.S. Biological Defense Research Program, its purpose to protect citizens from the possible threat of biological warfare. More to the point, USAMRIID had the largest Bio Level 4 containment laboratory in the country.

'Can't do it unless it's terrorism,' Fujitsubo said to me. 'Outbreaks go to CDC. Sounds like that's who you need to be talking to.'

'And I'm sure I will be, eventually,' I said. 'And I'm sure most of them have been furloughed too, which is why I couldn't get through earlier. But they're in Atlanta, and you're in Maryland, not far from here, and I need to get this body out of here as fast as I can.'

He was silent.

'No one hopes I'm wrong more than I do,' I went on in a cold sweat. 'But if I'm not and we haven't taken the proper precautions . . .'

'I'm clear, I'm clear,' he quickly said. 'Damn. Right now we're a skeleton crew. Okay, give us a few hours. I'll call CDC. We'll deploy a team. When was the last time you were vaccinated for smallpox?'

'When I was too young to remember it.'

'You're coming in with the body.'

'She's my case.'

But I knew what he meant. They would want to quarantine me.

'Let's just get her off the island, and we'll worry about other things later,' I added.

'Where will you be?'

'Her house is in the center of town near the school.'

'God, that's unfortunate. We got any idea how many people might have been exposed?'

'No idea. Listen. There's a tidal creek nearby. Look for that and the Methodist church. It has a tall steeple. According to the map there's another church, but it doesn't have a steeple. There's an airstrip, but the closer you can get to the house, the better, so we don't have to carry her past where people might see.'

'Right. We sure as hell don't need a panic.' He paused, his voice softening a little. 'Are you all right?'

'I sure hope so.' I felt tears in my eyes, my hands trembling.

'I want you to calm down, try to relax now and stop worrying. We'll get you taken care of,' he said as my phone went dead.

It had always been a theoretical possibility that after all the murder and madness I had seen in my career, it would be a disease that quietly killed me in the end. I never knew what I was exposing myself to when I opened a body and handled its blood and breathed the air. I was careful about cuts and needle sticks, but there was more to worry about than hepatitis and HIV. New viruses were discovered all the time, and I often wondered if they would one day rule, at last winning a war with us that began with time.

For a while, I sat in the kitchen listening to the clock tick-tock while the light changed beyond the window as the day fled. I was in the throes of a full-blown anxiety attack when Crockett's peculiar voice suddenly hailed me from outside.

'Ma'am? Ma'am?'

When I went to the porch and looked out the door, I saw

179

on the top step a small brown paper bag and a drink with a lid and a straw. I carried them in as Crockett climbed back inside his truck. He had gone off long enough to bring me supper, which wasn't smart, but kind. I waved at him as if he were a guardian angel, and felt a little better. I sat on the glider, rocking back and forth, and sipping sweetened iced tea from the Fisherman's Corner. The sandwich was fried flounder on white bread, with fried scallops on the side. I didn't think I'd ever tasted anything so fresh and fine.

I rocked and sipped tea, watching the street through the rusting screen as the sun slid down the church steeple in a shimmering ball of red, and geese were black V's flying overhead. Crockett turned his headlights on as windows lit up in homes, and two girls on bicycles pedaled quickly past, their faces turned toward me as they flew. I was certain they knew. The whole island did. Word had spread about doctors and the Coast Guard arriving because of what was in the Pruitt bed.

Going back inside, I put on fresh gloves, slipped the mask back over my mouth and nose and returned to the kitchen to see what I might find in the garbage. The plastic can was lined with a paper bag and tucked under the sink. I sat on the floor, sifting through it one item at a time to see if I could get any sense at all of how long Pruitt had been sick. Clearly, she had not emptied her trash for a while. Empty cans and frozen food wrappers were dry and crusty, peelings of raw turnips and carrots wizened and hard like Naugahyde.

I wandered through every room in her house, rooting through every wastepaper basket I could find. But it was the one in her living room that was the saddest. In it were several handwritten recipes on strips of paper, for Easy Flounder, Crab Cakes and Lila's Clam Stew. She had made mistakes, scratched through words on each one, which was why, I supposed, she had pitched them. In the bottom of the can was a small cardboard tube for a manufacturer's sample she had gotten in the mail.

Getting a flashlight out of my bag, I went outside and stood on the steps, waiting until Crockett got out of his truck.

'There's going to be a lot of commotion here soon,' I said.

He stared at me as if I might be mad, and in lighted windows I could see the faces of people peering out. I went down the steps, to the fence at the edge of the yard, around to the front of it and began shining the flashlight inside the cubbyholes where Pruitt had sold her recipes. Crockett moved back.

'I'm trying to see if I can get any idea how long she's been sick,' I said to him.

There were plenty of recipes in the slots, and only three quarters in the wooden money box.

'When did the last ferry boat come here with tourists?' I shone the light into another cubbyhole, finding maybe half a dozen recipes for Lila's Easy Soft-Shell Crabs.

'In a week ago. Never nothing since weeks,' he said.

'Do the neighbors buy her recipes?' I asked.

He frowned as if this were an odd thing to ask. 'They already got theirs.'

Now people had come out on their porches, slipping quietly into the dark shadows of their yards to watch this wild woman in surgical gown, hair cover and gloves shining a flashlight in their neighbor's cubbyholes and talking to their chief.

'There's going to be a lot of commotion here soon,' I

repeated to him. 'The Army's sending in a medical team any minute, and we're going to need you to make sure people stay calm and remain in their homes. What I want you to do right now is go get the Coast Guard, tell them they're going to need to help you, okay?'

Davy Crockett drove off so fast, his tires spun.

T HEY DESCENDED LOUDLY from the moonlit night at almost nine P.M. The Army Blackhawk thundered over the Methodist church, whipping trees in its terrible turbulence of flying blades as a powerful light probed for a place to land. I watched it settle like a bird in a yard next door as hundreds of awed Tangiermen spilled out onto the streets.

From the porch, I peered out the screen, watching the medical evacuation team climb out of the helicopter as children hid behind parents, silently staring. The five scientists from USAMRIID and CDC did not look of this planet in their inflated orange plastic suits and hoods, and battery-operated air packs. They walked along the road, carrying a litter shrouded in a plastic bubble.

'Thank God you're here,' I said to them when they got to me.

Their feet made a slipping plastic sound on the porch's wooden floor, and they did not bother to introduce themselves as the only woman on the team handed me a folded orange suit.

'It's probably a little late,' I said.

'It can't hurt.' Her eyes met mine, and she didn't look much older than Lucy. 'Go ahead and put it on.'

It had the consistency of a shower liner, and I sat on the glider and pulled it over my shoes and clothes. The hood was transparent with a bib I tied securely around my chest. I turned on the pack at the back of my waist.

'She's upstairs,' I said over the noise of air rushing in my ears.

I led the way and they carried up the litter. For a moment, they were silent when they saw what was on the bed.

A scientist said, 'Jesus. I've never seen anything like that.'

Everyone started talking fast.

'Wrap her up in the sheets.'

'Pouched and sealed.'

'Everything on the bed, linens, gotta go in the autoclave.'

'Shit. What do we do? Burn the house?'

I went into the bathroom and collected towels off the floor while they lifted her shrouded body. She was slippery and uncooperative as they struggled to get her from the bed inside the portable isolator designed with the living in mind. They sealed plastic flaps, and the sight of a pouched body inside what looked like an oxygen tent was jolting, even to me. They lifted the litter by either end and we made our way back down the stairs and out onto the street.

'What about after we leave?' I asked.

'Three of us will stay,' one of them replied. 'We got another chopper coming in tomorrow.'

We were intercepted by another suited scientist carrying a metal canister not so different from what exterminators used. He decontaminated us and the litter, spraying a chemical while people continued to gather and stare. The Coast Guard was by Crockett's truck, Crockett and Martinez talking to each other. I went to speak to them, and they were clearly put off by my protective clothing, and not so subtly stepped away.

'This house has got to be sealed,' I said to Crockett. 'Until we know with certainty what we're dealing with here, no one goes in or near it.'

He had his hands in the pockets of his jacket and was blinking a lot.

'I need to be notified immediately if anyone else here gets sick,' I said to him.

'This time of year they have sickness,' he said. 'They get the bug. Some take the cold.'

'If they get a fever, backache, break out in a rash,' I said to him, 'call me or my office right away. These people are here to help you.' I pointed to the team.

The expression on his face made it very clear he wanted no one staying here, on his island.

'Please try to understand,' I said. 'This is very, very important.'

He nodded as a young boy materialized behind him, from the darkness, and took his hand. The boy looked, at the most, seven, with tangles of unruly blond hair and wide pale eyes that were fixed on me as if I were the most terrifying apparition he had ever seen.

'Daddy, sky people.' The boy pointed at me.

'Darryl, get on,' Crockett said to his son. 'Get home.'

I followed the thudding of helicopter blades. Circulating air cooled my face, but the rest of me was miserable because the suit didn't breathe. I picked my way through the yard beside the church while blades hammered, and scrubby pines and weeds were ripped by the loud wind.

The Blackhawk was open and lit up inside, and the team was tying down the litter the same way they would have were the patient alive. I climbed aboard, took a crew seat to one side and strapped myself in as one of the scientists pulled shut the door. The helicopter was loud and shuddering as we lifted into the sky. It was impossible to hear without headsets on, and those would not work well over hoods.

This puzzled me at first. Our suits had been decontaminated, but the team did not want to take them off, and then it occurred to me. I had been exposed to Lila Pruitt, and the torso before that. No one wanted to breathe my air unless it was passed through a high efficiency particulate air filter, or HEPA, first. So we mutely looked around, glancing at each other and our patient. I shut my eyes as we sped toward Maryland.

I thought of Wesley, Lucy and Marino. They had no idea what was happening, and would be very upset. I worried about when I would see them next, and what condition I might be in. My legs were slippery, my feet baking, and I did not feel good. I could not help but fear that first fateful sign, a chill, an ache, the bleariness and thirst of fever. I had been immunized for smallpox as a child. So had Lila Pruitt. So had the woman whose torso was still in my freezer. I had seen their scars, those stretched, faded areas about the size of a quarter where they had been scratched with the disease.

It was barely eleven when we landed somewhere I could not see. I had slept just long enough to be disoriented, and the return to reality was loud and abrupt when I opened my eyes. The door slid open again, lights blinking white and blue on a helipad across the road from a big angular building. Many windows were lit up for such a late hour, as if people were awake and awaiting our arrival. Scientists unstrapped the litter and hastily loaded it in the back of a truck, while the female scientist escorted me, a gloved hand on my arm.

I did not see where the litter went, but I was led across the road to a ramp on the north side of the building. From there we did not have far to go along a hallway until I was shown into a shower and blasted with Envirochem. I stripped and was blasted again with hot, soapy water. There were shelves of scrubs and booties, and I dried my hair with a towel. As instructed, I left my clothes in the middle of the floor along with all of my possessions.

A nurse waited in the hall, and she briskly walked me past the surgery room, then walls of autoclaves that reminded me of steel diving bells, the air foul with the stench of scalded laboratory animals. I was to stay in the 200 Ward, where a red line just inside my room warned patients in isolation not to cross. I looked around at the small hospital bed with its moist heating blanket, and ventilator, refrigerator and small television suspended from a corner. I noticed the coiled yellow air lines attached to pipes on the walls, the steel pass box in the door, through which meal trays were delivered, and irradiated with UV light when removed.

I sat on the bed, alone and depressed, and unwilling to contemplate how much trouble I might be in. Minutes passed. An outer door loudly shut, and mine swung open wide.

'Welcome to the Slammer,' Colonel Fujitsubo announced as he walked in.

He wore a Racal hood and heavy blue vinyl suit, which he plugged into one of the coiled air lines.

'John,' I said. 'I'm not ready for this.'

'Kay, be sensible.'

His strong face seemed severe, even frightening behind plastic, and I felt vulnerable and alone.

'I need to let people know where I am,' I said.

He walked over to the bed, tearing open a paper packet, a small vial and medicine dropper in a gloved hand.

'Let's see your shoulder. It's time to revaccinate. And we're going to treat you to a little vaccinia immune globulin, too, for good measure.'

'My lucky day,' I said.

He rubbed my right shoulder with an alcohol pad. I stood very still as he incised my flesh twice with a scarifier and dripped in serum.

'Hopefully, this isn't necessary,' he added.

'No one hopes it more than me.'

'The good news is, you should have a lovely anamnestic response, with a higher level of the antibody than ever before. Vaccination within twenty-four to forty-eight hours of exposure will usually do the trick.'

I did not reply. He knew as well as I did that it might already be too late.

'We'll autopsy her at oh-nine-hundred hours and keep you for a few days beyond that, just to be sure,' he said, dropping wrappers in the trash. 'Are you having any symptoms at all?'

'My head hurts and I'm cranky,' I said.

He smiled, his eyes on mine. Fujitsubo was a brilliant physician who had sailed through the ranks of the Army's Armed Forces Institute of Pathology, or AFIP, before taking over the command of USAMRIID. He was divorced and a few years older than me. He got a folded blanket from the foot of the bed, shook it open and draped it around my shoulders. He pulled up a chair and straddled it, his arms on top of the backrest.

'John, I was exposed almost two weeks ago,' I said.

'By the homicide case.'

'I should have it by now.'

'Whatever *it* is. The last case of smallpox was in October 1977, in Somalia, Kay. Since then it has been eradicated from the face of the earth.'

'I know what I saw on the electron microscope. It could have been transmitted through unnatural exposure.'

'Deliberately, you're saying.'

'I don't know.' I was having a hard time keeping my eyes open. 'But don't you find it odd that the first person possibly infected was also murdered?'

'I find all of this odd.' He got up. 'But beyond offering biologically safe containment for the body and you, there isn't much we can do.'

'Of course there is. There isn't anything you can't do.' I did not want to hear of his jurisdictional conflicts.

'At the moment, this is a public health concern, not a military concern. You know we can't just yank this right out from under CDC. At the worst, what we've got is an outbreak of some sort. And that's what they do best.'

'Tangier Island should be quarantined.'

'We'll talk about that after the autopsy.'

'Which I plan to do,' I added.

'See how you feel,' he said as a nurse appeared at the door.

He conferred briefly with her on his way out, then she was walking in, dressed in another blue suit. Young and annoyingly cheerful, she was explaining that she worked out of Walter Reed Hospital but helped here when they had patients in special containment, which, fortunately, wasn't often.

'Last time was when those two lab workers got exposed to partially thawed field mice blood contaminated with Hantavirus,' she said. 'Those hemorrhagic diseases are nasty. I guess they stayed here about fifteen days. Dr Fujitsubo says you want a phone.' She laid a flimsy robe on the bed. 'I'll have to get that for you later. Here's some Advil and water.' She set them on the bedside table. 'Are you hungry?'

'Cheese and crackers, something like that, would be nice.' My stomach was so raw I was almost sick.

'How are you feeling besides the headache?'

'Fine, thanks.'

'Well, let's hope that doesn't change. Why don't you go on in the bathroom, empty your bladder, clean up and get under the covers. There's the TV.' She pointed, speaking simply as if I were in second grade.

'What about all my things?'

'They'll sterilize them, don't you worry.' She smiled at me.

I could not get warm, and took another shower. Nothing would wash away this wretched day, and I continued to see a sunken mouth gaping at me, eyes half open and blind, an arm hanging stiffly off a foul deathbed. When I emerged from the bathroom, a plate of cheese and crackers had been left for me, and the TV was on. But there was no phone.

'Oh hell,' I muttered as I got under the covers again.

The next morning, my breakfast arrived by pass box, and I set the tray on my lap as I watched the 'Today' show, which I ordinarily never got to do. Martha Stewart was whipping up something with meringue while I picked at a soft-boiled egg that wasn't quite warm. I could not eat, and did not know if my back ached because I was tired or from some other reason I would not contemplate.

'How are we doing?' The nurse appeared, breathing HEPA-filtered air.

'Don't you get hot in that thing?' I pointed my fork.

'I guess I would if I stayed in it for long periods of time.' She was carrying a digital thermometer. 'All right. This will just take a minute.'

She inserted it into my mouth while I stared up at the TV. Now a doctor was being interviewed about this year's flu shot, and I shut my eyes until a beep said my time was up.

'Ninety-seven point nine. Your temperature's actually a little low. Ninety-eight point six is normal.'

She wrapped a BP cuff around my upper arm.

'And your blood pressure.' She vigorously squeezed the bulb, pumping air. 'One hundred and eight over seventy. I believe you're almost dead.'

'Thanks,' I mumbled. 'I need a phone. No one knows where I am.'

'What you need is to get lots of rest.' Now she had out the stethoscope, which she pushed down the front of my scrubs. 'Deep breaths.' It was cold everywhere she moved it, her face serious as she listened. 'Again.' Then she moved it to my back as we continued the routine.

'Could you please have Colonel Fujitsubo stop by.'

'I'll certainly leave him a message. Now you cover up.' She pulled the blanket up to my chin. 'Let me get you some more water. How's your headache?'

'Fine,' I lied. 'You really must ask him to stop by.'

'I'm sure he will when he can. I know he's very busy.'

Her patronizing manner was beginning to really get to me. 'Excuse me,' I said in a demanding tone. 'I have repeatedly requested a phone, and I'm beginning to feel like I'm in prison.'

'You know what they call this place,' she sang. 'And usually, patients don't get . . .'

'I don't care what they usually get.' I stared hard at her as her demeanor changed.

'You just calm right down.' Eyes glinted behind clear plastic, her voice raised.

'Isn't she an awful patient? Doctors always are,' Colonel Fujitsubo said as he strode into the room.

The nurse looked at him, stunned. Then her resentful eyes fixed on me as if she did not believe it could possibly be true.

'One phone coming up,' he went on as he carried in a fresh orange suit, which he laid on the foot of the bed. 'Beth, I guess you've been introduced to Dr Scarpetta, chief medical examiner of Virginia and consulting forensic pathologist for the FBI?' To me, he added, 'Put this on. I'll be back for you in two minutes.'

The nurse frowned as she picked up my tray. She cleared her throat, embarrassed.

'You didn't do a very good job on your eggs,' she said.

She set the tray in the pass box. I was pulling on the suit.

'Typically, once you're in here, they don't let you out.' She shut the drawer.

'This isn't typical.' I tied down the hood and turned on my air. 'The case this morning is mine.'

I could tell she was one of those nurses who resented women doctors, because she preferred to be told what to do by men. Or maybe she had wanted to be a doctor and was told that girls grow up to be nurses and marry doctors. I could only guess. But I remembered when I was in medical school at Johns Hopkins, and one day the head nurse grabbed my arm in the hospital. I'd never forget her hate when she snarled that her son hadn't gotten in because I had taken his slot.

Fujitsubo was walking back into the room, smiling at me as he handed me a telephone and plugged it into a jack.

'You got time for one.' He held up his index finger. 'Then we got to roll.'

I called Marino.

Bio Level 4 containment was in back of a normal lab, but the difference between the two areas was serious. BL-4 meant scientists doing open war with Ebola, Hantavirus and unknown diseases for which there was no cure. Air was single-pass and negative pressure to prevent highly infectious microorganisms from flowing into any other part of the building. It was checked by HEPA filters before it entered our bodies or the atmosphere, and everything was scalded by steam in autoclaves.

Though autopsies were infrequent, when they were performed it was in an air-locked space nicknamed 'the Sub,' behind two massive stainless steel doors with submarine seals. To enter, we had to go in another way, through a maze of change rooms and showers, with only colored lights to indicate which gender was in what. Men were green so I put my light on red and took everything off. I put on fresh sneakers and scrubs.

Steel doors automatically opened and closed as I passed through another air-lock, into the inner change, or hot side room where the heavy gauge blue vinyl suits with built-in feet and pointed hoods hung from hooks on a wall. Sitting on a bench, I pulled one on, zipping it up and securing flaps with what looked like a diagonal Tupperware seal. I worked my feet into rubber boots, then layers of heavy gloves, with outer ones taped to cuffs. I was already beginning to feel hot, doors shutting behind me as other ones of even thicker steel sucked open to let me into the most claustrophobic autopsy room I had ever seen.

I grabbed a yellow line and plugged it into the quick-release coupling at my hip, and rushing air reminded me of a deflating wading pool. Fujitsubo and another doctor were labeling tubes and hosing off the body. In her nakedness, her disease was even more appalling. For the most part, we worked in silence for we had not bothered with communication equipment, and the only way to speak was to crimp our air lines long enough to hear what someone else was saying.

We did this as we cut and weighed, and I recorded the pertinent information on a protocol. She suffered the typical degenerative changes of fatty streaks and fatty plaques of the aorta. Her heart was dilated, her congested lungs consistent with early pneumonia. She had ulcers in her mouth and lesions in her gastrointestinal tract. But it was her brain that told the most tragic story of her death. She had cortical atrophy, widening of the cerebral sulci and loss of the parenchyma, the telltale hints of Alzheimer's.

I could only imagine her confusion when she had gotten sick. She may not have remembered where she was or even who she was, and in her dementia may have believed some nightmarish creature was coming through her mirrors. Lymph nodes were swollen, spleen and liver cloudy and swollen with focal necrosis, all consistent with smallpox.

She looked like a natural death, the cause of which we could not prove yet, and two hours later, we were done. I left the same way I had come in, starting with the hot side room, where I took a five-minute chemical shower in my suit, standing on a rubber mat and scrubbing every inch with a stiff brush as steel nozzles pounded me. Dripping, I reentered the outer room, where I hung the suit to dry, showered again and washed my hair. I put on a sterile orange suit and returned to the Slammer.

The nurse was in my room when I walked in.

'Janet is here writing you a note,' she said.

'Janet?' I was stunned. 'Is Lucy with her?'

'She'll slide it through the pass box. All I know is there's a young woman named Janet. She's alone.'

'Where is she? I must see her.'

'You know that isn't possible just now.' She was taking my blood pressure again.

'Even prisons have a place for visitors,' I almost snapped. 'Isn't there some area where I can talk to her through

195

glass? Or can't she put on a suit and come in here like you do?'

Of course, all this required permission, yet again, from the colonel, who decided that the easiest solution was for me to wear a HEPA filter mask and go into the visitors' booth. This was inside the Clinical Research Ward, where studies were conducted on new vaccines. She led me through a BL-3 recreation room, where volunteers were playing Ping-Pong and pool, or reading magazines and watching TV.

The nurse opened the wooden door to Booth B, where Janet was seated on the other side of glass in an uncontaminated part of the building. We picked up our phones at the same time.

'I can't believe this,' was the first thing she said. 'Are you all right?'

The nurse was still standing behind me in my telephone-booth-sized space, and I turned around and asked her to leave. She didn't budge.

'Excuse me,' I said, and I'd about had it with her. 'This is a private conversation.'

Anger flashed in her eyes as she left and shut the door.

'I don't know how I am,' I said into the phone. 'But I don't feel too bad.'

'How long does it take?' Fear shone in her eyes.

'On average, ten days, at the most fourteen.'

'Well, that's good, then, isn't it?'

'I don't know.' I felt depressed. 'It depends on what we're dealing with. But if I'm still okay in a few days, I expect they will let me leave.'

Janet looked very grown-up and pretty in a dark blue suit, her pistol inconspicuous beneath her jacket. I knew she would not have come alone unless something was very wrong.

'Where's Lucy?' I asked.

'Well, actually, both of us are up here in Maryland, outside Baltimore, with Squad Nineteen.'

'Is she all right?'

'Yes,' Janet said. 'We're working on your files, trying to trace them through AOL and UNIX.'

'And?'

She hesitated. 'I think the quickest way to catch him is going to be online.'

I frowned, perplexed by this. 'I'm not sure I understand . . .'

'Is that thing uncomfortable?' She stared at my mask.

'Yes.'

I was sorrier for the way it looked. It covered half of my face like a hideous muzzle and kept knocking the phone as I talked.

'How can you catch him online unless he's still sending messages to me?'

She opened a file folder on her Formica ledge. 'Do you want to hear them?'

I nodded as my stomach tightened.

'*Microscopic worms, multiplying ferments and miasma,*' she read.

'Excuse me?' I said.

'That's it. E-mail sent this morning. The next one came this afternoon. *They are alive, but no one else will be.* And then about an hour after that, *Humans who seize from others and exploit are macro parasites. They kill their hosts.* All in lowercase with no punctuation except spaces.' She looked through the glass at me.

'Classical medical philosophy,' I said. 'Going back to

Hippocrates and other Western practitioners, their theories of what causes disease. The atmosphere. Reproducing poisonous particles generated by the decomposition of organic matter. Microscopic worms, et cetera. And then the historian McNeill wrote about the interaction of micro and macro parasites as a way of understanding the evolution of society.'

'Then deadoc has had medical training,' Janet said. 'And it sounds like he's alluding to whatever this disease is.'

'He couldn't know about it,' I said as I began to entertain a terrible new fear. 'I don't see how he possibly could.'

'There was something in the news,' she said.

I felt a rush of anger. 'Who opened his mouth this time? Don't tell me Ring knows about this, too.'

'The paper simply said your office was investigating an unusual death on Tangier Island, a strange disease that resulted in the body being airlifted out by the military.'

'Damn.'

'Point is, if deadoc has access to Virginia news, he could have known about it before he sent the e-mail messages.'

'I hope that's what happened,' I said.

'Why wouldn't it be?'

'I don't know, I don't know.' I was worn out and my stomach was upset.

'Dr Scarpetta.' She leaned closer to the glass. 'He wants to talk to you. That's why he keeps sending you mail.'

I was feeling chills again.

'Here's the idea.' Janet tucked the printouts back inside the file. 'I could get you in a private chat room with him. If we can keep you online long enough, we can trace him from telephone trunk to telephone trunk, until we get a town, then a location.'

'I don't believe for a moment that this person is going to participate,' I said. 'He's too smart for that.'

'Benton Wesley thinks he might.'

I was silent.

'He thinks deadoc is sufficiently fixated on you that he might get into a chat room. It's more than his wanting to know what you think. He wants you to know what he thinks, or at least this is Wesley's theory. I've got a laptop here, everything you need.'

'No.' I shook my head. 'I don't want to get into this, Janet.'

'You've got nothing else to do for the next few days.'

It irritated me when anyone ever accused me of not having enough to do. 'I don't want to communicate with the monster. It's far too risky. I could say the wrong thing and more people die.'

Janet's eyes were intense on mine. 'They're dying, anyway. Maybe others are, too, even as we speak, that we don't know about yet.'

I thought of Lila Pruitt alone in her house, wandering, demented with disease. I saw her in her mirror, shrieking.

'All you need to do is get him talking, a little bit at a time,' Janet went on. 'You know, act reluctant, as if he's caught you unaware, otherwise he'll get suspicious. Build it up for a few days, while we try to find out where he is. Get on AOL. Go into the chat rooms and find one called M.E., okay? Just hang out in there.'

'Then what?' I wanted to know.

'The hope is he'll come looking for you, thinking this is

where you do consultations with other doctors, scientists. He won't be able to resist. That's Wesley's theory and I agree with it.'

'Does he know I'm here?'

The question was ambiguous but she knew who I meant.

'Yes,' she said. 'Marino asked me to call him.'

'What did he say?' I asked into the phone.

'He wanted to know if you were okay.' She was getting evasive. 'He has this old case in Georgia. Something about two people stabbed to death in a liquor store, and organized crime is involved. In a little town near St Simons Island.'

'Oh, so he's on the road.'

'I guess so.'

'Where will you be?'

'With the squad. I'll actually be staying in Baltimore, on the harbor.'

'And Lucy?' I asked again, this time in a way she couldn't evade. 'Do you want to tell me what's really going on, Janet?'

I breathed my filtered air, looking through glass at someone I knew could never lie to me.

'Everything okay?' I pressed harder.

'Dr Scarpetta, I'm here by myself for two reasons,' she finally said. 'First, Lucy and I got into a huge fight about your going online with this guy. So everyone involved thought it would be better if she wasn't the one to talk to you about it.'

'I can understand that,' I said. 'And I agree.'

'My second reason is a far more unpleasant one,' she went on. 'It's about Carrie Grethen.'

I was astonished and enraged at the mere mention of

her name. Years ago, when Lucy was developing CAIN, she had worked with Carrie. Then ERF had been broken into, and Carrie had seen to it that my niece was blamed. There were murders, too, sadistic and terrible, that Carrie had been accomplice to with a psychopathic man.

'She's still in prison,' I said.

'I know. But her trial is scheduled for the spring,' Janet said.

'I'm well aware of that.' I didn't understand what she was getting at.

'You're the key witness. Without you, the Commonwealth doesn't have much of a case. At least not when you're talking about a jury trial.'

'Janet, I am most confused,' I said, and my headache was back with fury.

She took a deep breath. 'I'm sure you must be aware that there was a time when Lucy and Carrie were close.' She hesitated. 'Very close.'

'Of course,' I impatiently said. 'Lucy was a teenager and Carrie seduced her. Yes, yes, I know all about it.'

'So does Percy Ring.'

I looked at her, shocked.

'It seems that yesterday, Ring went to see the C.A. who's prosecuting the case, uh, Rob Schurmer. Ring tells him, one buddy to another, that he's got a major problem since the star witness's niece had an affair with the defendant.'

'My God in heaven.' I could not believe this. 'That fucking bastard.'

I was a lawyer. I knew what this meant. Lucy would have to take the stand and be questioned about her affair with another woman. The only way to avoid this was for me to be struck as a witness, allowing Carrie to get away with murder.

'What she did has nothing to do with Carrie's crimes,' I said, so angry with Ring I felt capable of violence.

Janet switched the phone to her other ear, trying to be smooth. But I could see her fear.

'I don't need to tell you how it is out there,' she said. 'Don't ask, don't tell. It's not tolerated, no matter what anybody says. Lucy and I are so careful. People may suspect, but they don't really know, and it's not like we walk around in leather and chains.'

'Not hardly.'

'I think this would ruin her,' she matter-of-factly stated. 'The publicity, and I can't imagine HRT when she shows up after that. All those big guys. Ring's just doing this to do her in, and maybe you, too. And maybe me. This won't exactly help my career, either.'

She didn't need to go on. I understood.

'Does anyone know what Schurmer's response was when Ring told him?'

'He freaked, called Marino and said he didn't know what he was going to do, that when the defense found out, he was cooked. Then Marino called me.'

'Marino has said nothing to me.'

'He didn't want to upset you right now,' she said. 'And he didn't think it was his place.'

'I see,' I said. 'Does Lucy know?'

'I told her.'

'And?'

'She kicked a hole in the bedroom wall,' Janet answered. 'Then she said if she had to, she'd take the stand.'

Janet pressed her palm against the glass, spreading her

fingers, waiting for me to do the same. It was as close as we could get to touching, and my eyes teared up.

'I feel as if I've committed a 'crime,' I said, clearing my throat.

10

THE NURSE CARRIED the computer equipment into my room and wordlessly handed it to me before walking right back out. For a moment, I stared at the laptop as if it were something that might hurt me. I was sitting up in bed, where I continued to perspire profusely while I was cold at the same time.

I didn't know if the way I felt was due to a microbe or if I were having some sort of emotional attack because of what Janet had just told me. Lucy had wanted to be an FBI agent since she was a child, and she was already one of the best ones they'd ever had. This was so unfair. She had done nothing but make the mistake of being drawn in by someone evil when she was only nineteen. I was desperate to get out of this room and find her. I wanted to go home. I was about to ring for the nurse when one walked in. She was new.

'Do you suppose I could have a fresh set of scrubs?' I asked her.

'I can get you a gown.'

'Scrubs, please.'

'Well, it's a little out of the ordinary.' She frowned.

'I know.'

I plugged the computer into the telephone jack, and pushed a button to turn it on.

'If they don't get beyond this budget impasse soon, there won't be anybody to autoclave scrubs or anything else.' The nurse kept talking in her blue suit, arranging covers over my legs. 'On the news this morning, the president said Meals on Wheels is going broke, EPA isn't cleaning up toxic waste dumps, federal courts may close and forget getting a tour of the White House. You ready for lunch?'

'Thank you,' I said as she continued her litany of bad news.

'Not to mention Medicaid, air pollution and tracking the winter flu epidemic or screening water supplies for the Cryptosporidium parasite. You're just lucky you're here now. Next week we might not be open.'

I didn't even want to think about budget feuds, since I devoted most of my time to them, haggling with department heads and firing at legislators during General Assembly. I worried that when the federal crisis slammed down to the state level, my new building would never be finished, my meager current funding further ruthlessly slashed. There were no lobbyists for the dead. My patients had no party and did not vote.

'You got two choices,' she was saying.

'I'm sorry.' I tuned her in again.

'Chicken or ham.'

'Chicken.' I wasn't the least bit hungry. 'And hot tea.'

She unplugged her air line and left me to the quiet. I set the laptop on the tray and logged onto America Online. I went straight to my mailbox. There was plenty, but nothing from deadoc that Squad 19 hadn't already opened. I followed menus to the chat rooms, pulled up a list of the member rooms and checked to see how many people were in the one called M.E.

No one was there, so I went in alone and leaned back against my pillows, staring at the blank screen with its row of icons across the top. Literally, there was no one to chat with, and I thought of how ridiculous this must seem to deadoc, were he somehow watching. Wasn't it obvious if I were alone in a room? Wouldn't it seem that I was waiting? I had no sooner entertained this thought when a sentence was written across my screen, and I began to answer.

QUINCY: Hi. What are we talking about today?
SCARPETTA: The budget impasse. How is it affecting
             you?
QUINCY: I work out of the D.C. office. A night-
             mare.
SCARPETTA: Are you a medical examiner?
QUINCY: Right. We've met at meetings. We know
             some of the same people. Not much of
             a crowd today, but it could always get
             better if one is patient.

That's when I knew Quincy was one of the undercover agents from Squad 19. We continued our session until lunch arrived, then resumed it afterwards for the better part of an hour. Quincy and I chatted about our problems, asking questions about solutions, anything we could think of that might seem like normal conversation between medical examiners or people they might confer with. But deadoc did not bite.

I took a nap and woke up a little past four. For a moment, I lay very still, forgetting where I was, then it came back to me with depressing alacrity. I sat up, cramped beneath my tray, the computer still open on top of it. I logged onto AOL again and went back into the chat room. This time I was joined by someone who called himself MEDEX, and we talked about the type of computer database I used in Virginia for capturing case information and doing statistical retrievals.

At exactly five minutes past five, a bell sounded off-key inside my computer, and the Instant Message window suddenly dominated my screen. I stared in disbelief as a communication from deadoc appeared, words that I knew no one else in the chat room could see.

DEADOC: you think you re so smart
SCARPETTA: Who are you?
DEADOC: you know who I am   I am what you do
SCARPETTA: What do I do?
DEADOC: death   doctor death   you are me
SCARPETTA: I am not you.
DEADOC: you think you re so smart

He abruptly got quiet, and when I clicked on the Available button, it showed that he had logged off. My heart was racing as I sent another message to MEDEX, saying I had been tied up with a visitor. I got no response, finding myself alone in the chat room again.

'Damn,' I exclaimed, under my breath.

I tried again as late as ten P.M., but no one appeared except QUINCY again, to tell me we should try another meeting in the morning. All of the other docs, he said, had gone home. The same nurse checked on me, and she was sweet. I felt sorry for her long hours, and her inconvenience of having to wear a blue suit every time she came into my room.

'Where is the new shift?' I asked, as she took my temperature.

'I'm it. We're all just doing the best we can.'

I nodded as she alluded to the furlough yet one more time this day.

'There's hardly a lab worker here,' she went on. 'You could wake up tomorrow, the only person in the building.'

'Now I'm sure to have nightmares,' I said as she wrapped the BP cuff around my arm.

'Well, you're feeling okay, and that's the important thing. Ever since I started coming down here, I started imagining I was getting one thing or another. The slightest ache or pain or sniffle, and it's, oh my God. So what kind of doctor are you?'

I told her.

'I was going to be a pediatrician. Then I got married.'

'We'd be in a lot of trouble were it not for good nurses like you,' I smiled and said.

'Most doctors never bother to notice that. They have these attitudes.'

'Some of them certainly do,' I agreed.

I tried to go to sleep, and was restless throughout the night. Street lights from the parking lot beyond my window seeped through the blinds, and no matter which way I turned, I could not relax. It was hard to breathe and my heart would not slow down. At five A.M., I finally sat up and turned on my light. Within minutes, the nurse was back inside my room.

'You all right?' She looked exhausted.

'Can't sleep.'

'Want something?'

I turned on the computer as I shook my head. I logged onto AOL and went back to the chat room, which was empty. Clicking on the Available button, I checked to see if deadoc was on line, and if so, where he might be. There was no sign of him, and I began scrolling through the various chat rooms available to subscribers and their families.

There was truly something for everyone, places for flirts, singles, gays, lesbians, Native Americans, African Americans, and for evil. People who preferred bondage, sadomasochism, group sex, bestiality, incest, were welcome to find each other and exchange pornographic art. The FBI could do nothing about it. All of it was legal.

Dejected, I sat up, propped against my pillows and, without intending to, dozed off. When I opened my eyes again an hour later, I was in a chat room called ARTLOVE. A message was quietly waiting for me on my screen. Deadoc had found me.

DEADOC: a picture s worth a thousand words

I hastily checked to see if he was still logged on, and found him quietly coiled in cyberspace, waiting for me. I typed my response.

SCARPETTA: What are you trading?

He didn't respond right away. I sat staring at the screen for three or four minutes. Then he was back.

DEADOC: I don t trade with traitors I give freely what do you think happens to people like that

SCARPETTA: Why don't you tell me?

Silence, and I watched as he left the room, and a minute later was back. He was breaking the trace. He knew exactly what we were doing.

DEADOC: I think you know
SCARPETTA: I don't.
DEADOC: you will
SCARPETTA: I saw the photos you sent. They weren't very clear. What was your point?

But he did not answer and I felt slow and dull-witted. I had him and could not engage him. I could not keep him on. I was feeling frustrated and discouraged when another instant message appeared on my screen, this one from the squad again.

QUINCY: A.K.A., Scarpetta. Still need to go over that case with you. The self-immolation.

That's when I realized that Quincy was Lucy. A.K.A. was

Aunt Kay Always, her code for me. She was watching over me, as I had watched over her all these years, and she was telling me not to go up in flames. I typed a message back.

SCARPETTA: I agree. Your case is very troublesome. How are you handling it?

QUINCY: Just watch me in court. More later.

I smiled as I signed off and leaned back in the pillows. I did not feel quite so alone or crazed.

'Good morning.' The first nurse was back.

'Same to you.' My spirits dipped lower.

'Let's check those vitals. How are we feeling today?'

'We're fine.'

'You've got a choice of eggs or cereal.'

'Fruit,' I said.

'That wasn't a choice. But we can probably scrape up a banana.'

The thermometer went into my mouth, the cuff around my arm. All the while she kept talking.

'It's so cold out it could snow,' she was saying. 'Thirty-three degrees. You believe that? I had frost on my windshield. The acorns are big this year. That always means a severe winter. You're still not even up to ninety-eight degrees yet. What's wrong with you?'

'Why wasn't the phone left in here?' I asked.

'I'll ask about it.' She took the cuff off. 'Blood pressure's low, too.'

'Please ask Colonel Fujitsubo to stop by this morning.'

She stood back and scrutinized me. 'You going to complain about me?'

'Good heavens, no,' I said. 'I just need to leave.'

'Well, I hate to tell you, but that's not up to me. Some people stay in here as long as two weeks.'

I would lose my mind, I thought.

The colonel did not appear before lunch, which was a broiled chicken breast, carrots and rice. I hardly ate as my tension mounted, and the TV flashed silently in the background because I had turned off the sound. The nurse came back at two P.M. and announced I had another visitor. So I put on the HEPA filter mask again and followed her back down the hall into the clinic.

This time I was in Booth A, and Wesley was waiting for me on the other side. He smiled when our eyes met, and both of us picked up our phones. I was so relieved and surprised to see him that I stammered at first.

'I hope you've come to rescue me,' I said.

'I don't take on doctors. You taught me that.'

'I thought you were in Georgia.'

'I was. Took a look at the liquor store where the two people were stabbed, scouted around the area, in general. Now I'm here.'

'And?'

'And?' He raised an eyebrow. 'Organized crime.'

'I wasn't thinking about Georgia.'

'Tell me what you are thinking. I seem to be losing the art of mind reading. And you look particularly lovely today, let me add,' he said to my mask.

'I'm going to go crazy if I don't get out of here soon,' I said. 'I've got to get to CDC.'

'Lucy tells me you've been communicating with deadoc.' The playful light vanished from his eyes.

'To no great extent and with not much luck,' I angrily said.

To communicate with this killer was infuriating for it was exactly what he wanted. I had made it my mission in life not to reward people like him.

'Don't give up,' Wesley said.

'He makes allusions to medical matters, such as diseases and germs,' I said. 'Doesn't this concern you in light of what is going on?'

'He no doubt follows the news.' He made the same point Janet had.

'But what if it's more than that?' I asked. 'The woman he dismembered seems to have the same disease that the victim from Tangier does.'

'And you can't verify that yet.'

'You know, I didn't get where I am by making assumptions and leaping to conclusions.' I was getting very out of sorts. 'I will verify this disease as soon as I can, but I think we should be guided by common sense in the meantime.'

'I'm not certain I understand what you're saying.' His eyes never left mine.

'I'm saying that we might be dealing with biological warfare. A Unabomber who uses a disease.'

'I hope to God we're not.'

'But the thought has crossed your mind too. Don't tell me you think that a fatal disease somehow linked with a dismemberment is coincidental.'

I studied his face, and I knew he had a headache. The same vein on his forehead always stood out like a bluish rope.

'And you're sure you're feeling all right,' he said.

'Yes. I'm more worried about you.'

'What about this disease? What about the risk to you?' He was getting irritated with me, the way he always did when he thought I was in danger.

214

'I've been revaccinated.'

'You've been vaccinated for smallpox,' he said. 'What if that's not what it is?'

'Then we're in a world of trouble. Janet came by.'

'I know,' he said into his phone. 'I'm sorry. The last thing you needed right now . . .'

'No, Benton,' I interrupted him. 'I had to be told. There's never a good time for news like that. What do you think will happen?'

But he did not want to say.

'Then you think it will ruin her, too,' I said in despair.

'I doubt she'll be terminated. What usually happens is you stop getting promoted, get lousy assignments, field offices out in the middle of nowhere. She and Janet will end up three thousand miles apart. One or both will quit.'

'How's that better than being fired?' I said in pained outrage.

'We'll take it as it comes, Kay.' He looked at me. 'I'm dismissing Ring from CASKU.'

'Be careful what you do because of me.'

'It's done,' he said.

Fujitsubo did not stop by my room again until early the next morning, and then he was smiling and opening blinds to let in sunlight so dazzling it hurt my eyes.

'Good morning, and so far, so good,' he said. 'I'm very pleased that you do not seem to be getting sick on us, Kay.'

'Then I can go,' I said, ready to leap out of bed right then.

'Not so fast.' He was reviewing my chart. 'I know how hard this is for you, but I'm not comfortable letting you go quite so soon. Stick it out a little longer, and you can leave the day after tomorrow, if all goes well.'

I felt like crying when he left because I did not see how I could endure one more hour of quarantine. Miserable, I sat up under the covers and looked out at the day. The sky was bright blue with wisps of clouds beneath the pale shadow of a morning moon. Trees beyond my window were bare and rocking in a gentle wind. I thought of my home in Richmond, of plants to be potted and work piling up on mý desk. I wanted to take a walk in the cold, to cook broccoli and homemade barley soup. I wanted spaghetti with ricotta or stuffed frittata, and music and wine.

For half the day, I simply felt sorry for myself and did not do a thing except stare at television and doze. Then the nurse for the next shift came in with the phone and said there was a call for me. I waited until it was transferred and snatched up the receiver as if this were the most exciting thing that had ever happened in my life.

'It's me,' Lucy said.

'Thank God.' I was thrilled to hear her voice.

'Grans says hi. Rumor has it that you win the bad patient award.'

'The rumor is accurate. All the work in my office. If only I had it here.'

'You need to rest,' she said. 'To keep your defenses up.'

This made me worry about Wingo again.

'How come you haven't been on the laptop?' She then got to the point.

I was quiet.

'Aunt Kay, he's not going to talk to us. He's only going to talk to you.'

'Then one of you sign on as me,' I replied.

'No way. If he senses that's what's going on, we lose him for good. This guy is scary, he's so clever.'

My silence was my comment, and Lucy rushed to fill it.

'What?' she said with feeling. 'I'm supposed to pretend I'm a forensic pathologist with a law degree who's already worked at least one of this guy's cases? I don't think so.'

'I don't want to connect with him, Lucy,' I said. 'People like him get off on that, they want it, want the attention. The more I play his game, the more it might encourage him. Have you thought about that?'

'Yes. But think about this. Whether he's dismembered one person or twenty, he's going to do something else bad. People like him don't just stop. And we have no idea, not one clue, as to where the hell he is.'

'It's not that I'm scared for myself,' I started to say.

'It's all right if you are.'

'I just don't want to do anything to make it worse,' I repeated.

That, of course, was always the risk when one was creative or aggressive in an investigation. The perpetrator was never completely predictable. Maybe it was simply something I sensed, an intuitive vibration I was picking up deep inside. But I felt that this killer was different and motivated by something beyond our ken. I feared he knew exactly what we were doing and was enjoying himself.

'Now, tell me about you,' I said. 'Janet was here.'

'I don't want to get into it.' Cold fury crept into her tone. 'I have better ways to spend my time.'

'I'm with you, Lucy, whatever you want to do.'

'That much I've always been sure of. And this much everybody else can be sure of. No matter what it takes, Carrie's going to rot in jail and hell after that.'

The nurse had returned to my room to whisk the telephone away again.

'I don't understand this,' I complained as I hung up. 'I have a calling card, if that's what you're worried about.'

She smiled. 'Colonel's orders. He wants you to rest and knows you won't if you can be on the phone all day.'

'I am resting,' I said, but she was gone.

I wondered why he allowed me to keep the laptop and was suspicious Lucy or someone had spoken to him. As I logged onto AOL, I felt conspired against. I had barely entered the M.E. chat room when deadoc appeared, this time not as an invisible instant message, but as a member who could be heard and seen by anybody else who decided to walk in.

DEADOC:	where have you been
SCARPETTA:	Who are you?
DEADOC:	I ve already told you that
SCARPETTA:	You are not me.
DEADOC:	he gave them power over unclean spirits to cast them out and to heal all manner of sickness and all manner of disease pathophysiological manifestations viruses like hiv our darwinian struggle against them they are evil or are we
SCARPETTA:	Explain what you mean.
DEADOC:	there are twelve

But he had no intention of explaining, at least not now. The system alerted me that he had left the room. I waited inside it a while longer to see if he might return, as I wondered what he meant by *twelve*. Pushing a button on my headboard, I summoned the nurse, who was beginning to cause me guilt. I didn't know where she waited outside the room, or if she climbed in and out of her blue suit every time she appeared and left. But none of this could have been pleasant, including my disposition.

'Listen,' I said when she got to me. 'Might there be a Bible around here somewhere.'

She hesitated, as if she'd never heard of such a thing. 'Gee, now that I don't know.'

'Could you check?'

'Are you feeling all right?' She looked suspiciously at me.

'Absolutely.'

'They've got a library. Maybe there's one in there some-where. I'm sorry. I'm not very religious.' She continued talking as she went out again.

She returned maybe half an hour later with a black leather-bound Bible, Cambridge Red Letter edition, that she claimed to have borrowed from someone's office. I opened it and found a name in front written in calligraphy, and a date that showed the Bible had been given to its owner on a special occasion almost ten years before. As I began to turn its pages, I realized I had not been to Mass in months. I envied people with a faith so strong that they kept their Bibles at work.

'Now you're sure you're feeling okay?' said the nurse as she hovered near the door.

'You've never told me your name,' I said.

'Sally.'

'You've been very helpful and I certainly appreciate it. I know it's no fun working on Thanksgiving.'

This seemed to please her a great deal and gave her enough confidence to say, 'I haven't wanted to poke my nose into anything, but I can't help but hear what people are talking about. That island in Virginia where your case came from. All they do is crabbing there?'

'Pretty much,' I said.

219

'Blue crab.'

'And soft-shell crab.'

'Anybody bothering to worry about that?'

I knew what she was getting at, and yes, I was worried. I had a personal reason to be worried about Wesley and me.

'They ship those things all over the country, right?' she went on.

I nodded.

'What if whatever that lady had is transmitted through water or food?' Her eyes were bright behind her hood. 'I didn't see her body, but I heard. That's really scary.'

'I know,' I said. 'I hope we can get an answer to that soon.'

'By the way, lunch is turkey. Don't expect much.'

She unplugged her air line and stopped talking. Opening the door, she gave me a little wave and went out. I turned back to the Concordance and had to search for a while under various words before I found the passage deadoc had quoted to me. It was Matthew 10, verse one, and in its entirety it read: *And when he had called unto him his twelve disciples, he gave them power against unclean spirits, to cast them out, and to heal all manner of sickness and all manner of disease.*

The next verse went on to identify the disciples by name, and then Jesus invoked them to go out and find lost sheep, and to preach to them that the kingdom of heaven was at hand. He directed his disciples to heal the sick, cleanse the lepers, raise the dead, cast out devils. As I read, I did not know if this killer who called himself deadoc had a message he believed, if *twelve* referred to the disciples, or if he was simply playing games.

I got up and paced, looking out the window as light waned. Night came early now, and it had become a habit for me to

220

watch people walk out to their cars. Their breath was frosted, and the lot was almost empty because of the furlough. Two women chatted while one held open the door to a Honda, and they shrugged and gestured with intensity, as if trying to resolve life's big problems. I stood looking through blinds until they drove away.

I tried to go to sleep early to escape. But I was fitful again, rearranging myself and the covers every few hours. Images floated past the inside of my eyelids, projected like old movies, unedited and illogically arranged. I saw two women talking by a mailbox. One had a mole on her cheek that became eruptions all over her face as she shielded her eyes with a hand. Then palm trees were writhing in fierce winds as a hurricane roared in from the sea, fronds ripped off and flying. A trunk stripped bare, a bloody table lined with severed hands and feet.

I sat up sweating, and waited for my muscles to stop twitching. It was as if there were an electrical disturbance in my entire system, and I might have a heart attack or a stroke. Taking deep, slow breaths, I blanked out my mind. I did not move. When the vision had passed, I rang for the nurse.

When she saw the look on my face, she did not argue about the phone. She brought it right away and I called Marino after she left.

'You still in jail?' he said over the line.

'I think he killed his guinea pig,' I said.

'Whoa. How 'bout starting over again.'

'Deadoc. The woman he shot and dismembered may have been his guinea pig. Someone he knew and had easy access to.'

'I gotta confess, Doc, I got no idea what the hell you're

221

talking about.' I could tell by his tone he was worried about my state of mind.

'It makes sense that he couldn't look at her. The M.O. makes a lot of sense.'

'Now you really got me confused.'

'If you wanted to find a way to murder people through a virus,' I explained, 'first you would have to figure out a way. The route of transmission, for example. Is it a food, a drink, dust? With smallpox, transmission is airborne, spread by droplets or by fluid from the lesions. The disease can be carried on a person or his clothes.'

'Start with this,' he said. 'Where did this person get the virus to begin with? Not exactly something you order through the mail.'

'I don't know. To my knowledge there are only two places in the world that keep archival smallpox. CDC and a laboratory in Moscow.'

'So maybe this is all a Russian plot,' he said, sardonically.

'Let me give you a scenario,' I said. 'The killer has a grudge, maybe even some delusion that he has a religious calling to bring back one of the worst diseases this planet has ever known. He's got to figure out a way to randomly infect people and be sure that it can work.'

'So he needs a guinea pig,' Marino said.

'Yes. And let's suppose he has a neighbor, a relative, someone elderly and not well. Maybe he even takes care of her. What better way to test the virus than on that person? And if it works, you kill her and stage her death to look like something else. After all, he certainly can't have her die of smallpox. Not if there is a connection between him and her. We might figure out who he is. So he shoots her in the head, dismembers her so we'll think it's the serial killings again.'

'Then how do you get from that to the lady on Tangier?'

'She was exposed,' I simply said.

'How? Was something delivered to her? Did she get something in the mail? Was it carried on the air? Was she pricked in her sleep?'

'I don't know how.'

'You think deadoc lives on Tangier?' Marino then asked.

'No, I don't,' I said. 'I think he picked it because the island is the perfect place to start an epidemic. Small, self-contained. Also easy to quarantine, meaning the killer doesn't intend to annihilate all of society with one blow. He's trying a little bit at a time, cutting us up in small pieces.'

'Yeah. Like he did the old lady, if you're right.'

'He wants something,' I said. 'Tangier is an attention-getter.'

'No offense, Doc, but I hope you're wrong about all of this.'

'I'm heading to Atlanta in the morning. How about checking with Vander, see if he's had any luck with the thumb-print.'

'So far he hasn't. It's looking like the victim doesn't have any prints on file. Anything comes up, I'll call your pager.'

'Damn,' I muttered, for the nurse had taken that, too.

The rest of the day moved interminably slowly, and it wasn't until after supper that Fujitsubo came to say goodbye. Although the act of releasing me implied I was neither infected nor infectious, he was in a blue suit, which he plugged into an air line.

'I should keep you longer,' he said right off, filling my heart with dread. 'Incubation, on average, is twelve to thirteen days. But it can be as long as twenty-one. What I'm saying to you is that you could still get sick.'

'I understand that,' I said, reaching for my water.

'The revaccination may or may not help depending on what stage you were in when I gave it to you.'

I nodded. 'And I wouldn't be in such a hurry to leave if you would just take this on instead of sending me to CDC.'

'Kay, I can't.' His voice was muffled through plastic. 'You know it has nothing to do with what I feel like doing. But I can no more pull something out from under CDC than you can grab a case that isn't your jurisdiction. I've talked to them. They are most concerned over a possible outbreak and will begin testing the moment you arrive with the samples.'

'I fear terrorism may be involved.' I refused to back down.

'Until there is evidence of it – and I hope there won't be – we can do nothing more for you here.' His regret was sincere. 'Go to Atlanta and see what they have to say. They're operating with a skeleton crew, too. The timing couldn't be worse.'

'Or perhaps more deliberate,' I said. 'If you were a bad person planning to commit serial crimes with a virus, what better time than when the significant federal health agencies are in extremis? And this furlough's been going on for a while and not predicted to end anytime soon.'

He was silent.

'John,' I went on, 'you helped with the autopsy. Have you ever seen a disease like this?'

'Only in textbooks,' he grimly replied.

'How does smallpox suddenly just reappear on its own?'

'If that's what it is.'

'Whatever it is, it's virulent and it kills,' I tried to reason with him.

But he could do nothing more, and the rest of the night I wandered from room to room in AOL. Every hour, I checked my e-mail. Deadoc remained silent until six o'clock the next morning when he walked into the M.E. room. My heart jumped as his name appeared on screen. My adrenaline began to pump the way it always did when he talked to me. He was on the line, it was up to me. I could catch him, if only I could trip him.

DEADOC:	Sunday I went to church bet you didn't
SCARPETTA:	What was the homily about?
DEADOC:	sermon
SCARPETTA:	You are not Catholic.
DEADOC:	beware of men
SCARPETTA:	Matthew 10. Tell me what you mean.
DEADOC:	to say he s sorry
SCARPETTA:	Who is he? And what did he do?
DEADOC:	ye shall indeed drink of the cup that I drink of

Before I could answer, he was gone, and I began flipping through the Bible. The verse he quoted this time was from Mark, and again, it was Jesus speaking, which hinted to me, if nothing else, that deadoc wasn't Jewish. Nor was he Catholic, based on his comments about church. I was no theologian, but drinking of the cup seemed to refer to Christ's eventual crucifixion. So deadoc had been crucified and I would be, too?

It was my last few hours here and my nurse, Sally, was more liberal with the phone. I paged Lucy, who called me back almost instantly.

'I'm talking to him,' I said. 'Are you guys there?'

'We're there. He's got to stay on longer,' my niece said. 'There are so many trunk lines, and we got to line up all the phone companies to trap and trace. Your last call was coming in from Dallas.'

'You're kidding,' I said in dismay.

'That's not the origin, just a switch it was routed through. We didn't get any farther because he disconnected. Keep trying. Sounds like this guy's some kind of religious nut.'

LATER THAT MORNING I left in a taxi as the
sun was getting high in the clouds. I had nothing
but the clothes on my back, all of which had been
sterilized in the autoclave or gassed. I was in
a hurry, and guarding a large white cardboard box printed
with PERISHABLE RUSH! RUSH! and IMPORTANT KEEP
UPRIGHT and other big blue warnings.

Like a Chinese puzzle, my package was boxes within
boxes containing BioPacks. Inside these were Bio-tubes of
Lila Pruitt's liver, spleen and spinal fluid, protected by
fiber-board shields, and bubble and corrugated wrap. All
of it was packed in dry ice with INFECTIOUS SUBSTANCE
and DANGER stickers warning anyone who got beyond

the first layer. Obviously, I could not let my cargo out of sight. In addition to its well-proven hazard, it could be evidence should it turn out that Pruitt was a homicide. At the Baltimore-Washington International airport, I found a pay phone and called Rose.

'USAMRIID has my medical bag and microscope.' I didn't waste time. 'See what you can do about getting them shipped overnight. I'm at BWI, en route to CDC.'

'I've been trying to page you,' she said.

'Maybe they can return that to me, too.' I tried to remember what else I was missing. 'And the phone,' I added.

'You got a report back that you might find interesting. The animal hairs that turned up with the torso. Rabbit and monkey hairs.'

'Bizarre,' was the only thing I could think to say.

'I hate to tell you this news. The media's been calling about the Carrie Grethen case. Apparently, something's been leaked.'

'Goddamn it!' I exclaimed as I thought about Ring.

'What do you want me to do?' she asked.

'How about calling Benton. I don't know what to say. I'm a little overwhelmed.'

'You sound that way.'

I looked at my watch. 'Rose, I've got to go fight my way on a plane. They didn't want to let me through X-ray, and I know what's going to happen when I try to board with this thing.'

It was exactly what I expected. When I walked into the cabin, a flight attendant took one look and smiled.

'Here.' She held out her hands. 'Let me put this in baggage for you.'

'It's got to stay with me,' I said.

'It won't fit in an overhead rack or under your seat, ma'am.' Her smile got tight, the line behind me getting longer.

'Can we discuss this out of traffic?' I said, moving into the kitchen.

She was right next to me, hovering close. 'Ma'am, this flight is overbooked. We simply don't have room.'

'Here,' I said, showing her the paperwork.

Her eyes scanned the red-bordered Declaration For Dangerous Goods, and froze halfway down a column where it was typed that I was transporting 'Infectious substances affecting humans.' She glanced nervously around the kitchen and moved me closer to the rest rooms.

'Regulations require that only a trained person can handle dangerous goods like these,' I reasonably explained. 'So it has to stay with me.'

'What is it?' she whispered, her eyes round.

'Autopsy specimens.'

'Mother of God.'

She immediately grabbed her seating chart. Soon after, I was escorted to an empty row in first class, near the back.

'Just put it on the seat next to you. It's not going to leak or anything?' she asked.

'I'll guard it with my life,' I promised.

'We should have a lot of vacancies up here unless a bunch of people upgrade. But don't you worry. I'll steer everyone.' She motioned with her arms, as if she were driving.

No one came near me or my box. I drank coffee during a very peaceful flight to Atlanta, feeling naked without my pager or phone, but overjoyed to be on my own. In the Atlanta airport, I took one moving sidewalk and escalator after another, traveling what seemed miles, before I got outside and found a taxi.

We followed 85 North to Druid Hills Road, where soon we were passing pawnshops and auto rentals, then vast jungles of poison oak and kudzu, and strip malls. The Center for Disease Control and Prevention was in the midst of the parking decks and parking lots of Emory University. Across the street from the American Cancer Society, CDC was six floors of tan brick trimmed with gray. I checked in at a desk that had guards and closed circuit TV.

'This is going to Bio Level 4, where I'm meeting Dr Bret Martin in the atrium,' I explained.

'Ma'am, you'll need an escort,' one of the guards said.

'Good,' I said as he reached for the phone. 'I always get lost.'

I followed him to the back of the building, where the facility was new and under intense surveillance. There were cameras everywhere, the glass bulletproof, and corridors were catwalks with grated floors. We passed bacteria and influenza labs, and the red brick and concrete area for rabies and AIDS.

'This is impressive,' I said, for I had not been here in several years.

'Yeah, it is. They got all the security you might want. Cameras, motion detectors at all exits and entrances. All the trash is boiled and burned, and they use these filters for the air so anything that comes in is killed. Except the scientists.' He laughed as he used a card key to open a door. 'So what bad news you carrying in?'

'That's what I'm here to find out,' I said, and we were in the atrium now.

BL-4 was really nothing more than a huge laminar flow

hood with thick walls of concrete and steel. It was a building within a building, its windows covered with blinds. Labs were behind thick walls of glass, and the only blue-suited scientists working this furloughed day were those who had cared enough to come in anyway.

'This thing with the government,' the guard was saying as he shook his head. 'What they think? These diseases like Ebola gonna wait until the budget gets straight?' He shook his head some more.

He escorted me past containment rooms that were dark, and labs with no one in them, then empty rabbit cages in a corridor and rooms for large primates. A monkey looked at me through bars and glass, his eyes so human they unnerved me, and I thought of what Rose had said. Deadoc had transferred monkey and rabbit hairs to a victim I knew he had touched. He might work in a place like this.

'They throw waste at you,' the guard said as we walked on. 'Same thing their animal rights activists do. Kinda fits, don't you think?'

My anxiety was getting stronger.

'Where are we going?' I asked.

'Where the good doctor told me to bring you, ma'am,' he said, and we were on another level of catwalk now, heading into another part of the building.

We passed through a door, where Revco ultra low temperature freezers looked like computers the size of large copying machines. They were locked and out of place in this corridor, where a heavy man in a lab coat was waiting for me. He had baby-fine blond hair, and was perspiring.

'I'm Bret Martin,' he said, offering me his hand. 'Thanks.' He nodded at the guard, indicating he was dismissed.

I handed Martin my cardboard box.

'This is where we keep our smallpox stock,' he said, nodding at the freezers as he set my box on top of one of them. 'Locked up at seventy degrees centigrade below zero. What can I say?' He shrugged. 'These freezers are out in the hall because we have no room anyplace else in maximum containment. Rather coincidental you should give this to me. Not that I'm expecting your disease to be the same.'

'All of this is smallpox?' I asked, amazed as I looked around.

'Not all, and not for long, though, since for the first time ever on this planet we've made a conscious decision to eliminate a species.'

'The irony,' I said. 'When the species you're talking about has eliminated millions.'

'So you think we should just take all this source disease and autoclave it.'

His expression said what I was used to hearing. Life was much more complicated than I presented it, and only people like him recognized the subtler shades.

'I'm not saying we should destroy anything,' I replied. 'Not at all. Actually, probably we shouldn't. Because of this.' I looked at the box I had just given him. 'Our autoclaving smallpox certainly won't mean it's gone. I guess it's like any other weapon.'

'You and me both. I'd sure like to know where the Russians are hiding their variola stock virus these days, and if they've sold any of it to the Middle East, North Korea.'

'You'll do PCR on this?' I said.

'Yes.'

'Right away?'

'As fast as we can.'

'Please,' I said. 'This is an emergency.'

'That's why I'm standing here now,' he said. 'The government considers me nonessential. I should be at home.'

'I've got photographs that USAMRIID was kind enough to develop while I was in the Slammer,' I said with a trace of irony.

'I want to see them.'

We took the elevator back up, getting off on the fourth floor. He led me into a conference room where staff met to devise strategies against terrible scourges they couldn't always identify. Usually bacteriologists, epidemiologists, people in charge of quarantines, communications, special pathogens and PCR assembled in the room. But it was quiet, no one was here but us.

'Right now,' Martin said, 'I'm all you've got.'

I got a thick envelope out of my purse, and he began to go through the photographs. For a moment, he stared as if transfixed, at color prints of the torso and those of Lila Pruitt.

'Good God,' he said. 'I think we should look at transpiration routes right away. Everybody who might have had contact. And I mean, fast.'

'We can do that on Tangier,' I said. 'Maybe.'

'Definitely not chicken pox or measles. No way, Jose,' he said. 'Definitely pox-related.'

He went through photographs of the severed hands and feet, his eyes wide.

'Wow.' He stared without blinking, light reflecting on his glasses. 'What the hell is this?'

'He calls himself deadoc,' I said. 'He sent me graphic files through AOL. Anonymously, of course. The FBI's trying to track him.'

'And this victim here, he dismembered?'

I nodded.

'She also has manifestations similar to the victim on Tangier.' He was looking at vesicles on the torso.

'So far, yes.'

'You know, monkeypox has been worrying me for years,' he said. 'We survey the hell out of West Africa, from Zaire to Sierra Leone, where cases have occurred, along with whitepox. But so far, no variola virus has turned up. My fear, though, is that one of these days, some poxvirus in the animal kingdom is going to figure out a way to infect people.'

Again, I thought about my telephone conversation with Rose, about murder and animal hairs.

'All that's got to happen is the microorganism gets in the air, let's say, and finds a susceptible host.'

He went back to Lila Pruitt, to her disfigured, tormented body on her foul bed.

'Now she was obviously exposed to enough virus to cause devastating disease,' he said, and he was so engrossed, he seemed to be talking to himself.

'Dr Martin,' I said. 'Do monkeys get monkeypox or are they just the carrier?'

'They get it and they give it where there is animal contact, such as in the rain forests of Africa. There are nine known virulent poxviruses on this planet and transmission to humans happens only in two. The variola virus, or smallpox, which, thank God, we don't see anymore, and molluscum contagiosum.'

'Trace evidence clinging to the torso has been identified as monkey hair.'

He turned to look at me and frowned. 'What?'

'And rabbit hair, too. I'm just wondering if someone out there is conducting their own laboratory experiments.'

He got up from the table.

'We'll start on this now. Where can you be reached?'

'Back in Richmond.' I handed him my card as we walked out of the conference room. 'Could someone maybe call for a taxi?'

'Sure. One of the guards at the desk. Afraid none of the clerical staff is in.'

Carrying the box, he pushed the elevator button with his elbow. 'It's a nightmare. We got salmonella in Orlando from unpasteurized orange juice, another potential cruise ship outbreak of E. coli O-one-five-seven-H-seven, probably undercooked ground beef again. Botulism in Rhode Island, and some respiratory disease in an old folks' home. And Congress doesn't want to fund us.'

'Tell me about it,' I said.

We stopped at each floor, waiting as other people got on. Martin kept talking.

'Imagine this,' he went on. 'A resort in Iowa where we've got suspected shigella because a lot of rain overflowed in private wells. And try to get the EPA involved.'

'It's called *mission impossible*,' someone sardonically said as the doors opened again.

'If they even exist anymore,' Martin quipped. 'We get fourteen thousand calls a year and have only two operators. Actually, right now we got none. Anybody who comes in, answers the phone. Including me.'

'Please don't let this wait,' I said as we reached the lobby.

'Don't worry.' He was into it. 'I got three guys I'm calling in from home right away.'

For half an hour, I waited in the lobby and used a phone, and at last my taxi was here. I rode in silence, staring out at plazas of polished granite and marble, and sports complexes that reminded me of the Olympics, and buildings of silver and glass. Atlanta was a city where everything aspired higher, and lavish fountains seemed a symbol of generosity and no fear. I was feeling light-headed and chilled and unusually tired for one who had just spent the better part of a week in bed. By the time I reached my Delta gate, my back had begun to ache. I could not get warm or think very clearly, and I knew I had a fever.

I was ill by the time I reached Richmond. When Marino met me at the gate, the expression on his face turned to abject fear.

'Geez, Doc,' he said. 'You look like hell.'

'I feel like hell.'

'You got any bags?'

'No. You got any news?'

'Yeah,' he said. 'One tidbit that will piss you off. Ring arrested Keith Pleasants last night.'

'For what?' I exclaimed as I coughed.

'Attempting to elude. Supposedly, Ring was following him out of the landfill after work and tried to pull him for speeding. Supposedly, Pleasants wouldn't stop. So he's in jail, bond set at five grand, if you can believe that. He ain't going nowhere anytime soon.'

'Harassment.' I blew my nose. 'Ring is picking on him. Picking on Lucy. Picking on me.'

'No kidding. Maybe you should've stayed in Maryland, in bed,' he said as we boarded the escalator. 'No offense, but I ain't gonna catch this, am I?'

Marino was terrified of anything he could not see, whether it was radiation or a virus.

'I don't know what I've got,' I said. 'Maybe the flu.'

'Last time I got that I was out for two weeks.' His pace

slowed, so he did not keep up with me. 'Plus, you been around other things.'

'Then don't come close, touch or kiss me,' I said, shortly.

'Hey, don't worry.'

This continued as we walked out into the cold afternoon.

'Look. I'm going to take a taxi home,' I said and I was so mad at him I was next to tears.

'I don't want you doing that.' Marino looked frightened and was jumpy.

I waved in the air, swallowing hard and hiding my face as a Blue Bird cab veered toward me.

'You don't need the flu. Rose doesn't need it. No one needs it,' I said, furiously. 'You know, I'm almost out of cash. This is awful. Look at my suit. You think an autoclave presses anything and leaves a pleasant smell? The hell with my hose. I got no coat, no gloves. Here I am, and it's what?' I yanked open the back door of a cab that was Carolina blue. 'Thirty degrees?'

Marino stared at me as I got in. He handed me a twenty-dollar bill, careful his fingers did not brush mine.

'You need anything at the store?' he called out as I drove off.

My throat and eyes swelled with tears. Digging tissues out of my purse, I blew my nose and quietly wept.

'Don't mean to bug ya, lady,' said my driver, a portly old man. 'But where are we going?'

'Windsor Farms. I'll show you when we get there,' I choked as I said.

'Fights.' He shook his head. 'Dontcha hate 'em? I 'member one time me and the wife got to arguing in one these all-you-can-eat fish camps. She takes the car. Me, I take a hike. Five miles home through a bad part of town.'

He was nodding, eyeing me in the rearview mirror as he assumed that Marino and I were having a lovers' quarrel.

'So, you're married to a cop?' he then said. 'I saw him drive in. Not an unmarked car on the road that can fool this guy.' He thumped his chest.

My head was splitting, my face burning. I settled back in the seat and shut my eyes while he droned on about an earlier life in Philadelphia, and his hopes that this winter would not bring much snow. I settled into a feverish sleep. When I awoke, I did not know where I was.

'Ma'am. Ma'am. We're here,' the driver was saying loudly to wake me up. 'Where to next?'

He had just turned onto Canterbury and was sitting at a stop sign.

'Up here, take a right on Dover,' I replied.

I directed him into my neighborhood, the look on his face increasingly baffled as he drove past Georgian and Tudor estates behind walls in the city's wealthiest neighborhood. When he stopped at my front door, he stared at fieldstone, at the wooded land around my home, and he watched me closely as I climbed out.

'Don't worry,' he said as I handed him a twenty and told him to keep the change. 'I seen it all lady, and never say nothing.' He zipped his lips, winking at me.

I was a rich man's wife having a tempestuous affair with a detective.

'A good credo,' I said, coughing.

The burglar alarm welcomed me with its warning beep, and never in my life had I been more relieved to be home. I wasted no time getting out of my scalded clothes, and straight into a hot shower, where I inhaled steam and tried to clear the rattle from my lungs. When I was wrapping up in a thick terry cloth robe, the telephone rang. It was exactly four P.M.

'Dr Scarpetta?' It was Fielding.

'I just got home,' I said.

'You don't sound good.'

'I'm not.'

'Well, my news isn't going to help,' he said. 'They've got possibly two more cases on Tangier.'

'Oh no,' I said.

'A mother and daughter. Fever of a hundred and five, a rash. CDC's deployed a team with bed isolators, the whole nine yards.'

'How's Wingo?' I asked.

He paused, as if puzzled. 'Fine. Why?'

'He helped with the torso,' I reminded him.

'Oh yeah. Well, he's the same as always.'

Relieved, I sat down and shut my eyes.

'What's going on with the samples you took to Atlanta?' Fielding asked.

'They're doing tests, I hope, with what few people they can muster now.'

'So we still don't know what this is.'

'Jack, everything points to smallpox,' I said to him. 'That's the way it looks so far.'

'I've never seen it. Have you?'

'Not before now. Maybe leprosy is worse. It's bad enough to die of a disease, but to be disfigured in the process is cruel.' I coughed again and was very thirsty. 'I'll see you in the morning, and we'll figure out what we're going to do.'

'It doesn't sound to me like you should be going any-where.'

'You're absolutely right. And I don't have a choice.'

I hung up and tried Bret Martin at CDC, but his phone was answered by voice mail, and he did not call me back. I also left a message for Fujitsubo, but he did not return my call, either, and I figured he was at home, like most of his colleagues. The budget war raged on.

'Damn,' I swore as I put a kettle of water on the stove and dug in a cupboard for tea. 'Damn, damn, damn.'

It was not quite five when I called Wesley. At Quantico, at least, people were still working.

'Thank God someone is answering the phones somewhere,' I blurted out to his secretary.

'They haven't figured out how nonessential I am yet,' she said.

'Is he in?' I asked.

Wesley got on the phone, and sounded so energetic and cheery that it instantly got on my nerves.

'You have no right to feel this good,' I said.

'You have the flu.'

'I don't know what I've got.'

'That's what it is, right?' He was worried and his mood went bad.

'I don't know. We can only assume.'

'I don't mean to be an alarmist . . .'

'Then don't,' I cut him off.

'Kay,' his voice was firm. 'You've got to face this. What if it's not?'

I said nothing because I could not bear to think such thoughts.

'Please,' he said. 'Don't blow this off. Don't pretend it's nothing like you do with most things in your life.'

'Now you're making me mad,' I snapped. 'I fly into this goddamn airport and Marino doesn't want me in his car so

I take a taxi and the driver thinks we're having an affair and my rich husband doesn't know, and all the while I have a fever and hurt like hell and just want to go home.'

'The taxi driver thinks you're having an affair?'

'Just forget it.'

'How do you know you've got the flu? That it's not something else?'

'I don't have a rash. Is that what you want to hear?'

There was a long silence. Then he said, 'What if you get one?'

'Then I'm probably going to die, Benton.' I coughed again. 'You'll probably never touch me again. And I'd never want you to see me again, if it goes its course. It's easier to worry about stalkers, serial killers, people you can blow away with a gun. But the invisible ones are who I've always feared. They take you on a sunny day in a public place. They slide in with your lemonade. I've been vaccinated for hepatitis B. But that's just one killer in a huge population. What about tuberculosis and HIV, and Hanta and Ebola? What about this? God.' I took a deep breath. 'It started with a torso and I did not know.'

'I heard about the two new cases,' he said, and his voice had gotten quiet and gentle. 'I can be there in two hours. Do you want to see me?'

'Right now I don't want to see anyone.'

'Doesn't matter. I'm on my way.'

'Benton,' I said, 'don't.'

But he had his mind made up, and when he pulled into my driveway in his throaty BMW, it was almost midnight. I met him at the door, and we did not touch.

'Let's sit in front of the fire,' he said.

We did, and he was kind enough to make me another cup

241

of decaffeinated tea. I sat on the couch, he was in a side chair, and flames fed by gas enveloped an artificial log. I had turned the lights low.

'I don't doubt your theory,' he said as he lingered over cognac.

'Maybe tomorrow, we'll know more.' I was perspiring as I shivered, staring into the fire.

'Right now I don't give a shit about any of that.' He looked fiercely at me.

'You have to give a shit about that.' I wiped my brow with a sleeve.

'No.'

I was silent as he stared at me.

'What I care about is you,' he said.

Still, I did not respond.

'Kay.' He gripped my arm.

'Don't touch me, Benton.' I shut my eyes. 'Don't. I don't want you sick, too.'

'See, and that's convenient for you. To be sick. And I can't touch you. And you the noble doctor caring more about my well-being than your own.'

I was quiet, determined not to cry.

'Convenient. You want to be sick right now so nobody can get close. Marino won't even give you a ride home. And I can't put my hands on you. And Lucy won't see you and Janet has to talk to you behind glass.'

'What is your point?' I looked at him.

'Functional illness.'

'Oh. I guess you studied that in school. Maybe during your master's in psychology or something.'

'Don't make fun of me.'

'I never have.'

I could feel his hurt as I turned my face to the fire, my eyes closed tight.

'Kay. Don't you die on me.'

I did not speak.

'Don't you dare.' His voice shook. 'Don't you dare!'

'You won't get off the hook that easy,' I said, getting out of my chair. 'Let's go to bed.'

He slept in the room where Lucy usually stayed, and I was up most of the night coughing and trying to get comfortable, which simply was not possible. The next morning at half past six he was up, and coffee was brewing when I walked into the kitchen. Light filtered through trees beyond windows, and I could tell by the tight curl of rhododendron leaves that it was bitterly cold.

'I'm cooking,' Wesley announced. 'What will it be?'

'I don't think I can.' I was weak, and when I coughed, it felt as if my lungs were ripping.

'Obviously, you are worse.' Concern flickered in his eyes. 'You should go to a doctor.'

'I am a doctor, and it's too soon to go to one.'

I took aspirin, decongestants and a thousand milligrams of vitamin C. I ate a bagel and was beginning to feel almost human when Rose called and ruined me.

'Dr Scarpetta? The mother from Tangier died early this morning.'

'Oh God no.' I was sitting at the kitchen table and running my fingers through my hair. 'What about the daughter?'

'Condition's serious. Or at least it was several hours ago.'

'And the body?'

Wesley was behind me, rubbing my sore shoulders and neck.

'No one's moved it yet. No one's sure what to do, and

the Baltimore Medical Examiner's Office has been trying to reach you. So has CDC.'

'Who at CDC?' I asked.

'A Dr Martin.'

'I need to call him first, Rose. Meanwhile, you get hold of Baltimore and tell them that under no circumstances are they to have that body sent into their morgue until they've heard from me. What is Dr Martin's number?'

She gave it to me and I dialed it immediately. He answered on the first ring and sounded keyed up.

'We did PCR on the samples you brought in. Three primers and two of them match with smallpox, but one of them didn't.'

'Then is it smallpox or not?'

'We ran its genomic sequence, and it doesn't match up with any poxvirus in any reference lab in the world. Dr Scarpetta, I believe you got a virus that's a mutant.'

'Meaning, the smallpox vaccination isn't going to work,' I said as my heart seemed to drop right out of me.

'All we can do is test in the animal lab. We're talking at least a week before we know and can even begin thinking about a new vaccine. For practical purposes, we're calling this smallpox, but we really don't know what the hell it is. I'll also remind you we've been working on an AIDS vaccine since 1986 and are no closer now than we were back then.'

'Tangier Island needs to be quarantined immediately. We've got to contain this,' I exclaimed, alarmed to the edge of panic.

'Believe me, we know. We're getting a team together right now and will mobilize the Coast Guard.'

I hung up and was frantic when I said to Wesley, 'I've got to go. We've got an outbreak of something no one's ever

244

heard of. It's already killed at least two people. Maybe three. Maybe four.'

He was following me down the hall as I talked.

'It's smallpox but not smallpox. We've got to find out how it's being transmitted. Did Lila Pruitt know the mother who just died? Did they have any contact at all, or did the daughter? Did they even live near each other? What about the water supply? A water tower. Blue. I remember seeing one.'

I was getting dressed. Wesley stood in the doorway, his face almost gray and like stone.

'You're going to go back out there,' he said.

'I need to get downtown first.' I looked at him.

'I'll drive,' he said.

W ESLEY DROPPED ME off and said he was going to the Richmond Field Office for a while and would check with me later. My heels were loud as I walked down the corridor, bidding good morning to members of my staff. Rose was on the phone when I walked in, and the glimpse of my desk through her adjoining doorway was devastating. Hundreds of reports and death certificates awaited my initials and signature, and mail and phone messages were cascading out of my in-basket.

'What is this?' I said as she hung up. 'You'd think I've been gone a year.'

'It feels like you have.'

She was rubbing lotion into her hands and I noticed the small canister of Vita aromatherapy facial spray on the edge of my desk, the open mailing tube next to it. There was also one on Rose's desk, next to her bottle of Vaseline Intensive Care. I stared back and forth, from my Vita spray to hers, my subconscious processing what I was seeing before my reason did. Reality seemed to turn inside out, and I grabbed the door frame. Rose was on her feet, her chair flying back on its rollers as she lunged around her desk for me.

'Dr Scarpetta!'

'Where did you get this?' I asked, staring at the spray.

'It's just a sample.' She looked bewildered. 'A bunch of them came in the mail.'

'Have you used it?'

Now she was really worried as she looked at me. 'Well, it just got here. I haven't tried it yet.'

'Don't touch it!' I said, severely. 'Who else got one?'

'Gosh, I really don't know. What is it? What's wrong?' She raised her voice.

Getting gloves from my office, I grabbed the facial spray off her desk and triple-bagged it.

'Everybody in the conference room, now!'

I ran down the hall to the front office, and made the same announcement. Within minutes, my entire staff, including doctors still in scrubs, was assembled. Some people were out of breath, and everyone was staring at me, unnerved and frazzled.

I held up the transparent evidence bag containing the sample size of Vita spray.

'Who has one of these?' I asked, looking around the room.

Four people raised their hands.

'Who has used it?' I then asked. 'I need to know if absolutely anybody has.'

Cleta, a clerk from the front office, looked frightened. 'Why? What's the matter?'

'Have you sprayed this on your face,' I said to her.

'On my plants,' she said.

'Plants get bagged and burned,' I said. 'Where's Wingo?'

'MCV.'

'I don't know this for a fact,' I spoke to everyone, 'and I pray I'm wrong. But we might be dealing with product tampering. Please don't panic, but under no circumstances does anyone touch this spray. Do we know exactly how they were delivered?'

It was Cleta who spoke. 'This morning I came in before anybody up front. There were police reports shoved through the slot, as always. And these had been, too. They were in little mailing tubes. There were eleven of them. I know because I counted to see if there was enough to go around.'

'And the mailman didn't bring them. They had just been shoved through the slot of the front door.'

'I don't know who brought them. But they looked like they'd been mailed.'

'Any tubes you still have, please bring them to me,' I said.

I was told that no one had used one, and all were collected and brought to my office. Putting on cotton gloves and glasses, I studied the mailing tube meant for me. Postage was bulk rate and clearly a manufacturer's sample, and I found it most unusual for something like that to be addressed to a specific individual. I looked inside the tube, and there was a coupon for the spray. As I held it up to the light, I noticed edges imperceptibly uneven,

249

as if the coupon had been clipped with scissors versus a machine.

'Rose?' I called out.

She walked into my office.

'The tube you got,' I said. 'Who was it addressed to?'

'Resident, I think.' Her face was stressed.

'Then the only one with a name on it is mine.'

'I think so. This is awful.'

'Yes, it is.' I picked up the mailing tube. 'Look at this. Letters all the same size, the postmark on the same label as the address. I've never seen that.'

'Like it came off a computer,' she said as her amazement grew.

'I'm going across the street to the DNA lab.' I got up. 'Call USAMRIID right away and tell Colonel Fujitsubo we need to schedule a conference call between him, us, CDC, Quantico, now.'

'Where do you want to do it?' she asked as I hurried out the door.

'Not here. See what Benton says.'

Outside, I ran down the sidewalk past my parking lot, and crossed Fourteenth Street. I entered the Seaboard Building where DNA and other forensic labs had relocated several years before. At the security desk, I called the section chief, Dr Douglas Wheat, who had been given a male family name, despite her gender.

'I need a closed air system and a hood,' I explained to her.

'Come on back.'

A long sloping hallway always polished bright led to a series of glass-enclosed laboratories. Inside, scientists were prepossessed with pipettes and gels and radioactive probes as they coaxed sequences of genetic code to unravel their

250

identities. Wheat, who battled paperwork almost as much as I did, was sitting at her desk, typing something on her computer. She was an attractive woman in a strong way, forty and friendly.

'What trouble are you getting into this time?' She smiled at me, then eyed my bag. 'I'm afraid to ask.'

'Possible product tampering,' I said. 'I need to spray some on a slide, but it absolutely can't get in the air or on me or anyone.'

'What is it?' She was very somber now, getting up.

'Possibly a virus.'

'As in the one on Tangier?'

'That's my fear.'

'You don't think it might be wiser to get this to CDC, let them . . .'

'Douglas, yes, it would be wiser,' I patiently explained as I coughed again. 'But we haven't got time. I've got to know. We have no idea how many of these might be in the hands of consumers.'

Her DNA lab had a number of closed air system hoods surrounded by glass bioguards, because the evidence tested here was blood. She led me to one in the back of a room, and we put on masks and gloves, and she gave me a lab coat. She turned on a fan that sucked air up into the hood, passing it through HEPA filters.

'Ready?' I asked, taking the facial spray out of the bag. 'We'll make this quick.'

I held a clean slide and the small canister under the hood and sprayed.

'Let's dip this in a ten percent bleach solution,' I said when I was done. 'Then we'll triple bag it, get it and the other ten off to Atlanta.'

'Coming up,' Wheat said, walking off.

The slide took almost no time to dry, and I dripped Nicolaou stain on it and sealed it with a cover slip. I was already looking at it under a microscope when Wheat returned with a container of bleach solution. She dipped the Vita spray in it several times while fears coalesced, rolling into a dark, awful thunderhead as my pulse throbbed in my neck. I peered at the Guarnieri bodies I had come to dread.

When I looked up at Wheat, she could tell by the expression on my face.

'Not good,' she said.

'Not good.' I turned off the microscope and dropped my mask and gloves into biohazardous waste.

The Vita sprays from my office were airlifted to Atlanta, and a preliminary warning was broadcast nationwide to anyone who might have had such a sample delivered to them. The manufacturer had issued an immediate recall, and international airlines were removing the sprays from overseas travel bags given to business and first-class passengers. The potential spread of this disease, should deadoc have somehow tampered with hundreds, thousands of the facial sprays, was staggering. We could, once again, find ourselves facing a worldwide epidemic.

The meeting took place at one P.M. in the FBI's field office off Staples Mill Road. State and federal flags fought from tall poles out front as a sharp wind tore brown leaves off trees and made the afternoon seem much colder than it was. The brick building was new, and had a secure conference room equipped with audio-visual capabilities, so we could see remote people while we talked to them. A young female

252

agent sat at the head of the table, at a console. Wesley and I pulled out chairs and moved microphones close. Above us on walls were video monitors.

'Who else are we expecting?' Wesley asked as the special agent in charge, or S.A.C., walked in with an armload of paperwork.

'Miles,' said the S.A.C., referring to the Health Commissioner, my immediate boss. 'And the Coast Guard.' He glanced at his paperwork. 'Regional chief out of Crisfield, Maryland. A chopper's bringing him in. Shouldn't take him more than thirty minutes in one of those big birds.'

He had no sooner said this than we could hear blades thudding faintly in the distance. Minutes later, the Jayhawk was thundering overhead and settling in the helipad behind the building. I could not remember a Coast Guard recovery helicopter ever landing in our city or even flying over it low, and the sight of it must have been awesome to people on the road. Chief Martinez was slipping off his coat as he joined us. I noted his dark blue commando sweater and uniform pants, and maps rolled up in tubes, and the situation only got grimmer.

The agent at the console was working controls as Commissioner Miles strode in and took a chair next to mine. He was an older man with abundant gray hair that was more contentious than most of the people he managed. Today, tufts were sticking out in all directions, his brow heavy and stern as he put on thick black glasses.

'You look a little under the weather,' he said to me as he made notes to himself.

'The usual stuff going around,' I said.

'Had I known that, I wouldn't have sat next to you.' He meant it.

'I'm beyond the contagious stage.' I said, but he wasn't listening.

Monitors were coming on around the room, and I recognized the face of Colonel Fujitsubo on one of them. Then Bret Martin blinked on, staring straight at us.

The agent at the console said, 'Camera on. Mikes on. Someone want to count for me.'

'Five-four-three-two-one,' the S.A.C. said into his mike. 'How's that level?'

'Fine here,' Fujitsubo said from Frederick, Maryland.

'Fine,' said Martin from Atlanta.

'We're ready anytime.' The agent at the console glanced around the table.

'Just to make sure all of us are up to speed,' I began. 'We have an outbreak of what appears to be a smallpox-like virus that so far seems to be restricted to the island of Tangier, eighteen miles off the coast of Virginia. Two deaths reported so far, with another person ill. It is also likely that a recent homicide victim was infected with this virus. The mode of transmission is suspected to be the deliberate contamination of samples of Vita aromatherapy facial spray.'

'That hasn't been determined yet.' It was Miles who spoke.

'The samples should be getting here any minute,' Martin said from Atlanta. 'We'll begin testing immediately, and will hopefully have an answer by the end of tomorrow. Meanwhile, they're being taken out of circulation until we know exactly what we're dealing with.'

'You can do PCR to see if it's the same virus,' Miles said to the video screens.

Martin nodded. 'That we can do.'

Miles looked around the room. 'So what are we saying here? We got some loonytune out there, some Tylenol killer who's decided to use a disease? How do we know these little spray bottles aren't the hell all over the place?'

'I think the killer wants to take his time.' Wesley began what he did best. 'He started with one victim. When that paid off, he began on a tiny island. Now that's paying off, so he hits a downtown health department office.' He looked at me. 'He will go to the next stage if we don't stop him or develop a vaccine. Another reason I suspect this is still local, is it appears the facial sprays are hand-delivered, with bogus bulk-rate postage on the tubes to give the appearence that they were mailed.'

'You're definitely calling this product tampering, then,' Colonel Fujitsubo said to him.

'I'm calling this terrorism.'

'The point of it being what?'

'We don't know that yet,' Wesley told him.

'But this is far worse than any Tylenol killer or Unabomber,' I said. 'The destruction they cause is limited to whoever takes the capsules or opens the package. With a virus, it's going to spread far beyond the primary victim.'

'Dr Martin, what can you tell us about this particular virus?' Miles said.

'We have four traditional methods for testing for small-pox.' He stared stiffly at us from his screen. 'Electron micros-copy, with which we have observed a direct visualization of variola.'

'Smallpox?' Miles almost shouted. 'You're sure about that?'

'Hold on,' Martin interrupted him. 'Let me finish. We also got a verification of antigenic identity using agar gel. Now, chick embryo chorioallantoic membrane culture, other tissue cultures are going to take two, three days. So we don't have those results now, but we do have PCR. It verified a pox. We just don't know which one. It's very odd, nothing currently known, not monkeypox, whitepox. Not classic variola major or minor, although it seems to be related.'

'Dr Scarpetta,' Fujitsubo spoke. 'Can you tell me what's in this facial spray, as best you know?'

'Distilled water and a fragrance. There were no ingredients listed, but generally that's what sprays like this are,' I said.

He was making notes. 'Sterile?' He looked back at us from the monitor.

'I would hope so, since the directions encourage you to spray it over your face and contact lenses,' I replied.

'Then my question,' Fujitsubo went on via satellite, 'is what kind of shelf life might we expect these contaminated sprays to have? Variola isn't all that stable in moist conditions.'

'A good point,' Martin said, adjusting his ear piece. 'It does very well when dried, and at room temperature can survive months to a year. It is sensitive to sunlight, but inside the atomizers, that wouldn't be a problem. Doesn't like heat, which, unfortunately, makes this an ideal time of year.'

'Then depending on what people do when they have these delivered,' I said, 'there could be a lot of duds out there.'

'Could be,' Martin hoped.

Wesley said, 'Clearly, the offender we're looking for is knowledgeable of infectious diseases.'

'Has to be,' Fujitsubo said. 'The virus had to be cultured, propagated, and if this is, in fact, terrorism, then the perpetrator is very familiar with basic laboratory techniques. He knew how to handle something like this and keep himself protected. We're assuming only one person is involved?'

'My theory, but the answer is, we don't know,' Wesley said.

'He calls himself *deadoc*,' I said.

'As in Doctor Death?' Fujitsubo frowned. 'He's telling us he's a doctor?'

Again, it was hard to say, but the question that was most troublesome was also the hardest to ask.

'Dr Martin,' I said as Martinez silently leaned back in his chair, listening. 'Allegedly, your facility and a laboratory in Russia are the only two sources of the viral isolates. Any thoughts on how someone got hold of this?'

'Exactly,' Wesley said. 'Unpleasant thought that it may be, we need to check your list of employees. Any recent firings, layoffs? Anybody quit during recent months and years?'

'Our source supply of variola virus is as meticulously monitored and inventoried as plutonium.' Martin answered with confidence. 'I personally have already checked into this and can tell you with certainty that nothing has been tampered with. Nothing is missing. And it is not possible to get into one of the locked freezers without authorization and knowledge of alarm codes.'

No one spoke right away.

Then Wesley said, 'I think it would be a good idea for us to have a list of those people who have had such authorization over the past five years. Initially, based on experience, I am profiling this individual as a white male, possibly in his early forties. Most likely he lives alone, but if he doesn't or he dates, he has a part of his residence that is off limits, his lab . . .'

'So we're probably talking about a former lab worker,' the S.A.C. said.

'Or someone like that,' Wesley said. 'Someone educated,

trained. This person is introverted, and I base this on a number of things, not the least of which is his tendency to write in the lower case. His refusal to use punctuation indicates his belief that he is not like other people and the same rules do not apply to him. He is not talkative and may be considered aloof or shy by associates. He has time on his hands, and most important, feels he has been mistreated by the system. He feels he is due an apology by the highest office in the land, by our government, and I believe this is key to this perpetrator's motivation.'

'Then this is revenge,' I said. 'Plain and simple.'

'It's never plain or simple. I wish it were,' Wesley said. 'But I do think revenge is key, which is why it is important that all government agencies that deal with infectious diseases get us the records of any employees reprimanded, fired, laid off, furloughed or whatever, in recent months and years.'

Fujitsubo cleared his throat. 'Well, let's talk logistics, then.'

It was the Coast Guard's turn to present a plan. Martinez got up from his chair and fastened large maps to flip charts, as camera angles were adjusted so our remote guests could see.

'Can you get these in?' Martinez asked the agent at the console.

'Got them,' she said. 'How about you?' She looked up at the monitors.

'Fine.'

'I don't know. Maybe if you could zoom in more.'

She moved the camera in closer as Martinez got out a laser pointer. He directed its intense pink dot at the Maryland–Virginia line in the Chesapeake Bay that cut through Smith Island, just north of Tangier.

'We got a number of islands going up this way toward Fishing Bay and the Nanticoke River, in Maryland. There's Smith Island. South Marsh Island. Bloodsworth Island.' The pink dot hopped to each one. 'Then we're on the mainland. And you got Crisfield down here, which is only fifteen nautical miles from Tangier.' He looked at us. 'Crisfield's where a lot of watermen bring in their crabs. And a lot of Tangier folks have relatives in Crisfield. I'm real worried about that.'

'And I'm worried that the Tangiermen are not going to cooperate,' Miles said. 'A quarantine is going to cut off their only source of income.'

'Yes, sir,' Martinez said, looking at his watch. 'And we're cutting it off even as we speak. We got boats, cutters coming in from as far away as Elizabeth City to help us circle the island.'

'So as of now, no one's leaving,' Fujitsubo said as his face continued to reign over us from the video screen.

'That's right.'

'Good.'

'What if people resist?' I asked the obvious question. 'What are you going to do with them? You can't take them into custody and risk exposure.'

Martinez hesitated. He looked up at Fujitsubo on the video screen. 'Commander, would you like to field this one, sir?' he asked.

'We've actually already discussed this at great length,' Fujitsubo said to us. 'I have spoken to the secretary of the Department of Transportation, to Vice Admiral Perry, and of course, the Secretary of Defense. Basically, this thing is speeding its way up to the White House for authorization.'

'Authorization for what?' It was Miles who asked.

'To use deadly force, if all else fails,' Martinez said to all of us.

'Christ,' Wesley muttered.

I listened in disbelief, staring up at doomsday gods.

'We have no choice,' Fujitsubo spoke calmly. 'If people panic and start fleeing the island and do not heed Coast Guard warnings, they *will* – not if – but *will* bring smallpox onto the mainland. And we're talking about a population which either has not been vaccinated in thirty years. Or an immunization done so long ago it's no longer effective. Or a disease that has mutated to the extent that our present vaccine is not protective. There isn't a good scenario, in other words.'

I didn't know if I felt sick to my stomach because I wasn't well or because of what I'd just heard. I thought of that weather-beaten fishing village with its leaning headstones and wild, quiet people who just wanted to be left alone. They weren't the sort to obey anyone, for they answered to a higher power of God and storms.

'There must be another way,' I said.

But there wasn't.

'By reputation, smallpox is a highly contagious infectious disease. This outbreak must be contained,' Fujitsubo exclaimed the obvious. 'We've got to worry about houseflies hovering around patients, and crabs headed for the mainland. How do we know we don't have to worry about the possibility of mosquito transmission, as in Tanapox, for God's sake? We don't even know what all we've got to worry about since we can't fully identify the disease yet.'

Martin looked at me. 'We've already got teams out there, nurses, doctors, bed isolators so we can keep these people out of hospitals and leave them in their homes.'

'What about dead bodies, contamination?' I asked him.

'In terms of United States law, this consitutes a Class One public health emergency.'

'I realize that,' I said, impatiently, for he was getting bureaucratic on me. 'Cut to the chase.'

'Burn all but the patient. Bodies will be cremated. The Pruitt house will be torched.'

Fujitsubo tried to reassure us. 'USAMRIID's got a team heading out. We'll be talking to citizens, trying to make them understand.'

I thought of Davy Crockett and his son, of people and their panic when space-suited scientists took over their island and started burning their homes.

'And we know for a fact that the smallpox vaccine isn't going to work?' Wesley said.

'We don't know that for a fact yet.' Martin answered. 'Tests on laboratory animals will take days to weeks. And even if vaccination is protective in an animal model, this may not translate into protection for humans.'

'Since the DNA of the virus has been altered,' Fujitsubo warned, 'I am not hopeful that vaccinia virus will be effective.'

'I'm not a doctor or anything,' Martinez said, 'but I'm just wondering if you could vaccinate everyone anyway, just in case it might work.'

'Too risky,' Martin said. 'If it's not smallpox, why deliberately expose people to smallpox, thereby possibly causing some people to get the disease? And when we develop the new vaccine, we're not going to want to come back several weeks later and vaccinate people again, this time with a different pox.'

'In other words,' Fujitsubo said, 'we can't use the people

of Tangier like laboratory animals. If we keep them on that island and then get a vaccine out to them as soon as possible, we should be able to contain this thing. The good news about smallpox is it's a stupid virus, kills its hosts so fast it will burn itself out if you can keep it restricted to one area.'

'Right. So an entire island gets destroyed while we sit back and watch it burn,' Miles angrily said to me. 'I can't believe this. Goddamn it.' He pounded his fist on the table. 'This can't be happening in Virginia!'

He got out of his chair. 'Gentlemen. I would like to know what we should do if we start getting patients in other parts of this state. The health of Virginia, after all, is what the governor appointed me to take care of.' His face was dark red and he was sweating. 'Are we supposed to just do like the Yankees and start burning down our cities and towns?'

'Should this spread,' Fujitsubo said, 'clearly we'll have to utilize our hospitals, have wards, just as we did during earlier times. CDC and my people are already alerting local medical personnel, and will work with them closely.'

'We realize that hospital personnel are at the greatest risk,' Martin added. 'Sure would be nice if Congress would end this goddamn furlough so I don't have one hand and both legs tied behind my back.'

'Believe me, the president, Congress, knows.'

'Senator Nagle assures me it will end by tomorrow morning.'

'They're always certain, say the same thing every time.'

The swelling and itching of the revaccination site on my arm was a constant reminder that I had been inoculated with a virus probably for nothing. I complained to Wesley all the way out to the parking lot.

'I've been reexposed, and I'm sick with something, meaning I'm probably immunosuppressed, on top of it all.'

'How do you know you don't have it?' he carefully asked.

'I don't know.'

'Then you could be infectious.'

'No, I couldn't be. A rash is the first sign of that, and I check myself daily. At the slightest hint of such a thing, I would go back into isolation. I would not come within one hundred feet of you or anybody else, Benton,' I said, my anger unreasonably spiking at his suggestion that I might risk infecting anyone with even a mundane cold.

He glanced over at me as he unlocked doors, and I knew that he was far more upset than he would let on. 'What do you want me to do, Kay?'

'Take me home so I can get my car,' I said.

Daylight was fading fast as I followed miles of woods thick with pines. Fields were fallow with tufts of cotton still clinging to dead stalks, and the sky was moist and cold like thawing cake. When I had gotten home from the meeting, there had been a message from Rose. At two P.M., Keith Pleasants had called from jail, desperately requesting that I come see him, and Wingo had gone home with the flu.

I had been inside the old Sussex County Courthouse many times over the years, and had grown fond of its antebellum quaintness and inconveniences. Built in 1825 by Thomas Jefferson's master brick mason, it was red with white trim and columns, and had survived the Civil War, although the Yankees had managed to destroy all its records first. I thought of cold winter days spent out on the lawn with detectives as I waited to be called to the witness stand. I remembered the cases by name that I had brought before this court.

Now such proceedings took place in the spacious new building next door, and as I drove past, heading to the back, I felt sad. Such constructions were a monument to rising crime, and I missed simpler times when I had first moved to Virginia and was awed by its old brick and its old war that would not end. I had smoked back then. I supposed I romanticized the past like most people tended to do. But I missed smoking and waiting around in miserable weather outside a courthouse that barely had heat. Change made me feel old.

The sheriff's department was the same red brick and white trim, its parking lot and jail surrounded by a fence topped with razor wire. Imprisoned within, two inmates in orange jumpsuits were wiping down an unmarked car they had just washed and waxed. They eyed me slyly as I parked in front, one of them popping the other with a shammy cloth.

'Yo. What's going,' one of them muttered to me as I walked past.

'Good afternoon.' I looked at both of them.

They turned away, not interested in someone they could not intimidate, and I pulled open the front door. Inside, the department was modest on the verge of depressing, and like virtually all other public facilities in the world, had profoundly outgrown its environment. Inside were Coke and snack machines, walls plastered with wanted posters and a portrait of an officer slain while responding to a call. I stopped at the duty post, where a young woman was shuffling through paperwork and chewing on her pen.

'Excuse me,' I said. 'I'm here to see Keith Pleasants.'

'Are you on his guest list?' Her contact lenses made her squint, and she wore pink braces on her teeth.

'He asked me to come, so I should hope I am.'

She flipped pages in a loose-leaf binder, stopping when she got to the right one.

'Your name.'

I told her as her finger moved down a page.

'Here you are.' She got up from her chair. 'Come with me.'

She came around her desk and unlocked a door with bars in the window. Inside was a cramped processing area for fingerprints and mug shots, a banged-up metal desk manned by a heavyset deputy. Beyond was another heavy door with bars, and through it I could hear the noises of the jail.

'You're gonna have to leave your bag here,' the deputy said to me. He got on his radio. 'Can you get on over here?'

'Ten-four. On my way,' a woman answered back.

I set my pocketbook on the desk and dug my hands in the pockets of my coat. I was going to be searched and I did not like it.

'We got a little room here where they meet with their lawyers,' the deputy said, jabbing his thumb as if he were hitching a ride. 'But some a these critters listen to ever word, and if that's a problem, go upstairs. We got an area up there.'

'I think upstairs might be better,' I said as a female deputy, hefty with short frosted hair, came around the corner with her hand-held metal detector.

'Arms out,' she said to me. 'Got anything metal in your pockets?'

'No,' I said as the detector snarled like a mechanical cat.

She tried it up and down one side and the other. It kept going off.

'Let's get rid of your coat.'

265

I draped it on the desk as she tried again. The detector continued to make its startling sound as she frowned and kept trying.

'What about jewelry,' she said.

I shook my head as I suddenly remembered I was wearing an underwire bra that I had no intention of announcing. She put down the detector and began to pat me down while the other deputy sat at his desk and watched slack-jawed, as if he were gawking at a dirty movie.

'Okay,' she said, satisfied that I was harmless. 'Follow me.'

To get upstairs, we had to walk through the women's side of the jail. Keys jangled as she unlocked a heavy metal door that loudly banged shut behind us. Inmates were young and hard in institutional denim, their cells scarcely big enough for an animal, with a white toilet, bed and sink. Women played solitaire, and leaned against their cages. They had hung their clothes from bars, and trash barrels were close and crammed with what they hadn't wanted for dinner. The smell of old food made my stomach flop.

'Hey mama.'

'What we got here?'

'A *fine* lady. Umm-umm-umm.'

'Hubba-hubba-hubba!'

Hands came through bars, trying to touch me as I went past, and someone was making kissing sounds while other women emitted harsh, wounded outbursts that were supposed to be laughs.

'Leave her in here. Just fifteen minutes. Ooohhh come to mama!'

'I need cigarettes.'

'Shut up, Wanda. You always needin' something.'

'Y'all quiet on down,' the deputy said in a bored singsong as she unlocked another door.

I followed her upstairs and realized I was trembling. The room she put me in was cluttered and disorganized, as if it might have had a function in an earlier time. Cork boards were propped against a wall, a hand cart parked in a corner, and some sort of pamphlets and bulletins were scattered everywhere. I sat in a folding chair at a wooden table scarred with names and crude messages in ballpoint pen.

'Just make yourself at home and he'll be up,' she said, leaving me alone.

I realized that cough drops and tissues were in my pocketbook and coat, neither of which I had with me now. Sniffing, I shut my eyes until I heard heavy feet. When the male deputy escorted Keith Pleasants in, I almost did not recognize him. He was pale and drawn, thin in baggy denims, his hands cuffed awkwardly in front of him. His eyes filled with tears when he looked at me, and his lips quivered when he tried to smile.

'You sit down and stay down,' the deputy ordered him. 'Don't you let me hear no problem up here. Got it? Or I'm back and the visit's history.'

Pleasants grabbed a chair, almost falling.

'Does he really need to be cuffed?' I said to the deputy. 'He's here for a traffic violation.'

'Ma'am, he's out of the secure area. That's why he's cuffed. Be back in twenty minutes,' he said as he left.

'I've never been through anything like this before. You mind if I smoke?' Pleasants laughed with a nervousness that bordered on hysteria as he sat.

'Help yourself.'

His hands were shaking so badly, I had to light it for him.

'Doesn't look like they got an ashtray. Maybe you're not supposed to smoke up here.' He worried, eyes darting around. 'They got me in this cell with this guy who's a drug dealer? He's got all these tattoos and won't leave me alone? Picking on me, calling me sissy names?' He inhaled a lot of smoke and briefly shut his eyes. 'I wasn't eluding anybody.' He looked at me.

I spotted a Styrofoam coffee cup on the floor and retrieved it for him to use as an ashtray.

'Thanks,' he said.

'Keith, tell me what happened.'

'I was just driving home like I always do, from the landfill, and all of a sudden there's this unmarked car behind me with sirens and lights on. So I pulled over right away. It was that asshole investigator who's been driving me crazy.'

'Ring.' My fury began to pound.

Pleasants nodded. 'Said he'd been following me for more than a mile and I wouldn't heed to his lights. Well I'm telling you, that's just a flat-out lie.' His eyes were bright. 'He's got me so jumpy these days there's no way in hell I wouldn't know if he was behind my car.'

'Did he say anything else to you when he pulled you?' I asked.

'Yes, ma'am, he did. He said my troubles had just begun. His exact words.'

'Why did you want to see me?' I thought I knew, but I wanted to hear what he would say.

'I'm in a world of trouble, Dr Scarpetta.' He teared up again. 'My mama's old and got no one to care for her but me, and there are people thinking I'm a murderer! I never killed anything in my life! Not even birds! People don't want to be around me at work anymore.'

'Is your mother bedridden?' I asked.

'No, ma'am. But she's almost seventy and has emphysema. From doing these things.' He sucked on the cigarette again. 'She doesn't drive anymore.'

'Who's looking after her now?'

He shook his head and wiped his eyes. His legs were crossed, one foot jumping like it was about to take off.

'She has no one to bring her food?' I said.

'Just me.' He choked on the words.

I looked around again, this time for something to write with, and found a purple crayon and a brown paper towel.

'Give me her address and phone number,' I said. 'And I promise someone will check in with her to make sure she's all right.'

He was vastly relieved as he gave me the information and I scribbled it down.

'I called you because I didn't know where else to go,' he started talking again. 'Can't somebody do something to get me out of here?'

'I understand your bond has been set at five thousand dollars.'

'That's just it! Like ten times what it usually is for this, according to the guy in my cell. I don't have any money or any way to get it. Means I got to stay here until court, and that could be weeks. Months.' Tears welled in his eyes again, and he was terrified.

'Keith, do you use the Internet?' I said.

'The what?'

'Computers.'

'At the landfill I do. Remember, I was telling you about our satellite system.'

'Then you do use the Internet.'

He did not seem to know what that was.

'E-mail,' I tried again.

'We use GPS.' He looked confused. 'And you know the truck that dumped the body? I'm pretty sure now it was definitely Cole's, and the Dumpster may have come from a construction site. They pick up at a bunch of construction sites on South Side in Richmond. That would be a good place to get rid of something, on a construction site. Just pull up your car after hours and who's to see?'

'Did you tell Investigator Ring this?' I asked.

Hate passed over his face. 'I don't tell him anything. Not anymore. Everything he's been doing is just to set me up.'

'Why do you think he would want to set you up?'

'He's got to arrest someone for this. He wants to be the hero.' He was suddenly evasive. 'Says everybody else doesn't know what they're doing.' He hesitated. 'Including you.'

'What else has he said?' I felt myself turning to cold, hard stone, the way I did when I had moved from anger to determined rage.

'See, when I was showing him around the house and all, he would talk. He really likes to talk.'

He took his cigarette butt and clumsily set it end-up on the table, so it would go out without burning Styrofoam. I helped him light another one.

'He told me you have this niece,' Pleasants went on. 'And that she's a real fox but has no more business in the FBI than you have being a chief medical examiner. Because. Well.'

'Go on,' I said in a controlled voice.

'Because she's not into men. I guess he thinks you aren't, either.'

'That's interesting.'

'He was laughing about it, said he knew from personal experience that neither of you dated because he'd been around both of you. And that I should just sit back and watch what happens to perverts. Because the same thing was about to happen to me.'

'Wait one minute.' I stopped him. 'Did Ring actually threaten you because you're gay or he thinks you are?'

'My mama doesn't know.' He hung his head. 'But some people do. I've been in bars. In fact, I know Wingo.'

I hoped not intimately.

'I'm worried about Mama.' He teared up again. 'She's upset about what's happening to me, and that's not good for her condition.'

'I tell you what. I'm going to check on her myself, on my way home,' I said, coughing again.

A tear slid down his cheek and he roughly wiped it with the backs of cuffed hands.

'One other thing I'm going to do,' I said as footsteps sounded on the stairs again. 'I'm going to see what I can do about you. I don't believe you killed anyone, Keith. And I'm going to post your bond and make sure you have a lawyer.'

His lips parted in disbelief as the deputies loudly entered the room.

'You really are?' Pleasants asked as he almost staggered to his feet, his eyes wide on mine.

'If you swear you're telling the truth.'

'Oh yes, ma'am!'

'Yeah, yeah,' a deputy said. 'You and all the rest of 'em.'

'It will have to be tomorrow,' I said to Pleasants. 'I'm afraid the magistrate's gone home for the night.'

'Come on. Downstairs.' A deputy grabbed his arm.

Pleasants said one last thing to me. 'Mama likes chocolate milk with Hershey's syrup. Not much else she keeps down anymore.'

Then he was gone, and I was led back downstairs and through the women's section of the jail again. Inmates were sullen this time, as if I no longer were fun. It occurred to me someone had told them who I was, when they turned their backs on me and someone spat.

S HERIFF ROB ROY was a legend in Sussex County and ran uncontested every election year. He had been to my morgue many times, and I thought he was one of the finest law enforcement officers I knew. At half-past six, I found him at the Virginia Diner, where he was sitting at the local table, which literally was where the locals gathered.

This was in a long room of red-checked cloths and white chairs, and he was eating a fried ham sandwich and drinking coffee, black, his portable radio upright on the table and full of chatter.

'Can't do that, no sir. Then what? They just keep selling

crack, that's what,' he was saying to a gaunt weathered man in a John Deere cap.

'Let 'em.'

'Let 'em?' Roy reached for his coffee, as wiry and bald as he ever was. 'You can't mean that.'

'I sure as hell can.'

'Might I interrupt?' I said, pulling out a chair.

Roy's mouth fell open, and for an instant he did not believe whom he was looking at. 'Well, I'll be damned.' He stood and shook my hand. 'What in tarnation are you doing out in these parts?'

'Looking for you.'

'If you'll excuse me.' The other man tipped his hat to me and got up to leave.

'Don't you tell me you're out here on business,' the sheriff said.

'What else would it be?'

He was sobered by my mood. 'Something I don't know about?'

'You know,' I said.

'Well, what then? What do you want to eat? I recommend the fried chicken sandwich,' he said as a waitress appeared.

'Hot tea.' I wondered if I would ever eat again.

'You don't look like you're feeling too good.'

'I feel like shit.'

'There's this bug going around.'

'You don't even know the half of it,' I said.

'What can I do?' He leaned closer to me, his attention completely focused.

'I'm posting bond for Keith Pleasants,' I said. 'Now this obviously won't happen before tomorrow, I'm sorry to say. But I think you need to understand, Rob, that this is an innocent man who has been set up. He's being persecuted because Investigator Ring is on a witch hunt and wants to make a name for himself.'

Roy looked baffled. 'Since when are you defending inmates?'

'Since whenever they aren't guilty,' I said. 'And this guy is no more a serial killer than you or I. He didn't try to elude the police and probably wasn't even speeding. Ring's hassling him and lying. Look how high the bond was set for a traffic violation.'

He was silent, listening.

'Pleasants has an old, infirm mother who has no one to take care of her. He's about to lose his job. Now I know Ring's uncle is the secretary of public safety, and he's also a former sheriff,' I said. 'And I know how that goes, Rob. I need you to help me out here. Ring has got to be stopped.'

Roy pushed his plate away as his radio called him. 'You really believe that.'

'Yes, I do.'

'This is fifty-one,' he said into the radio, adjusting his belt and the revolver on it.

'We got anything on that robbery yet?' a voice came back.

'Still waiting for it.'

He signed off and said to me, 'You got no doubt in your mind that this boy didn't commit any crime.'

I nodded again. 'No doubt. The killer who dismembered that lady communicates with me on the Internet. Pleasants doesn't even know what that is. There's a very big picture that I can't get into now. But believe me, what's going on has nothing to do with this kid.'

275

'You're sure about Ring. I mean, you got to be if I'm going to do this.' His eyes were steady on mine.

'How many times do I have to say it?'

He slammed his napkin down on the table. 'Now, this really makes me mad.' He scooted back his chair. 'I don't like it when an innocent person's locked up in my jail and some cop's out there making the rest of us look bad.'

'Do you know Kitchen, the man who owns the landfill?' I said.

'Oh sure. We're in the same lodge.' He pulled out his wallet.

'Someone needs to talk to him so Keith doesn't lose his job. We have to make this thing right,' I said.

'Believe me, I'm going to.'

He left money on the table and strode angrily out the door. I sat long enough to finish my tea, looking around at displays of striped candy, barbecue sauce and peanuts of every description. My head hurt and my skin was hot when I found a grocery store on 460 and stopped for milk, Hershey's syrup, fresh vegetables and soup.

I charged up and down aisles, and next thing I knew my cart was full of everything from toilet paper to deli meats. Then I got out a map and the address Pleasants had given to me. His mother was not too far off the main route, and when I arrived she was asleep.

'Oh dear,' I said from the porch. 'I didn't mean to get you up.'

'Who is it?' She peered blindly into the night as she unhooked the door.

'Dr Kay Scarpetta. You have no reason . . .'

'What kind of doctor?'

Mrs Pleasants was wizened and stooped, her face wrinkled

like crepe paper. Long gray hair floated like gossamer, and I thought of the landfill and the old woman deadoc had killed.

'You can come on in.' She shoved open the door and looked frightened. 'Is Keith all right? Nothing happened to him, did it?'

'I saw him earlier, and he's fine,' I assured her. 'I brought groceries.' I had the bags in my hands.

'That boy.' She shook her head, motioning me into her small, tidy home. 'What would I do? You know, he's all I've got in this world. When he was born I said, "Keith, it's just you."'

She was scared and upset and didn't want me to know.

'Do you know where he is?' I gently said.

We entered her kitchen with its old, squat refrigerator and gas stove, and she did not answer me. She started putting groceries away, fumbling with cans and dropping celery and carrots to the floor.

'Here. Let me help,' I tried.

'He didn't do anything wrong.' She began to cry. 'I know he didn't. And that policeman won't leave him be, always coming over, banging on the door.'

She stood in the middle of her kitchen, wiping her face with her hands.

'Keith says you like chocolate milk, and I'm going to make you one. It's just what the doctor ordered.'

I fetched a glass and a spoon from the drain board.

'He'll be home tomorrow,' I said. 'And I don't imagine you'll be hearing from Investigator Ring anymore.'

She stared at me as if I were a miracle.

'I just wanted to make sure you have everything you need until your son gets here,' I said, handing her the glass of chocolate milk mixed medium dark.

'I'm just trying to figure out who you are,' she finally said. 'This is mighty good. Nothing in life any better.' She sipped and smiled and took her time.

I briefly explained how I knew Keith and what I did professionally, but she did not understand. She assumed I was sweet on him and issued medical licenses for a living. On my way home, I played CDs loudly to keep me awake as I drove through thick darkness, where for long stretches there was not a single light except stars. I reached for the phone.

Wingo's mother answered and told me he was sick in bed. But she got him on the line.

'Wingo, I'm worried about you,' I said with feeling.

'I feel terrible.' He sounded like it. 'I guess you can't do anything for the flu.'

'You're immunosuppressed. When I talked to Dr Riley last, your CD4 cell count was not good.' I wanted him to face reality. 'Describe your symptoms to me.'

'My head's killing me, my neck and back are killing me. Last time my temperature was taken it was a hundred and four. I'm so thirsty all the time.'

Everything he said was setting off alarms in my head, for the symptoms also described the early stages of smallpox. But if his exposure was the torso, I was surprised he hadn't gotten sick before now, especially in light of his compromised condition.

'You haven't touched one of those sprays we got at the office,' I said.

'What sprays?'

'The Vita facial sprays.'

He was clueless, and then I remembered that he was out of the office much of today. I explained what had happened.

'Oh my God,' he said suddenly, as fear shot through both of us. 'One came in the mail. Mom had it on the kitchen counter.'

'When?' I said in alarm.

'I don't know. A few days ago. When was that? I don't know. We'd never seen anything so fancy. Imagine, something sweet to cool your face.'

That made twelve canisters deadoc had delivered to my staff, and *twelve* had been his message to me. It was the number of full-time people in my central office, if I included myself. How could he know such trivia as the size of my staff, and even some of their names and where they lived, if he were far away and anonymous?

I dreaded my next question because I already thought I knew. 'Wingo, did you touch it in any way?'

'I tried it. Just to see.' His voice was shaking badly and he was choking from coughing fits. 'When it was sitting there. I picked it up one time, just to see. It smelled like roses.'

'Who else in your house has tried it?'

'I don't know.'

'I want you to make certain no one touches that canister. Do you understand?'

'Yes.' He was sobbing.

'I'm going to send some people to your house to pick it up and take care of you and your family, okay?'

He was crying too hard to answer.

When I got home, it was minutes past midnight, and I was so out of sorts and sick that I did not know what to do first. I called Marino and Wesley, and Fujitsubo. I told everybody what was happening and that Wingo and his family needed a team at their home immediately. My bad news was returned by theirs. The girl on Tangier who had gotten sick had died, and now a fisherman had the disease. Depressed and feeling like hell, I checked my e-mail, and deadoc was there in his small, mean way. I was glad. His message had been sent while Keith Pleasants was in jail.

mirror mirror on the wall where have you been

'You bastard,' I screamed at him.

The day was too much. All of it was too much, and I was achy and woozy and completely fed up. So I should not have gone into that chat room, where I waited for him as if this were the O.K. Corral. I should have left it for another time. But I made my presence known and paced in my mind as I waited for the monster to appear. He did.

DEADOC:	toil and trouble
SCARPETTA:	What do you want?
DEADOC:	we are angry tonight
SCARPETTA:	Yes, we are.
DEADOC:	why should you care about ignorant fishermen and their ignorant families and those inept people who work for you
SCARPETTA:	Stop it. Tell me what you want to make this stop.
DEADOC:	it s too late the damage is done it was done long before this
SCARPETTA:	What was done to you?

But he did not answer. Oddly, he did not leave the room, but he did not respond to any further questions from me. I thought of Squad 19 and prayed they were listening and following from trunk to trunk, tracing him to his lair. Half an hour passed. I finally logged off as my telephone rang.

'You're a genius!' Lucy was so excited she was hurting

my ears. 'How the hell have you managed to keep him on that long?'

'What do you mean?' I asked, amazed.

'Eleven minutes so far. You win the prize.'

'I was only on with him maybe two minutes.' I tried to cool my forehead with the back of my hand. 'I don't know what you're talking about.'

But she didn't care. 'We nailed the son of a bitch!' She was ecstatic. 'A campground in Maryland, agents from Salisbury already en route. Janet and I gotta plane to catch.'

Before I got up the next morning, the World Health Organization put out another international alert about Vita aromatic facial spray. WHO reassured people that this virus would be eliminated, that we were working on the vaccine around the clock and would have it soon. But the panic began anyway.

The virus, dubbed by the press Mutantpox, was on the cover of *Newsweek* and *Time*, and the Senate was forming a subcommittee as the White House contemplated emergency measures. Vita was distributed in New York, but the manufacturer was actually French. The obvious concern was that deadoc was making good on his threat. Although there were yet no reports of the disease in France, economic and diplomatic relations were strained as a large plant was forced to shut down, and accusations about where the tampering was done were volleyed back and forth between countries.

Watermen were trying to flee Tangier in their fishing vessels, and the Coast Guard had called in more backups from stations as far south as Florida. I did not know all the details, but based on what I had heard, there was a standoff between law enforcement and Tangiermen in the Tangier

Sound, boats anchored and going nowhere as winter winds howled.

Meanwhile, CDC had deployed an isolation team of doctors and nurses to Wingo's house, and word was out. Headlines screamed and people were evacuating a city that would be difficult, if not impossible, to quarantine. I was as distressed and sick as I'd ever been in my life, drinking hot tea in a bathrobe early Friday morning.

My fever had peaked at a hundred and two, and Robitussin DM didn't do a thing except make me vomit. Muscles in my neck and back hurt as if I had been playing football against people with clubs. But I could not go to bed. There was far too much to do. I called a bondsman and received the bad news that the only way to get Keith Pleasants out of jail was for me to drive downtown and pay in person. So I went out to my car, only to have to turn around ten minutes later because I'd left my checkbook on the table.

'God, help me please,' I muttered as I sped up.

Rubber squealed as I drove too fast through my neighborhood, and then moments later, back out, flying around corners in Windsor Farms. I wondered what had happened in Maryland during the night as I worried about Lucy, for whom every event was an adventure. She wanted to use guns and go on foot pursuit, fly helicopters and planes. I feared such a spirit would be crushed in its prime, because I knew too much about life and how it ended. I wondered if deadoc had been caught, but believed if he had, I would have been told.

I had never needed a bondsman in my life, and this one, Vince Peeler, worked out of a shoe repair shop on Broad Street, along a strip of abandoned stores with nothing in their windows but graffiti and dust. He was a short, slight man with waxed black hair and a leather apron. Seated at an industrial-sized Singer sewing machine, he was stitching a new sole on a shoe. As I shut the door he gave me the piercing look of one accustomed to recognizing trouble.

'You Dr Scarpetta?' he asked as he sewed.

'Yes.'

I got out my checkbook and a pen, not feeling the least bit friendly as I wondered how many violent people this man had helped back out on the streets.

'That will be five hundred and thirty dollars,' he said. 'If you want to use a credit card, add three percent.'

He got up and came to his scarred counter piled with shoes and tins of Kiwi paste. I could feel his eyes crawling over me.

'Funny, I thought you'd be a lot older,' he considered. 'You know, you read about people in the news and sometimes get flat-out wrong impressions.'

'He'll be freed today.' It was an order as I tore out the check and handed it to him.

'Oh, sure.' His eyes darted and he looked at his watch. 'When?'

'When?' he echoed rhetorically.

'Yes,' I said. 'When will he be freed?'

He snapped his fingers. 'Like that.'

'Good,' I said as I blew my nose. 'I'm going to be watching for him to be freed like that.' I snapped my fingers, too. 'And if he isn't? Guess what? I'm also a lawyer and in a really, really shitty mood. And I'll come after you. Okay?'

He smiled at me and swallowed.

'What kind of lawyer?' he asked.

'The kind you don't want to know,' I said as I went out the door.

I got to the office maybe fifteen minutes later, and my pager vibrated and the phone rang as I sat behind my desk. Before I could do anything, Rose suddenly appeared and looked unusually stressed.

'Everybody's looking for you,' she said.

'They always are.' I frowned at the number on my pager's display. 'Now who the hell is that?'

'Marino's on his way here,' she went on. 'They're sending a helicopter. To the helipad at MCV. USAMRIID's in the air right now, heading here. They've let the Baltimore Medical Examiner's office know a special team's going to have to handle this, that the body will have to be autopsied in Frederick.'

I gave her my eyes as my blood seemed to freeze. 'Body?'

'Apparently there's some campground where the FBI traced a call.'

'I know about that.' I had no patience. 'In Maryland.'

'They think they've found the killer's camper. I'm not clear on all the details. But it has what might be a lab of some type. And there's a body inside.'

I couldn't believe what I was hearing. 'Whose body?'

'They think, his. A possible suicide. Shot.' She peered at me over the top of her glasses, and shook her head. 'You should be home in bed with a cup of my chicken soup.'

Marino picked me up in front of my office as wind gusted through downtown and whipped state flags on tops of buildings. I knew instantly that he was angry when he pulled out before I'd barely shut the door. Then he had nothing to say.

'Thanks,' I said, unwrapping a cough drop.

'You're still sick.' He turned onto Franklin Street.

'I certainly am. Thank you for asking.'

'I don't know why I'm doing this,' he said, and he was

not in uniform. 'Last thing I want to do is get near some goddamn lab where someone's been making viruses.'

'You'll have special protection,' I replied.

'I should probably have it now, being around you.'

'I have the flu and am no longer infectious. Trust me. I know these things. And don't be mad at me, because I have no intention of putting up with it.'

'You'd better hope the flu's what you got.'

'If I had something worse, I would be getting worse and my fever would be higher. I would have a rash.'

'Yeah, but if you're already sick, don't that mean you're more likely to catch something else? Like, I don't know why you want to be making this trip. 'Cause I sure the fuck don't. And I don't appreciate being dragged into it.'

'Then drop me off and be on your way,' I said. 'Don't even think about whining to me right now. Not when the entire world's going to hell.'

'How's Wingo?' he asked in a more conciliatory tone.

'I'm frankly scared to death for him,' I replied.

We drove through MCV, turning into a helipad behind a fence where patients and organs arrived when they were medflighted to the hospital. USAMRIID had not arrived yet, but in moments we could hear the powerful Blackhawk, and people in cars and walking along sidewalks stopped and stared. Several drivers pulled off the road to watch the magnificent machine darken the sky as it hammered in, blasting grass and debris as it landed.

The door slid open and Marino and I climbed inside, where crew seats were already occupied by scientists from USAMRIID. We were surrounded by rescue gear, and another portable isolator that was collapsed like an accordion. I was handed a helmet with a microphone, and I put this on and fastened my five-point harness. Then I helped Marino with his as he perched primly on a fold-down seat not built for people his size.

'God knows I hope reporters don't get wind of this,' someone said as the heavy door shut.

I plugged the cord of my microphone into a port in the ceiling. 'They will. Probably already have.'

Deadoc liked attention. I could not believe he would leave this world silently, or without his presidential apology. No, there was something else in store for us, and I did not want to imagine what that might be. The trip to Janes Island State Park was less than an hour, but complicated by the fact that the campground was densely wooded with pines. There was nowhere to land.

Our pilots set us down at the Coast Guard station in Crisfield, in a marina called Somer's Cove, where sailboats and yachts battened down for winter bobbed on the dark blue ruffled water of the Little Annemessex River. We went inside the tidy brick station long enough to put on exposure suits and life vests while Chief Martinez briefed us.

'We got a lot of problems going at the same time,' he was saying as he paced the carpet inside the communication room, where all of us were gathered. 'For one thing, Tangier folk have kin here, and we've had to station armed guards at roads leading out of town because now CDC is concerned about Crisfield people going anywhere.'

'No one's gotten sick here,' Marino said, as he struggled to get cuffs over his boots.

'No, but I'm worried that at the very start of this thing, some people snuck through the cracks, got out of Tangier and came here. Point being, don't expect much friendliness in these parts.'

'Who's at the campground?' someone else asked.

'Right now, the FBI agents that found the body.'

'What about other campers?' Marino said.

'Here's what I've been told,' Martinez said. 'When the agents went in, they found maybe half a dozen campers and only one with a phone hookup. That was campsite sixteen, and they banged on the door. Nothing, so they look in a window and see the body on the floor.'

'The agents didn't go inside?' I said.

'No. Realizing it might be the perp's, they worried it could be contaminated and didn't. But I'm afraid one of the rangers did.'

'Why?' I asked.

'You know what they say. Curiosity killed the cat. Apparently one of the agents had gone to the airstrip where you landed to pick up two other agents. Whatever. At some point, no one was looking and the ranger went inside, came right back out like a ball of fire. Said there was some kind of monster in there straight out of Stephen King. Don't ask me.' He shrugged and rolled his eyes.

I looked at the USAMRIID team.

'We'll take the ranger back with us,' said a young man whose Army pins identified him as a captain. 'By the way, my name is Clark. This is my crew,' he said to me. 'They'll take good care of him, put him in quarantine, keep an eye on him.'

'Campsite sixteen,' Marino said. 'We know anything about who rented that?'

'We don't have those details yet,' Martinez said. 'Everybody suited up?' He scanned us and it was time to go.

The Coast Guard took us in two Boston Whalers because where we were going was too shallow for a cutter or patrol boat. Martinez was piloting mine, standing up and calm as if racing forty miles an hour on choppy waters was a very normal thing to do. I honestly thought I might sail overboard at any moment as I held hard to the rail, sitting on the side. It was like riding a mechanical bull, air rushing so fast into my nose and mouth, I could barely breathe.

Marino was across the boat from me and looked like he might get sick. I tried to mouth a reassurance to him, but he stared blankly at me as he held on with all his strength. We eventually slowed in a cove called Flat Cat, thick with cat-tails and spartina grass, where there were NO WAKE signs as the park got near. I could see nothing but pines. Then as we got closer, there were paths and bathrooms, a small ranger station, and only one camper peeking through. Martinez glided us into the pier, and another Guardsman tied us to a piling as the engine quit.

'I'm gonna puke,' Marino said in my ear as we clumsily climbed out.

'No you're not.' I gripped his arm.

'I ain't going inside that trailer.'

I turned around and looked at his wan face.

'You're right. You're not,' I said. 'That's my job, but first we need to locate the ranger.'

Marino stalked off before the second boat had docked, and I looked through the woods toward the camper that was deadoc's. Rather old and missing whatever had towed it, it was parked as far from the rangers' station as was possible, tucked in the shadow of loblolly pines. When all of us were ashore, the USAMRIID team passed out the familiar orange suits, air packs and extra four-hour batteries.

'Here's what we're doing.' It was the USAMRIID team

leader named Clark who spoke. 'We suit up and get the body out.'

'I would like to go in first,' I said. 'Alone.'

'Right.' He nodded. 'Then we see if there's anything hazardous in there, which hopefully there's not. We get the body out, and the camper's hauled out of here.'

'It's evidence,' I said, looking at him. 'We can't just haul it out of here.'

I knew what he was thinking by the look on his face. The killer may be dead, the case closed. The camper was a biological hazard and should be burned.

'No,' I said to him. 'We don't close this so quickly. We can't.'

He hesitated, blowing out in frustration as he stared off at the camper.

'I'll go in,' I said. 'Then I'll tell you what we need to do.'

'Fair enough.' He raised his voice again. 'Guys? Let's go. No one inside but the M.E. until you hear otherwise.'

They followed us through the forest, the portable isolator in our wake, an eerie caisson not meant for this world. Pine needles were crisp beneath my feet, like shredded wheat, and the air was sharp and clean as the camper got closer. It was a Dutchman travel trailer, maybe eighteen feet long, with a fold-out orange-striped awning.

'That's old. Eight years, I bet,' said Marino, who knew about such things.

'What would it take to tow it?' I asked as we put on our suits.

'A pickup,' he said. 'Maybe a van. This doesn't need nothing with a lot of horsepower. What are we supposed to do? Put these over everything else we already got on?'

'Yes,' I said, zipping up. 'What I'd like to know is what happened to the vehicle that hauled this thing here.'

'Good question,' he said, huffing as he struggled. 'And where's the license plate?'

I had just turned on my air when a young man emerged from trees in a green uniform and smoky hat. He seemed rather dazed as he looked at all of us in our orange hoods and suits, and I sensed his fear. He did not get close to us as he introduced himself as the night shift park ranger.

Marino spoke to him first. 'You ever see the person staying in there?'

'No,' the ranger said.

'What about guys on the other shifts?'

'No one remembers seeing anyone, just lights on at night sometimes. Hard to say. As you can see it's parked pretty far from the station. You could go out to the showers or whatever and not necessarily be noticed.'

'No other campers here?' I asked over the rush of air inside my hood.

'Not now. There were maybe three other people when I found the body, but I encouraged them to leave because there might be some kind of disease.'

'Did you question them first?' Marino asked, and I could see he was irritated by this young ranger who had just chased off all of our witnesses.

'Nobody knew a thing, except one person did think he ran into him.' He nodded at the camper. 'Evening before last. In the bathroom. Big grubby guy with dark hair and a beard.'

'Taking a shower?' I asked.

'No, ma'am.' He hesitated. 'Taking a leak.'

'Doesn't the camper have a bathroom?'

'I really don't know.' He hesitated again. 'To tell you the

truth, I didn't stay in there. Minute I saw that. Well, whatever it was. I was gone like a second.'

'And you don't know what towed this thing?' Marino then asked.

The ranger was looking very uncomfortable now. 'This time of year it's usually quiet out here, and dark. I had no reason to notice what vehicle it was hooked up to, and in fact don't recall there even being one.'

'But you got a plate number.' Marino's stare was unfriendly through his hood.

'Sure do.' Relieved, the ranger pulled a folded piece of paper from his pocket. 'Got his registration right here.' He opened it. 'Ken A. Perley, Norfolk, Virginia.'

He handed the paper to Marino, who sarcastically said, 'Oh good. The name the asshole stole off a credit card. So I'm sure the plate number you got is accurate, too. How did he pay?'

'Cashier's check.'

'He gave this to someone in person?' Marino asked.

'No. He made the reservation by mail. No one ever saw anything except the paperwork in your hand. Like I said, we never saw him.'

'What about the envelope this thing came in?' Marino said. 'Did you save it so maybe we got a postmark?'

The ranger shook his head. He nervously glanced at suited scientists, who were listening to his every word. He stared at the trailer and wet his lips.

'You mind my asking what's in there. And what's going to happen to me 'cause I went in?' His voice cracked and he looked like he might cry.

'It could be contaminated with a virus.' I said to him. 'But we don't know that for sure. Everybody here is going to take care of you.'

'They said they were going to lock me up in some room, like solitary confinement.' Fear erupted, his eyes wild, voice loud. 'I want to know exactly what's in there that I might have got!'

'You'll be in exactly the same thing I was last week,' I assured him. 'A nice room with nice nurses. For a few days of observation. That's all.'

'Think of it as a vacation. It really ain't that big of a deal. Just because people are in these suits, don't go getting hinky,' Marino said as if he were one to talk.

He went on as if he were the great expert in infectious diseases, and I left the two of them and approached the camper alone. For a moment, I stood within feet of it and looked around. To my left were acres of trees, then the river where our boats were moored. Right of me, through more trees, I could hear the sounds of a highway. The camper was parked on a soft floor of pine needles, and what I noticed first was the scraped area on the white-painted tongue.

Getting close, I squatted and rubbed gloved fingers over deep gouges and scrapes in aluminum in an area where the Vehicle Identification Number, or VIN, should have been. Near the roof, I noticed a patch of vinyl had been scorched, and decided someone had taken a propane torch to the second VIN. I walked around to the other side.

The door was unlocked and not quite shut because it had been pried open by some sort of tool, and my nerves began to sing. My head cleared and I became completely focused, the way I got when evidence was screaming a different story than witnesses claimed. Mounting metal steps, I walked inside and stood very still as I looked around at a scene that might mean nothing to most, but to me confirmed a nightmare. This was deadoc's factory.

First, the heat was up as high as it would go, and I turned it off, startled when a pathetic white creature suddenly hopped across my feet. I jumped and gasped as it stupidly ran into a wall, and then sat, quivering and panting. The pitiful laboratory rabbit had been shaved in patches and scarified with infection, his eruptions horrible and dark. I noticed his wire cage, and that it seemed to have been knocked off a table, the door wide open.

'Come here.' Squatting, I held out my hand as he watched me with pink-rimmed eyes, long ears twitching.

Carefully, I inched my way closer because I could not leave him out. He was a living source of propagating disease.

'Come on, you poor little thing,' I said to the ranger's monster. 'I promise I won't hurt you.'

Then I gently had him in my hands, his heart beating staccato as he violently trembled. I returned him to his cage, then went to the rear of the camper. The doorway I stepped through was small, the body inside practically filling the bedroom. The man was facedown on gold shag carpet that was stained dark from blood. His hair was curly and dark, and when I turned him over, rigor mortis had come and already passed. He reminded me of a lumberjack in a filthy pea coat and trousers. His hands were huge with dirty nails, his beard and mustache unkempt.

I undressed him from the waist up to check the pattern of livor mortis, or blood settling by gravity after death. Face and chest were reddish purple, with areas of blanching where his body had been against the floor. I saw no indication that he had been moved after death. He had been shot once in the chest at close range, possibly with the Remington double-barreled shotgun by his side, next to his left hand.

The spread of pellets was tight, forming a large hole with

scalloped edges in the center of his chest. White plastic filler from the shotgun clung to clothing and skin, which again did not indicate a contact wound. Measuring the gun and his arms, I did not see how he could have reached the trigger. I saw nothing to indicate that he had rigged up anything to help him. Checking pockets, I found no wallet, no identification, only a Buck knife. The blade was scratched and bent.

I spent no more time with him but came outside, and the team from USAMRIID was restless, like people waiting to go somewhere and afraid they're going to miss their flight. They stared as I came down the steps, and Marino hung back. He was almost lost in trees, orange arms folded across his chest, the ranger standing beside him.

'This is a completely contaminated crime scene,' I announced. 'We have a dead white male with no identification. I need someone to help me get the body out. It needs to be contained.' I looked at the captain.

'It goes back with us,' he said.

I nodded. 'Your guys can do the autopsy and maybe get someone from the Baltimore Medical Examiner's office to witness. The camper's another problem. It's got to go somewhere it can be worked up safely. Evidence needs to be collected and decontaminated. This, frankly, is out of my range. Unless you have a containment facility that can accommodate something this big, maybe we'd better get this to Utah.'

'To Dugway?' he said, dubiously.

'Yes,' I said. 'Maybe Colonel Fujitsubo can help with that.'

Dugway Proving Ground was the Army's major range and test facility for chemical and biological defense. Unlike

USAMRIID, which was in the heart of urban America, Dugway had the vast land of the Great Salt Lake desert for testing lasers, smart bombs, smoke obscurance or illumination. More to the point, it had the only test chamber in the United States capable of processing a vehicle as large as a battle tank.

The captain thought for a moment, his eyes going from me to the camper as he made up his mind and formalized a plan.

'Frank, get on the phone and let's get this mobilized ASAP,' he said to one of the scientists. 'The colonel will have to work with the Air Force on transport, get something here fast because I don't want this thing sitting out here all night. And we're going to need a flatbed truck, a pickup truck.'

'Should be able to get that around here, with all the seafood they ship,' Marino said. 'I'll get on it.'

'Good,' the captain went on. 'Somebody get me three body bags and the isolator.' Then he said to me, 'I'll bet you need a hand.'

'I certainly do,' I said, and both of us began walking toward the camper.

I pulled open the bent aluminum door, and he followed me inside, and we did not linger as we passed through to the back. I could tell by Clark's eyes that he had never seen anything like this, but with his hood and air pack, at least he did not have to deal with the stench of decomposing human flesh. He knelt at one end and I at the other, the body heavy and the space impossibly cramped.

'Is it hot in here or is it just me?' he said loudly as we struggled with rubbery limbs.

'Someone turned the heat up as high as it would go.' I was already out of breath. 'To hasten viral contamination, decomposition. A popular way to screw up a crime scene. All right. Let's zip him in. This is going to be tight, but I think we can do it.'

We started working him into a second pouch, our hands and suits slippery with blood. It took us almost thirty minutes to get the body inside the isolator, and my muscles were trembling as we carried it out. My heart was pounding and I was dripping sweat. Outside, we were thoroughly doused with a chemical rinse, as was the isolaton which was transported by truck back to Crisfield. Then the team started work on the camper.

All of it, except for the wheels, was to be wrapped in heavy blue tinted vinyl that had a HEPA filter layer. I took off my suit with great relief, and retreated into the warm, well-lit rangers' station, where I scrubbed my hands and face. My nerves were jangled and I would have given anything to crawl into bed, down shots of NyQuil and sleep.

'If this ain't a mess,' Marino said as he came in with a lot of cold air.

'Please shut the door,' I said, shivering.

'What's eating you?' He sat on the other side of the room.

'Life.'

'I can't believe you're out here when you're sick. I think you've lost your friggin' mind.'

'Thank you for the words of comfort.' I said.

'Well, this ain't exactly a holiday for me, either. Stuck out here with people to interview, and I got no wheels.' He looked frayed.

'What are you going to do?'

'I'll find something. Rumor has it Lucy and Janet are in the area and have a ride.'

'Where?' I started to get up.

'Don't get excited. They're out trying to find people to interview, like I gotta do. God, I gotta smoke. It's been almost all day.'

'Not in here.' I pointed to a sign.

'People are dying of smallpox and you're bitching about cigarettes.'

I got out Motrin and popped three without water.

'So what will all these space cadets do now?' he asked.

'Some of them will stay in the area, tracking down any other people who may have been exposed either on Tangier or in the campground. They'll work in shifts with other team members. I guess you'll be in contact with them, too, in case you come across anyone who might have been exposed.'

'What? I'm supposed to walk around in an orange suit all week?' He yawned and cracked his neck. 'Man, aren't they a bitch? Hot as hell except up in the hood.' He was secretly proud that he had worn one.

'No, you won't be wearing a plastic suit,' I said.

'And what happens if I find out someone I'm interviewing was exposed?'

'Just don't kiss him.'

'I don't think this is funny.' He stared at me.

'It's anything but that.'

'What about the dead guy? They going to cremate him when we don't know who he is?'

'He'll be autopsied in the morning,' I said. 'I imagine they'll store his body for as long as they can.'

'The whole thing's just weird.' Marino rubbed his face in his hands. 'And you saw a computer in there.'

'Yes, a laptop. But no printer or scanner. I'm suspicious this is someone's getaway. The printer, the scanner, at home.'

'What about a phone?'

I thought for a minute. 'Don't remember seeing one.'

'Well, the phone line runs from the camper to the utility box. We'll see what we can find out about that, like whose account it is. I'll also tell Wesley what's going on.'

'If the phone line was used only for AOL,' Lucy said as she walked in and shut the door, 'there won't be any telephone account. The only account will be AOL, which will still come back to Perley, the guy whose credit card number got pinched.'

She looked alert but a little tousled in jeans and a leather jacket. Sitting next to me, she examined the whites of my eyes, and felt the glands in my neck.

'Stick out your tongue,' she seriously said.

'Stop it!' I pushed her away, coughing and laughing at the same time.

'How are you feeling?'

'Better. Where's Janet?' I said.

'Talking. Out somewhere. What kind of computer's in there?'

'I didn't take time to study it,' I replied. 'I didn't notice any of the particulars.'

'Was it on?'

'Don't know. I didn't check.'

'I need to get in it.'

'What do you want to do?' I asked, looking at her.

'I think I need to go with you.'

'Will they let you do that?' Marino asked.

'Who the hell is *they*?'

'The drones you work for,' he replied.

'They put me on the case. They expect me to break it.'

Her eyes never stopped moving to windows and the

door. Lucy had been infected and would succumb from her exposure to law enforcement. Beneath her jacket she wore a Sig Sauer nine-millimeter pistol in a leather holster with extra magazines. She probably had brass knuckles in her pocket. She tensed as the door opened and another ranger hurried in, his hair still wet from the shower, eyes nervous and excited.

'Can I help you?' he asked us, taking off his coat.

'Yeah,' Marino said, getting up from his chair. 'What kind of car you got?'

THE FLATBED TRUCK was waiting when we
arrived, the vinyl-shrouded camper on top of it
gleaming an eerie translucent blue beneath the
stars and moon and still hooked to a pickup
truck. We were parking nearby on a dirt road at the edge of
a field when a huge plane passed alarmingly low overhead,
its roar louder than a commercial jet.

'What the hell?' Marino exclaimed, opening the door of
the ranger's Jeep.

'I think that's our ride to Utah,' Lucy said from the back,
where she and I were sitting.

The ranger was staring up through his windshield,

incredulous, as if the rapture had come. 'Holy shit. Oh my God. We're being invaded!'

A HMMWV came down first, wrapped in corrugated cardboard, a heavy wooden platform underneath. It sounded like an explosion when it landed on the hard-packed dead grass of the field and was dragged by parachutes caught in the wind. Then green nylon wilted over the multiwheeled vehicle, and more rucksacks blossomed in the heavens as more cargo drifted down and tumbled to the ground. Paratroopers followed, oscillating two or three times before landing nimbly on their feet and running out of their harnesses. They gathered up billowing nylon as the sound of their C-17 receded beyond the moon.

The Air Force's Combat Control Team out of Charleston, South Carolina, had arrived at precisely thirteen minutes past midnight. We sat in the Jeep and watched, fascinated as airmen began double-checking the compactness of the field, for what was about to land on it weighed enough to demolish a normal landing strip or tarmac. Measurements were made, surveys taken, and the team set out sixteen ACR remote control landing lights, while a woman in camouflage unwrapped the HMMWV, started its loud diesel engine and drove it off its platform, out of the way.

'I got to find some joint to stay around here,' Marino said as he stared out at the spectacle. 'How the hell can they land some big military plane on such a little field?'

'Some of it I can tell you,' said Lucy, who was never at a loss for technical explanation. 'Apparently, the C-17's designed to land with cargo on unusually small, unapproved runways like this. Or a dry lake bed. In Korea, they've even used interstates.'

'Here we go,' Marino said with his usual sarcasm.

'Only other thing that could squeeze into a tight place like this is a C-130,' she went on. 'The C-17 can back up, isn't that cool?'

'No way a cargo plane can do all that.' Marino said.

'Well, this baby can,' she said as if she wanted to adopt it.

He began looking around. 'I'm so hungry I could eat a tire, and I'd give up my paycheck for a beer. I'm gonna roll down this window here and smoke.'

I sensed the ranger did not want anyone smoking in his well-cared-for Jeep, but he was too intimidated to say so.

'Marino, let's go outside,' I said. 'Fresh air would do us good.'

We climbed out and he lit a Marlboro, sucking on it as if it were mother's milk. Members of the USAMRIID team who were in charge of the flatbed truck and its creepy cargo were still in their protective suits and staying away from everyone. They were gathered on the rutted dirt road, watching airmen work on what looked like acres of flat land that in warmer months might be a playing field.

A dark unmarked Plymouth rolled up at almost two A.M., and Lucy trotted to it. I watched her talk to Janet through the open driver's window. Then the car drove away.

'I'm back,' Lucy spoke quietly, touching my arm.

'Everything okay?' I asked, and I knew the life they lived together had to be hard.

'Under control, so far,' she said.

'Double-O-Seven, it was nice of you to come out and help us today,' Marino said to Lucy, smoking as if it were his last hour to enjoy it.

'You know, it's a federal violation to be disrespectful to

federal agents,' she said. 'Especially minorities of Italian extraction.'

'I hope to hell you're a minority. Don't want others out there like you.' He flicked an ash as we heard a plane far off.

'Janet's staying here,' Lucy said to him. 'Meaning, the two of you will be working this together. No smoking in the car, and you hit on her, your life is over.'

'Shhhh,' I said to both of them.

The jet's return was loud from the north, and we stood silently, staring up at the sky as lights suddenly blazed on. They formed a fiery dotted line, marking green for approach, white for the safe zone, and finally warning red at the end of the landing strip. I thought how weird it would seem for anyone who had the misfortune of driving by as this plane was coming in. I could see its dark shadow and winking lights on wings as it dropped lower and its noise became awesome. The landing gear unfolded and emerald green light spilled out from the wheel well as the C-17 headed straight for us.

I had the paralyzing sensation that I was witnessing a crash, that this monstrous flat-gray machine with vertical wing tips and stubby shape was going to plow into the earth. It sounded like a hurricane as it roared right over our heads, and we put our fingers in our ears as its huge wheels touched down, grass and dirt flying, great chunks chewed out of ruts made by big wheels and 130 tons of aluminum and steel. Wing flaps were up, engines in thrust reverse as the jet screamed to a stop at the end of a field not big enough for football.

Then pilots threw it in reverse and began loudly backing it up along the grass, in our direction, so there would be enough of a landing strip for it to take off again. When its tail reached the edge of the dirt road, the C-17 stopped, jet exhaust directed up away from us. The back opened like the mouth of a shark as a metal ramp went down, the cargo bay completely open and lighted and gleaming of polished metal.

For a while we watched as the loadmaster and crew worked. They had put on chemical warfare gear, dark hoods and goggles and black gloves that looked rather scary, especially at night. They quickly backed the pickup and camper off the flatbed truck, unhooked them, and the HMMWV towed the camper inside the C-17.

'Come on,' Lucy said, tugging my arm. 'We don't want to miss our ride.'

We walked out onto the field, and I could not believe the power surging and the noise as we followed the automated ramp, picking our way around rollers and rings built into the flat, metal floor, miles of wires and insulation exposed overhead. The plane looked big enough to carry several helicopters, Red Cross buses, tanks, and there were at least fifty jump seats. But the crew was small tonight, only the loadmaster and paratroopers, and a first lieutenant named Laurel, who I assumed had been assigned to us.

She was an attractive young woman with short dark hair, and she shook each of our hands and smiled like a gracious hostess.

'Good news is you're not sitting down here,' she said. 'We'll be up with the pilots. More good news, I've got coffee.'

'That would be heaven,' I said, metal clanking as the crew secured the camper and HMMWV to the floor with chains and netting.

The steps leading up from the cargo bay were painted with the name of the plane, which in this case, appropriately, was *Heavy Metal*. The cockpit was huge, with an electronic flight control system, and head-up displays like fighter pilots used. Steering was done with sticks instead of yokes, and the instrumentation was completely intimidating.

I climbed up on a swivel seat, behind two pilots in green jumpsuits, who were too busy to pay us any mind.

'You got headsets so you can talk, but please don't when the pilots are,' Laurel told us. 'You don't have to wear them, but it's pretty loud in here.'

I was clamping on my five-point harness and noting the oxygen mask hanging by each chair.

'I'm going to be down here and will check on you from time to time,' the lieutenant went on. 'It's about three hours to Utah, and the landing shouldn't be too abrupt. They got a runway long enough for the space shuttle, or that's what they say. You know how the Army brags.'

She went back downstairs as pilots talked in jargon and codes that meant nothing to me. We began to take off a mere thirty amazing minutes after the plane had landed.

'We're going on the runway now,' a pilot said. 'Load?' I assumed he meant the loadmaster below. 'Is everything secure?'

'Yes, sir,' the voice sounded in my headset.

'Have we got that checklist completed?'

'Yes.'

'Okay. We're rolling.'

The plane surged forward, bumping over the field with gathering power that was unlike any takeoff I had ever known. It roared more than a hundred miles an hour, pulling up into the air at an angle so sharp it flattened me against the back of my chair. Suddenly, stars spangled the sky, the lights of Maryland a winking network.

'We're going about two hundred knots,' a pilot said. 'Command Post aircraft 30601. Flaps up. Execute.'

I glanced over at Lucy, who was behind the co-pilot and trying to see what he was doing as she listened to every word, probably committing it to memory. Laurel returned with cups of coffee, but nothing would have kept me up. I drifted to sleep at thirty-five thousand feet as the jet flew west at six hundred miles an hour. I came to as a tower was talking.

We were over Salt Lake City and descending, and Lucy would never come to earth again as she listened to cockpit talk. She caught me looking but was not to be distracted, and I had never really known anyone like her, not in my entire life. She had a voracious curiosity about anything that could be put together, taken apart, programmed and, in general, made to do something she wanted. People were about the only thing she couldn't figure out.

Clover Control turned us over to Dugway Range Control, and then we were receiving instructions about landing. Despite what we had been told about the length of the runway, it felt like we were going to be torn out of our seats as the jet crescendoed over a tarmac blinking with miles of lights, air roaring against raised slats. The stop was so abrupt, I didn't see how it was physically possible, and I wondered if the pilots might have been practicing.

'Tally ho,' one of them said cheerfully.

D UGWAY WAS THE size of Rhode Island with two thousand people living on the base. But we could see nothing when we got in at half past five A.M. Laurel turned us over to a soldier, who put us in a truck and drove to a place where we could rest and freshen up. There wasn't time for sleep. The plane would be taking off later in the day, and we needed to be on it.

Lucy and I were checked into the Antelope Inn, across from the Community Club. We had a room with twin beds on the first floor, furnished with light oak and wall-to-wall carpet, everything blue. It offered a view of barracks across the green, where lights were already beginning to come on with the dawn.

'You know, there really doesn't seem any point in taking a shower since we'll have to put on the same dirty things,' Lucy said, stretching out on top of her bed.

'You're absolutely right,' I agreed, taking off my shoes. 'You mind if I turn this lamp off?'

'I wish you would.'

The room was dark and I suddenly felt silly. 'This is like a slumber party.'

'Yeah, the one from hell.'

'Remember when you used to come stay with me when you were little?' I said. 'Sometimes we stayed up half the night. You never wanted to go to sleep, always wanting me to read one more story. You wore me out.'

'I remember it the other way around. I wanted to sleep and you wouldn't leave me alone.'

'Untrue.'

'Because you doted on me.'

'Did not. I could scarcely tolerate being in the same room,' I said. 'But I felt sorry for you and wanted to be kind.'

A pillow sailed through the dark and hit me on the head. I threw it back. Then Lucy pounced from her bed to mine, and when she got there didn't quite know what to do, because she was no longer ten and I wasn't Janet. She got up and went back to her bed, loudly fluffing pillows behind her.

'You sound like you're a lot better,' she said.

'Better, but not a lot. I'll live.'

'Aunt Kay, what are you going to do about Benton? You don't even seem to think about him anymore.'

'Oh yes I do,' I answered. 'But things have been a little out of control of late, to say the least.'

'That's always the excuse people give. I should know. I heard it all my life from my mother.'

'But not from me,' I said.

'That's my point. What do you want to do about him? You could get married.'

The mere thought unnerved me again. 'I don't think I can do that, Lucy.'

'Why not?'

'Maybe I'm too set in my ways, on a track I can't get off. Too much is demanded of me.'

'You need to have a life, too.'

'I feel like I do,' I said. 'But it may not be what everybody else thinks it should be.'

'You've always given me advice,' she said. 'Maybe now it's my turn. And I don't think you should get married.'

'Why?' I was more curious than surprised.

'I don't think you ever really buried Mark. And until you do, you shouldn't get married. All of you won't be there, you know?'

I felt sad and was glad she could not see me in the dark. For the first time in our lives, I talked to her as a trusted friend.

'I haven't gotten over him and probably never will,' I said. 'I guess he was my first love.'

'I know all about that,' my niece went on. 'I worry that if something happens, there will never be anybody else for me, either. And I don't want to go the rest of my life not having what I've got now. Not having someone you can talk to about anything, someone who cares and is kind.' She hestitated, and what she said next was honed to an edge. 'Someone who doesn't get jealous and use you.'

'Lucy,' I said, 'Ring won't wear a badge again in this lifetime, but only you can strip Carrie of her power over you.'

'She has no power over me.' Lucy's temper flared.

'Of course she does. And I can understand it. I'm furious with her, too.'

Lucy got quiet for a moment, and then she spoke in a smaller voice. 'Aunt Kay, what will happen to me?'

'I don't know, Lucy,' I said. 'I don't have the answers. But I promise I will be with you every step of the way.'

The twisted path that had led her to Carrie eventually bent us back around to Lucy's mother, who, of course, was my sister. I wandered the ridges and rills of my growing-up years, and was honest with Lucy about my marriage to her ex-uncle Tony. I spoke of how it felt to be my age and know I probably would not have children. By now, the sky was lighting up, and it was time to start the day. The base commander's driver was waiting in the lobby at nine, a young private who barely needed to shave.

'We got one other person who came in right after you did,' the private said, putting on Ray-Bans. 'From Washington, the FBI.'

He seemed to be very impressed with this and clearly had no idea what Lucy was, nor did the expression change on her face when I asked, 'What does he do with the FBI?'

'Some scientist or something. Pretty hot stuff,' he said, eyeing Lucy, who was striking-looking even when she'd been up all night.

The scientist was Nick Gallwey, head of the Bureau's Disaster Squad, and a forensic expert of considerable reputation. I had known him for years, and when he walked into the lobby, we gave each other a hug, and Lucy shook his hand.

'A pleasure, Special Agent Farinelli. And believe me, I've heard a lot about you,' he said to her. 'So Kay and I are going to do the dirty work while you play with the computer.'

'Yes, sir,' she sweetly said.

'Is there anywhere to have breakfast around here?' Gallwey asked the private, who was tangled in confusion and suddenly shy.

He drove us in the base commander's Suburban beneath an endless sky. Unsettled western mountain ranges surrounded us in the distance, high desert flora like sage, scrub pine and firs, dwarfed by lack of rain. The nearest traffic was forty miles away in this Home of the Mustangs, as the base was called, with its ammunition bunkers, weapons from World War II and air space restricted and vast. There were traces of salt from receding ancient waters, and we spotted an antelope and an eagle.

Stark Road, aptly named, led us toward the test facilities, which were some ten miles from the living area on base. The Ditto diner was on the way, and we stopped long enough for coffee and egg sandwiches. Then it was on to the test facilities, which were clustered in large, modern buildings behind a fence topped with razor wire.

Warning signs were everywhere, promising that trespassers were unwelcome and deadly force used. Codes on buildings indicated what was inside them, and I recognized symbols for mustard gas and nerve agents, and those for Ebola, Anthrax and Hantavirus. Walls were concrete, the private told us, and two feet thick, refrigerators inside explosion-proof. The routine was not so different from what I had experienced before. Guards led us through the toxic containment facilities, and Lucy and I went into the women's changing room while Gallwey went into the men's.

We stripped and put on house clothes that were Army green, and over these went suits, which were camouflage with goggled hoods, and heavy black rubber gloves and boots. Like the blue suits at CDC and USAMRIID, these were attached to air lines inside the chamber, which in this case was stainless steel from ceiling to floor. It was a completely closed system with double carbon filters, where contaminated vehicles like tanks could be bombarded with chemical agents and vapors. We were assured we could work here as long as we needed without placing anyone at risk.

It might even be possible that some evidence could be decontaminated and saved. But it was hard to say. None of us had ever worked a case like this before. We started by propping open the camper's door and arranging lights directed inside. It was peculiar moving around, the steel floor warping loudly like saw blades as we walked. Above us, an Army scientist sat in the control room behind glass, monitoring everything we did.

Again, I went in first because I wanted to thoroughly survey the crime scene. Gallwey began photographing tool marks on the door and dusting for fingerprints, while I climbed inside and looked around as if I had never been there before. The small living area that normally would have contained a couch and table had been gutted and turned into a laboratory with sophisticated equipment that was neither new nor cheap.

The rabbit was still alive, and I fed him and set his cage on top of a counter neatly built of plywood and painted black. Beneath it was a refrigerator, and in it I found Vero and human embryonic lung fibroblast cells. They were tissue cultures routinely used for feeding poxviruses, just as fertilizers are used for certain plants. To maintain these cultures, the mad farmer of this mobile lab had a good supply of Eagle minimal essential medium, supplemented with ten percent fetal calf serum. This and the rabbit told me that deadoc was doing more than maintaining his virus, he was still in the process of propagating it when disaster had struck.

He had kept the virus in a liquid nitrogen freezer that did not need to be plugged in, but refilled every few months. It looked like a ten-gallon stainless steel thermos, and when I unscrewed the lid, I pulled out seven cryotubes so old that instead of plastic, they were made of glass. Codes that should have identified the disease were unlike anything I'd ever seen, but there was a date of 1978, and the location of Birmingham, England, tiny abbreviations written in black ink, neatly, and in lowercase. I returned the tubes of living, frozen horror to their frigid place, and rooted around more, finding twenty sample sizes of Vita facial spray, and tuberculin syringes that the killer, no doubt, had used to inoculate the canisters with the disease.

Of course, there were pipettes and rubber bulbs, petri dishes, and the flasks with screw caps where the virus was actually growing. The medium inside them was pink. Had it begun to turn pale yellow, the PH balance would indicate waste products, acidity, meaning the virus-laden cells had not been bathed in their nutrient-rich tissue culture medium in a while.

I remembered enough from medical school and my training as a pathologist to know that when propagating a virus, the cells must be fed. This is done with the pink culture medium, which must be aspirated off every few days with a pipette, when the nutrients have been replaced by waste. For the medium still to be pink meant this had been done recently, at least within the last four days. Deadoc was meticulous. He had cultivated death with love and care. Yet there were two flasks broken on the floor, perhaps due to an infected rabbit hopping about, somehow accidentally out of its cage. I did not sense suicide here, but an unforeseen catastrophe that had caused deadoc to run.

Slowly, I moved around some more, through the kitchen, where a single bowl and fork had been washed and neatly left to dry on a dish towel by the sink. Cupboards were orderly, too, with rows of simple spices, boxes of cereal and rice and cans of vegetable soup. In the refrigerator was skim milk, apple juice, onions and carrots, but no meat. I closed the door as my mystification grew. Who was he? What did he do in this camper day after day besides make his viral bombs? Did he watch TV? Did he read?

I began to look for clothes, pulling open drawers with no luck. If this man had spent a lot of time here, why had he nothing to wear except what he had on? Why no photographs or personal mementoes? What about books, catalogues for ordering cell lines, tissue cultures, reference material for infectious diseases? Most obvious of all, what had happened to the vehicle that had towed this? Who had driven off in it and when?

I stayed in the bedroom longer, the carpet black from blood that had been tracked through other rooms when we had removed the body. I could not smell or hear anything but air circulating in my suit as I paused to change my four-hour battery. This room, like the rest of the camper, was generic, and I pulled back the flower-printed spread, discovering the pillow and sheets on one side were wrinkled from having been slept on. I found one short gray hair, and collected it with forceps as I remembered that the dead man's hair was longer and black.

A print of a seaside on the wall was cheap, and I took it down to see if I could tell where it had been framed. I tried the love seat beneath a window on the other side of the bed.

It was covered in bright green vinyl, and on top was a cactus plant that had to be the only thing alive in the camper except for what was in the cage, the incubator and the freezer. I stirred the soil with my finger and it was not too dry, then I placed it on the carpet and opened up the love seat.

Based on cobwebs and dust, no one had been inside in many years, and I sifted through a rubber cat toy, a faded blue hat and a chewed-on corncob pipe. I did not sense that any of this belonged to the person who lived here now, or had even been noticed by him. I wondered if the camper had been used or in the family, and got down on my hands and knees and crawled around until I found the shot shell and the wad. These, too, I sealed inside an evidence bag.

Lucy was just sitting down at the laptop computer when I returned to the laboratory area.

'Screen saver password,' she said into her voice-activated microphone.

'I was hoping you'd get something difficult,' I said.

She was already rebooting and going into DOS. Knowing her, she would have that password removed in minutes, as I'd seen her do before.

'Kay,' Gallwey's voice sounded inside my hood. 'Got something good out here.'

I went down the steps, careful to keep my air line from tangling. He was in front of the camper, squatting by the area of the tongue where the VIN had been obliterated. Having polished the metal mirror-smooth with fine grit sandpaper, he was now applying a solution of copper chloride and hydrochloric acid to dissolve scarred metal and restore the deeply stamped number underneath that the killer thought he had filed away.

'People don't realize how difficult it is to get rid of one of these things,' his voice filled my ears.

'Unless they're professional car thieves.' I said.

'Well, whoever did this didn't do a very good job.' He was taking photographs. 'I think we got it.'

'Let's hope the camper's registered,' I said.

'Who knows? Maybe we'll get lucky.'

'What about prints?'

The door and aluminum around it were smudged with black dusting powder.

'Some, but God knows whose,' he said getting up and straightening his back. 'In a minute, I'll tear up the inside.'

Meanwhile, Lucy was tearing up the computer, and like me, not coming up with anything that might tell us who deadoc was. But she did find files he had saved of our conversations in the chat rooms, and it was chilling to see them on screen, and wonder how often he had reread them. There were detailed lab notes documenting the propagation of the virus cells, and this was interesting. It appeared work had begun as recently as early in the fall, less than two months before the torso had turned up.

By late afternoon, we had done all we could do with no startling revelations. We took chemical showers as the camper was blasted with formalin gas. I stayed in my army-green house clothes because I did not want my suit after what it had been through.

'Kind of hell on your wardrobe,' Lucy commented as we left the changing room. 'Maybe you should try pearls with that. Dress it up a little.'

'Sometimes you sound like Marino,' I said.

Days crept into the weekend, and next I knew that was

gone too with no developments that were anything but maddening. I had missed my mother's birthday. Not once had it crossed my mind.

'What? You got Alzheimer's now?' she unkindly told me over the phone. 'You don't come down here. Now you don't even bother to call. It's not like I'm getting younger.'

She began to cry, and I felt like it.

'Christmas,' I said what I did every year. 'I'll work something out. I'll bring Lucy. I promise. It's not that far away.'

I drove downtown, uninspired and weary to the bone. Lucy had been right. The killer's only use of the phone line at the campground was to dial into AOL, and in the end, all that came back to was Perley's stolen credit card. Deadoc did not call anymore. I had gotten obsessive about checking and sometimes found myself waiting in that chat room when I could not even be sure the FBI was watching anymore.

The frozen virus source I found in the camper's nitrogen freezer remained unknown. Attempts at mapping its DNA continued, and scientists at CDC knew how the virus was different, but not what it was, and thus far, vaccinated primates remained susceptible to it. Four other people, including two watermen who turned up in Crisfield, had come down with only mild cases of the disease. No one else seemed to be getting sick as the quarantine of the fishing village continued and its economy foundered. As for Richmond, only Wingo was ill, his willowy body and gentle face ravaged by pustules. He would not let me see him, no matter how often I tried.

I was devastated, and found it hard to worry about other cases because this one would not end. We knew the dead man in the trailer could not be deadoc. Fingerprints had come back to a drifter with a long arrest record of crimes

319

mostly involving theft and drugs, and two counts of assault and attempted rape. He was out on parole when he had used his pocketknife to pry open the camper door, and no one doubted that his shotgun death was a homicide.

I walked into my office at eight-fifteen. When Rose heard me, she came through her doorway.

'I hope you got some rest,' she said, more worried about me than I'd ever seen.

'I did. Thanks.' I smiled, and her concern made me feel guilty and shamed, as if I were bad somehow. 'Any new developments?'

'Not about Tangier.' I could see the anxiety in her eyes. 'Try to get your mind off it, Dr Scarpetta. We've got five cases this morning. Look at the top of your desk. If you can find it. And I'm at least two weeks behind on correspondence and micros because of your not being here to dictate.'

'Rose, I know, I know,' I said, not unkindly. 'First things first. Try Phyllis again. And if they still say she's out sick, get a number where she can be reached. I've been trying her home number for days and no one answers.'

'If I get her, you want me to put her through?'

'Absolutely,' I said.

That happened fifteen minutes later when I was about to go into staff meeting. Rose got Phyllis Crowder on the line.

'Where on earth are you? And how are you?' I asked.

'This wretched flu,' she said. 'Don't get it.'

'I did and am still getting rid of it,' I said. 'I've tried your house in Richmond.'

'Oh, I'm at my mother's, in Newport News. You know, I work a four-day week and have been spending the other three days out here for years.'

I did not know that. But we had never socialized.

'Phyllis,' I said, 'I hate to bother you when you're not well, but I need your help with something. In 1978 there was a laboratory accident at the lab in Birmingham, England, where you once worked. I've pulled what I can on it, and know only that a medical photographer was working directly over a smallpox lab . . .'

'Yes, yes,' she interrupted me. 'I know all about it. Supposedly, the photographer was exposed through a ventilator duct, and she died. The virologist committed suicide. The case is cited all the time by people who argue in favor of destroying all frozen source virus.'

'Were you working in that lab when this happened?'

'No, thank goodness. That was some years after I left. I was already in the States by then.'

I was disappointed, and she went into a coughing spell and could hardly talk.

'Sorry.' She coughed. 'This is when you hate living alone.'

'You don't have anyone looking in on you?'

'No.'

'What about food?'

'I manage.'

'Why don't I bring you something,' I said.

'I wouldn't hear of it.'

'I'll help you if you'll help me,' I added. 'Do you have any files on Birmingham? Concerning the work going on when you were there? Anything you could look up?'

'Buried somewhere in this house, I'm sure,' she said.

'Unbury them and I'll bring stew.'

I was out the door in five minutes, running to my car. Heading home, I got several quarts of my homemade stew out of the freezer, then I filled the tank with gas before going east on 64. I told Marino on the car phone what I was doing.

'You've really lost it this time,' he exclaimed. 'Drive over a hundred miles to take someone food? You coulda called Domino's.'

'That's not the point. And believe me, I have one.' I put sunglasses on. 'There may be something here. She may know something that could help.'

'Yo, let me know,' he said. 'You got your pager on, right?'

'Right.'

Traffic was light this time of day, and I kept the cruise control on sixty-nine so I did not get a ticket. In less than an hour, I was bypassing Williamsburg, and about twenty minutes later, following directions Crowder had given me for her address in Newport News. The neighborhood was called Brandon Heights, where the economic class was mixed, and houses got bigger as they got nearer the James River. Hers was a modest two-story frame recently painted eggshell white, the yard and landscaping well maintained.

I parked behind a van and collected the stew, my pocketbook and briefcase slung over a shoulder. When Phyllis Crowder came to the door, she looked like hell, her face pale, and eyes burning with fever. She was dressed in a flannel robe and leather slippers that looked like they might once have belonged to a man.

'I can't believe how nice you are,' she said as she opened the door. 'Either that or crazy.'

'Depends on who you ask.'

I stepped inside, pausing to look at framed photographs along the dark paneled entrance hall. Most of them were of people hiking and fishing and had been taken in long years past. My eyes were fixed on one, an older man wearing a pale blue hat and holding a cat as he grinned around a corncob pipe.

'My father,' Crowder said. 'This was where my parents lived, and my mother's parents were here before that. That's them there.' She pointed. 'When my father's business started doing poorly in England, they came here and moved in with her family.'

'And what about you?' I said.

'I stayed on, was in school.'

I looked at her and did not think she was as old as she wanted me to believe.

'You're always trying to make me assume you're a dinosaur compared to me,' I said. 'But somehow I don't think so.'

'Maybe you just wear the years better than I do.' Her feverish dark eyes met mine.

'Is any of your family still living?' I asked, perusing more photographs.

'My grandparents have been gone about ten years, my father about five. After that, I came out here every weekend to take care of Mother. She hung on as long as she could.'

'That must have been hard with your busy career,' I said, as I looked at an early photograph of her laughing on a boat, holding up a rainbow trout.

'Would you like to come in and sit down?' she asked. 'Let me put this in the kitchen.'

'No, no, show me the way and save your strength,' I insisted.

She led me through a dining room that did not appear to have been used in years, the chandelier gone, exposed wires hanging out over a dusty table, and draperies replaced by blinds. By the time we walked into the large, old-fashioned kitchen, the hair was rising along my scalp and neck, and it was all I could do to remain calm as I set the stew on the counter.

'Tea?' she asked.

She was hardly coughing now, and though she might be ill, this wasn't why she initially had stayed away from her job.

'Not a thing,' I said.

She smiled at me but her eyes were penetrating, and as we sat at the breakfast table, I was frantically trying to figure out what to do. What I suspected couldn't be right, or should I have figured it out sooner? I had been friendly with her for more than fifteen years. We had worked on numerous cases together, shared information, commiserated as women. In the old days, we drank coffee together and smoked. I had found her charming, brilliant, and certainly never sensed anything sinister. Yet I realized this was the very sort of thing people said about the serial killer next door, the child molester, the rapist.

'So, let's talk about Birmingham,' I said to her.

'Let's.' She wasn't smiling now.

'The frozen source of this disease has been found,' I said. 'The vials have labels on them dated 1978, Birmingham. I'm wondering if the lab there might have been doing any research in mutant strains of smallpox, anything that you might know . . . ?'

'I wasn't there in 1978,' she interrupted me.

'Well, I think you were, Phyllis.'

'It doesn't matter.' She got up to put on a pot of tea.

I did not say anything, waiting until she sat back down.

'I'm sick, and by now, you ought to be,' she said, and I knew she was not referring to the flu.

'I'm surprised you didn't create your own vaccine before you started all this,' I said. 'Seems like that was a little reckless for someone so precise.'

'I wouldn't have needed it if that bastard hadn't broken in and ruined everything,' she snapped. 'That filthy, disgusting pig.' Enraged, she shook.

'While you were on AOL, talking to me,' I said. 'That's when you stayed on the line and never logged off, because he started prying open your door. And you shot him and fled in your van. I guess you just went out to Janes Island for your long weekends, so you could passage your lovely disease to new flasks, feed the little darlings.'

I was beginning to feel the rage as I spoke. She did not seem to care, but was enjoying it.

'After all these years in medicine, are people nothing more than slides and petri dishes? What happened to their faces, Phyllis? I have seen the people you did this to.' I leaned closer to her. 'An old woman who died alone in her soiled bed, no one to even hear her cries for water. And now Wingo, who will not let me look at him, a decent, kind young man, dying. You know him! He's been to your lab! What has he ever done to you!'

She was unmoved, her anger flashing, too.

'You left Lila Pruitt's Vita spray in one of the cubbyholes where she sold recipes for a quarter. Tell me if I don't get it right.' My words bit. 'She thought her mail had been delivered to the wrong box, then dropped off by a neighbor. What a nice little something to get for free, and she sprayed it on her face. She had it on her nightstand, spraying it again and again when she was in pain.'

My colleague was silent, her eyes gleaming.

'You probably delivered all of your little bombs to Tangier at once,' I said. 'Then dropped by the ones for me. And my staff. What was your plan after that? The world?'

'Maybe,' was all she had to say.

'Why?'

'People did it to me first. Tit for tat.'

'What did anybody do to you that's even close?' It was an effort to keep my voice controlled.

'I was at Birmingham when it happened. The accident. It was implied that I was partly to blame, and I was forced to leave. It was completely unfair, a total setback to me when I was young, on my own. Scared. My parents had left for the United States, to live here in this house. They liked the outdoors. Camping, fishing. All of them did.'

For a long moment, she stared off as if there, back in those days.

'I didn't matter much, but I had worked hard. I got another job in London, was three grades below what I had been.' Her eyes focused on me. 'It wasn't fair. It was the virologist who caused the accident. But because I was there that day, and he conveniently killed himself, it was easy to pin it all on me. Plus, I was just a kid, really.'

'So you stole the source virus on your way out,' I said. She smiled coldly.

'And you stored it all these years?'

'Not hard when every place you work has nitrogen freezers and you're always happy to monitor the inventory,' she said with pride. 'I saved it.'

'Why?'

'Why?' Her voice rose. 'I was the one working on it when the accident happened. It was mine. So I made sure I took some of it and my other experiments with me on my way out the door. Why should I let them keep it? They weren't smart enough to do what I did.'

'But this isn't smallpox. Not exactly,' I said.

'Well, that's even worse, now isn't it?' Her lips were

trembling with emotion as she recalled those days. 'I spliced the DNA of monkeypox into the smallpox genome.'

She was getting more overwrought, her hands trembling as she wiped her nose with a napkin.

'And then at the beginning of the new academic year, I get passed over as a department chairman,' she went on, eyes flaming with furious tears.

'Phyllis, that's not fair . . .'

'Shut up!' she screamed. 'All I've given to that bloody school? I'm the senior one who has potty-trained everyone, including you. And they give it to a man because I'm not a doctor. I'm *just* a Ph.D.,' she spat.

'They gave it to a Harvard-trained pathologist who is completely justified in getting the position,' I flatly stated. 'And it doesn't matter. There's no excuse for what you've done. You saved a virus all these years? To do this?'

The teakettle was whistling shrilly. I got up and turned the burner off.

'It's not the only exotic disease I've had in my research archives. I've been collecting,' she said. 'I actually thought I might do an important project someday. Study the world's most feared virus and learn something more about the human immune system that might save us from other scourges like AIDS. I thought I might win a Nobel Prize.' She had gotten oddly quiet, as if pleased with herself. 'But no, I wouldn't say that in Birmingham my intention was to one day create an epidemic.'

'Well, you didn't,' I replied.

Her eyes narrowed like evil as she looked at me.

'No one's gotten sick except for those people suspected of using the facial spray,' I said. 'I've been exposed several times to patients, and I'm okay. The virus you created is

327

a dead end, affecting only the primary person but not replicating. There's no secondary infection. No epidemic. What you created was a panic, disease and death for a handful of innocent victims. And crippled the fishing industry for an island full of people who probably have never even heard of a Nobel Prize.'

I leaned back in my chair, studying her, but she did not seem to care.

'Why did you send me photographs and messages?' I demanded. 'Photographs taken in your dining room, on that table. Who was your guinea pig? Your old and infirm mother? Did you spray her with the virus to see if it worked? And when it did, you shot her in the head. You dismembered her with an autopsy saw so no one ever connected that death with your eventual product tampering?'

'You think you're so smart,' she, deadoc, said.

'You murdered your own mother and wrapped her in a drop cloth because you could not bear to look at her as you sawed her apart.'

She averted her eyes as my pager vibrated. I pulled it out and read Marino's number. I got out my phone, my eyes never leaving her.

'Yes,' I said when he answered.

'We got a hit on the camper,' he said. 'Traced it back to a manufacturer, then to an address in Newport News. Thought you'd want to know. Agents should be there right about now.'

'Wish the Bureau had gotten that hit a little sooner,' I said. 'I'll see the agents at the door.'

'What did you say?'

I got off the phone.

'I communicated with you because I knew you would pay

attention.' Crowder kept talking at a higher pitch. 'And to make you try and for once finally lose. The famous doctor. The famous chief.'

'You were a colleague and friend,' I said.

'And I resent you!' Her face was flushed, bosom heaving as she raged. 'I always have! The way the system's always treated you better, all the attention you get. The great Dr Scarpetta. The legend. But ha! Look who won. In the end I outsmarted you, didn't I?'

I would not answer her.

'Ran you around, didn't I?' She stared, reaching for a bottle of aspirin and shaking out two. 'Brought you close to death's door and had you waiting in cyberspace. Waiting for me!' she said triumphantly.

Something metal loudly rapped on her front door. I pushed back my chair.

'What are they going to do? Shoot me? Or maybe you should. I bet you've got a gun in one of those bags.' She was getting hysterical. 'I've got one in the other room and I'm going to get it right now.'

She got up as the knocking continued, and a voice demanded, 'Open up, FBI.'

I grabbed her arm. 'No one's going to shoot you, Phyllis.'

'Let go of me!'

I steered her toward the door.

'Let go of me!'

'Your punishment will be to die the way they did.' I pulled her along.

'NO!' she screamed as the door crashed open, slamming against the wall and jarring framed photographs loose from their hooks.

Two FBI agents stepped inside with pistols drawn, and

one of them was Janet. They cuffed Dr Phyllis Crowder after she collapsed to the floor. An ambulance transported her to Sentara Norfolk General Hospital, where twenty-one days later she died, shackled in bed, covered with fulminating pustules. She was forty-four.

EPILOGUE

I COULD NOT make the decision right away but put it off until New Year's Eve when people are supposed to make changes, resolutions, promises they know they'll never keep. Snow was clicking against my slate roof as Wesley and I sat on the floor in front of the fire, sipping champagne.

'Benton,' I said, 'I need to go somewhere.'

He looked confused, as if I meant right now, and said, 'There's not much open, Kay.'

'No. A trip, in February, maybe. To London.'

He paused, knowing what I was thinking. He set his glass on the hearth and took my hand.

'I've been hoping you would,' he said. 'No matter how hard it is, you really should. So you can have closure, peace of mind.'

'I'm not sure it's possible for me to have peace of mind.'

I pulled my hand away and pushed back my hair. This was hard for him, too. It had to be.

'You must miss him,' I said. 'You never talk about it, but he was like a brother. I remember all the times we did things together, the three of us. Cooking, watching movies, sitting around talking about cases and the latest lousy thing government had done to us. Like furloughs, taxes, budget cuts.'

He smiled a little, staring into flames. 'And I would think about what a lucky bastard he was to have you. Wonder what it was like. Well, now I know, and I was right. He was lucky as hell. He's probably the only person I've ever really talked to, besides you. Kind of strange, in a way. Mark was one of the most self-centered people I've ever met, one of these beautiful creatures, narcissistic as hell. But he was good. He was smart. I don't think you ever stop missing someone like him.'

Wesley was wearing a white wool sweater and cream-colored khakis, and in firelight he was almost radiant.

'You go out tonight and you'll disappear,' I said.

He gave me a puzzled frown.

'Dressed like that in the snow. You fall in a ditch, no one will see you until spring. You should wear something dark on a night like this. You know, contrast.'

'Kay. How about I put on some coffee.'

'It's like people who want a four-wheel-drive vehicle for winter. So they buy something white. Tell me how that makes sense when you're sliding on a white road beneath a white sky with white stuff swirling everywhere.'

332

'What are you talking about?' His eyes were on me.

'I don't know.'

I lifted the bottle of champagne out of its bucket. Water dripped as I refilled our glasses, and I was ahead of him, about two to one. The CD player was stacked with hits from the seventies, and Three Dog Night was vibrating speakers in the walls. It was one of those rare times I might get drunk. I could not stop thinking about it and seeing it in my mind. I did not know until I was in that room with the wires hanging out of the ceiling and saw where gory severed hands and feet had been lined in a row. It was not until then that the truth seared my mind. I could not forgive myself.

'Benton,' I quietly said, 'I should have known it was her. I should have known before I got to her house and walked in there and saw the photographs and that room. I mean, a part of me must have known, and I didn't listen.'

He did not answer, and I took this as a further indictment.

'I should have known it was her,' I muttered again. 'People might not have died.'

'*Should* is always easy to say after the fact.' His tone was gentle but unwavering. 'People who live next door to the Gacys, the Bundys, the Dahmers of the world are always the last to figure it out, Kay.'

'And they don't know what I do, Benton.' I sipped champagne. 'She killed Wingo.'

'You did the best you could,' he reminded me.

'I miss him,' I said with a sad sigh. 'I haven't been to Wingo's grave.'

'Why don't we switch to coffee?' Wesley said again.

'Can't I just drift now and then?' I didn't want to be present.

He started rubbing the back of my neck, and I shut my eyes.

'Why do I always have to make sense?' I muttered. 'Precise about this, exact about that. *Consistent with*, and *characteristic of*. Words cold and sharp like the steel blades I use. And what good will they do me in court? When it's Lucy in the balance? Her career, her life? All because of that bastard, Ring. Me, the expert witness. The loving aunt.' A tear slid down my cheek. 'Oh God, Benton. I'm so tired.'

He moved over and put his arms around me, pulling me into his lap so I could lean back my head.

'I'll go with you,' he quietly said into my hair.

We took a black cab to London's Victoria Station on February 18, the anniversary of a bombing that had ripped through a trash can and collapsed an underground entrance, a tavern and a coffee bar. Rubble had flown, shattered glass from the roof raining down in shrapnel and missiles with terrible force. The IRA had not targeted Mark. His death had nothing to do with his being FBI. He simply had been in the wrong place at the wrong time like so many people who are victims.

The station was crowded with commuters who almost ran me over as we made our way to the central area where Railtrack ticket agents were busy in their booths, and displays on a wall showed times and trains. Kiosks were selling sweets and flowers, and one could get a passport picture taken or have money changed. Trash cans were tucked inside McDonald's and places like that, but I did not see a single one out in the open.

'No good place to hide a bomb now.' Wesley was observing the same thing.

'Live and learn,' I said as I began to tremble inside.

I silently stared around me as pigeons flapped overhead and trotted after crumbs. The entrance for the Grosvenor Hotel was next to the Victoria Tavern, and it was here that it had happened. No one was completely certain what Mark had been doing at the time, but it was speculated that he had been sitting at one of the small, high tables in front of the tavern when the bomb exploded.

We knew he had been waiting for the train from Brighton to arrive because he was meeting someone. To this day I did not know who, because the individual's identity could not be revealed for security reasons. That's what I had been told. I had never understood many things, such as the coincidence of timing, and whether this clandestine person Mark was meeting may have been killed, too. I scanned the roof of steel girders and glass, the old clock on the granite wall, and archways. The bombing had left no permanent scars, except on people.

'Brighton is a rather odd place to be in February,' I commented to Wesley in an unsteady voice. 'Why would someone be coming from a seaside resort that time of year?'

'I don't know why,' he said, looking around. 'This was all about terrorism. As you know, that was what Mark was working on. So no one's saying much.'

'Right. That was what he was working on, and that was how he died,' I said. 'And no one seems to think there was a link. That maybe it wasn't random.'

He did not respond, and I looked at him, my soul heavy and sinking down into the darkness of a fathomless sea. People, and pigeons, and constant announcements on the

PA blended into a dizzying din, and for an instant, all went black. Wesley caught me as I swayed.

'Are you all right?'

'I want to know who he was seeing.' I said.

'Come on, Kay,' he said, gently. 'Let's go someplace where you can sit down.'

'I want to know if the bombing was deliberate because a certain train was arriving at a certain time,' I persisted. 'I want to know if this is all fiction.'

'Fiction?' he asked.

Tears were in my eyes. 'How do I know this isn't some cover-up, some ruse, because he's alive and in hiding? A protected witness with a new identity.'

'He's not.' Wesley's face was sad, and he held my hand. 'Let's go.'

But I wouldn't move. 'I must know the truth. If it really happened. Who was he meeting and where is that person now?'

'Don't do this.'

People were weaving around us, not paying any attention. Feet crashed like an angry surf, and steel clanged as construction workers laid new rail.

'I don't believe he was meeting anyone.' My voice shook and I wiped my eyes. 'I believe this is some great big Bureau lie.'

He sighed, staring off. 'It's not a lie, Kay.'

'Then who! I have to know!' I cried.

Now people were looking our way, and Wesley moved me out of traffic, toward platform 8, where the 11:46 train was leaving for Denmark Hill and Peckham Rye. He led me up a blue and white tile ramp into a room of benches and lockers, where travelers could store belongings and claim left baggage. I was sobbing, and could not help myself. I was confused and furious as we went into a deserted corner and he kindly sat me on a bench.

'Tell me,' I said. 'Benton, please. I've got to know. Don't make me go the rest of my life not knowing the truth,' I choked between tears.

He took both my hands. 'You can put this to rest right now. Mark is dead. I swear. Do you really think I could have this relationship with you if I knew he were alive somewhere?' he passionately said. 'Jesus. How can you even imagine I could do something like that!'

'What happened to the person he was meeting?' I kept pushing.

He hesitated. 'Dead, I'm afraid. They were together when the bomb went off.'

'Then why all the secrecy about who he was?' I exclaimed. 'This isn't making sense!'

He hesitated again, this time longer, and for an instant, his eyes were filled with pity for me and it looked like he might cry. 'Kay, it wasn't a he. Mark was with a woman.'

'Another agent.' I did not understand.

'No.'

'What are you saying?'

The realization was slow because I did not want it, and when he was silent, I knew.

'I didn't want you to find out,' he said. 'I didn't think you needed to know that he was with another woman when he died. They were coming out of the Grosvenor Hotel when the bomb went off. It had nothing to do with him. He was just there.'

'Who was she?' I felt relieved and nauseated at the same time.

'Her name was Julie McFee. She was a thirty-one-year-old solicitor from London. They met through a case he was working. Or maybe through another agent. I'm really not sure.'

I looked into his eyes. 'How long had you known about them?'

'For a while. Mark was going to tell you, and it wasn't my place to.' He touched my cheek, wiping away tears. 'I'm sorry. You have no idea how this makes me feel. As if you haven't suffered enough.'

'In a way it makes it easier,' I said.

A teenager with body piercing and a mohawk slammed a locker door. We waited until he sauntered off with his girl in black leather.

'Typical of my relationship with him, in truth.' I felt drained and could scarcely think as I got up. 'He couldn't commit, take a risk. Never would have, not for anyone. He missed out on so much, and that's what makes me saddest.'

Outside it was damp with a numbing wind blowing, and the line of cabs around the station did not end. We walked hand in hand and bought bottles of Hooper's Hooch, because one could drink alcoholic lemonade on the streets of England. Police on dappled horses clopped past Buckingham Palace, and in St. James's Park a band of guards in bearskin caps were marching while people pointed cameras. Trees swayed and drums faded as we walked back to the Athenaeum Hotel on Piccadilly.

'Thank you.' I slipped my arm around him. 'I love you, Benton,' I said.

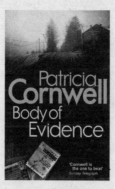

A reclusive writer is dead. And her final manuscript has
disappeared . . .

Someone is stalking Beryl Madison. Spying on her and making
threatening, obscene phone calls. Terrified, Beryl flees to Key
West – but on the very night she returns to her Richmond
home, Beryl inexplicably invites her killer in.

Now Dr Kay Scarpetta must take on a case that is as convoluted
as it is bizarre. Why would Beryl open the door to someone
who brutally slashed and then nearly decapitated her? Did she
know her killer? Adding to the intrigue is Beryl's enigmatic
relationship with a prize-winning author and the disappearance
of her own manuscript.

As Scarpetta retraces Beryl's footsteps, an investigation that
begins in the laboratory with microscopes and lasers leads her
deep into a nightmare that soon becomes her own.

'A great writer . . . read these books only in broad daylight'
Daily Mail

The 'book of the dead' is the morgue log, the ledger in which all cases are entered by hand. For Kay Scarpetta, however, it is about to have a new meaning.

Fresh from her bruising battle with a psychopath in Florida, Scarpetta decides it's time for a change of pace. Moving to the historic city of Charleston, South Carolina, she opens a unique private forensic pathology practice, one in which she and her colleagues offer expert crime scene investigation and autopsies to communities lacking local access to competent death investigation and modern technology. It seems like an ideal situation, until the murders and other violent deaths begin.

A woman is ritualistically murdered in her multi-million-dollar beach home. The body of an abused young boy is found dumped in a desolate marsh. A sixteen-year-old tennis star is found nude and mutilated near Piazza Navona in Rome.

Scarpetta has dealt with many brutal and unusual crimes before, but never a string of them as baffling, or as terrifying, as the ones before her now. Before she is through, that book of the dead will contain many names – and the pen may be poised to write her own.

'Patricia Cornwell is the queen of gritty, grisly, crime fiction writing and her latest offering doesn't disappoint.
Book of the Dead will keep you gripped throughout'
Heat

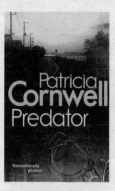

Florida is full of human predators from the animals who thrive
in its humid heat to the humans that stalk the air-conditioned
malls, and they all give Dr Kay Scarpetta the opportunity and
the means to do what she does best – persuading the dead to
speak to her.

In the icy chill of Boston, Benton Wesley is working on a
secret project involving convicted killers. It is a project which
gives Scarpetta deep disquiet, as does the behaviour of her
niece, Lucy, who is spending too much time in cheap bars
looking for casual pick-ups.

The Academy is called when a woman's body is found in Boston.
She has been tortured, sexually abused, her body tattooed with
handprints. The same sort of handprints Lucy had seen on the
flesh of her latest pick-up . . .

'Sensationally plotted, with a twist at the end that
will leave you gasping for breath'
Daily Express

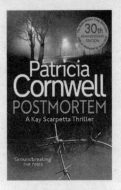

A serial killer is on the loose in Richmond, Virginia. Three women have died, brutalised and strangled in their own bedroom. There is no pattern: the killer appears to strike at random – but always early on Saturday mornings.

So when Dr Kay Scarpetta, chief medical officer, is awakened at 2.33 am, she knows the news is bad: there is a fourth victim. And she fears now for those that will follow unless she can dig up new forensic evidence to aid the police.

But not everyone is pleased to see a woman in this powerful job. Someone may even want to ruin her career and reputation . . .

'Terrific first novel, full of suspense, in which even the scientific bits grip' *The Times*

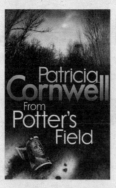

It's Christmas and a naked body is discovered in Central Park ...

Although a holiday for most, the festivities always seem to heighten the alienation felt by society's criminals; and that usually means more work for Dr Kay Scarpetta, Virginia's Chief Medical Examiner and consulting forensic pathologist for the FBI.

The body is found propped against a fountain in a bleak area of New York's Central Park. The unknown female's apparent manner of death points to a modus operandi that is chillingly familiar: the gunshot wound to the head, the sections of skin excised from the body, the displayed corpse – all suggest that Temple Brooks Gault, Scarpetta's nemesis, is back at work.

Calling on all her reserves of courage and skill, and the able assistance of colleagues Marino and Wesley, Scarpetta must track this most dangerous of killers, in pursuit of survival as well as justice – heading inexorably to an electrifying climax amid the dark, menacing labyrinths of the New York subway.

'Cornwell is on magnificent form' *Evening Standard*